Other Titles by C

The Medieval Herb
Lavender Vows (ebook only)
A Whisper of Rosemary
Sanctuary of Roses
A Lily on the Heath

The Regency Draculia
(historical vampire romance)
The Vampire Voss
The Vampire Dimitri
The Vampire Narcise

Marina Alexander Adventures
Siberian Treasure
Amazon Roulette (forthcoming)

Modern Gothic Romantic Suspense
The Shop of Shades and Secrets
The Cards of Life and Death

———

Writing as Joss Ware
The Envy Chronicles
(paranormal romance)
Beyond the Night
Embrace the Night Eternal
Abandon the Night
Night Betrayed
Night Forbidden
Night Resurrected (March 2013)

A LILY ON THE HEATH

The Medieval Herb Garden Series

COLLEEN GLEASON

AVID PRESS

To be alerted to new book releases, send an
email to alert@colleengleason.com.

ISBN: 978-1-931419-12-3

PROLOGUE

England
April 1166

"I SHALL have her murdered!" the queen raged. The long, pointed edges of her sleeves brushed the stone floor, flowing and sweeping as she stalked across the solar. "When I find that woman who tempts my husband from my side, 'twill be her bitter end!"

Judith of Kentworth, Lady of Lilyfare, did not flinch at her mistress's fury. It was not the first time she'd seen Eleanor of Aquitaine, Queen of England and wife of Henry the Plantagenet, boiling with anger. Nay, she did not flinch or skulk or hide from the queen's wrath as the maids and even some of the more spineless ladies did. She listened sympathetically, as a confidante and friend would do, for there were few whom the queen could truly count as both.

"I will have her banished," seethed the queen. "Or married to a coarse Welshman and sent off to the mountains."

"But my lady, your highness, surely no man would be tempted from the side of a woman as beautiful and wealthy as yourself," ventured Lady Amice from the silk cassock on which she perched, edging as far from the raging queen as possible.

Judith barely kept from rolling her eyes. She would have turned on the boulder-headed Amice herself, but the queen, in as fine a fettle as Judith had ever seen her, was already shrieking at the hapless woman.

"You fool! Do you not have eyes in your vacant head? The whole of his court knows of his wandering eye and his pinching fingers. Get you out of here!" Eleanor cried. Now, true tears, not those born of rage, threatened her blue eyes. "Get from my sight!"

Judith pulled to her feet for 'twas past time to intervene. Glowering at Amice, the only other of Eleanor's ladies to remain after she launched into her tirade, Judith snapped her fingers to send the foolish woman from the chamber.

She and the queen were alone.

"My lady…Eleanor. Do you sit. This raging cannot be good for the babe." Judith gently took Eleanor's slender arm, ready to release it if the queen wasn't ready to succumb, and urged her toward a large chair piled with cushions. Any intervention with the queen must be done gently.

"The babe of my faithless husband," Eleanor muttered, smoothing her hands over the small, tight bulge under her gown. But she heeded Judith's advice and sank onto the bean-filled cushions.

"Some wine, my lady? Mayhap another apple?" The queen had shown a particular fondness for apples during this breeding time. This was a difficulty, as it was early spring and fresh apples were out of season. The dried, bruised ones kept in the cellars beneath the kitchens did not ease her longing, but the king had had several baskets shipped from the Holy Lands.

"See you, the king loves you, my lady," Judith reminded her truthfully as she selected one of the red-orange fruit to slice in two. "Else he would not make certain that every ship from Jerusalem carries your apples."

"Nay, 'tis his heir he loves," Eleanor snapped. Her face, arguably the most beautiful in all of Christendom, shined with a streak of tear-tracks on each cheek. Rounder now, due to pregnancy, her countenance bore traces of harshness and anger. Her wide blue eyes narrowed, and a soft curl of honey-blonde hair had loosed uncharacteristically from her intricate coiffure. "He cannot keep his cock stuffed inside his breeches. 'Tis a wonder there are not thrice as many bastards as heirs in this court!"

That was saying quite a lot, for the king and queen already had a surplus of living children: Henry, Matilda, Richard, Geoffrey, and Eleanor.

Judith offered the queen a bejeweled salver, with the halved apple resting on it. "My lady, this truth I speak, and I know you will hear it from me…the king might have a wandering eye, but his hands and cock do not always follow. And indeed, 'tis always your bed to which he returns. And you on which his eyes settle. 'Tis you to whom he goes for advice. You have his head and his heart, your highness."

Eleanor pushed away the plate, and Judith replaced it on the table betwixt them. She nodded, yet her eyes were sad. "Aye, Judith, I wish to believe you. Despite my strong ways, he does bear me some love. And 'tis my great cross that I must love him so, so that it pains me thus when he seeks release elsewhere."

"But you are his queen, and ever will be," Judith added gently. She lifted the errant wisp of blond hair and smoothed it into place, rearranging a jeweled pin to hold it as Eleanor sighed.

The queen nodded, and Judith, who had only seen her so sad and lost once before, was relieved to see a spark of determination flare back in her eyes. "Aye. Though I grow large with child, and longer in tooth, I am still Hank's queen, and I remain his partner. 'Tis true he comes to me for advice as oft as he does his Chancellor. 'Tis a cross I must come to accept, then. His wandering hands."

"Longer in tooth? My lady, you are hardly over two score. The king's mother Matilda still lives, and she is nearly sixty years."

Eleanor smiled and reached to pat Judith's arm. "Thank you, my dear. You have done your duty and pulled me from my sulks. You know that I count you as friend as much as attendant, Judith."

"I am most privileged, your highness," she replied.

But Judith could not help but compare the benefits with the drawbacks of such a position. Being close to the queen was a double-edged sword, and she must step lively to assure she did not meet the wrong side of it.

"Should I live to be such a ripe age as Matilda, I'll have skin trailed with wrinkles and breasts sagging to my belly, but now I am still young enough to turn the heads of the men both young and old. If Hank does not tend to his queen, mayhap she will find another lion of her own."

Being witness to such a threat was an example of the wrong side of the sword—the one that Judith did not want slicing into her flesh, literally or nay. Though the king might sow his oats wildly, he would not accept being cuckolded himself. "My lady, I know this has been a difficult breeding for you…mayhap once you have birthed this babe, you will feel differently."

Eleanor's laugh held a raw edge. "Aye, after I have birthed this babe, Hank will no doubt eagerly find his way back to my bed."

"'Tis where he belongs, my lady. An' he knows it too."

The queen sighed, smoothing her hand over her belly once more. "Aye. Thank you, Judith. I am relieved I can trust you to listen even when I rage."

"You ever have my loyalty, Eleanor," she replied. "That I vow."

ONE

Fourteen months later
June, 1167

"AND THUS it begins."

Malcolm de Monde, Lord of Warwick, drew on the reins and halted his horse. They were on a small rise overlooking the walled castle at Clarendon, where King Henry, Queen Eleanor and the royal court were currently in residence.

From here, he could see countless tendrils of smoke rising into a clear blue sky from the walled cluster of buildings. The castle rose above them, and men at arms watched from the roof. Carts and wagons trundled in and out of the main gate, men-at-arms in groups clattered over the drawbridge, and peasants and tradesmen hurried about their business in the town below.

"I detest court," Malcolm added as he glanced over at his squire, who'd brought his horse up next to him. But Mal's grumbling was unnecessary, for Gambert knew precisely how his master felt about the necessity of leaving Warwick in order to immerse himself in the false niceties, manipulations, and stifling closeness of the royal court.

But he had no choice. Sarah had been dead these four summers, and it was past time for him to take another wife and beget an heir. Although he could certainly do the latter without royal permission—and he was considering a particular Lady Beatrice, the heiress of Delbring—a vassal of Mal's stature couldn't wed without the blessing of the king unless he wished to be taxed and fined up to his eyes for such an impudence. Henry had to fund his continuous warring here in England as well as in France—where he and his wife had massive land holdings. Thus the king took any opportunity to impose fines and taxes and liens upon his vassals.

A shadow overhead caught Mal's attention and he looked up in time to see a golden-brown merlin hawk shooting down from the sky. Entranced by its grace and speed, he watched as the bird skimmed over a small meadow to the north, grazing the tops of its grasses, and then with the slightest hitch in its long, low arc, jerked and then swooped back up. Now, a small creature—rabbit, most likely—dangled from its beak.

Mal watched as the hawk darted toward the edge of the meadow, likely to settle in a treetop nest to tear its meal into edible pieces. Or mayhap it was a hunter bird, trained by a royal falconer, and would return to settle on a leather cuff worn to protect the falconer's skin from the talons. Malcolm found himself rising in the stirrups to see where the bird went—out of curiosity as much as to delay the inevitable of riding onward.

His procrastination was rewarded, for the slight addition to his height gave him a better view into the small meadow cupped by stands of pines, oaks, and other thick trees. At the edge was revealed two men, one in a slouching hood and the other bareheaded. As Mal watched, the handsome raptor landed on the ground near his master, catch still firmly in its talons. The hooded hunter knelt to retrieve the kill before the hawk finished it off. Moments later, he stood, and then, with a shimmer of wings, the raptor flew up and settled onto his outstretched hand. Even from here, Mal could see the merlin eating its reward—likely a chunk of rabbit or squirrel—from the fist of its master.

The sight couldn't help but remind him of a girl he'd known once, when he was a squire hardly older than Gambert. Quick-witted and vivacious, with a beacon of red-gold hair that was as bold as her personality, Judith of Kentworth had nevertheless been mild and patient with the hunting birds her father bred and trained. Mal had fostered along with Gregory of Lundhame, Judith's betrothed, at Kentworth. He'd felt the quick edge of her tongue more often than he'd landed on his arse during sword practice—and that was saying a lot. Mal was shy, light of weight and much too gangly in those years, and he'd spent more time than he cared to admit on the wrong end of a practice sword. More often than not, it was one held by Gregory.

Though his clumsiness and ineptitude had long ago been replaced by speed and skill, he still remembered the jeers and jests from his peers.

The sounds of the rest of their party approaching—the jingle of harnesses, the dull clopping of hooves—drew Mal's attention from his memories of the past.

"Why do you stop here, my lord, when we're so near?" asked Sir Nevril, his master-at-arms, as he joined Mal. He had his hand on the hilt of his sword. "Is aught amiss?"

"Nay," Mal replied, gathering up his reins reluctantly. The sight of the busy, close town below already had the effect of making him feel as itchy as if he'd just donned wet wool. Infested with lice.

"Naught is indeed amiss, other than Warwick's great aversion to all pomp and circumstance and having to lay his pallet in a chamber with a dozen other unwashed men," jested another voice.

Malcolm made a rude gesture to his friend, Dirick, the new Lord of Ludingdon. "I cannot deny my mislike of having every breath of my days and nights managed for me while in attendance to the king. Did you not nearly miss your own father's funeral because of the king's demands?"

Dirick had pulled his horse close enough to Mal's so the two sets of equine ears were nearly aligned. "Aye. The sword of loyalty's blade can swing both ways when one is favored by the king. But I cannot complain on my latest acquisition," he added with a cheeky grin.

"Nay, I should say not," Malcolm replied with a wry smile. For all his time and loyalty given to Henry, Dirick had recently been rewarded with not only a title and fief, but a beautiful, well-landed heiress.

Mal had met Lady Maris and had been astounded by the fact that the lovely woman was not only comely but intelligent as well— and had no qualms about speaking her mind. His Sarah had been sweet-tempered and pretty, but there'd never been an argument betwixt the two of them in which she'd raised her voice above a modulated tone. Mal had been witness to the fact that this was not so with Dirick of Ludingdon and his new bride when Lady Maris, who had been quite heavy with child, decided she meant to ride out some distance from the walls of the keep to tend to an ill farmer. Dirick had taken exception to her intent, and a loud row had ensued, leaving Mal gawking in shock at the lady's stubbornness.

To his further astonishment, she'd gotten her way, with Dirick insisting on accompanying her to the ill farmer whilst she—an accomplished healer— rode in a small cart, leaving his guests to their own meal. Even now, Mal mentally raised his brows at the very memory.

Still, he'd never known Dirick to be happier, and Malcolm was well aware of the benefits of having a wife to warm his bed and manage his household. This was the only reason he'd forced himself to leave the lush green meadows and velvety rolling hillocks of Warwick and his other holdings in northern England to travel to the chaos of the king's court.

The season was early summer, and Malcolm had every intention of being back in Warwick with a wedded, bedded and—God willing—breeding woman before the first snowfall.

~*~

"WHO IS that man?"

Judith winced at the unexpected jab in her side and turned to Lady Ursula. The younger woman's pretty round face was alit with curiosity. "Which man?" she asked, looking around the room.

This was not as simple a task as it would seem, for they were gathering at supper in the great hall at Clarendon. The ceiling rose high above their heads, and the vast chamber was filled with people squeezing into their seats at row after row of trestle tables. Lords and ladies, maidens, knights, monks, men-at-arms, jongleurs, bards, and acrobats, serfs, pages, and stewards—and even a small pack of hunting dogs, a trio of kestrels, and a pride of fat mousers—filled the chamber. Not to mention the *noise.*

It was fair deafening.

The king and queen sat on the dais at the high table, accompanied by the most wealthy and powerful of their guests including Thomas à Becket, the Bishop of Canterbury. And then, row by row, with the richest and most loyal vassals sitting nearest the dais and the meanest serfs and servants in the crowded rear of the chamber, everyone else settled in their places by rank. The further from the archbishop and royal couple, the closer and narrower the tables, and the less plentiful and appetizing the food.

Judith and a group of the queen's ladies sat only three rows from the dais. Further down their table and at the bench behind them were some of the unmarried vassals and higher-ranking knights favored by the king and queen. She knew everyone in the vicinity, for they dined, hunted, socialized, and worshipped together.

"Look you there—he's the tall man bowing to her majesty, standing with Ludingdon. He's even as tall as Ludingdon," Ursula said. Judith resisted the urge to elbow her into keeping her voice low. It was so loud in here, surely no one would hear. "Do you know him? You must know him, Judith. You've been with the queen so long, you know everyone."

She forbore to respond to a comment that, if delivered by any other woman would be considered a gentle insult—but which was meant only in the most innocent of ways coming from Ursula of Tenavaux. Sixteen, undeniably pretty and the daughter of one of the king's French vassals, Ursula was six years younger than the twenty-two-year-old Judith and extremely marriageable. She still found the royal court mesmerizing and exciting, filled with colorful opportunity and gaiety and excitement.

Judith had long ago lost such ingenuousness. But she straightened in her seat on the rough wooden bench and peered toward the front to see if she did, indeed, know who the newcomer was.

"He's sitting next to the king," hissed Ursula unnecessarily. "He must be someone important!"

"That's Lord Warwick," said a low voice that nevertheless reached Judith's ear from across the table and beneath the dull roar of conversation, laughter, shouts, and the metallic clang of utensil and tray. "I heard him announced earlier today. He arrived with Ludingdon."

Judith glanced at Lady Alynne, one of Eleanor's other favorite ladies, and then, turning back to look at the dais, replied, "Warwick?"

She could be forgiven if there was a note of disbelief in her voice, for she'd met both John de Monde, the Lord of Warwick, and his son and heir, Malcolm, when the latter fostered with her father at Kentworth nearly a decade past. The imposing, muscular man settling into his seat next to the king was much too young to be Lord John, and he didn't at all resemble the awkward, earnest young man she'd known years ago.

As Lady Ursula had noted, the newcomer was tall, and Judith suspected he'd top the king by at least a full head. And, unlike Henry and most of the other men in court, he was clean-shaven. His hair, the rich brown color of well-tanned leather, was overly long, just covering his ears and nearly brushing his shoulders in the back. This gave him an unfashionable, almost wild appearance next to the other neatly trimmed and groomed attendants at the high table.

Trying not to appear too interested—for the sharp eyes and quick tongues of the court were always on the spy for gossip—Judith nevertheless continued to steal looks toward the dais throughout the meal. It was curiosity that got the best of her, for despite their differences in personality and appearance, Malcolm de Monde and Judith's betrothed husband, Gregory of Lundhame, had been friends during their fostering.

It wasn't until the man in question turned so she saw the clean shape of his profile that Judith was convinced of his identity. Although his shoulders had broadened greatly and the rest of his body had filled out and matured, the sharp, prominent jut of his nose and squared jaw hadn't changed.

She mused silently at this revelation. So Malcolm was now Lord Warwick. Judith didn't recall hearing of his father's death, but it could have happened during the time she was away from court. Home at Kentworth, grieving over the death of Gregory.

As Judith drew her attention from the guest at the high table, her glance slid over the king. He was looking at her.

Startled, Judith smiled in acknowledgment and half-rose in her seat to make a brief curtsy. The king smiled back and, still looking at her—or at least in her direction—lifted his wine goblet and drank.

"Judith, did you see the new fabrics Tyrinia brought to the queen today?" asked Alynne, drawing her attention from the high table. "I vow, I've not ever seen such delicate material. 'Tis like cobwebs, but shot with emerald and sapphire threads."

"Nay, and I'm sorry I didn't. It sounds lovely, if not expensive. I didn't know Tyrinia was visiting today," Judith said with genuine disappointment. "I might have waited until the morrow for my hunt if I'd remembered."

"That fabric costs more for a bolt than does a good warhorse," Ursula said, a bit of wistfulness in her voice. "And though it glitters like the sea in sunlight, the cloth is so fragile and transparent it isn't suitable for anything other than a veil or overtunic."

"But it would need no embroidery—which is thankful, for it is too delicate to handle much stitching," added Alynne.

"It sounds magnificent," Judith said. For all the time she spent tramping through field and meadow with her hawks, she also enjoyed fashion and clothing just as much. "Verily 'tis as well I didn't see the samples and be left to moon over them." She sighed. "The nearest I shall come to wearing such a fabric is if her majesty has an overtunic made and a bit of it drags over my slipper." They all laughed merrily.

"*Bon soir*, lovely ladies," said a deep voice behind her. "Is there a place for a weary, bedraggled knight to sit at your table?"

Judith turned and looked up as Hugh de Rigonier, baron of Rigonier-Chatte, slid onto the bench between her and Ursula. "Good evening, Lord Hugh," she said with a smile. "Thank you for joining us."

In the realm of the gossipy, whispering, back-stabbing court, Hugh was one of the people whose company she truly enjoyed. "We were just bemoaning the lack of courtly presence at our table tonight, and here you've arrived in the nick of time to keep us from talking only of the latest weave of fabric from Milan and bejeweled hair fashions," Judith jested, using a long red curl to gesture teasingly at him. The lock was enclosed in a slender metal cuff that glinted with tiny gems.

He reached for a hunk of cheese and, breaking off a large piece, gave her an easy grin. His curling golden hair and sparkling blue eyes made him look just as Judith imagined a grown-up cherubic angel would appear—and despite his comment, he wasn't the least bit bedraggled. In fact, his beard and mustache were neatly trimmed and possibly even combed. Nary a hair was out of place.

"I'm relieved to hear it," he said, brushing the cheese dust from his tunic with a slender, elegant hand. "I'd hate to imagine that you lovely ladies must needs resort to such unimaginative discussions."

"You've saved us from that fate," Judith told him, grinning at Ursula, who never failed to gawk at the handsome baron. "But now it falls to you, Lord Hugh, to determine what the topic of conversation will be. Mind you, it must be sparkling and witty and relevant."

"*Merde*, my lady Judith…could you not have set me to a lesser task?" he teased, beckoning for a serf to fill his wine goblet. She merely tilted her head and smiled expectantly. "Very well then," he said with mock exasperation. "Tell me of your hunt this day. Did you go after all? How did Hecate fly for you?"

"Two rabbits and a rat," she told him proudly. "She was eager to be out after being locked in the mews for a se'ennight. But it was the only way for her foot to heal, keeping her silent and in the dark."

"Excellent. But tell me you did not go on the hunt alone, my lady," Hugh replied, looking at her with the most intent and serious expression since he sat down. "You did take Tessing with you, and some men-at-arms? Whence the royal court goes, also goes those who scuttle in its shadow. You'd be a fine temptation for ransom or to wive, my dear."

Judith sighed. "I suspect 'tis the only way I'll become a wife again—if some nefarious brigand or mayhap a rich lord were to snatch me up for himself." She was only partly jesting, for the queen had made it quite clear she preferred Judith to remain her close attendant in the stead of being married off to some other vassal of the king.

Judith hadn't been home to her fief of Lilyfare for more than six years. Instead, the keep and its small village had been managed by Roger of Hyrford, a castellan assigned many years ago by Judith's father.

Hugh chuckled, though his eyes remained serious. "Nay, I trow even that plot wouldn't come to fruition. A fortnight with you and your ever-working, stubborn tongue, and any kidnapper would *pay* the king to take you back." He patted her hand as she glared at him in mock insult and Ursula giggled. "Nay, Judith, you know I jest. 'Tis your lively conversation that keeps me lingering at table more oft than not. But I do not jest when I remind you that you *are* a valuable prize for any man who wishes power, wealth, or influence with her majesty. Now tell me true—did you bring chaperones with you today when you went beyond the walls of the castle, or did you not?"

"Tessing accompanied me, as did Holbert and Piall," she told him. "I might have an energetic tongue, but I'm not a fool."

"I have never counted you as a fool, Lady Judith," he told her. The concern in his eyes eased. "I'm glad to know you took no chances. Now, 'tis your turn to select a topic of conversation, for I mean to apply myself to this meal." He was watching the line of serfs coming from the kitchen, carrying trays and platters.

"Very well then. Mayhap you'll tell us what you know of the lately come Lord Warwick. Lady Ursula and I are quite curious." She smiled secretly at the young, unwed Ursula—for she knew her companion was curious about the newcomer for a very different reason than Judith might be.

A serf pushed between the two rows of benches, setting a platter of small roasted quails down on their table, then another on the next table. Then followed a wooden tray with more thick slices of bread, and Hugh, always the courtier, snatched up three of them and put one on his, Judith's and Ursula's plates as he said, "Ah, aye, Warwick. He's just arrived today—and why should I not be surprised that you wish to know all the gossip, Judith, my dear? If there was ever a woman who knew more of what goes on in this court than the queen, 'twould be you." He grinned again.

Judith passed him the dish of quail stewed in wine and mushrooms, and he scooped out generous servings for her and Ursula before serving himself, pouring the fowl over their bread trenchers. "And who is my best source but you," she said, passing the stew across to Alynne.

"I've not met Warwick personally." Hugh glanced up at the man in question and studied the unkempt lord for a moment, using his eating knife to spear a small piece of quail. "By the rood, if the man can shave his face, then he could surely have his hair trimmed," he murmured, chewing thoughtfully. "In truth, Judith, I know little of the man. But why do you ask me?" he said, turning on her with suddenly sharp eyes. "Was he not of an age with Gregory? Surely they knew each other."

"Aye, they fostered together at Kentworth." Before she could finish her thought, the king rose from his seat. He was wiping his hands with a cloth, and as the hall settled into expectant silence, he handed the rag to one of the pages who stood at attendance behind the high table.

"This night we have been gifted with the presence of the jongleur Duchande, and he has offered to entertain us this evening. The tables shall be moved back and the *rondelets* and *estampies* shall commence!"

A roar of approval filled the hall, and the serfs and pages moved quickly to pull tables away from the dais. This left an empty space large enough for two dozen or more people to dance. Judith climbed eagerly over the bench, gathering her skirts with her, as several of her friends vacated their finished meals as well.

"The last time we danced was on Easter," said Lady Ursula, her eyes sparkling. "I hope I remember the steps for the *estampie*."

"'Tis very simple," Judith told her, catching Ursula's hand on the left and Alynne's on the right. They were forming a large circle, or *rondele*. "Follow the music, and stamp your foot on the third count, then hop on the fourth. Ah, you'll remember once the music begins."

And so it began. Duchande the jongleur wasn't traveling alone, for though he played the psaltery, another of his companions played kettledrums and another had a wooden flute. As Judith hopped and stamped and promenaded through the vigorous steps of the fast-paced *estampie*, she couldn't help but smile broadly. Dancing thus was nearly as enjoyable as watching Hecate take flight, then dart down after her prey, ending with the satisfying sensation of the agile bird settling back onto her leather-covered fist.

Judith glanced at the high table as she danced past, aware that her veil had slipped down and several of her braids were loosening and swirling about her shoulders and elbows. The king and queen were watching the dancers, and so was Lord Warwick. She caught his eye and with a breathless laugh, she stamped her foot hard in time to the music and spun into the next step. Ignoring the stinging vibration from slippered foot meeting solid stone, she dipped and hopped and continued in the circle as the music went on and on.

As she circled around, stamping and hopping and twirling, Judith couldn't help but feel the attention from the high table settling heavily, implacably upon her.

~*~

THE LAST bloody thing Malcolm wanted or expected was to be seated next to the king during dinner, but a benefit of that dubious honor was the excellent view of the Great Hall. Another benefit was being served first, and with the most choice of courses and best vintages of wine.

When Mal realized he was quite hungry and that the quality of the food far surpassed anything he'd eaten in months—yet another reason to obtain a wife—he ceased his inward grumbling about having to make conversation with Henry. More oft than not in his experience such conversations ended expensively—either by virtue of costly services such as men-at-arms being committed, time pledged, or fines and taxes levied as the result of a careless tongue boasting about a particularly good harvest or imported goods.

And there was always the danger of Henry deciding one's estate would be an excellent place to stay while journeying through his kingdom—making that the most expensive prospect of all. Mal had known lords who'd emptied their coffers to the last coin to pay for an extended royal visit, and he didn't want to be one of them. Particularly since he'd just spent the last three years attempting to refill his own after five summers of drought. However, Henry had hardly been in England for two years, and seemed to be intent on his problems in France, so it was likely he wouldn't be traveling to the north any time soon. Thus Mal settled in to enjoy his meal and allowed the king to complain about the upstart French vassals in Aquitaine that continued to challenge his authority.

It was partway through the second course of stewed quail that Malcolm noticed the vivacious young woman seated three rows away from the dais. She seemed to be greatly enjoying herself, conversing with ladies and men alike, laughing, jesting, gesturing. Everyone seemed to want to speak to her. It wasn't until she turned and a bit of red-gold hair slipped from beneath her veil that he felt a stab of recognition.

Surely it wasn't Lady Judith. Mal shook his head mentally and sopped up the last bit of gravy with a crust of bread. The falconer in the meadow had merely put him in mind of her earlier today, and that, combined with the color of this woman's hair—albeit a color he'd never witnessed on anyone other than Lady Judith—made him see a resemblance where there was none.

But he found himself unable to keep from studying her in the same way a dog couldn't cease from gnawing on a flea bite. When the music started and she came near the dais to dance with her friends, Mal saw her face clearly for the first time as she stomped and twirled about.

It *was* Judith. How could he have doubted it? The woman was as she had ever been—surrounded by a crowd, talking and motioning energetically. Just watching her lithe, graceful figure made Mal twitchy and irritated. Apparently the years had done naught to relax her tongue or settle her boisterous spirit. Even the death of her betrothed at the hand of her powerful cousin Gavin Mal Verne seemed not to have dampened her spirit.

Although Malcolm and Gregory had been peers and trained together as pages then squires before being knighted, they had never been particularly close friends. Gregory had a slick way about him Mal didn't care for, as well as an overly critical tongue. Aside from that, he'd been betrothed to the beautiful, wealthy young woman who was a favorite of Queen Matilda—a far sight different from Malcolm, whose father had selected a plain, if not biddable, wife for him whose dowry was only a small chest of gold coins and a pair of warhorses.

Still, he would never have wished Gregory harm. And to be slain by his betrothed wife's cousin was no happy occurrence, regardless of the reason for it. Judith must have been overset and distraught, although clearly she had come to terms with his death.

Malcolm wasn't able to extricate himself from the company of King Henry until long after the platters and trays had been cleared away, the bottles of wine emptied, and the dancers pled exhaustion. Many of them, including the fiery-haired Lady Judith, left the hall. When Duchante the jongleur sat himself up on a stool to sing a final ballad for the night, Mal couldn't have been more relieved.

As soon as the song ended, he begged leave of the king and queen, citing the need to check on his horse in the stable.

Outside, Mal breathed in the fresh night, glad to be quit of the loud, crowded hall with its heavy, smoke-filled air. The enclosed yard, or bailey, was fairly empty except for men-at-arms taking their turn standing watch on the walls above and an occasional serf or other figure rushing off somewhere. Flickering torches studded the turrets and were assisted by a full, pearly moon and a swath of sparkling stars. The night was very well lit.

He had to ask directions to the particular stable where Alpha had been taken, and was told by one of the marshals "'tis the low yonder one, on the way passing the hawk mews."

Of course that direction put him in mind once again of Lady Judith, and as he strode toward the stable, he wondered if she kept any of her raptors with her at court. Or if she even hunted any longer. And he wasn't certain why he continued to think of her.

"Malcolm?"

The voice interrupted his thoughts, bringing him to a sharp standstill.

"Lord Warwick?"

As if he'd conjured her up with all of his musings, suddenly there was Lady Judith standing at the shadowy doorway to what was presumably the mews.

"Lady Judith," he said. All at once, he felt tense and uncomfortable, which irritated him even more than…well, than the whole idea of being here. Away from Warwick. And Violet.

"My pardon, my lord, I shouldn't have greeted you thus. Until this night, I didn't realize you were Warwick now," she said, stepping closer and into better light.

"Good evening Lady Judith," he said, pausing reluctantly. "It has been a long time since we've spoken."

"Aye," she said, and from behind her, he heard movements inside the mews. "I'll return in a moment, Tessing," she called into the building.

Mal had a sense of relief she wasn't out of the keep in the middle of the night without company. Still, if Tessing was the same falconer who'd worked with Judith at Kentworth, the man must be near sixty by now, hardly a deterrent to any drunk or rapacious man-at-arms who meant to cause mischief—or worse. "Where is your man?" he asked. "Are you here in the bailey alone?"

"Alone but for my constant companion." She produced a slender glint of metal in the form of a dagger. "And Tessing. As well as Sir Holbert. I'm not foolish enough to go about without him or Sir Piall, even in the king's yard."

Mal nodded and realized his mind had gone irritatingly blank. He'd never had much to say to Judith—not that her busy tongue would have allowed him any opportunity to speak—and part of the reason was still terribly evident: he found her to be utterly, intimidatingly beautiful. Limned by silvery moonlight, her veil slipped carelessly down to her shoulders. With her elegant, perfectly formed nose and high cheekbones outlined by the pearly light, she appeared even more comely than he recalled. Her brilliant red-gold hair blazed even in the gray night. He forced himself to look away, settling his attention onto the relative safety of her shoulder.

"I hope you are well, Lord Warwick," she said, stepping even closer. Now he must look at her lips, curved into a soft, welcoming smile, and the shape of her eyes—like that of a perfect peach pit. She gave a little laugh. "It feels odd to name you so; for I have still and always did think of you only as Malcolm, a friend of my—of Gregory's."

"I care not if you call me Malcolm," he said with a shrug. Then, realizing she'd given him an opening, he added, "'Twas a tragedy, Gregory's death. I have heard…." He hesitated. "Is it true Mal Verne slayed him?"

She nodded, her smile fading slightly. "Aye. 'Twas even before Gregory and I were able to marry. But Gavin has overpaid his penance for the deed—and 'twas an unfortunate circumstance all around. Gregory was involved in an ugly scheme—one he should never have been part of. Thus, I hold no grudge against Gavin, and he has finally come to accept that. He is well now, and recently wed. And tell me of your father. Lord John? What happened?"

The pang of grief still nudged at him, though it had been years. "A growth overtook his belly, and he died in his bed after a long illness. 'Twas five years past."

"I've heard you only arrived in Clarendon this day. What brings you so far from home?" she asked, and Mal wondered if she meant to keep him conversing all the night.

Why did he feel so itchy, so impatient? So…unsure of himself? 'Sblood, he wasn't the awkward, green boy he'd been when last they met. His irritation with himself grew and he responded more bluntly than he meant. "I've come to petition the king, for I'm in need of a wife."

The moment those words left his lips he realized that for the first time 'twas a possibility—although a far-reaching one—that Judith of Kentworth could be his wife. As soon as the thought formed, a heady rush of heat flooded his body, making him light of head…then was followed immediately by a sharp chill that left him feeling slightly ill. Nay. He wouldn't even consider the prospect. She was…not suitable for him.

"Did you not wed Sarah of Glawstering?" she asked, seemingly insistent on learning every event that had overtaken his life in the last seven years. Would she soon ask him how many moons it had been since he last saw his mother? Or how many times he'd gone to a shire's faire?

But despite his desire to end the conversation and get away from the woman, he must respond. "Lady Sarah and I were wed as planned, but a fever claimed her four summers ago."

"I'm very sorry," Judith said, her eyes so very large and steady, fastened upon him. Although he couldn't see their color, he knew they couldn't have changed from the clear blue sapphire hue they'd been when he and she were younger. "Did you have any children?"

A daughter. But he didn't say it aloud. "Lady Judith, do you not allow me to keep you from your business," he said, gesturing to the mews. "I am certain we shall speak again while I'm here at court." *But as little as possible for the duration of my visit.* For he didn't care for the unsettled way she made him feel. As if he were a young, green, awkward boy again. "Mayhap I should allow you to continue with your task so Holbert can be relieved before the moon rises too high."

Judith looked at him speculatively, but to his surprise, she merely nodded at his suggestion. "I'm certain Sir Holbert will appreciate your conscientiousness. I'll be certain to tell him of your concern." Her eyes danced, yet her words sounded sincere.

Malcolm was fair ready to be on his way and he cared little whether she was jesting with him or nay. "Very well then, my lady. I bid you good evening." And he hurried off toward the stable, determined to take a different route when he returned to the keep.

TWO

THE NEXT morning, as was her habit, Judith rose just after the sun filtered through the narrow slit of her window.

As a favorite of the queen and a permanent resident of the court, she was granted the luxury of a private chamber for herself and her maid, Tabatha, who slept on a thick pallet in a small antechamber just inside the door. In a pile of rags next to her pallet snored a decrepit dog named Bear and another unidentifiable ball of fur.

"Good morrow, milady," Tabatha said, already digging in one of Judith's trunks as she hummed softly. She straightened, holding a dark red bliaut that glittered with gold embroidery at the hem and cuffs. "Will this suit for today?"

"Aye." Judith was already unplaiting her thick braid in preparation for the maid to comb it out and fashion it into a more complicated style. She sat in her plain, linen kirtle by the fire, which needed to be naught more than a small, whimpering blaze on this warm June morning. Though in summer the stone walled chambers of the keep could feel damp and cool, a roaring fire was hardly necessary.

The activity in the chamber prompted Bear to stir. He gave a deep, annoyed groan that clearly bespoke his opinion of early risers. The ball of fur curled up next to him unrolled into the fluff of an amber-striped kitten, who stumbled sleepily from his resting place.

"Lotty is so steady on her feet already," Judith said as the small cat padded over toward her. "She's healed more quickly than I'd imagined. 'Twas good of you to bring the poor mite here, Tabby."

Her maid smiled in affection at the little creature, who was batting at the hem of Judith's shift with a tiny white paw. "Aye, look at her now. 'Tis hard t'believe she was only a scrawny, bloody little thing just a se'ennight past."

"You have a gift for healing animals, that's certain," Judith said as she stood and pulled off the kirtle in which she slept. "Even if your patients tend to overrun my chamber betimes," she added drily.

"Ah, ye wouldn't be near as happy if ye didn't have something to badger me about, milady. Ye love the critters as much as I do." Tabatha spoke tartly as she helped her mistress into the bliaut, which was a long, fitted tunic that laced up the side to give the gown shape. Its sleeves were laced tight from elbow to wrist and the hem covered her slippers, dragging on the ground behind her.

"I cannot argue with that, but I beg you not to befriend any more mother skunks preparing to give birth...at the least until we return to Lilyfare. Then I shall grant you an entire out-building for your animal caretaking." Judith made the comment in jest, but nevertheless, a wave of sadness and frustration surged over her.

"Lilyfare?" Tabby snorted, her blue eyes flashing. "'Twill be the end of the world—or at least her reign—before the queen allows you to see those green hills again."

"Aye. But I miss it so much...and, it seems, more as of late than ever before."

"As do I, milady," the maid said softly, folding up the discarded kirtle. "But 'tis our lot to serve the queen."

"Aye. To be a bird, caged at her majesty's whim and allowed not even to hunt...but only to sing the songs she wishes to hear." Judith bit her lip, suddenly irritated with her discontent. She was blessed in numerous ways being a member of the queen's close retinue. She had more freedom than many other ladies, coming and going with her raptors almost as she pleased, her own chamber, and the ear of the queen (who had the even more important ear of the king)—as well as a cluster of friends with whom she might make merry.

Though that cluster of friends might sift and change as they wed and left court, there were always newcomers to befriend. An ever-changing sea of lords and ladies currying favor with the royal couple and their confidantes. And at court, one always had good food and new fashions, priests when they were needed, and the best medical care from physicians of both Paris and London as well as Antioch. Even exotic foodstuffs, such as oranges, olives, and cinnamon, were readily available.

Truly, Judith had naught of which to complain. And so she lifted her chin and lectured herself into compliance. If she were at Lilyfare, she reminded herself, she'd never have tasted a fresh fig. And that would have been a tragedy.

Judith approved Tabby's choice of a simple gold-link girdle to wrap around her waist, then slipped her eating knife into a sheath affixed to the chain and hung a small pouch of coins next to it. As she slid her feet into soft leather shoes, the furious sound of metal clanging rose from below.

She peered out the narrow window slit, her fingers brushing the cool stone, and looked down. In the courtyard, knights and men-at-arms trained. Their metal blades gleamed though the early morning light was dull with rainclouds, and she heard shouts and jests floating up in deep masculine voices.

"The men are training early this morn," Tabby commented. "Even before mass."

"From the look of the clouds, it'll rain betimes," Judith told her. "Then they'll be cooped inside like a bunch of riotous chickens. Better to work off some of their bile before then, or there will be fights in the hall. Men are such war-mongering fools," she added wryly. "Not a one is happy if he isn't brandishing a blade and making off to fight some battle—whether real or imagined. Never do they care if their women are left behind, waiting for word of them." As she had been when Gregory went off to fight. And never returned.

"'Tis one of the things I find comforting about my station," Tabby said with the frank honesty they shared from more than a decade of being servant and mistress. She'd been Judith's maid since she was eight and her lady was ten—although at that time, she'd merely been learning how to be a good tiring woman. "The chance of any husband of mine riding off to protect his lands—or even the king's—will happen nearly about the time Her Majesty releases you to Lilyfare. Should I ever find a husband, he'll be naught but a marshal, smith or miller—and devoid of warlust."

"And that blessing I pray for you, Tabby, dearling," Judith said. "That you must never lift the mail *sherte* off or onto the shoulders of your husband. And now, I must see to Hecate before mass, for I fear the rain will come soon."

Judith's slippered feet were light on the curving stone stairs as she bounded down them. Tapestries—some wrought by Queen Eleanor, but mostly by her ladies—as well as the flaming wall sconces fluttered in Judith's energetic wake. When she reached the bottom, instead of pausing in the hall where serfs prepared for the breaking of the fast after mass, she went out into the bailey.

She had to pass by the training yard on her way to the mews... well, mayhap that wasn't quite true. She could have cut across between the fore stable and the bakery, but then she wouldn't have had the opportunity to walk past the pairs of men battling with broadsword and shield. And aside from that, the strip of grass between the stable and bakery was sure to be wet from the dew, which would soak her slippers.

Thus, Judith had ample opportunity to observe the two dozen or so knights and men-at-arms as she went on her way. Many of them wore only mail chausses and boots, leaving their shoulders and chests bare. If it were midday, they likely wouldn't have been so bold—for fear one of the women might see them. But Ursula, Alynne, and the other ladies were most likely still abed, or at the least dressing for mass.

But Judith was no prude—after all, she'd grown up watching men train in her father's yard, oft in various states of undress. As well, she and Gregory were betrothed for more than a year before he died, and they'd been intimate on more than one occasion. Before she came to court, Judith had even attended to visiting lords or other important men at her father's estate, often bathing them herself as a sign of honor and hospitality.

Thus she counted herself fortunate rather than mortified to see and admire the sleek muscles, broad, square shoulders, and dark patches of hair covering many of the bare chests of some of the king's best warriors. Sweat gleamed, muscles bulged, and powerful arms swung swords nearly as heavy as Judith herself.

She knew many of the men: Hugh de Rigonier, James of Revrielle, Clancy de Monfronte, and at the furthest edge of the group, Malcolm of Warwick. Judith found herself wanting to pause and watch him for a moment—simply out of curiosity, of course, for she'd oft seen the other men during their swordplay—but she dared not be noticed gawking. Still, Judith took note of Mal's sleek bunches of muscle, rippling down his arms and over his shoulders. He moved with speed and surprising grace for one so tall, his too-long hair plastered over his eyes and across one cheek.

As she continued past, now eyeing the lunging and spinning movements of the other warriors, she noticed a pair of younger fighters. Squires, likely, and mayhap barely fifteen years of age. They were surrounded by a small group of others of their age; not the full-grown, knighted men, but younger ones still aspiring to receive their accolade. One of the two fighters was long and gangly and overmatched by his more agile partner. As Judith approached, she was reminded of the days at Kentworth when Gregory was fostering. She'd watch him practice whenever she could, utterly besotted by his handsome face and curling blond hair. He was quick and lithe, even if he used his feet to trip his sparring partner as oft as he did his sword.

If he had not done such foolish, dangerous things and gotten killed, she would be married. They would likely have a babe or two. And she would be home at Lilyfare, with a man who—if he did not love her, at the least he cared for her somewhat.

A shout caught her attention, and Judith looked over in time to see the taller, slighter young fighter tumble into a heap on the muddy ground. His sword lay well out of reach, and it appeared he'd tripped on his own feet instead of being disarmed by his opponent.

None of the other young men went so far as to laugh or even jeer at him—but mayhap that was even worse. Instead, Judith caught some laughing, slanted looks cast between them along with a few expressions of disgust.

Someone handed the boy his sword as he picked himself off the ground. From the amount of dirt on his tunic and chausses, it was clear it wasn't the first time he'd taken a spill.

"Better luck next time, Rike," the other boy said jovially. But even from where she stood, Judith could tell he was trying hard not to smile.

She looked away quickly, for fear Rike would see her watching and be even more mortified. But at the same time, her mind was working. He needed someone to train with—someone who knew what he was doing and could teach him how to move his too-long legs and control his awkward arms. Mayhap she would ask Hugh to take him under his wing, or—nay. Not Hugh. Malcolm.

Nay, *Warwick*. She must remember to think of him as Lord Warwick now.

But it was a good thought, no mater how she named the man in her mind. How many times had Mal—Warwick—ended up accidentally dropping his sword or tripping over its tip when he was younger? Judith had oft seen it happen when he was fostering with Gregory. Once, he'd tried to do a spinning lunge and ended up flat on his face, his sword bouncing across the dirt, his own shield cutting him across the cheek as he fell. If anyone could advise Rike, 'twould be Warwick.

She kept walking, frowning in thought. But would he even be willing? Did he have the temperament? During their brief conversation last evening by the mews, she'd sensed impatience and discomfort fairly rolling off him. Whether it was caused by herself or nay, Judith didn't know. But she must find out before putting any plan into action. The poor boy didn't need any further bruise to his ego, that was certain.

By now she'd reached the mews. Tessing was there of course, his sparse white hair standing in soft, curly tufts at the back of his head like the underdown of a baby merlin. His watery gray eyes were bright as he looked up from sweeping to greet her.

He preferred to sleep on a small pallet in the falcon house, and Judith didn't dissuade him. He liked to be among the feathers, he told her, for they didn't talk back to him. (That had been a veiled reprimand to her in remembrance of Judith's stubbornness and saucy tongue when she was younger and just learning her way around the birds—thinking she knew better than he. How soon she learned otherwise.) And 'twas good for the birds to be around men as much as possible. As well, Tessing's presence also protected them from any cat or other beast—including a two-legged one—that might wish to partake of the valuable hunters.

By the time Judith finished checking Hecate's foot and feeding her and the three other falcons, what was left of the anemic yellow sun had turned gray. She stayed with her birds for another few moments, settling them one by one in turn on a leather-gloved fist and speaking quietly while they ate a small treat, just as her father had taught her to do. When she finally came back out of the mews, the clouds hung thick and heavy. The scent of impending damp filled the air.

Nevertheless, Judith took her time wandering back to the hall. She'd missed mass, but there was another at terce and she could always go to confession if she missed that one too. Since she was bound to be closed up the rest of the day if the clouds were any indication, she wanted to enjoy the fresh air—and she suspected God might appreciate that sentiment as much or more than her presence at daily mass. At the least, she hoped so. She certainly wasn't brave enough to raise the question with Father Anselm.

Some of the men were still training, and Judith slowed her pace without appearing to do so. She looked around for Rike, wanting to assure herself he wasn't moping in a corner of the yard—or, worse, tumbled on the ground again or cut by his own blade. At first she didn't see him, and Judith slowed even more.

Hugh caught sight of her and paused mid-battle, swiping a forearm over his perspiring forehead. He grinned and waved, then charged back toward his opponent, who was no match for Hugh's quick feet.

She returned the hail and finally caught sight of Rike. He was standing near the edge of the training yard, away from the others, but he wasn't alone. Malcolm of Warwick stood there, speaking to him, gesturing with his large, broad hands, and the younger man was nodding earnestly. Malcolm towered over the boy just enough that Judith suspected Rike might grow as tall as he some day, for he was well on his way there.

Well. Mayhap they'd both had the same idea. Judith smiled to herself, determined to find out if that was the case.

"And what does such a lovely woman find so amusing on this dreary day?"

Judith halted in her tracks, then sank into an efficient curtsy. "My lord," she said, her voice directed toward the ground due to her pose of obeisance. She could see the fine leather shoes of the king just outside her field of vision. When he took her hand to draw her to her feet, she looked up to find him smiling down at her.

"Well, Lady Judith, what is it that brings such a beautiful smile to an already lovely face?" he asked again.

"Good morrow, my lord," she said, trying to gather her scattered wits. She'd spoken with the king numerous times, and she was a confidante of his wife. The mere royal presence wasn't enough to set her mind to the wind; it was that he'd come upon her so quickly and intruded upon her thoughts. Thoughts which she preferred not to share. "I was merely thinking about…a jest Lord Hugh made last evening, at the expense of the jongleur," she manufactured quickly.

"And pray what was that?" pressed the king. His attention was focused so heavily on her Judith found it difficult to breathe.

"Naught but his assertion that if the man could shave his face, then why could he not cut his hair?" Hugh had said that about Warwick in an almost admiring fashion, but the king didn't know that and Judith needed an answer.

"Indeed," replied Henry. He stroked his reddish beard, a darker, duller shade than Judith's own hair. He hadn't released her hand, and Judith felt an odd tripping of her heart as she became aware of this. "Hugh is a witty man, 'tis true. Lady Judith," he said, command replacing his conversational tone, "'tis our good fortune to have come upon you this morrow. Had we attended mass as Becket suggested, in the stead of coming to view our men, we shouldn't have had such a happy moment."

"Ah," Judith replied, managing to slip her fingers from his grip under the guise of adjusting her girdle, "I wonder what the archbishop would say on that, knowing you chose the task of war over that of worship." She kept her tone light, knowing the king appreciated jests. "But mayhap you could convince him your intent was to worship amid God's natural house on this cloudy day, and not mention that it was in the same yard as your fighting men."

Henry chuckled, his blue eyes lighting with humor. "Beautiful and witty. 'Tis no wonder our queen admires you, Lady Judith."

She relaxed. She'd misunderstood the warmth in his eyes and the too-long clasp of her hand. Even the king wouldn't tread upon his wife's ground. "Not nearly as much as I love her, your majesty," she replied.

"And pretty with the compliments as well," he acknowledged. "Well, then, Lady Judith, let us tell you of the thought we've had. The queen has just informed us of her news—that she expects another confinement in seven or eight months. So soon after Joan's birth, aye? But I daresay, 'tis not only the fault of the queen. And mayhap you are already aware of this," he added with a twinkle in the eye.

Judith wasn't certain whether to acknowledge that she was, indeed, aware of the queen's condition and so she remained silent with a vague smile curving her lips.

"We now tell you—if she produces another son and heir for us, his name shall be John. But if she is blessed with a daughter, her name shall be Mary. 'Tis no matter now...but the reason we wish to speak with you is simple. We wish to gift her with a fine, well-trained falcon, fit for a queen, in celebration of this news. And we know of no other lady who should be the one to find and train this huntress bird."

"Oh my lord, you honor me," Judith said, sweeping into another curtsy. Inside, she was alive and fairly bouncing with enthusiasm. "I would be very grateful to take on such a task! It would give me such pleasure to do so for her majesty—and for you as well. I thank you."

"Please, rise, my lady," he said, pulling her to her feet again. "We have great confidence in your abilities. You may begin this task this day—if," he added as a large raindrop splashed onto their joined hands, "the weather allows."

Before she could reply, the clouds opened up, releasing a heavy downpour. Judith gave a soft shriek in surprise, and the king chuckled. "Apparently, 'tis not to be. Off with you, my lady," he said, gesturing her back to the keep.

She heard his laughter behind her as she took his advice, picked up her skirts, and ran.

~*~

MAL DIDN'T mind the rain, and to the lad Rike's obvious surprise, he kept him in the training yard even after the other men peeled away and went inside. A crash of thunder rolled nearby, followed by a streak of lightning—but it was distant. They had time.

"You'll fight in the rain too," he told Rike, showing the boy once more how to use the weight of the broadsword to lever it into a powerful upward swing. "And in the dark. And when you're weary or injured or hungry. Thus 'tis best to train under all conditions as well."

"Aye, my lord," Rike replied soberly, trying the demonstrated move once more.

Mal watched him try it twice, then thrice, and nodded with satisfaction. "Aye. 'Tis much improved even today."

The rain pelted onto them, dripping from their hair into their eyes, soaking through to their hose. Mal could have remained in the training yard all the day, for the downpour felt cool and refreshing after the closeness of the great hall and sleeping chambers. But Rike, still wearing his tunic, looked like an angular, half-drowned dog, so he took pity on the miserable boy. "Go on with you, then. But I'll meet up with you here tomorrow at dawn if you wish some more advice."

"Oh, aye, Lord Warwick, I do." The young man's reply was filled with genuine hope and enthusiasm. "Thank you."

"Be off," Mal said with a grin. "And do you take care not to trip on those boat-feet of yours." He watched Rike hurry away, remembering with more than a touch of discomfort his early days of training. He had the same massive feet, the same uncontrollable arms of ridiculous length, and hands that just couldn't seem to do what he wanted.

There'd been no kind lord to mentor him while at Kentworth, but at last a grizzled master-at-arms had taken him aside—much as Mal had done to Rike today—and found him a sword better suited for his weight and height. And Mal had practiced and practiced and practiced.

A bolt of lightning flashed closer now and Mal glared up at it. "Very well," he growled to the heavens. "Back into shelter I go. But if you'll be so kind as to find me a wife, I can soon quit this place." He collected his *sherte* and tunic. He preferred to train without them whenever possible, because they became soaked with perspiration and, often, blood and dirt as well. But today, they were just as wet as if he'd worn them. And as he didn't wish to walk into the keep with his torso bare, he struggled into the soaking clothing and slid his sword into its sheath.

When he came into the Great Hall, dripping but not the least bit chilled, Malcolm found it just as he expected: filled with people everywhere, the space loud and close. Yet he hadn't broken his fast and there was food to be had, so he tamped down his irritation and searched for an empty place among the trestle tables.

"Warwick!" someone called, and he turned to see Lady Judith.

For some unaccountable reason, his chest tightened and he meant to keep walking...but before he could force himself to do so, his feet turned and brought him over to her. It was rude, he told himself, to ignore a gentlelady's hail. She sat at a small table next to one of the lesser fireplaces, a chessboard arranged in front of her.

He swiped the long, sopping hair from his forehead, careful not to stand so close he'd drip all over her and the table as he gave a brief bow. "Good morrow, Lady Judith," he said politely, noticing her own clothing was still damp.

Of course he'd seen her walking by the training yard earlier—how could one ignore that beacon of fiery hair, especially in a colorless morn such as this? Little wisps of it fell from her coiffure, settling over her shoulders in frizzing curls. She wore no veil this morrow.

"I beg of you, my lord—a game of chess?" she asked. He opened his mouth to decline, but as was Judith's way, she barreled on, "I've taken two games already this morning from my opponents, and no one else is brave enough to challenge me. 'Twill be a long day cooped in here if I've naught to occupy my time, for the queen is locked away with her steward and has no need of me this morrow."

Mal could think of a variety of ways she could occupy her time—dancing, jesting, flirting and talking with all of her friends, sewing and whatever else ladies did when they weren't torturing men—but declined to mention them. Instead, he shook his head. "Nay, my lady, I dare not. I'm soaked to the skin and would be a poor opponent, dripping all over the table as I am."

"But there is a seat for you right next to the fire," Judith pointed out with a smile. "You'll dry in a trice, and as I suspect you haven't broken your fast, there will also be cheese and apples from the page who hovers just yonder."

He looked down at her, realizing he'd been maneuvered quite neatly into doing her bidding. There was no honorable way out of the situation, and he realized it wasn't such an unfortunate thing after all. "Very well, Lady Judith. But I trow, if you play chess as well as you maneuvered me, I doubt I'll have a chance for checkmate."

She laughed merrily and he felt his own lips tugging into a smile. Like a bolt of sunshine, her good humor and vivacity were near impossible to resist, and he felt himself relaxing a little. "You're too kind, Mal—er, Warwick. But I challenged you because I hope for a good battle on this game, at the least."

Before he was even settled in his seat, the page approached and set a goblet of wine and a small plate of white cheese and sliced apples nearby. Mal glanced at Judith, wondering if this too was part of her grand plan, then returned to arranging his chess pieces.

They made their first few moves, playing in silence for a while. Mal had the stray thought that it was unusual for Judith to be quiet for such a stretch, but when he glanced up and saw her coppery brows drawn together, he realized she was concentrating on her game. He grinned, determined to be the one to give her a good battle this day. And as she pondered her next move, he had the opportunity to look upon her without feeling awkward.

He noticed her slender hand, delicate and graceful as it hovered over her queen's rook. There were scratches and one deep scar near the wrist and he wondered if it were from her raptors or some other mishap. Her skin wasn't the same pearly white as that of most ladies, who spent much of their time indoors. Instead, her hands, throat, and face were a pleasing golden color, faintly brushed with amber and honey freckles.

Mal's mind wandered, wondering if the freckles and sun-kissed coloring extended beneath her clothing, where he could see the curve of her breasts and well knew the shape of her hips, for they swayed enticingly as she walked…then when he realized his folly, he snatched his thoughts back to the game. *Foolish, man.*

She was not a suitable wife for him. She was too…loud and energetic and, he sensed, she would demand much from any husband she might take. Attention. Conversation. Chess games.

"I saw you this morrow," Judith said, taking his king's bishop with a flourish. "In the training yard."

"Aye," he replied, considering his next move. She'd done what he expected, fallen into his own trap on the board…but he must decide whether to spring it yet, or lull her into a false sense of security. He grinned to himself. She was a worthy opponent thus far, however, causing him to rethink his strategy more than once.

"I believe you will make a fine husband indeed," she said, startling him so his hand jerked. He nearly knocked over his queen and sent two other pieces awry.

"A fine husband?" he managed to say in a normal voice. But he didn't have quite the courage to look at her, for he feared what she might see in his eyes. And yet, his thoughts flew to that secret desire, long tamped away and nearly forgotten until only yesterday. *Mad. You are mad to even think of it.*

"Yes indeed. Is that not why you are here? At court? To find a wife? That's what you said last evening." Her voice was amused—until she looked down and saw that he'd taken *her* bishop. "A pox on you, Mal! I had plans for that holy man!"

He couldn't hold back a rumbling chuckle. "Well, then, mayhap you should put your attention on the game in the stead of my business, Lady Judith."

"But I vow I could help you with your business," she told him, chewing on a fingernail as she looked at the board. "I am well-acquainted with all the ladies at court, and many others. I have been known to help make many a match of them. And I could," she added, looking up at him even as her face was angled toward the board, "help you determine which would be worthy of a man such as you."

Mal was caught for a moment by those blue eyes, soft and warm and smiling. *A man such as you.* Something inside him creaked pleasantly.

"After all," she continued, looking back down, thank the Blessed Lord, and grasping the head of her queen, "you *are* Warwick. You control near as much land in England as my cousin Gavin Mal Verne and Lord Salisbury, and you have the wealth to go with it. As well, you are quite a skilled warrior, as was evident in the yard this morrow, and would surely be able to defend any threat to you or your wife. And then there is the matter of the unfortunate young man named Rike."

"Rike?" he said after a beat of a moment, comprehension catching up with his thoughts.

"Aye. I saw you speaking with him, working with him. It was very kind of you, Mal—my lord. And you appeared to have done so with tact and care, so as not to mortify the poor boy. Check."

Mal's attention whipped back down to the game. How the bloody rood had she done *that?* Well, 'twas no matter. He could easily maneuver himself out of that threat and continue on. He shifted a pawn and replied, "The boy's barely a squire and won't make it to knighthood without some guidance. He's as like to fall on his own sword than use it to defend himself."

"I saw him too, and, ah, well...Mal, I was going to approach you and suggest the very thing. But you had already done so." She was looking at him again with those warm eyes, only a game-board distance away.

"Because he reminded you of me, when I was such an age?" he asked, not quite able to keep a tinge of bitterness from his voice.

"Mayhap some trifle bit," she replied carelessly, sliding her knight into place with a grand gesture. "But most of all because of who you'd become. Check, sirrah!"

"You hardly know who I've become," he retorted, swiftly moving his king out of danger.

"'Tis true...but even as we sit here, I learn more of you. And all the ladies are asking about you, too, my lord; do you not allow yourself to think otherwise. Any new face at court—particularly one as pleasing as yours—will garner such interest. Because we are old friends, though, I wish only for the best for you. And therefore, 'tis my intent to drive you clear from certain potential wives...such as...." She leaned over the table, her face coming so close that he could see that the single, dainty freckle on her eyelid was amber and not brown, "Gladys of Darvington and Winifred d'Alsineaux." Judith's voice had dropped to a husky whisper, and she held his gaze with hers. "Keep yourself far from them, my lord, I beg of you, and you will be much happier." She grinned then as her hand swooped down and snatched up his queen, replacing it with her knight. She looked up at him with dancing, triumphant eyes.

He nodded gravely, reaching for the board. "Thank you very much for the warning, my lady. Check...*mate.*"

Her eyes popped wide and she nearly burst from her seat. "Nay! You did not!" But as she looked frantically at the board, her hand hovering from place to place as if to find some move to free her from the trap, her lips pursed in acceptance. "Fie! You are fortunate, my lord, for my very next move would have been to put an end to you myself."

"I am well aware of that," he replied, entertained by how quickly her mood had changed from earnest advice to mischief to irritation. "Nevertheless, you are a formidable opponent, my lady."

"As are you, my lord." He detected the bit of a pout in her tone and he couldn't completely smother a smile. "Laugh at me all you wish," she told him tartly, "but I vow our next meeting will finish quite differently!"

"I dare not laugh at you, Lady Judith," he told her, doing just that—and was surprised with himself for doing so. And surprised that he had not taken her words as an opportunity to take his leave—for there was no reason to stay now that the game was finished. He was eager to be on his way. Yet, he did not rise. "Did you not beg me to play with you in order to offer you a better challenge than your last opponents?"

"Mmph." She made a comical expression, then reached to pluck the last slice of apple from his tray. "Now that I have told you whom to avoid, my lord, mayhap you should tell me what you seek in a wife. Surely she must be beautiful and come with a large dowry chest or a fief of her own...but what more do you seek? Shall she have hair the color of honey or eyes as green as the heath-grass?"

"I care not the color of her hair or eyes," he replied impatiently. "'Tis of no import to me. I care not whether she is homely or comely. But she must be modest and biddable. And she must know how to manage an estate, for I need a good chatelaine to oversee the household." Beatrice of Delbring, whose estate was only two days' ride from Warwick, met all of those requirements. And she would be a good mother to Violet, for, as a cousin of Sarah's, she'd oft visited Warwick. But...there were other options here at court.

"Aye," Judith said, nodding sagely. "The Warwick holdings are vast, and you must oft travel between them."

"Not so oft as one might suppose," he replied. "There is much to keep me occupied at Warwick Castle, and I have long-serving, trustworthy castellans at my other holdings. In sooth, I prefer not to leave Warwick at all. 'Tis where I belong, my home. I would never have come *here* had I not been in sore need of a wife, and permission from the king to take one." Mal closed his mouth at that point, astonished that he'd spoken so many words—and to a woman—and at the same time discomfited by the raw honesty of the contents of his speech.

He looked up at Judith to see what her reaction would be to his bluntness. Her expression had turned sober. Even a little sad. "Aye. 'Tis difficult to be away from one's home."

Something in her tone prompted him to ask, "Have you not been to Lilyfare as of late?"

Judith laughed, but it was humor tinged with bitterness. "Nay, my lord. I've not been to my lands for six years. The queen has made this court my home, and I fear I will never see the green heath of Lilyfare until I am buried there. If perchance the queen will even allow *that*." She laughed again, but he heard the strain beneath the lightness.

"I am sorry for that, my lady. But surely there are benefits to being in the confidence of the queen?" Malcolm could hardly fathom what benefits might overweigh the comfort and privacy of home, but he was doing his best to be gallant.

"Oh, aye, I mustn't sound like I'm unhappy. I'm truly not," Judith replied brightly. "There is always entertainment here and people to talk with—and play chess with," she added with a sassy, more genuine smile. "And her majesty has been very good to me on many occasions."

"And surely you have done aught for her, my lady, or she would not be so attached to you," he reminded her.

"I copy her private letters for her betimes, and if she consults with someone, I often sit with her so I can help her recall the conversation. She considers me a friend as much as she considers anyone, I trow. I am very blessed to be in my position, my lord. Please excuse my moment of complaint."

"Not at all, my lady. If it 'twere I, trapped here in this gilded cage of court, I should have more than a few complaints."

She looked at him, startled. "I said very near the same thing to my maid this morrow—of being trapped in a gilded cage. Never being allowed to fly free." Then she seemed to shake herself from the melancholy that overtook her. "But on the topic of flying free," she said, her expression lighting up again, "the king made a most wondrous request of me this morn."

Mal had noticed the king speaking to her and couldn't help but wonder on the topic, for their conversation had seemed almost intimate in nature. "Indeed?"

"Aye. He has asked of me to find and train a hunting falcon for her majesty, because she is—oh!" Her eyes flew open and her hand covered her mouth. When she drew her fingers away, her full lips were curved in a secretive smile. "There goes my flapping tongue again! Gavin never ceases to remind me that I cannot seem to keep my mouth closed. Verily, my lord, I cannot say precisely the occasion for which the king wants the gift for his wife, but it is quite an honor to be asked."

"Indeed," Mal said again. He decided not to ask what—or, more accurately, *whether*—the king would pay for such a gift, for Judith seemed so pleased with the honor. "If your raptors are as well trained as those of your father, then the king would be foolish to ask it of any other falconer. The raptors of Lilyfare are well known."

She smiled, her eyes crinkling sweetly at the corners. "Thank you, Mal—my lord. That is very kind of you to say. And aye—my birds are as well trained as those of Father's. Mostly due to Tessing and his guidance," she added modestly. "Mayhap you would care to come on a hunt with me? Then you may see for yourself…and mayhap you'll request such a bridal gift for your future wife? If 'tis a fine enough present for the queen, then 'twould be a fine bride's gift." Her eyes were wide and ingenuous.

Mal couldn't hold back a laugh. "Very well, Lady Judith. I shall take your recommendation into account." Just then, Hugh de Rigonier moved into view, meeting his eyes purposefully. Mal nodded in assent and stood. "And now, I believe there is another gentleman who wishes to take on your challenge. Good morrow, my lady."

THREE

THE NEXT morning was rainy and gray, and stayed that way all through the day. Judith found herself cloistered with the queen, who was still in the early months of her pregnancy and required much entertainment, fawning, and solace. By the time she returned to her chamber that night, Judith was exhausted and in dire need of privacy. She didn't even regret missing dinner in the Great Hall and the visiting acrobats who entertained the court.

However, the next day dawned as different from the days before as possible: sunny with blue skies and nary a cloud to be seen.

"'Tis a perfect day to hunt for the queen's falcon," Judith told Tabatha as she looked out the window slit.

Her maid knew what that meant and pulled an old pair of men's hose and a heavy *sherte* that fell nearly to Judith's knees. She donned the masculine clothing then fastened an unfashionably wide leather belt around her waist. Its holes and ties were useful for attaching tools and other implements. She wore a pair of well-worn but sturdy boots and tucked the end of her single braid into the back of her belt to keep it from swinging into her way. Over this ensemble she pulled a wool cloak with a hood then fastened it at her throat with a heavy brooch.

When she searched for hunting birds, Judith was known to climb trees or over rocky terrain into small mountains in order to find their nests. It was no easy task, but one she enjoyed on most occasions. There was something exhilarating about being so high in a tree she could see for what seemed like leagues…not to mention wearing clothing that allowed such freedom of movement.

"Now, lady, I'm getting too old to folla you up into them branches," Tessing told her when she informed him of her plans. They stood in the mews while she gathered up the items she needed for her task.

"And right you are," she told him. "You're to stay on the ground so if I fall, you can catch me." This last she said with a jest and he rolled his eyes and shook his head, *tsk*ing.

"If'n yer pap was alive, he'd send me up after ye anyway," said the elderly man. "Old bones or nay. Tell me if'n one hair on yer head was bent, I'd be hung by m'toes."

"And now you're jesting with me, Tessing, because we all know all my hair is bent and curly," she teased her mentor. "And asides, Papa used to send *me* up in the trees for him when the branches were too delicate to bear his weight."

"An' he'd be on the ground the whole time, pacin', waitin' to catch you if'n you fell."

"And I never did," she reminded him, swinging a small leather bag over her shoulder. Inside was a hunk of cheese, two apples and some dried beef. She'd tucked a skin of watered-down wine into her belt. Now she took two live mice and a vole from the cages where Tessing kept them and stuffed them into a small wooden box-cage. The small rodents would be good bait for her trap, or food for a young hawk if she needed it, and then her captured bird could ride back in the empty cage. "I want you to stay here anyway, Tessing. Someone must take care of Hecate, Gall and Petrus. You know I may not return until late tonight, or even tomorrow."

The nearest forest that could be inhabited by raptors was a two hours' ride away. But it was near a shallow ridge of rocky hills, and there was a good chance one or both places would offer a selection of nests for Judith to raid.

"Sir Piall is coming with me," she told him when he began to protest. "And dressed as a boy like I am, and him as a simple man-at-arms, the two of us will attract no unwanted attention. We'll ride quicker if it's only us, and I am not about to be naysaid," she finished, her voice going a little steely. "This is a special gift for the queen, and I must find the right hawk. If I don't find one today or on the morrow, then I'll go back on another time." Though she didn't say so, Judith was determined not to return until she found the best hunter…even if it meant sleeping on the ground. Hence the heavy cloak.

Tessing *tsk*ed again, but his mistress had spoken and Judith knew she made good sense. "Very well. Don' break any of yer bones, my lady," the old man told her. "Or Tabatha will have my head because I didn't go with ye."

Since Tabby was Tessing's granddaughter, Judith suspected he was correct. "I vow to return with no broken bones," she told him, and pressed a kiss to his warm, weathered cheek. Then she was back out in the sunlight where Piall waited with their horses.

Sir Piall was one of her men-at-arms, currently at court with her from Lilyfare, but he'd been on many hawk-hunting trips. He knew what to expect from the excursion, and as well, he was an excellent warrior and a kind man. Judith was no rock-head when it came to her safety and that of her mare and hawks. She trusted Piall as implicitly as she trusted Sir Holbert and Tessing.

Because of her clothing, she was able to ride astride; although with the long cloak covering her and the back of her mount, no one could tell. When she and Piall rode past the training yard where the men sweated, clanged, and clashed, no one seemed to recognize or even notice her hidden beneath the heavy hood. The disguise was purposeful because in order for her to be relieved of duty to Eleanor long enough to see to her task—and not have to make an explanation to the queen—Judith directed Tabby to respond that she was ill and resting if someone sent for her.

The last men she saw as she and Piall trotted toward the main portcullis gate were Malcolm and Rike, feinting and parrying in the near corner of the yard. Mal, she noticed with rapt interest, was the only one not wearing a *sherte* while training this morrow. He was also nearer to her pathway than the last time she'd seen him, giving Judith an excellent view of his tanned, golden skin and slabs of rippling muscle. Dark hair covered the upper part of his formidable chest, and as she rode past, she realized her mouth had fallen partly open and that she was staring.

Thankful for the enveloping hood so neither Malcolm nor Piall could see her gawking, Judith closed her mouth and turned her attention so it was focused where it should be: precisely between the upright ears of her mare and the task at hand. But despite her redirection, the image remained in her mind far longer than she preferred.

Malcolm of Warwick would make a fine husband indeed.

Once beyond the main gate, Judith kicked her mare into a canter, then a full gallop just for the fun of the moment. The trees streamed by, the air was fresh and scented with something floral, and it brushed over her face, pushing the hood from her head. Her braid worked out from the cloak, bouncing along behind her. But because they had a long distance to go, she reined Crusty into a brisk trot before they'd galloped very far.

She and Piall briefly discussed the best route to take, with him making the suggestions and her agreeing with his opinion. They should reach the edge of the forest well before midday. Part of their journey would take them on well-traveled roads between Clarendon and the compact fief of Marchmonte, but they would also cross several meadows and skirt the edge of a small forest. As they rode, she divided her attention between the road ahead of them and the sky above, watching for the sight of the graceful birds she sought, swooping and diving after their prey.

There were two ways to find a new hunter, and each had its challenges and benefits. She could find a young raptor that wasn't yet flying—an eyas—in its nest, and hope the mother or father wouldn't be around to attack her. Or she could trap an older bird that was already flying, but that could be difficult to do without injuring it or breaking a feather. Aside from that, trapping could be a losing prospect, for she had no way of choosing which hawk took the bait. If he was too old or not strong or large enough, she could release him. But every time a hawk was trapped, there was the chance of injury to a wing, which would leave the bird vulnerable in the wild.

True to Piall's estimate, the sun was high overhead when the tallest trees loomed just ahead of them. Pines, oaks and walnuts stood sentinel at the base of the low, rocky hills. They'd passed several wagons and a small group of men-at-arms escorting a wealthy youngest son to the court at Clarendon; but other than that, their journey thus far had been uneventful.

But now, as Judith spotted the first nest, high in a cluster of branches, she knew it was about to become more interesting. A thrill of excitement rushed through her as she saw the shadow of a hawk ripple over the meadow next to her.

"There," she said, pointing to a group of trees. "I see a nest there, and another over there. It's a good place to begin."

"Aye," Piall said, scrubbing his wiry brown and gray beard thoughtfully. "You do not intend to entrap a bird?"

"First I'll see what's to be found in those nests." Judith was full aware the main reason she wanted to do so was for the joy of climbing the trees. "It's early in the summer and mayhap they'll be empty of all but eggs. But I intend to look."

While Piall fed and watered the horses, she prepared for her climb. The first tree she meant to scale was a tall, scrubby pine with many horizontal branches at regular intervals. 'Twould be nearly like climbing a ladder, but nevertheless, Judith intended to be prepared. If she fell and broke her neck, the queen would never get her special hawk, and that would be a shame.

She donned the special boots her father and Tessing had designed: heavy leather ones with small spur-like spikes on the bottom and at the toe to help keep her feet from slipping on the tree bark. She'd never seen such footwear elsewhere—nor gloves like the special ones she used for climbing. They were smooth and supple leather, fitting her hand perfectly so as to give her a good grip. Tessing had sewn a patch of rough chain mail just over the palm and the undersides of the fingers in order to help keep her hands from slipping.

Judith slung a small linen sack over her shoulder. Inside was a light, loosely woven cloth to wrap the eyas in so he wouldn't injure himself when she put him inside the sack for the climb down. Her final necessity was the light rope she wrapped around her waist. When she reached the nest, she'd tie herself to the tree trunk for stability while she removed the hawk and wrapped him up.

"Up I shall go," she told Piall brightly.

He shielded his eyes against the sun, looking up into the branches. "'Tis a long height, my lady. Be slow and take care," he said as he always did before she embarked on such a task. Then he moved to stand near the tree, making a cup with his two joined hands onto which she could step.

"Aye," she told him, placing her foot carefully on his palms so as not to stab him with one of the spikes. "Always. Up!"

Piall had done this many times before, and he gave her a good, sharp boost up to the lowest branch. She curled her hands around it and pulled herself up.

And then she was on her way, easily scrabbling from one limb to the another. Before she knew it, Judith was as high in the pine as her chamber window was above the ground. Up here, the trunk was more slender and the upper part of the tree swayed gently in the wind. In the distance, she heard a pack of dogs barking raucously and the way-off call of a bird. Judith could see as far away as forever, it seemed: the green-brown heath, the small blue ribbon of a creek they'd splashed through, a thick forest to the north and rough, rocky hills to the east.

To the south lay Clarendon, nearly two hours away and where, Judith sincerely hoped, the queen had found someone else to amuse her. What a fine temper Eleanor had been in yesterday, flouncing around the chamber, railing about the fact that her belly would grow huge again and her husband wouldn't care for her….

Judith shook her head and reached for the next branch. Little bits of bark wafted down like dust every time she gripped the tree, thanks to her rough gloves. This would be Eleanor's tenth pregnancy. One would think she'd be used to it by now.

A surprise pang of grief caught Judith by surprise. It had been a long time since she'd thought about having a baby herself. A long time since she'd had the luxury to even think it a real possibility. For after Gregory died, Judith had certainly grieved…but she expected she would soon be betrothed to someone else, then wed and be bearing children within a year or two. For that was how it worked and that was the best for Lilyfare: to have a lord and lady and heir.

But her father had been dead for three years when Gregory was killed, so there was no one to speak for Judith except her cousin Gavin, Lord of Mal Verne…and at that time, he was so wrapped in his ball of guilt and grief he gave little thought to Judith's marital state.

Meanwhile, the queen had become very fond of Judith and decided she must stay with her at court. The king had no argument with this, for that meant he had an heiress for a bargaining chip as well as a greater portion of the rents from Lilyfare and Kentworth to flow into his coffers.

And now, six years after Gregory's death, Judith knew she'd never have to worry about her belly growing to the size of basket.

Don't think on it, she told herself fiercely. *'Twill do you no good to stew. Your lot is your lot…and it could be much, much worse.*

And so she climbed higher, and higher…and finally the nest was just above her head. One more branch and she'd be just high enough to look down into it. She couldn't see Piall on the ground any longer, but she knew he was still below.

As she approached the nest, Judith hadn't seen any sign of a parental hawk coming or going. Her optimism waned that she'd find anything in the large bundle of sticks, but she'd come too far not to check. The branches were strong and steady beneath her feet, and she hoisted herself up once more and peered into the nest.

"Greetings there, young chick," she said softly in surprise. A bundle of gold, black, brown and rust-colored feathers tufted with thick white baby molting nestled in its rudimentary basket. "Or shall I say, *chicks*."

There were two of them, shifting and moving about hungrily. Judith looked around again, expecting to see a parent charging toward her at any moment, talons and fierce beak at the ready…but the sky was clear.

She pulled herself up onto the branch nearest the vee-shaped crook where the nest was situated and got a better view into the bedding. "Oh," she said sadly when she saw that there were—or had been—two other eyases. Their soft corpses had fallen down half beneath their siblings as the survivors begged for food, jockeying for position.

"Something happened to your parents, then," Judith said. And glanced around once more. It wasn't an uncommon thing. Between disease and predators, not to mention injuries—for even the graceful hawks flew into trees while hunting, often killing or damaging themselves—it was rare for an entire family of raptors to live out their first year. As she looked down at the babies, she noticed the barking dogs were closer now and fancied she heard them rustling through the forest nearby. Perhaps it was the lord of Marchmonte on a hunt with his dogs.

"Hail, Lady Judith," came Piall's call from below. "What do you see?"

"Two fledglings," she shouted down. "Orphans. I'll feed them a bit then be down in a trice."

Judith took a minute to loop the rope around the trunk then her waist, tying it securely the way her father and Tessing had shown her. Now she could move about more easily without fear of falling. She pulled off her climbing gloves and tucked them into their place on her belt, then loosened the drawstring on her food pouch. The hawks would prefer fresh meat, but the dried beef would do in a pinch.

She had just slipped a morsel of food into the second eyas's wide-open mouth when a horrible, snarling barking sound came up from below. Piall shouted and then Judith heard the unmistakable scream of a horse.

The sound of a dying horse was enough to haunt one's dreams, and Judith jerked upright against the tree, her heart pounding. The snarling and growling became even louder and more fierce as she cried, "What is it? Piall!"

Her knight shouted something, but whatever he said was drowned out by squealing, snarling, barking and growling. She heard more snarling and wild barking, thrashing in the brush below. Then the clang of a sword and an agonized human cry.

"*Piall!*" Judith screamed and untied herself quickly from the tree trunk. She began to work herself down, branch by branch. All the while, the horrible sounds continued below—clearly a ferocious battle between a pack of dogs, her man-at-arms, and the horses.

By the time she got low enough to see what was actually going on, her heart was in her throat. Piall hadn't responded to her multiple cries, and although the snarling and barking continued, the fight seemed to have died down. Ill with fear, she looked down through the branches and gasped at the sight below.

"Piall!" she half-sobbed, half-cried…but his body, on the ground near the base of the tree, was bloody and unmoving.

One of the dogs—nay. Oh, *nay*. Those weren't mere dogs she realized now that she was closer. They were a pack of wild, rabid, wolf-like canines. White foam dripped from the mouth of the one nearest the tree…the one who saw her just above him.

With a snarl and shuddering cry that sounded pain-filled and desperate, he leapt up at Judith's branch. He came close enough that she saw the burning red of his eyes and the gleam of his feral teeth.

The others in his pack—just as wild and rabid as he—must have caught her scent, for all at once they were all there: surrounding her tree, scrabbling at the trunk, leaping and vaulting up toward her. Trampling the torn, bloody body of her man Piall.

And Judith was trapped.

FOUR

TABBY DREW in a deep breath, inhaling the scent of daisies and honeysuckle. Like her mistress, she enjoyed any opportunity to be out of the chill stone walls of the keep. And after two days of rain and cloudiness, it was a blessing to be able to walk through the grasses and vast gardens beyond the hard dirt of the bailey.

This morrow, with Lady Judith gone on her hawk-hunting mission, Tabby was left with fewer responsibilities than usual. Normally, she must be available if her mistress needed a change of clothing or wanted to send a message to someone within the court. Not that Tabby would deliver it herself, but she was often sent off to locate a page to do the actual running. She was also responsible for maintaining the chamber and ensuring her lady's clothing, bedding and other belongings were clean and organized. And then there was the matter of her furry charges, the elderly mutt, the spunky kitten—and any others she might adopt.

But with Lady Judith away for much of the day, Tabby finished her work shortly after the midday meal. Just before she left the chamber for a much-desired walk, wherein she hoped she might find a sweet pear on one of the trees, the expected message came from the queen. Tabby did as she'd been instructed and sent word back that her mistress was indisposed and Lady Judith begged forgiveness for being unable to attend her majesty today.

Moments later, Tabby went out one of the side doors used by the kitchen serfs. Soon she was walking among rosemary, thyme and fragrant lavender. Beyond the worn pathways in the herb garden were the orchards, lined with trees of pears, plums and apples. And past the rows of fruit trees, currently boasting fruits in various stages of growth, was a small meadow bordered by a forest.

Tabby passed a cluster of ladies sitting on a bench surrounded by rose bushes. She saw two maidservants picking herbs, likely for the monks or the physicians who attended the king and queen. An orange-striped cat stalked something through the tall grasses to the north of a row of apple trees. Two boys played hide and seek. On the meadow, a group of five men-at-arms stood, pointing and talking. Two of them held bows and wore quivers filled with arrows.

She skirted all of them—particularly the men-at-arms. Her papa, a skilled fighter, had been killed years ago while defending Lady Judith's father's estate, Kentwood, during a siege. Tabby spent the next five summers caring for her grieving mother even while she served the young Lady Judith, and the experience gave her a strong mislike for any man who wielded a sword.

As she meandered along the edge of the meadow, Tabby alternately hummed and sang under her breath, for she always had a song in her head. Keeping a wary eye on the men, she picked a handful of flowers and looked for strawberries. Lady Judith would surely appreciate a small bouquet of daisies and wild lilies, and perhaps even some of the feathery, silky grasses that shimmered in the sunshine. And there was little more pleasurable than a handful of sun-warmed berries.

Something rustled in the tall grass and she caught sight of a white cottontail as a brown hare bounded off into the forest. Now Tabby was singing in a normal tone, for no one was close enough to hear her. She could see people in the distance; she wasn't alone or unsafe. Lady Judith oft warned her not to go about or beyond the bailey alone, for there were unscrupulous men who'd hardly think twice about tumbling an unaccompanied maid—whether she wanted to lift her skirts or nay.

Then, right at the edge of the forest, she heard more rustling. It was more frantic this time. And the creature remained in one place instead of rushing away from her approach. Curious, Tabby stopped singing and walked carefully toward the jolting, jerking brush. Now she could hear sounds of distress, and as she drew closer she heard a soft squeaking.

When she parted the grasses and saw what they hid, she gave a soft gasp and fell to her knees. "Oh, nay," she cried softly. "Poor soul!"

A white rabbit lay huddled on its side, kicking ineffectually, trembling with obvious pain. Its fur was stained with fresh blood, bright red against its soft coat. A broken arrow was embedded in its left haunch. Tabby cursed the men and their sport, sending a glare in the general direction of the five men-at-arms.

Despite its agony, the terrified creature tried valiantly to elude her hands when she tried to help him...but he couldn't move quickly enough. Tabby was able to examine the protruding arrow, noting with relief that it hadn't gone all the way through the rabbit's leg. But there would be blood when she pulled it out....

Biting her lip then clenching her teeth, Tabby held her breath and positioned her hand as leverage against the rabbit's fragile leg. She sent up a prayer and yanked the arrow away with one sharp, smooth movement. The creature squeaked and gave a horrid squeal, then lay there panting and trembling. He watched her with one unblinking pink eye as if to measure her friend or foe. Tabby was relieved to see blood oozing from the wound, but not gushing forth as she'd feared. Maybe it could heal.

"'Tis all I can do for you here," she said, stroking the creature's soft fur. "And I trow Lady Judith will have aught to say on her return to find yet another occupant in her chamber, but you must come with me for the rest."

Taking great care, she was just gathering the shuddering creature up into the long skirt of her tunic when she heard footsteps swishing in the grass behind her. She turned, shielding her eyes against the sun.

"What do you here, good wench?" called the man as he approached. She recognized him as one of the men-at-arms she'd noticed earlier. He wore a livery she didn't immediately recognize—therefore he and his master or mistress were new to court. Or were not part of the king's retinue at all, and mayhap he hailed from a nearby estate. The man's hair was the color of pale wheat, but his skin was tanned golden and his beard and mustache were honey-colored. He carried a bow and wore a sword at the waist. And, as evidence of his warring ways, there was a long-healed scar along his jaw, running up toward the ear.

Tabby's heart thudded and her palms went damp. She looked around quickly, suddenly realizing she was out of sight of the others. Nevertheless, she had her own knife—small as it was—tucked into her girdle. She eased it from its sheath, keeping it hidden. The man had made no threatening move, but she meant to be prepared should that change. "I was out for a walk and I found evidence of your sport," she said—then immediately regretted it.

How many times had Lady Judith bewailed her own thoughtless tongue? And now Tabatha had done the precise thing her mistress warned her against.

"My sport?" rumbled the man. Now he stood so close, his shadow loomed over her.

Tabby swallowed hard. He was big and burly, and the scar made him appear even more forbidding. *Fool! You should not have angered him!* She gripped her knife more tightly and, cuddling the rabbit close in her skirt, rose. "Prithee, let me pass," she said.

"What do you have there?" he asked. Despite his demand, his voice was kind. Almost gentle. To her relief, he didn't make a move toward her.

She relaxed a little, but still held the knife behind her. "'Tis naught of interest to you, I trow." Tabby edged to the side, hoping he would allow her to pass.

"Are you injured?" asked the man suddenly. He stepped closer, now reaching toward her tunic.

"Nay, 'tis not from me," she replied, realizing blood from the rabbit had seeped through her linen clothing. "'Tis only the fault of you." And now she moved her arm away to reveal the injured rabbit.

"'Sblood, what do you mean to do with that?" he said with amusement in his voice. "Verily, 'twould make a fine stew."

"Nay," she cried and stepped back. "'Tis because of you he is injured at all. Can you not leave the poor beast free of your violent hand?" Tabby edged further away.

"Ah, miss, I meant it only as a jest," he said, clearly taken aback by her violent response. "Have you never eaten rabbit stew?"

"'Twas a sad jest," she spat in return. She was no longer wary of the man, she was furious with him. How dare he say such a thing?

He nodded gravely and rubbed his beard. "'Twas a sad jest indeed. Mayhap I have been in the company of men too long to have a care for what comes off my tongue."

"Then I pity your wife if you return to her with such unpleasant words about such a helpless creature," Tabby told him. "Now, pray, allow me to pass. I mean to heal the mess you've made of this poor beast."

The man bent toward the grass, and when he straightened he was holding the arrow she'd pulled from the rabbit's haunch. "'Tis a pity I must correct you," he said, reaching into the quiver on his back. "For as you will see, should you care to look, 'tis not my arrow you withdrew from the creature."

Tabby hardly glanced at the two arrows he showed her: the broken one and the one from his supply. "Very well. 'T may not have been yours on this time, but it could well be in the future."

"Nay, miss. For I am a much better shot than whoever loosed that arrow," he said. And for the first time, Tabby caught a glint of humor in his eyes.

"And so you say. I doubt I should ever find out the truth of that statement or nay," she told him, slipping her small dagger back into its sheath. "Good day, sir."

She'd walked hardly three steps away when he called after her. "What is your name, then, comely miss?"

She hesitated, then flung an answer over her shoulder, "I am called Tabatha." Her feet kept at a rapid pace, but somehow when she heard movement in the grass behind her, she wasn't surprised he'd followed.

"Truly, what do you intend to do with that mangled creature, Tabatha?" asked the man as he fell into step with her. His long legs took one pace for every two of her shorter ones. "Methinks there's little hope for the wee beastie."

"If I cannot heal him, then at the least he will die in comfort and safety. Which is more than I could say for my papa, who died alone and on a field of battle." Tabby's eyes widened, for she couldn't believe those words had spilled from her mouth. Was Lady Judith's loose tongue now become contagious to her?

"I'm very sorry for your papa," her unwanted companion replied.

Tabby made a sound of dismissal and continued to walk at a fast pace. They'd reached the edge of the orchard now and there were others in view. She kept the still-trembling rabbit wrapped closely next to her, however, for she cared not to draw more attention to herself.

"Good day, O nameless sir," she said, turning away at a large clump of yellow-sprigged myrtle.

"I am called Nevril," he called after her. "Best of luck with the wee critter."

~*~

WITH THE furious, feral dogs snarling just below her perch, Judith could not go down…but she could go back up.

And so she did, climbing back up into the tall, swaying pine. She took much more care this time, knowing if she fell not only would Piall—oh, *dear Piall!*—not be there to catch her, but the rabid canines would. And so she went very slowly, branch by branch, trying not to think about the dire situation.

She'd lost one of her most trusted men. Judith's eyes filled with tears and her stomach lurched, horror at the manner of his death at last sinking in.

And at least one horse was gone…for she'd seen the remains, torn into shreds by the possessed beasts. 'Twas clear to Judith the pack of dogs weren't hungry and desirous of eating, but that they were well and truly maddened. Wild animals only killed what was necessary for survival, but these creatures were different. Bent only on destruction.

Judith's hope was to climb high enough that they'd forget about her and eventually leave. Then she must take the chance and climb back down, and hope…what? That she could somehow make her way to help? She had no horse to ride. She wasn't certain where to go. She and Piall had traveled nearly two hours from Clarendon. Judith didn't know the way back. They'd passed no town or village on the way, although she remembered Piall pointing out the direction of Marchmonte.

She drew in a deep breath, inhaling the fresh pine scent. *Cease your worrying. You are resourceful and smart. You will find a way out of this.*

With that private lecture, Judith gathered her resolve and climbed still higher. The snarling and barking continued below, but she was safely far away from the beasts.

When she reached the nest, Judith once more tied herself to the pine trunk. To her relief, the two eyases were still alive but no longer as desperate for food. They seemed to have settled to rest.

She used the advantage of height in the tree to decide which direction she must go once she was able to climb down. Hills rolled in seemingly infinite waves, and the scrub of trees studding the rocky hills didn't appear welcoming. There was a roadway in the distance, and Judith realized it was her best opportunity. If she could find her way to the road, eventually it would lead her to help.

Now, all she could do was wait. She opened her wineskin and drank—but not as much as she wanted to. There was no telling how long she'd be trapped here, and she'd need water. Nibbling on a piece of bread, Judith had another idea. If she could climb from this branch to another tree, and then to another and another…mayhap she could elude the dogs that way.

But when she looked around, she saw there weren't any other tree's branches close enough that would bear her weight.

The little niggle of worry began to spread into something larger and heavier. Once more Judith forced herself to ignore it. The dogs had to leave sooner or later.

And when they did, she'd find her way down and away. She would. She must.

Now she had naught left to do but wait. So, tied securely to the tree, she let her head tip back against the trunk and closed her eyes.

~*~

TABBY ALWAYS enjoyed watching her grandpapa do his work for the Lilyfare hawks. One of her earliest memories was the sight of him sitting on a short wooden stool near the fire, a myriad of candles around him as he carefully stitched a pair of jesses for Lady Judith's father.

Her grandpapa had a great love for the raptors and was grateful for his position as Master Falconer for the Lord of Kentworth and now the lord's daughter, Lady Judith. Since it was illegal for any but the gentry to own the large hunting birds, Tessing was able to spend as much time with the falcons and peregrines as he chose. He had a goshawk for his own hunting purposes, but Lady Judith's Hecate and Fencer were very nearly as much his as they were hers.

After Tabby settled the injured rabbit in a small basket next to her pallet, she came to her grandpapa for advice. It was through him she'd learned how to care for the injured creatures she found.

"I pulled an arrow from his leg," she told Tessing, watching as he cleaned out the mews. The floor was covered with sawdust and hay, along with the castings regurgitated by the birds. "The bleeding has stopped and I wrapped it up gently with a cloth. But methinks a poultice might serve him better. What did you put on Hecate?"

"A paste of dried woad and lavender," he replied. "Pull its fur away from the wound to make certain it doesn't stick inside as it heals."

"Aye. And for food, I've pulled some arugula and dandelion leaves and left them where he can reach."

"And where is Bear during this? Surely you don't want him to decide to gnaw on a rabbit leg?" Tessing teased.

Tabby frowned, thinking of the man named Nevril who'd made a similar jest. "What is it with men—is it always only food that sits in their minds?"

"Food, ale—and copulatin'," her grandfather replied with a wheezing laugh. He must have found that particularly amusing, for he kept chuckling even as he continued sweeping up the pellets on the floor.

"And their bloody swords," Tabby added tartly. As she went to adjust the rows of leather jesses—long strips that connected the raptor's feet to his master's gloves—there was an alarmed shout in the bailey.

This was nothing unusual—someone was always shouting, warning, arguing or otherwise making a loud noise. But the tone had her and Tessing both hurrying out of the mews to see what caused the commotion.

A cluster of men-at-arms and knights stood talking and gesticulating. The first person Tabby recognized was Sir Holbert, Lady Judith's master-at-arms. He seemed to be the one speaking most animatedly.

"God's stones," breathed Tessing. He reached over and curled his fingers around Tabby's arm. He was pointing to a sight right next to the men, right by the stables. A trio of grooms and one man-at-arms were gathered around a horse. "That's Crusty."

"*Nay,*" she gasped, looking around in hopes of seeing Lady Judith. "*My lady….*" Tabby's heart thudded so hard she thought she might be ill. She ran over, her eyes fixed on the battered, staggering mare.

Because the grooms were already attending to Crusty, Tabatha didn't get close enough to see much more than a gash in the mare's side and another injury on her right flank. But 'twas clear something awful had befallen both the horse and her mistress.

"Sir Piall!" Tabby cried and spun, rushing over to Sir Holbert.

He heard and immediately turned on her. "Tabby—where is Lady Judith?" His eyes were dull with worry and fear, and she saw he'd already begun to prepare himself to ride out, having donned his mail and cloth hauberk. He was carrying a shield. "Has she yet returned?"

"She and Sir Piall went to capture a hawk," she told him, aware that the attention of every man in the group was fixed on her. "I don't know where they went."

"They traveled to the forest at the foot of those hills." Grandpapa, bless him, was next to her now. His voice, calm and yet laden with gravity, soothed her some small bit. "Sir Piall would allow nothing to happen to my lady."

"But there is her mare," said a man who towered over the others. Like the others, he was garbed in full mail and had obviously been training in the yard. "And aught has clearly happened to *her*." His voice was tight and his green-brown eyes cool and sharp. His fine surcoat and the shield he carried indicated his status as a great lord.

Though Tabby didn't know him, she recognized the standard on his shield and surcoat. It was the same as the livery worn by the man named Nevril. With a start, she realized that very man was standing in the group as well. He glanced over, but made no move to speak to her. Nevril's face was serious, and he returned his attention to his lord.

"We must ride after them," Sir Holbert said unnecessarily, for the group had already begun to call for the grooms to bring their horses. "God knows what has befallen them."

"'Tis a two-hour ride to the hills," said Nevril's master, peering into the distance from beneath a hand shielding the sun. Despite the grave situation, he appeared calm and thoughtful. "What time did they leave?"

When he turned suddenly to Tabby, she was startled at being addressed so directly by such a powerful lord. She stammered, "'Twas well after mass." Peering at the sun's position, she calculated quickly. "They've been gone at the least five hours."

"How did they mean to travel?" he demanded. "Do you know? By road?"

Thankfully, Tessing once again spoke up. "They would follow the road as far as they could. And then when the forest at the foot of the hills was near, they would head toward the tallest trees wherein one might see the nest of a raptor. If not there, then they would go toward the highest of the hills, where a nest might also be among the rocky peak."

"We ride. Nevril, Gambert, *now*," said the lord just as three of the grooms brought his fierce, dancing warhorse from the stable. Tabby shied away from the dark brown beast, whose hooves were the size of dinner plates and whose strength required the three men to keep him under control—and even then 'twas no easy task. "There's no time to be lost."

"We're with you, Warwick," said Sir Holbert, then turned to holler for the other men-at-arms from Lilyfare.

"As am I," announced Lord Hugh. Standing with him was Lord Richard of Castendown. "If we ride fast we'll be to the hills well before dusk." He took the reins of his own massive horse.

"We'll ride fast," Lord Warwick told him as he vaulted onto the back of his mount. The prancing, whuffling horse settled as soon as he felt his master's weight. "Do your best to keep pace. H*yah*!"

The horse leapt forward and everyone scattered as the stallion and Lord Warwick flew across the bailey yard, clattering beneath the raised portcullis and out over the drawbridge.

~*~

MALCOLM WASN'T entirely certain why he felt such a numbing yet blazing fear as he bent over Alpha's neck, the warhorse's muscles bunching and stretching with each movement. His chest was banded tight and his mind blank but for the focus of: *ride, ride, ride!*

Of course he always feared for any woman or child—or even a man, even his deadliest of enemies—who would be mauled or so terribly injured, as was clearly what happened to Judith's mare. And quite possibly to her as well.

And that was where the blinding terror came in. Nay. Not to Judith. Not to exuberant, imperious, confounding Judith.

But it was precisely that unexpected, white-hot fear which drove him now—the fear of what they would find. The images of her, pale and bloody, ripped and slashed...dead. Her life seeping into the grass even as her glorious hair spread around her cold body like fire.

It was only once Clarendon was far in the distance that Mal realized he couldn't force Alpha to keep such a breakneck pace all the way to…wherever they were going. With regret, he slowed the trusty destrier to a brisk canter and, breathing heavily from the effort of the mad ride and his anxiety, took the opportunity to marshal his thoughts.

On the road coming up behind him—from much too far back—galloped Nevril and Gambert, along with Holbert, whom he'd gleaned was Judith's master-at-arms, and several more of her men. There was also de Rigonier, Castendown, Ludingdon, and Fleurwelling, and their squires. Mal could have felt a little foolish at his mad dash, blasting out of Clarendon as he'd done, but it wasn't in his nature to worry on others' opinions of him.

Nevertheless, when Dirick of Ludingdon and the others caught up with him at last, his friend looked curiously at Mal. "Kind of you to wait for us," he commented in that understated way of his.

"Alpha needed to run," Mal replied with a shrug. "Else he'd be champing and stomping all the day. Asides, the longer the delay, the more likely we are to find what we do not wish. I meant to waste no time. If either lay injured or near death, the sooner we find them…."

"Aye," Dirick replied, but in his sober expression there lurked a hint of levity. "Let us pray we do not find the worst."

"My lord," said Nevril, riding up alongside them. He was panting from the exertion of the mad ride as well. "The lady's maid was beside herself. On the orders of Lady Judith, she sent word to the queen her lady was indisposed today and could not attend her. She is terrified Queen Eleanor will learn of the lie and fears both she and Lady Judith will feel the queen's wrath if the truth comes out."

Mal shook his head grimly. "Let us hope that is the least of her worries, Nevril." He looked ahead and saw, perhaps a half hour in the distance, the tall trees brushing the sky just at the foot of rough hills. "They were searching for raptors. How will we ever find them?"

"We'll split up," de Rigonier said, drawing even with Mal and Dirick as Nevril fell back. "Lady Judith prefers to capture her birds by climbing rather than trapping. If we sight nests, we can have a good sense of whither she and Piall have gone. And then we must follow their trail."

Mal nodded in agreement and they rode along in near silence for a time. For once he almost wished for conversation—that aught might take his mind from the worry churning within. But in the stead of gnawing on what he might find—for he would learn soon enough if his fears would come to pass—Mal distracted himself by wondering on the relationship between Judith and Hugh de Rigonier.

He'd witnessed them laughing, jesting, and conversing together. Their informality and ease with the other would be enviable if Mal cared about such things. But for him, a woman—a wife—meant someone to warm his bed, provide an heir, and keep his household running smoothly. Nor would he refuse a fat dowry chest or some other valuable bride's price if she brought it. Whether they amused each other or even cared for each other beyond a basic affection was of little interest to him. He was a practical man.

Yet since he was a man, and a practical one, he couldn't help but wonder if Judith and de Rigonier were lovers. It wouldn't surprise Mal, for it was well-known that Eleanor's and Henry's court wasn't the strictly moral one the queen had left behind when she divorced the pious Louis of France. The priests and bishops—even the flamboyant Archbishop of Canterbury, Thomas à Becket— decried the current mode of dress in which women wore tightly-laced gowns to show off their curves. The holy men claimed it was salacious and immodest and contributed to the growing immorality of the court.

That was yet another reason Mal preferred the quiet privacy of his beloved Warwick. *The sooner I can return, the happier I shall be.* He'd hoped to have his audience with the king on this day, for he needed permission to find a bride and marry as he wished.

But this journey to find Judith was much more important than obtaining permission to wed someone like Lady Beatrice of Delbring.

"There," he cried, pointing to a clump high in a pine tree, just a half-league north of where they road. "A raptor nest. Where there is one, mayhap shall be Lady Judith."

"And there is another," said de Rigonier. "And another. We must divide ourselves."

This was quickly accomplished, with Mal, Nevril and Gambert heading north on their own. His heart thudding with purpose, Mal kicked Alpha into a full gallop and once again left the others in his dust. As they headed toward the forest of tall, scraggly trees, he felt a moment of bliss at the glorious speed and grace from his warhorse. Oft the destriers were so large and muscular they didn't have the speed and elegance one needed for such a task, but Alpha was one of a few that had all the skills a battle-bound lord would need.

As they galloped among the tall trees and thickening brush, Mal kept his eyes trained on the nest he spied. It was the first he'd seen from the road, and his senses tingled. Mayhap Judith had seen it too. As they drew closer, he saw something else that made his insides seize up: birds. Circling. Diving down among the treetops then reappearing.

God, nay. Something inside him tripped and he urged Alpha faster, all the while praying also for sure-footedness. They leapt smoothly over a large tree trunk and easily skirted bushes and trees, clumps of dirt flying up from the destrier's hooves behind them. He bent low over the stallion's neck to keep from being swept off by a low branch.

Over the pounding of Alpha's massive hooves, Mal heard frenzied barking and snarling in the distance. The snarling grew closer and louder, and Mal and Alpha smelled it at the same time: blood. In the air. Thick and heavy. *Nay.* He kept his mind blank as his horse reacted to the smell of blood—the smell of war. What he'd been trained for. Alpha slowed and snorted, then roared on faster.

Suddenly, they burst into a clearing near the tree he sought, and Mal saw the bloodied corpse of a horse. But they blazed past it, scaring away the hawks picking at the carrion, and headed for the feral pack of dogs crowding around a tree. The wolf-like beasts snarled and clawed as if trying to launch themselves up the rough bark. Nearby on the ground was a human corpse—that of a man, praise God—but it was unattended and the wild canines seemed more interested in what was in the tree.

Mal had his sword in hand by then and was ready when the first of the wild, rabid creatures noticed him and launched in his direction. Alpha screamed and reared up on his two back legs, then crashed down, crushing the dog that had come too close. Mal, who easily kept his seat, cried out as he slashed with his broadsword, neatly cleaving the head from the next dog.

At the same time, he heard a voice…from above. A female voice. "I am here! Up here!"

He glanced into the branches, his heart leaping with hope— for it sounded like Judith—but he couldn't take his eyes from the snarling canines for long enough to see if his prayers had been answered. The rabid creatures terrified him for another reason: should one of them bite Alpha, the destrier would surely become rabid himself. Then Mal would lose one of his most valuable possessions. He wheeled his mount around and galloped back out of the clearing before the worst happened.

Two of the mayhap dozen dogs followed on his tail, leaping and snarling at Alpha's heels. Yet in the end, the horse was much too fast for them and the gap between them widened. But Mal had to get his mount to safety while going back to rescue whoever was in the tree. He wheeled his horse around sharply, feeling the shudder as Alpha stumbled and nearly fell. Heart in his throat, Mal sent up a prayer of gratitude and patted his horse on the neck, murmuring a thanks to the beast as well.

"Off with you," he said as they headed at a breakneck speed toward a low, thick tree branch directly in front of them. "*Go, Alpha.*"

Sword in hand, the dogs barking madly in their wake, Mal half-crouched, rising, in his stirrups, his weight on the balls of his feet. As they barreled toward the branch, he braced himself.

The bark was rough and hard, and he slammed into it hard enough that half his breath was knocked out, but he caught it as planned, curving his arm around it. Alpha streaked on past and as soon as the horse was out from beneath Mal, he dropped to the ground.

Just in time to face the raving beasts.

FIVE

JUDITH GRIPPED the tree trunk tightly as a horseman blasted into the clearing below. Relief swept through her, followed by admiration when she watched the mail-clad knight remain in his saddle even as his massive warhorse snorted, rearing violently in the midst of the feral dogs. She heard the sickening thud as one of its hooves crushed a canine to the ground.

From her perch high up in the branches, Judith could see little detail other than the blur of blue and gray from the knight's shield, the sleek, dark coat of his horse, and a flash of steel as he swung his broadsword to behead one of the mad dogs. The sounds were horrible: squealing, thudding, snarling.

Then just as quickly as he'd come, her presumed savior and his mount bolted out of the clearing. Two of Judith's four-legged captors followed, barking and streaking behind, but the others remained. Their frenzied snarls, red eyes, and foaming mouths didn't seem to have lessened in the hours they'd had her trapped. Every time the pack began to quiet or edge away, something would happen to start them up again, and thus she'd been stranded.

Judith hadn't been on the ground for nearly four hours, and she was tired, hungry, and frustrated. And frightened. If she hadn't had the rope to tie herself to the trunk, surely she would have tumbled down by now. But now that help had arrived—or so she thought—Judith had a sudden burst of strength.

Shortly after the warrior on the horse galloped away, she heard a sharp whistle in the distance, followed by the bellow of a horn echoing among the trees. Moments later, a man ran into the clearing brandishing his sword. At first, Judith wasn't certain whether it was the same man who'd been on the horse. She climbed down to the lower branches, watching in hope, fear and amazement as he drew the dogs' attention to him with a ferocious war cry.

Between shield and sword, he fought off two of the dogs before the others were able to twist their writhing bodies away from the tree and bound over to him. But then they all seemed to swarm toward her rescuer at once, and Judith's heart was in her throat as five canines leapt toward him. He was much more vulnerable on foot, and from above she watched tensely. He spun and slashed, blocking snarling fangs and maniac claws neatly with his shield, then slicing and slashing with his weapon. The dogs cried and squealed, thumping to the ground or staggering away, howling in pain.

The sound of more horses thudding through the forest caught Judith's attention, and she climbed up two more branches in order to see. A group of men-at-arms streaked toward them, bounding through the woods.

More help. Aye, Judith was saved.

A loud, victorious cry from below drew her attention back to the man as he stabbed the last dog, heaving the beast away from the end of his sword.

"Judith!" he bellowed up into the tree, his face tilted toward her for the first time.

Her heart leapt. *Malcolm?* Nay, impossible. But she was already clambering down as quickly as she could on stiff legs and arms, her heart light and relieved.

"Judith, are you there?" he shouted again as the other horses arrived in the clearing. It *was* Malcolm!

"Aye! 'Tis me!" she called as her foot slipped and she skimmed wildly down the trunk. Judith gasped in pain as the rough bark scraped down her arms and a cheek, but she caught herself before tumbling all the way to the ground. That would have been most mortifying.

By the time she recovered and stepped onto the lowest branch, however, he was waiting there. She didn't even have the chance to ease herself off the branch before Malcolm snatched her down.

Judith staggered a bit as he placed her quickly and unceremoniously on her feet, but before he could speak, she launched herself back into his arms. "Thank you, Mal," she cried, throwing her arms up around his broad shoulders. "Oh, I do not know how you—all of you," she added, looking beyond his mail-covered arm at the others in the clearing, "came to be here, but thank you! 'Tis a miracle you found me!"

Mal, who seemed to have naught to say, set her back from him almost as quickly as she'd gotten there, but Judith cared not. Now that she was on the ground, she had other things on her mind. After all, she'd been up a tree for four hours. "I must needs have some privacy," she said, gesturing to the woods.

But though she started off quickly, Judith halted at Piall's body. One of the younger men—Mal's squire, she thought—had already begun to cover it, but that did little good to hide the horrible sight. Her stomach lurched and she pressed a hand against her mouth, sickened by the carnage as well as the knowledge he was gone. "Oh, Piall," she managed to say, closing her eyes tightly. Her breath hitched and her insides churned. 'Twas a terrible, needless loss.

"There's no need for you to look at him, my lady," someone said kindly. A large hand brushed her shoulder and gently directed her toward the forest. She glanced up at Lord Dirick, whose handsome face was serious and sympathetic. "See to your needs, and we will attend to your man."

The reality of the situation settling heavy on her, Judith walked into the woods on unsteady feet and did what she needed to do. She cried a bit, too, wiping her eyes on her sleeve. Piall had given his life for her—because of her whim to go hunting, and because he was insistent on being her protector. The guilt weighed heavily on her, and Judith stayed in the woods mayhap longer than she needed to. When she returned to the clearing, she caught Mal's eye; he'd been watching for her. He stood to the side, tying up the reins of a massive warhorse to a sturdy tree. She nodded at him, allowing her grief to show, then turned to find that the carnage from the slain dogs was being attended to.

"They must be burned," Mal told her as he came over. She felt his attention settle on her scraped cheek, but he said naught about it. "For if another animal eats the tainted meat, the madness will spread." As if to emphasize his words, the horses standing to the side of the clearing stomped and snorted, their eyes a little wild at the scent of tainted blood.

"Aye," Judith said, then turned to eye the tree once more. She considered for a moment, then drew in a breath and exhaled. Her decision was made. Piall's death would not be completely in vain.

"What are you doing, my lady?" Mal demanded when he saw her approach the tall pine. He'd been helping to dig a burial hole with the point of his long, triangular shield and now he stood upright.

Despite the pain in her arms from the slide down the trunk, Judith knew she must climb up again. "Holbert, if you please?" she ordered.

Her man knew what she wished, and the next thing she knew, Judith was back in the lower branch of the tree. Her metal-tipped boots worked just as well as they had before, and though she'd been up and down the span of branches many times since arriving here, Judith climbed once more. This time, though, her muscles protested and trembled with effort. But she was stubborn. This journey would yield some good, she hoped.

A short time later, once more at the nest which held the two eyases—now no longer as hungry, due to her sharing the bit of dried meat with them—she carefully scooped them out. Their mouths opened wide and silent, they froze in obvious terror as she bundled them into the soft linen cloth from her pouch. "Poor things," she murmured, taking care not to injure the delicate wings. 'Twas a risk to take them from the nest so small, but if she left them there, they would surely die.

Then, just as carefully—and with no little bit of pain—she made her way back down to the ground.

"Judith!" a voice exclaimed as her feet touched the blood-soaked grass.

She turned to see Hugh de Rigonier, along with Fleuwelling and Castendown and a contingent of other men now gathered in the clearing. Mayhap the horn she'd heard earlier had been a signal to them.

Still carefully holding the bundle of baby raptors, she greeted Hugh as he maneuvered over, still mounted on his horse. His arms strained to keep the massive beast under control, and she was forced to step back from the dancing hooves.

"You are safe," he said, looking down at her. "Praise be."

"All in thanks to Warwick," she told him. "But Piall is dead."

"I am aggrieved to hear that." Hugh tightened the reins in his hand and leaned down toward her. "But you are unhurt?"

"'Tis time to ride," Malcolm announced. "If we mean to return to Clarendon before 'tis full dark. Nevril, you and Barth stay with Castendown and Fleuwelling and see that all the remains are buried." He glanced at Judith. "I fear the same must be done for your man as well," he said. "For he was attacked by the mad dogs and carries the taint."

She nodded, her eyes filling with sudden tears. Even worse than she'd imagined. "Aye. Though he has died unshriven, I will speak with Father Anselm about paying an indulgence for him. Mayhap there is yet hope of saving his soul."

Malcolm nodded, his expression softening slightly. He looked as if he were about to speak, but Hugh interrupted. "Lady Judith rides with me." He dismounted, his feet thudding onto the ground with the jangle of chain mail.

"Wait, Hugh," she said as he reached for her. She hesitated, then went to Holbert. "Piall had a small cage. Mayhap—"

"Aye, my lady. I'll find it. Or make one," Holbert assured her, carefully taking the bundle of birds she offered. "But now you must get you back to the keep. I smell rain in the air again, and night is due to fall." His expression was as grim as she felt and she patted his arm.

"Many thanks," she told him, then swept her attention over the men in the clearing. Several of them were still digging graves for the dogs, and it would take them some time. "Thank you all."

Hugh lifted her onto his horse, and the beast shifted and pranced at her light weight. But she'd hardly settled on the back, riding astride due to her man's breeches, when Hugh swung up in front of her. She wrapped her arms around his waist and prepared for a long ride back to Clarendon.

~*~

MAL RODE at the head of the small contingent. Dirick of Ludingdon was next to him, but they trotted along in silence. Somewhere behind was Lady Judith, sitting on the back of de Rigonier's horse, her hose-clad legs clamped around the beast in an unfeminine manner, her arms around the man. That, Mal found, was a mental image nearly as bothersome as the one he'd had on the journey to find her. And so he trained his attention on other matters.

They would be fortunate to reach Clarendon before sundown, but at the least they were a large enough group—as well as armed and armored—that they needn't fear any threat from bandits or wild animals.

The group was less than an hour into its journey when a shout from behind caught Mal's attention. He reined in Alpha and turned to see a cluster of his companions standing in the road. Some had dismounted and others merely gathered around de Rigonier's horse. He could see Judith's bright hair among the group. She was standing on the ground aback from the men, and though any other woman might be complaining or weeping about the delay, about being tired or cold or hungry…she was merely standing there watching.

Muttering a curse, Mal directed Alpha back to them.

"Horse threw a shoe," de Rigonier's squire told him as Mal and Dirick drew up.

"Bad luck, that," Mal said, then glanced at Judith. She wouldn't be riding on the back of that horse any longer. He firmly squelched his rush of glee when he noticed how her shoulders slumped. She looked bedraggled and exhausted. Yet she held her chin high and made no complaint, and Mal felt a niggle of admiration for her composure. He'd known squires—aye, and even men—who'd been through less trauma and spewed complaints.

Dirick dismounted, handing the reins to his squire. "Lady Judith, may I help you up? I am fair certain Warwick's Alpha can easily handle another small weight such as yours."

Judith's attention flew from Dirick to Mal, her eyes widening as she took in the distance he sat off the ground. As if to emphasize his strength and size to the tiny woman, Alpha stamped and shimmied then gave a snort. Mal tightened the reins to check the beast, then before he could think better of it, reached down and scooped up Judith around the waist.

She gave a surprised squeak as she went airborne, clutching Mal's arm as he plopped her firmly on the saddle in front of him. "Well," she said, a little breathlessly. "That was unexpected."

Dirick's face was turned away as he took back his own reins, but Mal caught the hint of a smile curving his cheek. He grimaced, tamping down a burst of chagrin at his overeagerness to assist Lady Judith. *Fool.*

"Thus our party has shrunk yet again," Dirick said to the group at large after vaulting into his saddle. "Warwick and I will continue on. Bethrel, Fredrick, Mark, come you with us. The others will catch up to you soon enough, once their task in the forest is done," he added to the grounded de Rigonier, who was surrounded by his squire and two men-at-arms.

Mal was only vaguely aware of these arrangements as they were being made, for there were arrangements of his own that must be attended to. Lady Judith, once settled onto the saddle in front of him, had adjusted herself so she sat astride rather than sidesaddle. This meant that Mal, who sat behind and had an easy view down the front of her, couldn't help but notice the way her widespread thighs gripped the sides of their mount...something that would never have happened if she'd been wearing a proper gown.

He felt mortifyingly lightheaded for a moment as a variety of fantasies galloped through his mind, then firmly redirected his thoughts—and gaze—upward to the road in front of them. But as Judith jounced along in the seat, her curvy behind nestled into *his* widespread thighs, Mal had countless other disturbing thoughts with which to contend.

He was required to ride with one arm banded around her middle and the other holding the reins, blocking her in on one side. Despite his arm settling over the relatively innocent span of Judith's midriff, Mal couldn't be more aware of the curve of her breasts *just* above. And since she'd thrown herself into his arms upon her rescue, he was fully aware of how soft and curvy she was…everywhere. Once, she bent to the side to adjust her shoe or boot and the underside of one breast came perilously close to brushing against his mail-clad arm.

And then there was the matter of her hair. Directly below his chin bounced her head with its fiery braid, smelling of flowers and pine and some other scent that made his insides tighten and shiver. Wispy curls freed from their moorings fluttered into his face.

He couldn't bear to think about her warmth seeping into his thighs and groin—burning even through the hauberk, mail *sherte,* and chausses he wore. Or so it seemed. His cock responded accordingly, filling and straining uncomfortably inside his hose. But there was naught he could do to relieve the situation without announcing his condition to the very person who caused it.

Hell. He should have insisted she ride with Ludingdon, who hadn't even noticed another woman since his betrothal and wedding to Maris of Langumont. Yet at the same time, Mal realized this was the closest he'd likely ever be to the wench who'd taunted and teased him—knowingly and unknowingly—for more than a decade.

"Did you fall off your horse?"

Judith's question snatched Malcolm's attention abruptly from his private, tortuous musings to the present. "Fall off my horse?" he repeated, sure he hadn't heard her properly. "By the rood, what nonsense do you speak?"

She turned to look up at him, her hips sliding mercilessly around his inner thighs. Her hand reached across as she twisted so she could grip the arm he held alongside her. "When you first came into the clearing, you were on your horse. Then you came back without him. I bethought you fell—"

"Lady Judith," he interrupted, hardly able to keep his voice from a bellow, "I do not fall off my horse. Ever. I have not fallen from a mount since I was ten summers. And even that 'twas because I took too high a jump."

"Oh," she replied. She was silent for a moment—not nearly long enough, in his estimation—before she said, "Now I understand. You didn't wish for Alpha—is that his name, then?—to be injured by the dogs. And so you sent him away and came back on foot?"

"Aye," he replied tightly.

"But how did you get him back? He might have been lost in the forest, and you without a horse."

"Alpha—aye, that is his name—is trained to come at my whistle."

"I heard a whistle when I was still in the tree, and then a horn, but—"

Mal drew in a long, Judith-scented breath, then exhaled slowly. Could she not just sit and ride silently, leaving him to his private musings? "If you must know the entire tale, I caught a tree branch and let Alpha run out from beneath me."

"You did?" she said, her eyes widening in wonder. "At such a speed?"

He could not allow himself to indulge in the internal warmth that came with her admiration and responded brusquely, "Aye. Then I whistled a call to Gambert so that he and Nevril would know where I was—they were some distance behind me. He blew the horn to notify de Rigonier, Castendown, and the others, for we had divided ourselves into groups in our search for you. Did not you have this conversation already with de Rigonier?"

"Nay," Judith replied, still half-turned on his lap. Her mouth was tantalizingly close. Not to mention the sweet curve of her bottom. Mal forced his attention to the road ahead. "Hugh spent much of the journey thus far assuring himself that I was well, and then lecturing me about riding out with such little protection. I hardly was able to speak at all."

"De Rigonier had the right of it," Mal said sternly. "I dare not ask how you thought to be safe with a single man-at-arms at your side." Irritation flared, then he reminded himself he had no reason to be overly concerned with her safety. At the least, no more than he would be for any maiden.

"I have done so many a time," she retorted flatly. "And as I was dressed thusly, never would I have been mistaken for aught other than a boy riding with his father."

Mal gave a derisive snort, but forbore to point out that her long braid—not to mention the not-at-all-hidden curves—would have betrayed her gender in an instant. He was trying valiantly not to think about those curves. *Man, you have been without a woman for overlong.*

"We could not have expected the danger we found. How many packs of mad, wild dogs have you encountered in your journeys?" she demanded. "Wild boars, mayhap—and Piall could easily have evaded those lumbering creatures. But wild dogs? And a whole pack?"

"Not a one but for today," he admitted. "But one must remember that dangers are never expected, Lady Judith. That is why they are called dangers."

She *hmphed*, jolting in her seat. Then she turned back around toward the front.

Mal had hardly relaxed when she twisted to face him once more. This time, her breast came even more dangerously close to bumping his arm. And he was *not* going to think about where the pressure of her hip and bottom was. How close it was to hi—

"How did you come to find me? How did you even know I was in distress?"

"Your mare," he said, his voice thick. He swallowed, put the dangerous thoughts firmly from his mind. "Somehow she knew to return to Clarendon. She was recognized and we gathered our search party together. 'Twas mostly luck that I found you so quickly, but the birds of prey circling above the trees helped."

She was silent for a moment, then said, "Oh, no. *Crusty.* She was attacked—surely bit and scratched by the dogs."

Mal knew what she was asking without precisely doing so, and he also knew she was aware of the answer. "'Tis a shame when one loses a horse," was all he said. "And I'm sorry for that."

"But 'tis a greater shame when one loses a man," she replied.

"I cannot argue with that."

To his relief, Judith seemed willing to lapse into silence after that exchange. She turned back around and not long afterward, Mal felt her slump against him. Dead asleep, her negligible weight sagging against his chest and arm…all sweet-smelling, curvy, soft, blessedly quiet Judith. He closed his eyes briefly, allowing himself the luxury of holding her even as he berated himself for being so foolish as to even consider the thought of taking her to wife.

But, by God, the woman was lovely. And, apparently, she was intelligent *and* brave—if the events of the day were any indication. The cuts and scrapes on her hand and cheek from sliding down the tree trunk must hurt, but she'd not mentioned them once. Yet she was too loud and talkative for his taste. Too demanding. He could only imagine what it would be like to bed her. Would she have a running conversation, peppering him with questions about his day even as they coupled? She would want to know everything, she would want to have her fingers stirring up every part of his life, and surely—having been at court for so long—she'd want visitors at table all of the time.

Nay, Judith of Kentworth would not be a suitable wife for him.

Shortly after that, the rain promised by Nevril came. As they rode along, Mal reached behind to gather his cloak, then draped it over the front of him to cover his charge. By now, she'd turned to huddle against him and he helped her move sleepily, lifting her so both legs hung over one side.

She didn't awaken until they clattered across the drawbridge, rattling its heavy metal chains. Then she shifted and emerged from the cloak, her hair matted down and her eyes dull and sleepy. The rain had all but ceased, yet some drizzle still chilled the air. "We're home," she said, her voice rusty. "I slept."

"Indeed you did," he replied, aware that in a few precious moments, she'd be sliding away from him…forever. "You must see to the scrape on your cheek. And your arms as well. You slipped some distance on the tree."

She blinked as Alpha trotted across the bailey. "You saw me fall?"

"Aye."

"I climbed up and down seven times," she grumbled, pushing the cloak away. "And the one time I lose my footing is when it must be witnessed."

Mal nearly laughed, charmed by her irritation—and surprised at how easy it was becoming to converse with her. But…*seven times?* The woman must be as agile as the monkeys he'd seen once at court, many years ago. "Why did you climb up and down so many times?" he asked, his voice still light with humor.

"I was in the tree for more than four hours," she replied as they approached the stables. "Do you not think I tried to come down more than once? But the dogs were there every time I came into view, and so back up I went. Hoping they would lose sight of me and leave."

"You climbed the tree in order to capture a raptor for the king," Mal said grimly. They were at the stables now and he reluctantly turned Alpha to greet the grooms. He was dripping from the rain, but not at all chilled. "'Twas good fortune you were in the tree to begin with, my lady, else the dogs may have done more than tree you for hours."

"Aye," she replied, her voice quieting again. Surely she was remembering the cost of her folly.

Mal dismounted and handed his reins to the marshal, who gestured for help from a groom in case Alpha was still full of spirit. Then he turned to look up at Judith, meeting her eyes for a moment in the gray, drizzly light. "'Tis my hope, Lady Judith, that whatever becomes of your gift to the king and his queen, 'twas worth the sad events of this day." He lifted her from the saddle, setting her none too gently on the ground as the courtyard filled with the rest of their party.

"I do not think that is possible," she replied sadly. "Thank you, Malcolm."

~*~

"MY LADY!" Tabby greeted Judith with a relieved shriek when she came into her chamber. The maid flew into her mistress's arms as if *she'd* been the one lost and then found. "You are returned! I was so afeared for you, my lady, when Crusty returned and you did not!"

Judith embraced her in return, then extricated herself carefully, wincing at the pain in her arms and legs. "I am sore tired and—"

"And your face! And arms! What has befallen you?"

"I will tell you all of it, but I must have a bath. And some of your salve for my hurts. I've already ordered the water to be brought up." She stopped when the expected knock came at her chamber door.

Tabby rushed over to open it. "My *lord*!" she squeaked in shock.

Judith turned sharply, not certain whom she thought would be there after her maid's exclamation...but the last person she expected to see was *the king*.

"Your majesty," she exclaimed, collapsing into a curtsy.

"Rise, Lady Judith," said Henry in his low but commanding voice. "And tell your maid she need not have such a fit."

Indeed, Tabby was fairly prostrate on the floor, her breathing coming in short, quick gasps.

"Tabatha," Judith commanded in a steely voice, unable to fathom why on earth the king had seen fit to visit *her*. "Attend to... to...aught...."

"What is this? A menagerie? Is that a *rabbit* in yonder cage?" Henry was looking about the tiny antechamber where Bear, who had no sense of the greatness in his presence, had hardly lifted his head when the king entered the room. Unfortunately, the kitten was not so uninterested, and she stumbled from her place next to the dog and meowed up at the muscular, auburn-haired man. "And who is this?"

"Oh, my lord, your majesty, 'tis naught but a poor little cat I was nursing back to health," Tabby managed to say, scooping up the kitten just before she began to sharpen her claws on the royal legs. Her words came out in little more than a shaky whisper and Judith took pity on her.

"The men will be here with my bath any moment. Mayhap you shall meet them in the hall so they do not…er…splash water on his majesty." Judith turned her attention to the king, still stunned that she'd had to speak those words. "Your highness, to what do I owe this honor?"

Henry stepped into the chamber, the anteroom door closing partly behind him as Tabby went out through the main chamber door. He was dressed in informal clothing—a simple *sherte* and hose covered by a tunic, along with fine leather slippers. Nevertheless, his royal presence seemed to overtake the chamber, making the space shrink to just his size. "I just learned of your adventures this day, Lady Judith. I merely came to assure myself you have returned whole and unharmed."

Judith blinked and tried to hide her confusion. If the king made it his business to personally visit every one of his subjects when they returned from a journey, he would spend more time out of his chambers than in. "Aye, my lord, as you are well able to see, I am whole and unharmed."

"But for this bit of nastiness on your lovely face," he said, reaching to touch her scraped cheek. It was more of a caress than an inquisitive touch, and his fingers lingered on her skin, brushing the curve of her jaw.

Her heart skipped a beat and Judith felt herself flush with heat and confusion. He was looking at her…oddly. In a manner that made her insides flutter uncomfortably. "Aye," she managed to say, despite her dry mouth and pounding heart. "'Tis naught but the scrape of a pine tree trunk. I was…I climbed the tree in hopes of finding a baby falcon for the…for the queen."

"Indeed," Henry said. His hand fell away from her cheek and Judith breathed more easily. "We do hope it doesn't leave a scar. Such a beautiful countenance should never be marred thusly."

"You are very kind, your majesty," she replied, curtsying again briefly. "And you are very kind to take the time to visit me here."

"'Tis of naught account," he said. "Our queen is everything to us, and we wish only to ensure that our Lady Falconer is able to fulfill the request we have made of her."

"Of course, your highness," Judith told him, a little spark of excitement flaring inside her at the name 'Lady Falconer.' It might not be a formal title, but she would accept the honor nevertheless. Never had a woman been spoke of in such a manner. "And this day, I was able to capture two eyases. Surely one of them will suit for your lady wife."

"A pair of eyases? And mayhap we shall have a matching hunter for the king himself, then?" he said, his eyes glinting with pleasure.

"Indeed, my lord…if both falcons show promise. I vow it."

"Very well, then, Lady Judith. We shall leave you to your bath." His voice slowed and deepened on the word, and his attention skimmed the chamber. "And mayhap on the morrow, you shall tell us more of your adventures, and how you intend to train a pair of falcons for your sovereigns."

"Aye, my lord, and thank you for your kind attention this night," Judith said. She swept into one last curtsy, remaining thus until she saw his leather slippers turn and his feet carry him from the chamber, then out to the antechamber.

No sooner had the door closed behind King Henry than Judith collapsed onto the stool near the fire. What was the meaning of such an encounter? Her heart was pounding and her palms damp, but Judith drew in several slow, deep breaths to calm herself.

She was close enough to Eleanor to have met the king many times, but even more importantly, to have witnessed many of his majesty's various moods. He could be fiery and commanding, ruthless and violent…but he could also be wise and judicious—and kind and gentle, as he had been this night. He cared for his people in both England and France, and despite his thirst for power and land, Henry was a good king who was liked and respected by his most powerful barons. Judith's cousin Gavin, Lord Mal Verne, was one of the men who had the king's ear, and, along with Salisbury and Ludingdon, was respected by him as well. Among other things, they spoke optimistically of Henry's plans to redesign the legal system and applauded his move to institute a jury of peers in most trials.

As for the queen…. Henry loved and respected his wife as much as any man in a marriage arranged purely for power, wealth and land would do, and together they complemented each other in the manner in which they ruled.

By the time Judith had walked her mind through those rational thoughts, her breathing had slowed and the uncomfortable fluttering in her belly eased. Clearly, Henry cared for the well-being of one of his queen's closest confidantes—as well as the status of his own request of Judith.

A tentative knock startled her from her musings. "Enter," she called, tensing again.

Tabby burst in, still wide-eyed and carrying the kitten. "My lady," was all she said, looking around as if to see the king still lurking in the chamber. When she saw her mistress was alone, she said, "What—?"

"'Tis naught of your concern, Tabatha—the king's visit. He merely wished to ensure that I was unhurt. But 'tis not something I wish to be gossiped about. Do you understand?"

"Aye, of course, my lady," Tabby replied. Then her voice dropped. "No one saw his majesty enter or leave, my lady. I made certain of it."

"Where is my bath?" was Judith's only reply. The discussion was finished.

"'Tis without." Tabby opened the door then stood aside as a parade of pages and serfs marched into the chamber.

The first two were pages and carried a luxuriously large tub fashioned of metal. They wrestled it into position in front of the fire, where the blaze would help maintain the heat. Then followed a dozen serfs with buckets of hot water, dumping them one by one into the vessel until it was filled to its smooth, curled brim. Another series of serfs brought two smaller tubs: one empty and one filled with more steaming water for washing Judith's hair.

Tabby added a large bunch of fresh lavender branches, crushing some of the leaves and flowers between her fingers as she sprinkled it into the bath. Then, once the serfs left and the chamber door closed, Judith at last slid her sore, scraped body into the tub.

As she settled slowly into the steaming water, she groaned loudly—for the bath was both shockingly hot and wonderfully soothing. Once she was fully immersed, with only a small slop dripping over the side, she looked at Tabby and said, "And what is this about a rabbit? In my chamber?"

"Oh," replied her maid, her expression filled with consternation. "I didn't mean for you to find out so…unexpectedly."

"Indeed." Judith raised a brow as Tabby came behind her to comb out her braid and wash it. She settled in, resting her neck on a cushion at the side of the tub. As the maid went about her business, Judith closed her eyes, only half-listening to the long-winded explanation about an injured rabbit.

The hot water and its relaxing scent nearly had her slipping into repose. As she did so, the water lapping gently against her shoulders, Judith couldn't help remembering the rhythmic jolting of Malcolm's horse rocking her against him as she fell asleep. Despite the massive size of the beast, and the startling distance from the ground, she was able to relax and doze, safe in Mal's arms.

Such a feat was surprising, for Judith oft found it difficult to sleep even in her own bedchamber. She woke at any little noise, and if she wasn't comfortable, she didn't sleep well. *I was very tired this day.* Aye, she was tired and sore and she'd felt safe and comfortable huddled against his solid chest—a torso she could easily picture after having seen it bare in the training yard.

Judith's heart tripped a beat when she remembered the feeling, and when she thought about the way his powerful thighs angled behind and beneath hers as they rode. The unyielding texture of mail pressed into the back of her breeches, its chill warming as it brushed against her. At the time, she'd managed to push away the awareness of such intimacy by engaging him in conversation. But now, away from Mal, quiet and relaxed, she felt her entire body flush with heat. And it wasn't from the bath.

Malcolm of Warwick had matured into a powerful, courageous lord from the awkward young man she'd known. And he was kind too—taking Rike under his wing. He would be a fine husband for any gentlelady. Judith started, splashing a generous wave of water over the rim of the tub.

"What is it, my lady? Did I pull your hair?"

"Nay," she replied, biting her lip as she sank back down. "I was nearly asleep and almost slipped under the water."

Tabby replied, but Judith wasn't listening. *A fine husband.* She'd been so intent on matching him up with one of the other ladies at court, she'd never thought....

Judith's mind was working, her insides fluttered and bubbled and she gnawed on her lip. Then she stopped cold. And sagged back into the water.

The queen.

The queen would never allow Judith to wed and thus leave her side. To wed and then have an allegiance to a husband.

Tabby had been right: *'Twill be the end of the world—or at least her reign—before the queen allows you to see the green hills of Lilyfare.*

Or to wed.

SIX

THE NEXT morning, Tabby went to the kitchen garden to pick baby lettuce and other greens for her injured rabbit. On her way back to the keep, she made a detour around the north side of the bailey in hopes of accidentally encountering Bruin, the second marshal of the guest stables.

Bruin was five-and-twenty to Tabby's age of eighteen, and though he was shy around her, she found she could get him to smile on occasion—if she worked hard at it. He had a crooked tooth in the front that made him particularly endearing and a habit of shifting from foot to foot when she was speaking to him. Yet the man hardly said three words in her presence, for he seemed to prefer the company of the horses that were in his charge to any two-legged creature.

It was Tabby's desire to change that, and so she made certain to saunter past the stable whenever possible. Bruin was healthy, unmarried, gentle with the animals—and above all, he wasn't about to ever go off to war.

Today, however, when she walked past, Bruin was nowhere to be found. Mayhap he was brushing one of the horses, or attending to a broken bridle.

Nevertheless, Tabby found herself loitering a bit longer than necessary in hopes he might return. Behind her, she heard the clang of swords where the men-at-arms were training. The very sight of them, clashing with sword and shield, made her angry and sad all at the once. Thus, she resolutely kept her back to the embattled men, having no wish to watch them preparing for violence and bloodshed. Other women might admire their sleek muscles and powerful movements, but Tabby did not.

'Twas that folly which caused her to quite literally jump when a voice behind her said, "How fares the main ingredient of my rabbit stew?"

Tabby whirled and the basket slung over her arm crashed into the man standing behind her. Arugula, dandelion and lettuce leaves scattered into the dirt. With a sound of annoyance, she dropped into a crouch to gather them up, all the while doing her best not to speak out of turn. She nearly had to bite her tongue to keep from snapping at Sir Nevril.

But next she knew, he knelt beside her on the dirt-packed ground, carefully picking up the leaves and shaking the soil from them. "The beastie must still be living if ye're bringing the food to him. Or are these leaves for your mistress?"

"Nay," she replied, unable to hold her tongue any longer. "You'll not make rabbit stew of Maggin. He slept well last eve. His eyes are open and his nose quivers, and I trow he'll soon be hopping about the chamber."

"A rabbit hopping about your mistress's chamber," Nevril responded, placing a handful of the leaves back into her basket. "Imagine that. You gave the rabbit a name?"

She drew back, her brows pulling together in irritation. "Aye. Of course I did."

"You gave a rabbit *a name?*" he said again. This time, he stroked his beard, and his long finger rubbed against the scar along his cheek. "I don't believe I've ever known of a rabbit to be named." He looked as if he were about to laugh.

"Methinks 'tis because you see them only as fodder for your soup pot," she retorted. "Good day, Sir Nevril."

"Tabatha. One moment, if you will," he said, moving quickly to stall her. Something clinked and she noticed for the first time he was wearing mail, though it wasn't a surprise that he should be. He was, after all, Lord Warwick's master-at-arms. A heavy sword hung from its scabbard.

"I'm late. The poor thing is near starving," she told him, sidling to the right. "I've no time to talk with you."

"I doubt the beast will expire if you exchange two more words with me. You seemed not to be in a hurry before I approached. Aye, I saw you dandling about, trying not to look over at the training yard."

"Trying not to look at the training yard?" she exclaimed. "Pah! If you only knew.... I have no interest in watching any man learn to slay another with a sword! I care not for matters of war or battle. Now, sir, if you will allow me to be on my way."

He stepped aside, a surprised expression on his face. "Very well, then, Tabatha. But I merely meant to ask how your mistress was faring. I was with the party who found her yestereve, as you must recall, and my lord wondered aught to me this morn. I bethought you would know the whole of it and how she feels on this day."

Tabby stopped and turned, hugging the basket to her. "She is well."

"And her horse? The one which returned without her?"

"Surely you have heard, it must be put down for fear of the madness. Today they mean to do it. My lady will be resting in her chamber, for she cannot bear to watch."

"And there can be no funeral for Sir Piall," he said. "For we buried him there in the wood, giving him as much a blessing as we could."

"Aye," Tabby replied. "My lady mourns him, and at this moment is with Father Anselm to pray on his soul."

"Surely a man who gave his life in such an honorable way shall not be denied entrance to Heaven, whether unshriven or nay."

Tabby nodded fiercely, thinking of her father. "Aye, Sir Nevril. On that, at the least, we can agree."

"And the rabbit? Lady Judith isn't opposed to having such a four-legged beastie hopping about her chamber?" His eyes were grave.

"She was not altogether pleased," Tabby admitted. "But when the king had no real complaint, what more could she say?"

"The king?" Nevril looked at her in surprise.

Tabby wanted to give herself a firm kick—or mayhap the man in front of her should be the one to be kicked. "I should not have said anything." But then she felt she must explain, for the man was looking at her as if she were mad. "The king made a visit to our chamber last eve, to assure himself my lady was unhurt."

"How kind of the king," he replied.

"Please do not speak on it," she added in a rush. "My lady gave strict orders there should be no gossip about it, and I even ensured the pages and serfs who brought her bath did not encounter his majesty."

"I do not gossip," he replied, clearly insulted. "That is a woman's task. But since you are asking a boon of me, I must be allowed to ask one of you in return."

Tabby truly wished to kick him now. How had she come into such a pickle? "What sort of boon?"

"I should like to meet your—what was his name, did you say? Maggot?"

"Mag*gin*," she replied fiercely. "I do not trust you, sirrah. You might pluck him from his cage and drop him into your stew pot."

"I vow I will do nothing of the sort," he said soberly. "At the least, as long as Maggin is still kicking and his nose is quivering."

She couldn't control a sound of disgust and he laughed, which made her even more angry. "Why do you want to see him?"

The spark of humor drained away. "I merely wished to see how the fellow fares. Despite your belief, I do not like to see any creature in pain."

"Then mayhap you ought sheath your sword and put your bow and arrows away," she grumbled.

"Aye, and then what would you eat and who would protect the lands on which you live?" he countered.

Tabby huffed and rolled her eyes. "Very well. I will bring you to see him. On the morrow."

"I shall hold you to that, Tabatha," he said. "On the morrow. After morning mass. To your chamber."

Just as Nevril turned to go, Tabby noticed Bruin. He was standing at the open door of the stable, holding a bridle in his hand. He looked from her to Nevril and back again, then turned to go back into the dim building.

She glared up at the man she wanted to kick even more and said, "And now you have utterly ruined my day. Good morrow." She spun and stalked off, the basket of greens swaying violently from her arm.

~*~

MALCOLM OBTAINED his audience with King Henry late the day after Judith's rescue. He left his sword with the guard at the door as he strode into the royal court room, then bowed deeply.

"Warwick. What brings you to our presence?" demanded the king.

Mal took that as permission to straighten and did so, looking around the chamber. The queen was present, as she oft was when Henry held court, as well as the Archbishop of Canterbury (although he appeared to be distracted by a chess game with some other clergyman Mal didn't recognize). A scribe sat at a table to one side, inks, pens and rolls of parchment at the ready along with the king's seal and a pot of wax kept warm over a small candle.

The royal couple sat on two massive chairs raised on a small dais with Canterbury next to them. A large table near the queen held an array of food: white cheese, grapes, apples, and a round, dark loaf of bread. A page stood behind it at a smaller table laden with plates, goblets, and a trio of wine bottles.

"I've come to petition your majesty for the right to wed," Mal replied as he approached the dais.

"Is that so?" Henry said, his eyes narrowing thoughtfully. "You married Sarah of Glawstering quite some time ago…." The queen leaned over and spoke quickly to her husband, who sobered. "And our queen has reminded us that your wife died four years past. Our sympathies, Lord Warwick."

"Many thanks," Mal replied. "I received your letter of condolence at the time, and I was much appreciative for that as well as the one you sent on the death of my father. But it is four years gone, and 'tis time I set my mind to a new wife and begetting an heir."

"There was no issue from your previous consummation?" Henry frowned. "I recall aught of a daughter…."

Mal kept his expression smooth. "Aye. But she is very sickly and weak, and is not expected to…." Mortified when his voice trailed off, he swallowed hard and continued flatly, "She cannot inherit."

Henry looked at him, then at his wife. "I see," he said with notable gentleness. "'Tis never easy to lose a child, nor to see one waste away." He patted Eleanor's hand, reminding Mal that the king and queen had lost three of their own children in a variety of ways over the years. "In that case, we foresee no problem with such a request. Warwick is flush, well-managed, and pays its rents on time. You send mercenaries as needed. Your loyalty to the crown is unquestionable. Of course, the granting of such a privilege will require some recompense on your part."

Of course. A large, fat recompense, I am sure. Mal tried not to show that he was gritting his teeth as he bowed briefly, responding, "I would expect naught other than to show my gratitude for such grace, your majesty."

Eleanor leaned over again and murmured. Henry chuckled and muttered in response and she laughed in return. Then the king looked at Mal with shrewd eyes. "The queen wishes to know which lovely lady might have caught the eye of the Lord of Warwick."

"I've made no offers, my liege, as of yet. I am considering Beatrice of Delbring, for her estate adjoins my lands at Pranville, and her father is more than willing for the match. But 'twas another reason I came to petition your highness directly: I thought to see if there were other candidates here in your court."

"Beatrice of Delbring is a pitiful *mouse* of a girl," Eleanor said, surprising Mal with her bluntness. "But joining your lands with hers would be a smart decision. Yet there are others of an age to wed. Ursula of Tenevaux is sweet and pretty, but more importantly, she comes with an estate near the sea. A bit vacant-headed, but 'tis no great matter. And there is Lady Alynne…though a bit long in tooth, she is sturdy, wealthy, and would at the least not be crushed beneath your great…ehm…physique."

Mal wasn't certain whether to blush or laugh at the queen's assessment, for her eyes were bold as they swept over his figure. "I assure you, my lady queen, my previous wife did not expire due to being crushed under my…self."

Eleanor laughed, clearly surprised at his jest—though no more than Mal himself. He hardly considered himself a wit, let alone forward enough to make such a lewd jest in the company of the queen. But he had done so and, thank fortune, didn't appear to have offended. Even the king was chuckling as he called the scribe over.

"Very well, then, Warwick. The writ shall be prepared thus: a grant to wed as you wish, provided the maid is not otherwise betrothed or promised, and that her lands—if she brings any— reside in England. I do not wish you to expend resources traveling across the Channel to see to an estate when you have aught to keep you busy in England."

But of course, for that would mean less of my "resources" to flow to your coffers, my lord king. Yet Mal was sore pleased, even when the king named the very generous remuneration he must pay for the privilege of obtaining the writ—as well as a fine based on a portion of the lady's dowry when he actually exercised the entitlement. The grant gave him the freedom to negotiate with any number of fathers or brothers for a lady's hand, and allowed him the ability to make a decision quickly and expediently if necessary.

The king signed and sealed the charter, then called Canterbury and the queen to witness it as well. Mal took the precious paper with relief and begged leave of the king.

He was one step closer to returning to Warwick. And if he chose to wed Beatrice of Delbring, Mal realized, he could leave as soon as the morrow.

‒*‒

TWO DAYS after her ill-fated hunting trip, Judith was in the mews checking on Hecate and the other raptors when a long shadow fell across the space.

Startled, she turned to see Malcolm standing on the inner threshold. His shoulders were so broad he barely fit in the entrance, his head tilted slightly down to keep from bumping the top of it. His too-long hair hung in shaggy waves, curling about his neck and clean-shaven jaw. Her heart gave a sudden, warm lurch.

He wore an ambiguous expression as he said, "I didn't mean to frighten you."

"You didn't frighten me as much as startle me," she replied smartly, aware that her heart was pounding now. Why was her heart pounding? "I thought I was alone—and then all at once, there is a large, hulking man standing in the doorway."

"I am not so very hulking," he said stiffly.

Judith couldn't help but giggle as she looked him over. For some reason, she was ridiculously happy to see him. "Tall, then, my lord. You are very tall. And your shoulders are very wide, and if one doesn't call that hulking—"

"You're here alone?" he interrupted, looking around the space. His attention skimmed the sawdust floor and the five falcons sitting calmly on the long perch.

"At the moment. Tessing went to check the traps for pigeons." Judith opened the mews's three large windows, allowing more mellow light to illuminate the area. It was large enough for any of the falcons to bate—spread and flap its wings—without hitting the walls. The raptors preferred an open, well-lit space once they were full grown. "'Tis time to feed them. The raptors, not the pigeons," she added quickly, then felt foolish for babbling…but she couldn't seem to stop. "We feed the raptors the caught pigeons or sparrows, for they prefer fresh meat, still warm." What on earth was wrong with her?

"No hunting today?"

"Is that why you've come?" she replied, glad for the distraction—yet a little confused. Why *was* he here? Then she looked Hecate, who hadn't flown in two days because of Judith's trip. "Her weight is down," she said thoughtfully. "She hasn't started molting yet. Do you wish to hunt?" She tried to keep the eagerness from her voice, but likely didn't succeed. Yesterday had been an unhappy day, attending to the death of her man Piall as well as the loss of Crusty. A hunt would be an excellent diversion.

"Na—" Malcolm began, then seemed to change his mind. "Aye. 'Twas not the reason I came, but I could hunt." He shrugged easily, but his eyes lingered on Judith long enough that her insides gave another little flutter.

Pleased at this turn of events—but uncertain as to precisely why—she immediately began to make preparations, leaving the raptors in the mews while she did so. The supplies and tools she and Tessing used were in an adjoining room so as not to distract the falcons.

"The eyases I took from the nest are doing well," she told Malcolm, pulling on the heavy glove she wore over the fist where Hecate was trained to sit. "But 'twill be some time before we determine whether they'll suit for hunting. They still have their baby down, and to be taken from the nest so young, they may learn to screech. But if I had left them there, they surely would have died."

"Screech?" he asked, watching her as she tied the jesses to her glove.

"When a human comes near. 'Tis a bad habit, and makes for difficulty in training them if they screech and cry whenever a man— or woman—is about. So we leave them alone as much as possible, only visiting to quickly feed them two or three times per day. When they get their adult feathers, they can learn to fly freely, going out of the hack house and coming back for food. For we know they'll return to their nest."

"Until they become older and stronger. And then one must take the time to man them."

"Aye," she said, her cheeks warming. *Babble on, my lady.* "Mayhap you've trained falcons afore?"

"Nay." His lips curved in something like a smile. "'Twas a guess gleaned from other conversation. I hunt with raptors, but I have ne'er trained one. I'll call for Gambert. He'll accompany us." He went to leave, then paused. "Shall I arrange a mount for you, my lady?"

Judith's heart gave a pang over the reminder of Crusty but she nodded. "Aye. I shall have Hecate ready to go in a moment. Shall I bring a falcon for you, my lord?"

"Nay. 'Tis enough to watch your bird."

Though the day wasn't brilliantly sunny, there was no sign of rain as they rode out several minutes later. Wispy clouds streaked a light blue sky, and a gentle breeze ruffled the rich green meadow grass. A hooded Hecate was settled on Judith's leather-covered fist. She rode along next to Malcolm and Sir Nevril, along with Sir Holbert, who also had a falcon on his hand, and they discussed the imminent hunt. Gambert followed close behind.

Not far from the walls of Clarendon, they rode down a gentle slope into the field bordered by a stand of trees. After they halted the horses, Malcolm dismounted and offered Judith his assistance. She slid to the ground so smoothly Hecate hardly ruffled a feather.

When Judith removed the leather hood to reveal the new surroundings, Hecate bated. But her mistress was prepared, holding her fist far from her body, and the falcon's wings flapped harmlessly while she remained on her perch.

"The hood is a new fashion," Judith told Malcolm. "We've been using them only for two summers now, but 'tis a wonderful invention. Tessing learned about it when he met a falconer who'd been in the Holy Land. Apparently, they have been using hoods for many centuries in the Far East. It keeps the bird calm, as you have surely noted, even whilst riding to the hunt."

"She seems eager," Mal said. "And strong. What will she take, do you think?"

Judith couldn't hold back a smile of pride. "She's taken a partridge in the past, but as she is still recovering from an injury to her leg, I would be pleased with a fat hare."

"Do you not allow your maid to hear you say that," spoke up Nevril. "My lady," he added hastily, looking utterly abashed. With a glance at Malcolm, he pulled at his forelock and gave a brief bow. "My apologies."

But Judith wasn't insulted. "You know my maid, Sir Nevril? I was not aware of it. How know you Tabby?"

"Aye, my lady," the man replied, taking obvious care with his speech this time. She noticed the red line of an old scar along his jaw, from beard into the edge of his hair. "I came to know her on the day you went missing. She was protecting a rabbit in the meadow and I came upon her—"

"Ah! So 'twas you who ruined my maid's day," Judith interrupted, laughing merrily. "I trow you rue the day you crossed paths with Tabatha, then, Sir Nevril."

"Nay," he replied. "She is a pretty wench, despite her sharp and loose tongue."

"I cannot imagine where she might have learned such," Malcolm muttered.

Judith swore she heard Sir Holbert choke back a chuckle, but when she turned to look at him, he was innocently adjusting his mount's bridle, his face studiously blank of emotion. "Indeed," was all she said, still watching her master-at-arms. "Well, Sir Nevril, her loose tongue had plenty to say on you."

"I am not surprised. What is her arrangement with the marshal Bruin?" he asked, to her surprise. "Are they wed or betrothed?"

"Nay," Judith replied, now becoming more thoughtful. "But do you not look in her direction, Sir Nevril. For you must return to Warwick, and I, like the queen, shall never allow my serving woman to leave me. Although…if you *were* set on the maid, mayhap your lord would be less rigid." She cast Malcolm a teasing glance.

"Ah, my lady, I did not look at the wench so *very* closely. 'Twas a simple question is all," he said quickly. But Judith noticed he kept his gaze averted from his master.

"Very well, then," she said. "Let us hunt!"

They had no dogs with them to roust out any prey, but Gambert offered to ride about in the meadow and act the part.

"First you scheme to keep my master-at-arms here at Clarendon, and now my squire is becoming a hound," Mal said dryly to Judith. "Mayhap this hunt wasn't my best decision."

She laughed up at him, catching herself from touching his arm just in time. *He's not Hugh,* she had to remind herself. *Not as loose or informal.* But she surely enjoyed his company.

He was looking at her when she laughed, and their eyes met for a moment. His gaze was intense and warm, surprising her —and Judith's mouth went dry. Her insides flushed with a sudden heat and she felt her heart trip a little.

Then abruptly he looked away. "Well, lady, shall we hunt or nay?"

A little unsettled by her strong reaction to Malcolm, Judith turned her attention to Gambert. He was galloping across the field in zig-zag formation as if he never wished to stop. Holbert helped her untie Hecate's jesses, which was difficult to do with one hand.

Then she looked at Hecate and said, "Off!" She thrust her hand high and her falcon pushed up into the air. She felt the gentle dig from the raptor's claws from the effort, thankful for the thick glove to protect her from being footed. She had enough scars on her other hand from irritated falcons.

"I never tire of watching them soar," she murmured, looking up as her raptor circled the meadow, fast and high and free. And then without warning, Hecate dived. "Hie!" Judith cried, straining to see what had been flushed out. "A quail!"

Without being asked, Malcolm slung her back into her saddle and she kicked off, riding toward the bird and its prey. The others followed, and by the time she reached the area where Hecate had snatched at the quail, Mal was on Judith's tail.

She dismounted quickly and whistled for her bird, who returned promptly to her fist. Judith took the piece of raw meat Holbert had readied for her, giving it to Hecate as a reward for her catch. The raptor must be rewarded immediately after catching its prey, or on the next time, the bird might eat it before Judith could be there.

They hunted for another hour, with Hecate finding a small rabbit, and Holbert's falcon snatching up a squirrel and a vole.

"'Tis time to return, I trow," Mal said, squinting up at the sun. "It has been a good hunt, my lady."

"Aye," she replied, herself satisfied with the results. And the company. She cast him a look, acutely aware of the constant awareness she had of him. It was so different from how she felt around Hugh, when she teased and flirted. With Hugh, it was naught more than a way to pass time. But it was different with this sober man.

As they rode back, she and Mal led the way and the others fell behind. At first, they trotted along in silence. But after a short time, Judith's curiosity got the better of her.

"And so…if you did not mean to hunt," she asked as they neared the walls of Clarendon, "what brought you to the mews this morrow?"

He looked straight ahead. "I merely thought to see how your injuries were. And to share my sorrow over the loss of your mare."

"Ah. Thank you," she replied. They rode in silence for a moment, then, ready to think about aught other than the loss of Crusty and Piall, Judith said, "I bethought you might wish to compare my list of potential wives to that of the queen's." When he looked at her, startled, she added cheekily, "Beatrice of Delbring? *Truly?*"

Malcolm didn't seem to know how to respond, for his face was filled with consternation and his cheeks turned ruddy.

"The queen—and I—believe you could make a better match. And although her majesty has included Gladys of Darvington and Winifred d'Alsineaux on her list of candidates, you have already been warned away from them by me, have you not? I cannot imagine you wishing to face either of them at table day after day for years, for they are both miserable and unhappy women."

"The lady doesn't have to smile at me in order to fulfill the role of a wife," he commented.

"Verily 'tis true, my lord, but why not choose a wife who is at the least pleasing to converse with as well as one who is wealthy and fertile?" Judith knew she was speaking boldly, but as ever, her tongue had a mind of its own. "'Tis fortunate for you the queen shall never allow me to wed and leave her side, or you must needs find a reason to strike even *me* off your list of possible wives." She forced herself to laugh merrily.

If she'd hoped Mal would have said aught about finding no reason to strike her off his list, or even express some token dismay that she wasn't eligible to wed, Judith was bound to be disappointed, for he remained stoically silent. So she rattled on, inducing her tones to remain bright and cheery. "Now, Lady Ursula would be a fine choice. And though she has moments of cloud-headedness—and who among us does not—she is amusing to converse with. Her estate is fine, and best of all," she added mischievously, "she has seen you training in the yard."

"Of what import is that?" Mal demanded, glancing back as if to see whether his squire had heard. But Gambert was well behind them, talking with Sir Nevril and Sir Holbert. The open gate to Clarendon was just ahead.

"Why, she has been swooning and exclaiming over your… uhm…prowess with the sword," Judith told him with great innocence. "Her cheeks turn pink whenever someone mentions your name. And ere I told her about your skill fighting off an entire pack of mad dogs, she has asked me many times to re-tell the tale—each with more detail than on the last telling. I've had to describe how you leapt from the seat of your horse and allowed Alpha to run off in order to save him, even though I was not witness to that particular performance."

By now, Malcolm's face was more than ruddy and his features had tightened. "By the rood, how your tongue ever wags, Lady Judith," he said grimly. "The next I know, Duchante himself will be singing ballads of my supposed feats."

"But my Lord Warwick, how can that be a bad thing?" Judith teased as they clattered over the drawbridge into the bailey. She must keep her words jesting, for if she thought too closely about what she said, she might begin to believe it herself. "Methinks garnering the rapt attention of the ladies when one is in search of a wife can only be a happy occurrence."

"I care not whether a maid moons over me or nay," Malcolm said with stiffness in his tones. "'Tis her lands and the dowry she brings, not how the lady looks at me."

"'Tis rather like choosing a horse—or a falcon, then, is it, my lord? Selecting a wife because her estate is near yours or somehow complements it?" Judith had stopped her mount, for they were at the stables, and she looked up at Malcolm. "You have little concern for mutual affection or even personality—"

"I told you previously she must be mild and biddable. And a good chatelaine. And by the rood, of course I'll not wed a woman who despises me!"

"Well," Judith said, holding out her hand for him to help her dismount. "That, at the least, is promising."

~*~

JUDITH WAS in her chamber late in the evening when there was a knock on the door. Bear lifted his head and gave a half-hearted growl, then collapsed back on his pallet.

After her hunt with Malcolm, Judith had returned to the keep to find the queen in need of her. After several hours of attending Eleanor, she had a brief supper in the hall. And, as there'd been no entertainment this evening—nor had she spied Malcolm in the hall—she'd returned to her room shortly after the meal. It was well into the evening, nearly bedtime, and thus, she didn't expect a visitor. Tabby was somewhere—likely mooning over the groom Bruin, who'd been sitting at a trestle table near the rear of the hall this evening. Judith knew this because Tabby had pointed him out to her when they entered the hall for dinner, and then her maid had slipped off in order to sit "near" the young man.

Judith rose from her seat by the fire, where she'd been working on the embroidery for a small pouch she intended to hang from her waist. It would be large enough to carry some coin as well as her eating knife and the keys to the trunks containing her valuables, which she kept with her when she left her chamber. The kitten, who'd been alternately batting at Judith's hem and chasing the tail of her embroidery thread, scrambled out of the way.

She opened the door to find a page wearing the king's livery. "My lady, the king wishes you to attend him."

Judith froze, her hand clutching the solid wood of the door. "The king?" she repeated dumbly.

"The king wishes you to attend him," repeated the page, clearly having memorized the message and naught more.

Her insides churning, Judith sought frantically for an explanation for such a summons. None was forthcoming, unless he wished to speak with her on the matter of the queen's falcon. It was a possibility, for the king was known to have a mind that ne'er stopped working, and he would call for his advisors or servants at any time of day or night for any purpose. But…. She felt ill.

"My lady," the page said, shifting urgently on his feet.

"I…I am coming," Judith said slowly, turning to look about her chamber. Her palms had dampened, and that swirling, churning sensation inside her did not lessen. She snatched up her long cloak, then thrust it aside in favor of a different one—an old castoff she'd given Tabby that was less fine and ornate.

Pulling it around her shoulders, Judith fastened the brooch and gave one last glance about her chamber. Then she had no choice left but to follow the page.

He walked briskly through the corridors of the keep and she kept good pace with him, all the while considering and discarding explanations for why the king should call her to him at this time of the night.

There were few people about; the dim hallways, lit by wall sconces and sheathed in tapestries, were fairly empty. In the distance, Judith heard male laughter coming from the men's chamber—a vast room where the men-at-arms, knights and even unmarried lords slept on pallets until they could arrange for a more private chamber.

Nervousness seized her as she passed the queen's apartments. There was unusual silence coming from behind the heavy double door, beyond which was the chamber where Judith spent much of her days amusing or conversing with the queen. If she was not in those chambers, she was often with the queen in her private solar, copying her legal papers or contracts, or writing letters as Eleanor dictated them.

But it was quiet behind those doors, and the fear that aught had happened to the queen spurred Judith to walk faster. Mayhap that was the reason for the king's summons. Something had happened to his wife, who was four months gone with child.

Despite her current uncertainty, Judith couldn't help a smile. She had enjoyed the day, enjoyed the company, and most certainly found it amusing to tease Malcolm as she'd done. He was so very serious and sober, 'twas entertaining to try to pique him, to see him draw up those broad shoulders and make stiff-lipped retorts to her jests.

He would make some lady a fine husband. Judith bit her lip. *But not I.*

The page led Judith down a narrow corridor through which she'd never traveled and at last stopped before a small door. She noticed an armed guard standing just beyond the entrance at the end of the short passageway, cloaked in shadow.

"My lady," the page said with a bow. "You may enter. His majesty awaits you."

Judith's heart was pounding erratically once again, having surged up into her throat—or at the least, it felt that way. Her insides were in such turmoil she feared she might lose her supper. "Thank you," she said, then loosened the latch and stepped inside.

"Come in, Lady Judith," said a voice when she hesitated on the threshold. "Close the door."

She did so, slowly, her heart racing, her palms slippery.

The chamber was simply furnished with a myriad of wall sconces and candles providing a mellow golden illumination. A table and two chairs were arranged near a hearth with a roaring fire. A fine rug covered the stone floor. Another table near the wall, which had no windows nor even arrow slits, boasted an array of food.

And there was a bed.

The king stood in the center of the chamber, as if he'd just risen from one of the chairs and walked toward her. Once again, he was wearing a simple tunic over footed hose. His eyes were dark and fastened on her with intensity. "Lady Judith…come in. How kind of you to join me."

A corner of her frantic, racing mind wondered if Henry knew how ironic his words were. As if she'd had any choice in the matter.

Just as she had no choice in obeying his command to "come in." Yet she could hardly make her legs move.

"My lord," she said, forcing herself into a curtsy…wanting never to rise again. Because she greatly feared what would happen when she did.

But surely…*surely*…she was mistaken. Surely it was a misunderstanding.

Henry walked over to her and, taking her hand, lifted her to her feet with a firm grip. He was standing very close—so close she could smell the wine on his breath, the smokiness from the fire, the expensive scent wafting from his clothing. His beard and mustache were neatly trimmed and his thick hair curled around his forehead and ears.

"Your hurts have begun to heal," he said, reaching, as he had done only two nights earlier, to touch her cheek. This time, after trailing over the scrape, his fingers continued along her jaw and down over her neck where they settled at the clasp of her cloak. "'Tis glad I am of that."

With a short, neat movement, he unpinned the brooch at her throat and flung the cloak aside.

"My lord, your majesty," she stammered, stepping back slightly. "What may I—what is your—why have you called me here?"

Henry smiled at her. He was a handsome man, one with an energy many people of both genders found attractive. In truth, Judith had always considered the man magnetic in his personality and appearance. Even now, a part of her acknowledged this: she was in the presence of greatness, of her liege lord, her king, and he was a virile, alluring, muscular man.

But the rest of her…the greatest part of her…wasn't thinking of him in that way.

"Judith, will you have some wine?" he asked. Still holding the hand he'd taken when he raised her from the curtsy, he drew her across the room with him.

She must follow, though her knees shook and surely he could feel how icy her fingers were. "My lord," she managed to say. "To what do I owe this…h-honor?"

The king poured wine for both of them, then handed her a goblet. "A toast, my lady," he said, lifting his own drink. "To the fair Judith, Lady of Kentworth, Lady of Lilyfare, Lady Falconer…a most elegant, graceful lily in her own right."

He brought the wine to his lips and sipped, and Judith followed suit. She didn't know if she'd be able to swallow for her throat was so dry and constricted. The wine was rich and heavy, filled with the essence of berries, and it flushed warmth through her. She set the goblet on the table.

"You have the most beautiful hair I have e'er seen," said Henry, reaching to touch it. He filtered one of her finger-thick braids between the pad of thumb and forefinger, then at the end, removed the metal case that confined the plait. "'Tis like fire. I've naught seen any like it on any other head—man or woman—in all my travels."

Judith could do nothing but stand there as he pulled his fingers through the braid, loosening it into fiery waves over her shoulder and down over her breasts.

"My lord," she spoke again. "What do you do? Your wife—"

"We shall not speak of my queen this night," he interrupted sharply. His eyes flashed for a moment.

Judith swallowed hard and nodded miserably. "My lord… please…I am honored that you should…find my hair so beautiful. But I…." She swallowed, desperate for the words to let him know her feelings, yet not to insult. For he was her lord, her king. He held infinite power over her. He could order her banished, imprisoned— even her death. She was at his mercy in all things. "I am weary. I beg of you, allow me to return to my chamber and seek my bed."

Henry gave a short, low chuckle. "But there is a bed anon. Here in this very chamber. And, I promise it, 'tis more comfortable than any other in the whole of Clarendon."

"My lord," she tried again. "I do not believe I would…sleep overmuch in this chamber."

His eyes cooled a trifle. "Lady Judith, methinks you are thirsty. Drink you more of this very fine wine." He thrust the goblet back into her hand. She accepted it with trembling fingers and took another drink. When she would have taken the cup away, he reached up and tipped it toward her mouth once again. "There now, my lady. Mayhap you are warmer…and more pliable now?"

She set the empty goblet on the table and tried to keep her quivering knees from buckling.

"Now tell me, Lady Judith," said the king as he took her hand once more. He drew her across the chamber, over the fine, smooth rug, toward the bed. "Are you still in possession of your maidenhead?"

Her heart nearly choking her, Judith scrambled for a response. If he believed she was still a virgin, mayhap he would allow her to leave. A lady's maidenhead was very valuable, and not to be given lightly. But if Henry had no intention of allowing her to leave and he learned she was not a virgin, would he punish her for lying to him?

"Judith?" he pressed, unfastening a second braid. "I wish to know if you are a virgin."

"Nay," she whispered at last as he tugged his fingers through her hair. "I am no virgin."

Henry smiled, a warm, genuine smile that, under any other circumstance might have eased her. "I am very glad to hear that. For that will make this much more pleasurable…for both of us."

With that, he reached up and began to unlace her gown.

SEVEN

A HAND on his shoulder brought Malcolm immediately out of the depths of sleep and into wakefulness. He simultaneously opened his eyes and sat up, fully awake and aware in the instant. Such was the necessary skill of a leader, of a man trained to be a warrior, of one who slept oft on the ground and was responsible for the safety and well-being of an entire village and keep.

But Mal didn't immediately recognize the man who'd waked him. "Aye?" he said in a low growl, aware of the rows of other snoring, grunting, farting men who joined him in the chamber wherein he was relegated to sleeping. If he meant to stay at court much longer, he must needs find his own chamber.

"Lord Warwick, I am loathe to disturb you, but there is a problem in the stable. With your horse."

Now Mal recognized the young man as one of the night marshals for the public stable, where he housed Alpha and the other horses from Warwick. But recognition of the messenger was much less important than the message itself, and he rolled from his pallet, launching to his feet in a flash. He yanked on a tunic and hose—for like most of his chambermates, in the summer he slept nude—then shoved his feet in a pair of soft boots.

Less than two minutes after he'd been awakened, Mal was following the groom out of the chamber. The first thought he had on hearing the news was a terrible fear that Alpha had been injured by the rabid dogs after all, and that his trusty horse was showing signs of madness. The worry had him striding at such speed that the groom fairly ran in order to keep pace with him.

He could have asked the messenger, but that would have entailed slowing and conversing and mayhap the man didn't even know the answer to the question "What the hell is wrong with my horse?" His destrier was worth more than a small estate, aside from being his constant, trusted companion who'd carried him safely from countless dangerous situations. Losing Alpha would be a devastating blow, both financially and personally.

And so Mal hurried out through the great hall and into a dark summer night that was lit only by a sliver of moon and a distant swath of stars. Torches studding the ramparts above, manned by men-at-arms, added to the illumination of the bailey. But shadows fell long and wide, casting much of the area into darkness.

The stable was lit and Mal rushed in, expecting to find the worst. At his abrupt arrival, the other marshal jolted in surprise, looking over from where he waited at the entrance to Alpha's stall.

"What is it?" Mal demanded. "What ails my horse?"

"'Tis his leg, my lord," said the groom, gesturing to the stall. "'Tis raw and red, and the mad beast willna let me touch it."

Mal was aware of a tightening in his chest when he heard the term "mad," and he pushed past the groom—whose name, he remembered belatedly, was Bruin—and approached Alpha.

The destrier snorted in recognition when his master appeared and eased what had been a shaking, shimmying sort of dance in his stall. Mal opened the half-door of the enclosure and knelt in front of his horse. Most men would have been fools to do such a thing—placing oneself in front of those massive hooves—but Mal knew Alpha, and he was angled slightly aside, half inside the stall. The powerful beast could crush him against the wall, true, but Mal had a comforting hand on the horse's ribs as he spoke softly to him. He also knew how to move quickly if need be.

In the lantern light, he saw at once whereof the groom spoke. To his great relief, the injury was clearly not from a mad dog. "'Tis a boil on his joint," he murmured. "Surely you've seen aught before,

Bruin?" This last was directed to the groom, who, along with the messenger, stood safely in the aisle.

"Aye, my lord. I wished to put a poultice on him, but he near as kicked me through the wall," replied the young marshal.

"'Tis no wonder, for the beast is in rare pain." Mal sighed. Better that he attend to it and lose some bit of sleep—and on the morrow, Gambert or Nevril could assist—than to chance his valuable warhorse to be injured.

But the ailment, though not serious was no small inconvenience, for he meant to join Ludingdon, Fleurwelling, and several others on an excursion on the morrow. Earlier, the king received news of a band of raiders or brigands wreaking havoc in the area, and several of his barons—likely as bored as Mal—offered to go in search and put a stop to them. For his part, Mal was delighted with an excuse to leave Clarendon for a time. As well, it would give him the chance to speak with Castendown about taking on Rike's fostering when he returned to Warwick.

"Bring me the poultice," Mal said to Bruin, already considering which of the other mounts from Warwick would suffice for the trip.

"'Tis here," was the reply, and shortly thereafter, Mal found himself playing both groom and physician to Alpha.

Once the boil was carefully wrapped, the thick, aromatic salve oozing from the edges of the bandage, Mal shifted back and rose to his feet. Alpha seemed calmer—which was no surprise, for the bandage likely provided some cool relief to the fiery, pulsing boil—and he butted his head against his master's shoulder.

Mal spoke softly to him once more, feeding him an apple demanded from Bruin, and then took his leave. "Send to me immediately if there is any other problem," he directed as he walked out into the night.

The bailey was near as quiet as his own back at Warwick, and Mal took his time wandering back into the close, crowded, privacy-lacking keep. A pang of homesickness caught him by surprise, followed by a clutch of sadness when he thought of Violet. He must return soon to his little one.

There is little reason for me to remain here. I can leave as soon as Alpha is able to travel, and we will stop at Delbring on the return trip. Then all would, as he'd hoped, be arranged well before Christ's Mass and the winter.

But then a pair of laughing blue eyes, devilish and sparkling, popped into his mind. *Beatrice of Delbring? Truly?*

Mal allowed himself the luxury of reliving that moment, the memory of the day, riding beside Lady Judith in the sun and about the meadow. He'd enjoyed her company—even the teasing. And somehow, he'd become comfortable in her presence, no longer unsettled by her intense beauty and energetic tongue. Throughout the hunt, he'd admired her face and figure, laughed inwardly at her jests, been entertained by the hunt and the skill with which she managed her falcon, and felt himself growing more and more desirous of being with her.

'Tis no good to continue on this route. Naught will become of it.

She'd told him so herself, in her own blunt yet good-humored way: the queen would never allow her to wed. She said so with joy and amusement, clearly not unhappy with the arrangement. And so he dare not allow his mind to go there any longer.

But there were other options here at court—and was that not part of the reason he'd come? There was no cause to settle for the small estate of Delbring when he might have Tenevaux or another larger property. And a wife not unpleasant to look on. Mayhap even one with whom he could converse.

Funny. Until he spent time with Judith, Malcolm had never considered a pleasant, intelligent, witty woman a boon in a wife. And now....Now she was forcing him to look at things in an utterly different way.

By now Mal had reached the keep, and he drew in one last fresh breath of air before subjecting himself to the smoky, dank inside. There were nights like this when he missed the days of riding and fighting, sleeping under the stars while preparing for a siege or skirmish—and he looked forward to the task ahead on the morrow. But most days, he simply missed Warwick, and the chance to sleep in his own bed, to walk his own ramparts, to see to his own people, to ride and hunt in his own meadows.

I must leave from here.

He slipped into the hall, gaining sleepy bows from the pair of serf boys whose only job was to keep the fire going all the night. Without mail or spurs, Mal moved silently down the corridors back to the men's chamber. As he came around the corner, he nearly collided with a cloaked and hooded figure, hurrying along the way.

She—it was clearly a woman, based on size and grace and the small part of hand exposed by the cloak—didn't look up, nor even acknowledge his presence, but kept on walking. An armed man followed, clearly her escort, but not one to whom she spoke. He acknowledged Mal but walked past in the path of the woman.

Mal hesitated and turned to look. Something about the woman bothered him, something drew his attention. She was completely covered, her head bowed beneath a deep hood, but for her hand and a small bit of the hem of her gown, trailing from beneath the cloak.

It was an instant later that he realized he knew who it was. A deep scratch on her hand. A blue hem, embroidered with silver—one he recognized from earlier today.

What was Lady Judith doing about, and in such secrecy, at this time of night?

~*~

"JUDITH! WHAT ails you?" The queen's demand startled Judith so much she jolted her quill and made an ink blot on the paper.

"My pardon, my lady," Judith replied, dabbing at the blot with a wadded up piece of cloth. "I was…woolgathering."

"Well, do you not *wool*gather when I am waiting for you to finish your task," Eleanor huffed. "I am in need of your witty and amusing conversation, but I cannot indulge in that until you complete that letter." She glowered, smoothing her hand over the rounding of her belly. "You know I was ill yesterday. Today I must feel better."

"Of course, my lady," Judith replied, returning her attention to the parchment in front of her.

Normally, she would have been more than mildly intrigued by the contents of the message she was penning for the queen, for it was a reprimand to one of Eleanor's vassals. The vassal in question, the baron of Doucette, had neglected to pay his quarterly rents, claiming expenditures for a new stable and mill had taken every last bit of funds from the coffers—and did the queen not appreciate the fact that he was maintaining Doucette to the highest standard?

But the queen was as tight-fisted as her husband, determined to extract every fee due her, and the letter Judith copied was filled with pretty compliments for the baron's dedication to the estate— but also an underlying, steely threat. Usually Judith appreciated her majesty's skill at exposing excuses and deflating subterfuge with flattery and wit, but today she wanted nothing more than to curl up in her bed and be alone.

The *very* last thing she wanted was to attend the queen, who, when *enceinte* was particularly demanding and petulant. Judith was in no humor to make witty remarks and tell stories and listen to Eleanor rave about whatever bothered her—her weariness with the pregnancy. Her weight gain, her rounding belly. Dishonest vassals. Mealy apples. Stupid serving women.

Her husband.

The very thought of the king made Judith's belly tighten and swirl alarmingly. She pushed the thought away, forcing herself to ignore what had happened last night, hoping it would never happen again.

She'd returned to her chamber well past midnight. Other than the guard, whom the king had thoughtfully sent to accompany her back to her room, she encountered only one other person on the way. She remained enveloped inside her cloak, neither recognizing him nor being recognized herself. And though Tabby had been half-asleep, waiting up for her return, Judith merely slid into bed wearing only her kirtle.

She wanted a bath. *Oh,* how she wanted a bath. But it was too late, and as much as she wanted to wash, she was loathe to ask her maid in the middle of the night. Because then there would be questions. And concerns.

And Judith wanted to forget it all. Forget the royal hands everywhere on her body. The rough, muscular skin sliding against hers. The intimate sounds and smells, the discomfort and, worst of all, the unwanted stirrings within her. The king had promised pleasure, and though she certainly had not enjoyed the experience, neither was it rough or painful.

Pray, do not allow it to happen again.

"Judith!" The queen's voice was a near shriek this time. "I cannot fathom what it is that ails you this day! Put you that aside, then, if you cannot concentrate on a simple task such as copying my letter. It will wait another day. Instead, do you tell me of your adventure with the mad dogs in the forest. And be certain to tell *all* of the details on the rescue." Eleanor's lips curved mischievously, for she was a woman who enjoyed every aspect of the male species. "Ursula claims Warwick was a hero, and that you were carried off by de Rigonier."

"'Twas not precisely that way," Judith told her, forcing a smile. She launched into a description of the tale from her perspective, thankful to have aught to focus on besides her thoughts.

Pray, she thought as she took her leave of the queen much later—with barely time to dress for the evening meal—*do not let her find out.*

EIGHT

MALCOLM HAD looked for Lady Judith the morrow after he saw the cloaked and hooded figure at night, hoping to speak with her before leaving with Ludingdon and the others to track the brigands. But though his height gave him the advantage over most other men, he caught no sight of her flaming coppery hair in the great hall or elsewhere before it was time to prepare for the journey.

Nevertheless, Mal was glad to leave Clarendon and its politics behind him as he and his companions set off. A se'ennight away from the keep would give him the opportunity to consider possible marriage options as well as put Lady Judith and the temptation of her vivacity and smile from his mind.

And, in truth, there was no real need for him to speak with her. If it had been her he'd seen rushing back to her chamber in the dead of night, there must be some good reason for it. Likely the queen had called Judith to her side apurpose.

Whatever the reason for her nocturnal activity, Lady Judith's business was of no concern to Mal. He would do well to remind himself of that. Instead, he spoke of their strategy for tracking and capturing the brigands with Ludingdon and Castendown as they trotted along, trailed by a dozen knights and squires. All wore mail and carried swords and shields, for they eagerly anticipated a battle of some sort.

"'Tis my blessing Maris hasn't arrived yet from Ludingdon," Dirick said after they'd ridden for several hours. "Else I doubt I'd be off on this adventure. She is a skilled healer, but for some reason prefers not to have to mend me from any battle hurts. The woman seems to think I seek out danger and injury."

"And what is wrong with that?" Mal jested.

Castendown, who was older than both Dirick and Mal and had been wed far longer, laughed. "Aye. But 'tis better for the woman to *care* whether ye return with all yer arms and legs than not, aye? Especially one as comely as your Lady Maris." His grin couldn't quite be considered lascivious, but 'twas certainly appreciative.

"'Tis true, that," Dirick replied, laughing heartily. "Only methinks 'tis best all around for her not to know. Then at the least I won't get the tongue-lashing for rushing off on what she'd name a folly."

"A tongue-lashing is a small price to pay for such a woman warming your bed," Castendown replied archly.

"I cannot disagree on that. And as I sore miss the tongue-lashing—and all the good that comes of it later—I am well-pleased she and the babe should arrive at Clarendon within a fortnight. Though if she's learned from the queen, 'tis likely she'll travel even faster and may arrive before we return."

"In which case you'd receive the tongue-lashing *and* any necessary mending of your severed limbs," Mal reminded him dryly.

"Not to mention a warm bed," Dirick added with a satisfied grin.

Mal laughed, but the exchange with his friend gave him aught to think on in relation to marriage and wives and the benefits and drawbacks of them. He'd met Maris of Ludingdon and had been surprised—and mildly amused—by the obvious delight Dirick felt being wed to her. They were together more often than Mal had ever been with Sarah, or ever wanted to be. Malcolm had done his business, making war and managing the fiefs of Warwick, and Sarah had run the household. They coupled when necessary, ate together when it was convenient, and went their separate ways otherwise... but this was clearly not the case with Dirick and Maris. They were together as oft as Dirick was with his squire—mayhap even more.

The flash of an image of Judith, sitting at table in Warwick, came to his mind and he frowned then ignored it.

When the group broke to water the horses and trade a few bites of dried meat and bread, Mal had the opportunity to speak with Nevril about Alpha.

"I left him in the charge of the second marshal," Mal told his master-at-arms. "But mayhap you should have stayed back, for Alpha knows you and is less like to plant a hoof in your face."

Nevril grimaced, causing his scar to stretch taut. "Praise God I did not. Methinks the marshal should manage his own charges. If not," he said with a shrug, "a hoof on the foot or in the gut is only what the twit deserves."

Mal raised his brows, surprised at the vehemence from his normally even-tempered man. "And what is stuck in your craw this day, Nevril? You know as well as I how ornery Alpha can be with anyone—even myself betimes."

The man scratched his beard and glared into the wood. "That maid Tabatha seems to think Bruin could walk on water if he chose. A broken foot might teach her otherwise."

"Tabatha? Lady Judith's maid?" Mal frowned. Apparently, even away from Clarendon and the copper-haired witch he was not to have peace from her.

"Aye. That's the one. She was loitering at the stable again this morrow when I went to get Alpha's saddle for you. I heard her complainin' to Bruin that her lady came in very late to the chamber last eve."

So it had been Judith he'd seen. "Did the maid know where she'd been, so late in the night? Alone?"

Nevril began to reply, then looked sharply at him. "I ne'er said she was alone, my lord."

"You did not need to," Mal retorted flatly. "I saw her myself—or at the least, I believed it was her. Wrapped in a cloak as she was, hidden under a hood, I wasn't certain." He looked at Nevril expectantly. "But what she would be doing at such an hour, and alone…I cannot guess."

"Tabatha did not say whence her lady came. But...she was accompanied by one of the king's guards." Nevril glanced around and stepped closer. His voice dropped low as he said, "Some nights ago, the king came to their chamber. Alone."

Malcolm stared at him for a moment as the man's words sunk in. There was only one reason a man would go to a woman's chamber alone. "Indeed," he replied, aware that his expression had gone blank. A loud roaring seemed to fill his ears.

Fool. You fool! You saw the signs.

"The maid insisted I say naught to anyone on it, my lord, for it seemed to upset her—and I have not. Not until this very moment. I do not gossip. But...." Nevril's voice trailed off and he stared into the forest, as if to avoid seeing his master's face. "I bethought you should know."

Mal decided he'd prefer not to understand why his man thought that way. Instead, he nodded and, thankfully, at that moment, Castendown called for the group to mount up again. Mal swung into the saddle of his replacement mount, eager to be on his way—both in thought and in deed.

Praise God I must have naught to do with that woman.

˜*˜

JUDITH KNELT on the cold, hard floor of the chapel.

She held a string of prayer beads formed of stewed and dried rose petals, given her by her cousin Gavin's wife Madelyne. The faint scent of roses clung to the beads, wafting to Judith's nose every time she moved from one to the next.

Pater noster, she prayed, eyes closed, head bowed, "*qui es in caelis....*"

The chapel, a small secondary one tucked in a far corner of the keep, was silent and dark. She was alone in the place which had become her sanctuary. Even the king wouldn't find her here. And if he did, surely even he wouldn't order her to come to him from a church.

It had been a week since Henry first summoned her to his private chamber. Since then, Judith had spent three more nights with him.

"I cannot cease thinking of you," the king had told her after the third night they were together. They were abed, furs and cushions mounded around them; some even on the floor, for Henry was a vigorous lover. "You are my obsession, my fiery lady."

A silk cloth was her only covering, from waist to foot, and Judith had no choice but to lie there as he trailed a finger over a shoulder and down to circle her breast. Her skin rose in little bumps in its wake.

"You fill my dreams and my thoughts, so that e'en when I meet with my barons or hold court you are never far from my mind." He leaned forward to press a kiss to the side of her neck, then her shoulder, his tongue slipping out in a gentle caress. Judith shivered a little, for her skin was sensitive there.

"Why do you never smile when you are here with me?" he demanded. "You are known for your wit and vivacity, and yet you are dull and quiet in my chambers."

"I have little cause to smile," she replied with fearful honesty.

"I have given you baubles and jewels. I have fed you delicacies, told you of private matters. I have even done as you begged, against my better judgment—allowing you to come and go from me in great secrecy. You are a leman to the King of England, the most powerful man in Christendom. How can you have no cause to smile?" He sounded wounded, and yet genuinely astonished.

"I do not wish to be with you in this manner," she said. Despite the fact that she'd told him thus in many words and in many ways, he did not—or would not—comprehend.

Nay, 'twas not a lack of comprehension. It was a lack of conscience.

"I am your king," he reminded her. "Your liege lord. You are my vassal. You are beholden to me, you have sworn fealty to me. Do you not forget that." His voice had cooled and now when he reached for her, his touch was not quite so gentle.

Now, in the chapel, in her sanctuary, Judith closed her eyes and pushed away the memory. She must accept her fate. Such was her life, her lot as a woman—for women had little or no choice in whom they wed. In truth, she reminded herself over and over, lying with the king was no worse than being wed to a man for whom she had no affection or care. She must do as her lord or husband commanded, must copulate with him as he wished, must bear his heirs as necessary…must even accept a slap or blow as her due, if he so chose.

Many women suffered such a fate—or worse. And being with the king was mayhap a better fate than being wed to a man she misliked—for surely Henry would soon tire of her, as he had each of his other mistresses.

And at the least, the king wasn't rough or cruel. There were times when she could nearly forget he wasn't someone with whom she wished to be, when she even felt a niggling of pleasure. But those times were rare, and only after Henry urged her to drink more wine than she needed.

She'd had no maidenhead when coming to the king's bed. For that Judith must thank Gregory. Though they lay together only two times before he went off to join the traitor Fantin de Belgrume's cause—and was eventually killed—she was no shy virgin at Henry's hands.

Thus far, he'd been willing to keep their liaison a secret. That alone was, mayhap, testament to his attraction to her. For in the past, his lemans were never a mystery; everyone at court knew who they were. The women oft couldn't conceal their pride and self-importance at being chosen to warm the king's bed. It was an honor.

But Judith felt no honor in her predicament.

Pray the queen didn't find out.

Pray the king didn't get Judith with child.

Those were the petitions she asked, over and over. *I can bear it…I will bear it willingly, Father, if You will allow those cups to pass me by.*

~*~

NEARLY A fortnight after leaving Clarendon, Malcolm and his companions rode over the drawbridge into the bailey. With them were the four brigands who'd survived after a violent clash near the town of Vartington. The other three thieves had perished in the skirmish.

None from the royal party died, though Claude, one of Dirick of Ludingdon's squires, and a man-at-arms from Castendown were seriously injured. Mal, for his part, had no more than a cut on his thigh and an ugly scrape along the right side of his torso from the edge of his shield when he was nearly knocked off Alpha's substitute.

A fortnight spent beneath the stars and sun, chasing down outlaws, tracking them for miles across the open land, fighting victoriously in a battle that could hardly be called thus—and all the while, jesting and conversing with peers of a like mind—had put him in a fine mood.

But now, as he dismounted from the stalwart horse named Theseus—who, though sturdy and strong was no Alpha—Malcolm's fine mood ebbed.

He delayed going into the keep, taking the time to visit his warhorse and assure himself the leg was healed. Ludingdon and Castendown would report to the king, bringing the prisoners to him for their sentencing. Mal was relieved he wouldn't have to face King Henry quite yet. He wasn't certain he could hide his festering dislike for the man.

But that was naught compared to what he'd come to feel toward Judith. Sunny-faced, flirtatious, flamboyant Judith. A trusted confidante of the queen, cuckolding her mistress with the king. A two-faced, treacherous viper. He would never have guessed it of the girl he'd known at Kentworth or the teasing woman who connived to help an awkward young squire learn to fight with his sword.

'Twas no wonder Judith was all smiles when she spoke of the queen's refusal to allow her to marry. If she should wed, Judith would be forced to leave her position as the king's leman.

Once assured of Alpha's good health, Mal had no further excuse to remain in the stable. Yet he took his time walking to the keep.

Without realizing it, the roundabout path he took brought him past the rear of the mews.

As luck would have it, just as he walked by, Judith appeared. She slipped out of the building, closing the side door quickly behind her in an effort to keep the raptors from escaping.

Mal could have kept walking; in fact, he should have increased his speed and passed her by before she caught sight of him. But his traitorous feet did not obey the logic of this internal command, and when Judith turned, she saw him immediately.

"Warwick," she said, clearly surprised. "You've returned."

"Lady Judith," he replied in steady tones. In spite of his feelings and what he knew and had come to understand, Mal couldn't help but drink in the sight of her. It was at that moment he realized how fully gone he was when it came to this woman.

And because he looked at her so closely—his eyes tracing rapidly over the simple loops of blazing braid over her ears, the delicate, curvaceous figure in its dark blue bliaut—he saw that her face was thinner, her cheekbones and jaw seemed sharper. Her eyes had no sparkle and in the stead of a warm smile, her lips barely curved.

"Did you catch the brigands?" she asked after an awkward moment of silence.

"Aye. The survivors are brought to the—to the king." Mal cursed himself for the stumble. *Fool.* "His majesty will pass judgment and sentence them," he forced himself to continue.

"Very good," she said, and turned toward the keep. "Pray, I beg your leave. I must needs return. The queen awaits me."

Mal stared after her, very nearly as stunned as if she'd thwacked him aside the head with a log. Not only had she not required him to engage in an overlong conversation, but she'd not made one jest about the condition of his tunic sleeve. And she'd called him Warwick.

Warwick instead of Malcolm...or even my lord.

~*~

JUDITH WASN'T lying when she told Malcolm the queen awaited. Eleanor did expect her attendance—but not for another hour.

In truth, it was the unexpected sight of him that set Judith's thoughts to scattering…and then converging into one desire: escape. She didn't want to talk with him, didn't want to be tempted into jesting or teasing him as she had done in the past. She wasn't even certain she was capable of doing so any longer. At least not now.

Two weeks of warming the king's bed had become a heavy burden. The late nights. The secrecy. The mixed feelings, the confusing emotions. The dull, ugly scraping in her belly every time a knock came to her chamber door or a page approached. And Henry's obsession with her seemed not to have waned in the least.

Last eve, he'd even insisted she sit at the high table—next to him. Fortunately, inviting a peer to join him and the queen and archbishop at the dais wasn't an unusual occurrence. But Judith had hardly been able to choke her food down a throat dry as sawdust. Particularly when the king rested his hand on her thigh…and elsewhere…during the meal.

Pray God the queen hadn't noticed. Nor anyone else.

When she came upon Malcolm unexpectedly, Judith surprised herself when her heart gave a great, happy surge. But almost immediately, the warmth evaporated. Yet, he was a sight for sorely weary eyes: tall and broad, confidence exuding from his very stance. His too-long hair, the color of walnuts, might even have been trimmed since she last saw him—for it hardly brushed past his jaw. But he hadn't shaved this day, and he was dusty and grimy from riding and fighting. Still, her heart had made that great leap.

And now she rushed back into the keep, wondering why he mattered so much.

~*~

WHEN JUDITH arrived at the queen's solar less than an hour later, she found her mistress in a fine fettle.

The other ladies in waiting were gathered in the chamber, seated on hassocks or chairs, embroidering and gossiping as usual. Some were eating, others had their attention on the queen attempting to amuse her, and Lady Amice plucked at a lute in the corner. Judith smiled briefly at Maris of Ludingdon, who'd arrived only two days earlier with her infant son and had settled in with the court as if she'd never left it. But Eleanor, still slender and quick despite the rounding belly showing beneath her gown, was pacing while gesticulating energetically.

"Judith! What has kept you!" she said as Judith stepped across the threshold. "You are late!"

"My apologies, my lady," she said, sweeping into a curtsy. She was not late, but one did not argue with the queen, and most particularly when she was in this state of mind. "I brought you a bit of a nosegay to brighten your chambers."

She offered a small bouquet of sweet-scented orange lilies with black and yellow spots, picked at the last minute from the herb garden. Eleanor glanced at the flowers then flapped her hand at one of the pages. "See to them."

Judith relinquished the nosegay and rose from her curtsy. "How may I serve you this day, my lady? Shall I peel an apple for you? Or mayhap you wish to—"

"Nay, nay," Eleanor said, still swirling about. Her graceful hands clasped and unclasped in agitation. "I am not hungry."

"The party who went after the brigands has returned," Judith suggested. "Mayhap Lady Maris has some news? Was not your husband in the group?" She turned her attention to the other lady, who was one of the more level-headed—if not blunt—women who gathered around the queen.

"I did not know they've returned," said Maris. Her eyes lit with pleasure. "But with her majesty's permission, I shall take my Rogan to see his papa—and to hear any news." Before the queen responded, the woman was on her feet, preparing to leave.

"Nay, pray, stay you one moment," said Eleanor, at last ceasing her incessant pacing. "For there is one thing you may take with you."

"Of course, your majesty," Maris said, pausing next to Judith.

"You may take this *lying*, cock-licking, backstabbing *slut* of a *bitch* from my sight!" Eleanor erupted. And before Judith realized what she said, the queen lashed out, striking her sharply across the cheek.

The blow sent Judith reeling as every occupant of the chamber gasped. She nearly tumbled to the floor, bumping into Maris, who caught her as she went off-balance.

"Get out!" shrieked the queen. "Get out of my sight!"

Holding a hand to her throbbing cheek, Judith straightened with as much dignity as she could manage. "Your majesty," she began, looking directly at the queen. Fighting back tears, struggling to keep her voice steady, she said, "Whatever you may think of me, please know I regret hurting you from the bottom of my heart."

"Get you out of my sight!" Eleanor cried. Her cheeks were bright red, her eyes glassy with madness. Her movements were frenetic, near insanity.

"My lady, the babe," Maris said, turning to the queen. "Have a care for the babe." She tried to soothe the woman, casting Judith a pointed glance.

Judith turned and, removing her hand—which was wet with blood—from her cheek, walked toward the door. It seemed to take forever; every step seemed to draw her further away from the exit rather than toward it. Her eyes stung, her insides were in turmoil. The ugly gnawing in her belly was back with a vengeance, threatening to empty its contents at any moment.

At last, she was out of the chamber. The doors closed behind her and, stunned, hurt and heartsore, Judith made her way back to her chamber.

~*~

"OH, MY lady!" cried Tabby when she opened the chamber door and saw Judith's face. "What has befallen you?"

"The queen," Judith replied, still fighting to hold back the tears.

"The queen? Wh—" Tabby repeated, then cut off whatever else she was about to say. Instead, she helped her mistress to the stool by the fire. "She found out, didn't she?" the maid asked quietly. "About the king."

Judith looked at her in surprise, her misery swelling. "You know?"

Her maid's eyes, still concerned, flared with indignation. "By the rood, I'm your tiring woman. Of course I know. I've known since the beginning. The nights you cried—trying to keep silent. I heard you. I wanted to tell you there was no need to hide it from me, but I didn't know how. I'm sorry, my lady."

Judith lost the tenuous hold on her emotions and for the first time since her *affaire* with the king began, she began to sob. Loudly, harshly, with big, choking, gasping sobs. Tabby, bless her, was there next to her. Like an older sister, the maid stroked her hair, even embracing her mistress as she slid off the stool and onto the rug in front of the hearth.

"There, my lady," she said when Judith could cry no more. "I'll see to your face. And a bath too, aye?"

"I prayed she would never find out," Judith said. Her throat was raw and her voice gritty, but she lifted her face from where it was buried in her arms. "But 'tis a secret that cannot be kept. I would not have hurt her," she added fiercely.

"I know, my lady. I know. Damn the king," she whispered fiercely. "'T may be treason to say so, but damn him." After a moment, Tabby pulled to her feet. "I will call for a bath. And I must get a paste for your cheek. Was the queen wearing a ring?"

"Aye," Judith replied dully, reaching to touch the mark on her cheek. It was wet with blood mingled with tears. "She must have been."

A knock at the chamber door had both women freezing. Tabby looked at her mistress, whose heart ceased pounding for a moment. "Answer it," Judith said, wiping her eyes. "If 'tis…him…." Her voice trailed off and she shook her head. "Answer it." Her voice was strong.

But, praise God, it wasn't the king nor any of his messengers at the door.

"Lady Maris," Judith said, rising from her stool.

"If you will allow me, I'll see to your cheek," said Maris as she whisked into the chamber. She smacked a kiss on the cheek of her chubby, bright-eyed babe, then thrust him at Tabby. "'Twould be a shame if the queen's rage left a scar," she said, moving directly to Judith.

"Have a care," Judith managed to say as Maris fairly shoved her back down onto the stool. "I do not wish for her wrath to fall upon you as well."

"Pish," Maris told her, peering closely at the cut on her cheek. "The queen can have no fault with me. I am Ludingdon's wife, a close favorite of the king. Aside from that…she does not know I am here." She smiled grimly.

Judith sat silently as Maris prepared a sweet-smelling paste from dried herbs and a dark aromatic tea. She sensed the other lady wished to talk, or at the least, wished Judith to talk, but she had naught to say. While this was happening, Tabby took the babe Rogan and showed him how to pet the kitten with his pudgy hand. He cooed and laughed, his legs kicking in excitement.

"There," said Maris a short while later as she finished applying a small piece of clean cloth over the paste. "Your hurts—on the outside, anyway—are tended. Mayhap you have others you wish to speak on?"

Judith bit her lip and shook her head. "Naught, other than I wished never to hurt the queen. But now the worst has come to pass, and I must lie in the bed made for me." She stood.

"As must we all." Maris reached into the wooden box from which she'd produced her medicinal herbs. She hesitated, then withdrew a small leather pouch. "I do not know if you have want or need of this," she said, watching Judith carefully, "but 'tis an herbal powder. If added to warm water and allowed to steep and you drink its tea every day, it will prevent a babe from growing in your belly."

Judith nearly snatched the bag from her, but caught herself in time. "Truly? Oh, aye, I would…I would be very grateful." She took the pouch. "But it may be too late," she added quietly, her hand settling over her belly.

"When came your last flux?"

"At the last full moon."

The other woman's face tightened and her eyes grew sober—for they both knew the moon was full this night, and for the next two. "Does your flux come at the appointed time, with the same moon phase each month?"

Judith glanced at Tabby, who'd been watching in open-mouthed interest even as she bounced the gurgling baby on her hip. "Aye." And she prayed for it to come—not only to prove the king had not planted his seed, but also for rest from his attentions.

Maris's lips tightened. "Then we shall ere know of that, at the least. Use the tea in the meanwhile, Lady Judith. Each day, drink one cup."

"I will," Judith told her fervently. "Thank you for your kindness, Lady Maris. I hope you do not find it to your detriment."

"I would I could do more," replied the other woman. Her sharp gaze searched Judith's eyes as if to read her thoughts. "Sit with me at the evening meal this night, if you will. Your cousin is close friends with my husband. You will find no judgment here."

~*~

"AND SO you could not resist the chance to chase brigands and play with your sword," Maris told her husband tartly, surveying the damage on his blood-stained *sherte.*

"Play is indeed the word," he replied mildly, plucking at the strings that laced her gown. "And I have other ideas for play in mind as well."

She danced out of his reach. "Not until I have seen to every inch of you—"

"Every inch?" he asked. "I have some inches for you to see to." He patted the growing bulge behind his hose, grinning lasciviously.

Maris laughed and cast him a hot, purposeful look that had him lunging for her. She whirled out of reach once more. "But of course, those inches must need special treatment. Very special treatment. But only *after* I've peeled the last bit of cloth from your skin. Why do men allow their wounds to bleed into the *sherte,* and then dry thus?" she asked, moving back within range of his randy hands in order to soak the cloth in warm water and pull it carefully away.

"Because we do not care, for we know we have sharp-tongued wives to do it for us. Inflicting torture is one of the things they do best," he said, sliding his hand around to cup her breast. "By God, you are still so full and round," he murmured, burying his face in her neck.

Maris shivered and sagged against him for a moment, her hand settling over his flat belly, her fingers brushing the top of his hose-covered cock. It had been overlong since they lay together, for the king had called Dirick to him only a month after Rogan's birth. Now the babe was a half-year old. She had sorely missed her husband, which was why she had made the journey to court.

But there was aught to be seen to before any special treatment so there was no blood over the bedcoverings. And Maris must assure herself there were no serious wounds on the man she loved, for after the injuries she'd tended to in his squire Claude, she feared what Dirick might be hiding beneath his bravado and clothing.

She slipped from his embrace, taking a piece of the *sherte* with her. He winced and glowered as she ripped it from his skin. "Not only do you put me off, but you torture me in the process," he grumbled.

"Then let us talk of aught else while I see to you—no more distractions. Sally will be back with Rogan soon, and I know he will want to see his papa."

"Only as long as you promise to give special attention to all of my inches."

"But of course, my lord," Maris replied primly. "*Every* inch shall get its due. Now, what do you know of Judith of Kentworth and her liaison with the king?"

"What say you?" Dirick stared at her, his lustful interest shifting to befuddlement. "Where do you hear this rumor?"

She shook her head. "'Tis no rumor. The queen confronted her in the solar this day. 'Twas an ugly scene."

"Judith of Kentworth. Hair the color of fire? Mal Verne's cousin?" Dirick repeated. "I would not have believed it."

"Nor would anyone else. The other ladies were stunned by the revelation. Even Ursula of Tenavaux, who is quite close to Judith, did not know."

"Not that the king isn't known for his...appetite," he mused as she pulled off another cloth-scab. "And she is a comely woman. Ouch!"

Maris grinned. "So sorry, my lord."

He grumbled again and reached around, firmly grasping her arse with both hands as he pulled her up against him. "You are not sorry in the least."

"For such a warrior, you are a quite a chicken-heart," she told him, poking his shoulder. "That would not have even hurt Rogan." Then, once again disengaging herself from his busy fingers—though 'twas getting more difficult to do—she turned her attention back to the matter at hand. "So Lady Judith did not flaunt her relationship with the king. She kept it secret. I wonder how long she has been warming his bed."

"I do not know, Maris. But what I do know is...someone must needs warm *my* bed. Right *now*."

And before she could make even a token protest, he scooped her up and tossed her onto the bed.

NINE

BY THE time of the evening meal, the gossip had spread like a blaze among tinder.

But Mal, who'd kept himself busy away from the doings of the court by working with Rike, first heard of the events in the queen's solar when he joined Dirick of Ludingdon and the man's wife at one of the trestle tables in the great hall.

"She'll likely have a bruise, and mayhap a scar," Lady Maris was saying to Lady Ursula as Mal stepped over the bench and settled into a place across from them. "I tended to her as well as I could, but only time will tell."

Dirick handed Mal a bottle of wine to fill his goblet as he asked his wife, "Will she show her face for dinner? Or will she remain abovestairs, for fear of meeting the wrath of the queen?"

"I do not—ah, well, there is the answer to your question." Maris nodded toward the front of the hall.

Mal, ignorant of the topic of conversation, didn't deign to turn behind him to look until Lady Maris added, "See you there? That does not look like a woman infatuated with her lover. The king fawns, and Judith looks miserable. And the queen is nowhere to be seen."

Mal had stiffened at the mention of Judith. But instead of looking, he busied himself by sawing through a loaf of bread with a dull knife. In the end, he resorted to tearing off a hunk of it and leaving the blade to rest. Then he reached for a platter of stewed rabbit and carrots, training his attention on the wealthy blond lady across from him. Lady Ursula was easy on the eyes, he told himself. He must set his mind to better acquainting himself with her. Or mayhap he could turn his eye to Lady Alynne, who had a sweet countenance and did not chatter quite as much.

"Her face! Why, look at her face," Lady Ursula gasped, her blue gaze widening. "It's green and purple! And the cut," she whispered. "Her majesty's ring was cruel. Poor Judith."

He didn't turn, yet there was a prickling at the back of his neck. Knowing she was there, and with the king. *That does not look like a woman infatuated with her lover.* The words hung in his mind, but he dismissed them.

'Tis more like she is ashamed of her conduct. Mortified that all at court know.

"But she is still a most beautiful woman," Dirick murmured. "'Tis no wonder the king is enamored."

"Indeed," Lady Maris replied archly.

"If one is drawn to a lady with flaming red hair," Dirick added, grinning idiotically at his wife. "And I cannot imagine who would be. Imagine the temper that would accompany hair of that color. Most particularly not I—for I seem to have an affinity for women with hair the color of pine bark and an imperious tongue."

"She is acting bashful and shy," said Lady Amice. "And she is not sitting with the king—only at the end of the high table." The new arrival gathered up her gown to climb over the bench, taking a spot next to Mal. "Better the whore of the king should flaunt her favor and power. What has his majesty's favorite to hide? With the king's protection, she is untouchable, even by the queen." Her voice was wistful and laced with unmitigated envy.

"I do believe Lady Judith would argue with that. Do you not see her face?" Lady Maris said coldly. "Lady Judith is no fool. And she is not one to flaunt anything. Most especially the cuckolding of her friend, her majesty the queen."

Whore of the king.

Suddenly Mal was no longer hungry, though he'd eaten naught since the morn. The nape of his neck itched, encouraging him to turn and survey the scene himself. But he resisted, taking a gulp from his goblet instead. He was aware of Dirick's regard, and an exchange of glances with Lady Maris, but Mal cared little for their private flirtations.

He rose abruptly and excused himself. There would be time later to woo Lady Ursula.

_*_

SOMEHOW JUDITH managed to survive the meal in the great hall. Fully aware everyone had heard of the queen's rage—and the reason for it—she wasn't certain whether she'd become a pariah or merely a curiosity. By inviting her to sit at the high table—though not next to him, praise God—the king had shown his support for her and yet some deference to the queen.

After all, Henry had had many mistresses over the years. And more oft than not, they were openly acknowledged—at least by the king and those close to him. Rumors flew, and understanding glances and knowing murmurs were exchanged among those of the court. And the leman herself most usually had naught to hide. To be chosen by the king was, to most women, an honor.

But because of Eleanor's fury and her public reaction, Judith didn't know what to expect from her friends and peers. She wanted not to care, but care she did. These were her friends. This was her life, though not one of her choosing. And she had not sought any of this attention.

Nevertheless, Judith held her head high and tried to ignore the incessant throbbing of her cheek as she nibbled on as much of her food as she could choke down. She already knew she'd be attending Henry this night. He had no reason for secrecy any longer.

Why could he not find someone else on which to turn his attention?

Judith saw Maris and Ludingdon sitting with Ursula, and she wished she could join them. Hugh de Rigonier was there as well, along with Alynne, the bitter-faced Lady Amice, Castendown…and Malcolm. *Nay, Warwick. He is Warwick to you.*

And what must he think of you now?

She saw him rise from his place before the first course was even finished, maneuvering his way between the rows of benches and out of the hall. She wished she could do the same.

She wished she could go with him.

She wished she could go *to* him.

~*~

LATER THAT night, Henry sent for her. This time, she was brought not to the small, secret chamber, but to his larger, royal apartments. They were more sumptuous and well-furnished, guarded by three men-at-arms at the outside of the door instead of a single one.

"I am sorry for this," he said, gently touching her swollen cheek. "The queen vented her spleen upon me as well—but not nearly so violently. I did duck when she threw the goblet, though." He chuckled, but Judith found no humor in his words.

"I would not have hurt her," she said, scraping up her last bit of pride in order to speak her mind. "She has been good to me. I considered her a friend as well as my liege lady."

"Eleanor is wise in the ways of the world, and of a marriage such as ours," Henry replied dismissively. "Ask her of her relationship with her uncle, and in whose beds *she* has played. She is not one to point fingers. Aye, she is angry now, but she will come to terms with it."

Judith wasn't inclined to agree, but she remained silent, closing her eyes and blocking away the feel of his hands on her bare skin. *How much longer?*

"And she will not lay a finger on you again," he added, sliding his hand over a most intimate place. His breathing changed, roughened, and he probed and stroked…and then he rose over her.

Judith closed her eyes and thought of flying free, like Hecate.

~*~

THE MORROW after the events in the queen's solar, Judith was alone in her chamber. The kitten—who was very nearly a cat now—sat on her lap, purring loudly. Judith wasn't certain who was receiving more benefit from the quiet moment—she or the furry beast. Petting the soft fur was comforting, and being with a living being that required naught from her was a relief.

When a knock came at the door, she stiffened…then relaxed. The king had released her from his attentions some hours ago, and she knew he was attending to some court business. He wouldn't be sending for her again so soon.

"Enter," Judith called from her favorite place by the fire.

The door opened and a page stood on the threshold. "The queen requests you attend her."

Judith stood slowly, putting the cat down without looking where her paws landed. The queen?

She glanced at herself in the polished silver mirror. The bruising had begun to subside overnight, and the cut no longer appeared as vivid and angry, thanks to Lady Maris's paste. But Judith had no desire to have her other cheek laid open with an emerald ring.

Yet, what choice had she?

Heart pounding, she drew herself up and left the chamber. The walk to the queen's apartments seemed to take forever, but they finally arrived.

Drawing in a deep breath, Judith entered upon command and sank into a curtsy in front of Eleanor. She had yet to look directly at the queen and so did not know what her mood was.

"Rise," commanded Eleanor.

Judith did so, looking about quickly. The chamber, the queen's private courtroom, was empty. No one was present but the two of them. Her attention came to the queen, who stood in front of her only a few paces away.

"And so you have just come from my husband's bed. Yet again."

"My lady…I would not ever hurt you. But he is my king and there is no denyin—" She stopped, drew in a breath and fell to her knees. The queen would hear no excuses, regardless of how true they might be. But mayhap there was another way. "Your majesty, will you allow me to return to Lilyfare? I beg you—send me away. Send me home."

When she raised her eyes, Judith found Eleanor looking down at her with a cold, remote expression. "Send you away? Never. Why should I give you what you so badly desire when you have betrayed me so…and when I am in need of you. You may service my husband whilst you service me. He will tire of your body long before I have finished with you. Thus your greedy rise to power and influence shall be short-lived…but you shall pay obeisance to me for far longer than you suck Henry's cock. Rise."

The queen's cruel words struck deeply. For a moment, Judith was so cold and weary she could hardly move. Yet she pulled to her feet. She would retain what little dignity she still possessed; the queen had taught her that, at least.

"Yonder are contracts," Eleanor said, pointing to a table in the corner of the chamber. "Five of them. Make ten copies each."

"Aye, my lady," Judith replied, walking over to the table. It took her only a moment to see each contract was three pages long of crimped script. It would take her most of the day, mayhap into the evening, to finish the task. Work such as this was normally assigned to scribes, for it wasn't a personal or private correspondence and required no particular skill or confidence. And never had Judith known of ten copies to be made. Mayhap four, or even five—but never ten.

She straightened her shoulders. So this was to be her punishment. Judith settled at the table and began the tedious work.

It took far longer than she expected, for when she was nearly finished with the ninth copy of the first contract, Eleanor decided there must be a change. And so Judith must begin again.

By the time she had completed the work, night had fallen and the evening meal was long past. Judith's belly was empty and her head felt light. She'd been allowed watered-down wine and half an apple to eat, but nothing more.

The queen returned from dinner and dismissed her, looking upon her as if a stranger. "Return on the morrow."

When Judith reached her chamber, exhausted and famished, her fingers cramped and her shoulders tight, Tabby was there, frantic with worry. Judith barely had time to explain when one of the king's guards arrived, bringing a summons from Henry.

She had no choice but to go.

The next day, the queen again kept her at work on the most tedious of tasks. Malicious and cold, Eleanor had a never-ending list of work for her. The king did not call for Judith when she was in the queen's chambers. Either he did not know her whereabouts, or he did not dare anger his wife further.

When she was released from her majesty well past the evening meal and returned to her own chamber, a guard waited for her outside. Judith had hardly the opportunity to enter before being whisked off to the pleasure of the king.

And after the three days of the full moon, Judith's flux had not come.

*

NEVRIL SPENT far too much time in the smithy this day, setting the man to task to finish a new shoe for his mount. When he at last came out of the glowing, oven-like place into full sunlight, he was in a foul mood.

One couldn't solely blame the mood on the rock-headed blacksmith, who could not see how the shoe he'd made was in the wrong damned shape, regardless of how many times Nevril sketched it out on the dirt floor—although that was more than a part of it. Nay, Nevril was full of spleen because by now he'd missed the midday meal—and also the breaking of the fast because his master Lord Malcolm had set him off on some mundane task that took much too long and was wholly unnecessary.

And then there was the fact that the maid Tabatha had hardly been about in the hall the last days. The only time Nevril had seen her, with her honey-bright hair and heart-shaped face, was when she mooned over the slow-witted marshal Bruin. While she cooed at Bruin, she gave Nevril only a cold, accusatory look every time she saw him.

All of those aspects contributed to his foul mood. His master himself had been no better than Nevril this morrow—and had been that way since their return from chasing the brigands. Lord

Malcolm might be a fair lord and master, but one would not know it from the last five days. If the man did not find himself a woman to wed—or at the least, bed—in the next se'ennight, Nevril, Gambert and the rest of those from Warwick were either going to kidnap a bride for him themselves, or send him a tribe of whores.

Or beg Ludingdon to take them on.

The only person onto whom Lord Malcolm did not seem to vent his spleen was the gawky squire Rike, with whom he seemed to have infinite patience.

In this black frame of mind, Nevril stalked through the bailey, wondering if he might go by the kitchen and beg a bit of cheese or ham from the cooks there. He was walking too quickly and came around the corner of the mews at such a rapid pace that he nearly bowled over a slight figure.

To his shock, and then cautious delight, he realized the woman he'd nearly trampled was none other than the impudent Tabatha. He was just about to make a pointed comment about rabbit stew, designed to infuriate her in an effort to prolong their meeting, when he noted her expression. Rather than defiant or irritated—as she was whenever she laid eyes on him—she was clearly in distress.

"What has befallen you, maid Tabatha?" he asked, taking her arm when she would have slipped past him. "What is it?"

She pulled from his grip, but at the least she did not run off. "'Tis naught of your concern. I was trying to find Sir Holbert, in hopes that he could find Lord Ludingdon and mayhap Lady Maris."

Nevril might have said aught about rabbit stew at that point, but then he noticed the red rims of her eyes and the weariness in her face. "I will help you. Warwick will surely know where Ludingdon is about."

Tabatha shook her head impatiently, and to his surprise, tears threatened her eyes. "Nay, I have already learned. Ludingdon and his wife have gone to Canterbury on a journey for the king. They will not return for two days or more."

"Whatever you are in need of Ludingdon for, I am certain Warwick will help. Come with me," Nevril said, then hesitated. Normally, he would not have a concern whether Lord Malcolm would have the patience and care to speak with a lowly maid. But his mood as of late….

"Come," Nevril said again, making the decision. At the very least, it would allow him an excuse to walk with Tabatha. And mayhap he would take his time finding the lord. He looked at the maid as she fell into step with him.

Nay. He would not dally. From the looks of her, the matter was urgent.

_*_

MALCOLM DUMPED a bucketful of water over his head, snorting to blow it out of his nose and mouth. The deluge was icy cold and refreshing after an intense bout of training beneath the warm sun. He'd taken on Rike for a time, and then Castendown, d'Allemande, and de Rigonier in turn. Now his muscles sang and his mind was clear. And he was hungry.

He dunked the bucket in the water trough once more and upended it again, mostly over shoulders and torso to cool and cleanse his sweaty skin. When he emerged from the torrent, he opened his eyes to find Nevril standing in front of him.

Mal recognized the woman with his master-at-arms as Lady Judith's maid. He whipped his head, flinging the sopping hair from his face, and reached for the *sherte* he'd left hanging on the gate during the training.

"My lord, Tabatha begs a moment of your time," Nevril said. There was an unusual tone in his voice—one almost of warning, and he looked at his master warily.

"What is it?" Mal asked, attempting to keep his voice neutral. But the sight of the maid, of course, reminded him of her mistress. And that was a consideration he'd found best left alone as of late.

"My lord," said Tabatha, curtsying in the dust of the training yard. "I come to you at your man's suggestion" —with this, she gave a quick, almost accusing glance at Nevril— "and because I have no other to whom I can speak. I wished to find Lady Maris of Ludingdon, for mayhap she would know what to do, but…is it true she is gone? With Lord Dirick? And they shall not return for some days?"

Mal felt a niggling in the pit of his belly, but he subdued it. "What is the problem?"

"My lady…she…." Tabatha's voice trailed off and she stepped back.

"Speak up, wench," Mal commanded, then saw Nevril glaring at him as he moved nearer, as if to protect the maid from his terrible master. This in turn told Mal that his own expression had become dark and forbidding, possibly terrifying the maid.

"Is aught wrong with your lady? Is she ill?" With effort, he kept his tones even. Yet already he knew he did not wish to hear the rest of the maid's story.

Let the king see to his woman's needs.

"My lady Judith…she is in the chapel. She has been there for hours, and she will not leave. The queen has sent for her, but my lady will not answer the summons. I fear…I fear for her mind and body, I fear what the queen will do if she does not come…and I bethought Lady Maris would help. I do not know what else to do."

"The *queen* has sent for her?" Mal repeated, pulling on the dry *sherte* over his wet torso. Something unpleasant prickled in the back of his mind. But surely Judith was not that much of a coward. A cuckold, aye. But a coward, to disobey the queen and refuse to face the woman she betrayed?

Tabatha shifted from one foot to the other. "Aye. The queen…." He waited, but the maid would say no more. She merely shook her head miserably, looking up at him and then at Nevril.

"Where is your lady now?"

"In the small chapel. 'Tis abovestairs in the square east tower. But she will not come away. And on the last I went to beg her to leave, she slapped me and ordered me to go. She has not slept for days, and hardly eaten. I am fair worried for her, and I bethought Lady Maris would speak to her. At the least, my lady won't hit *her*," she added tartly, but genuine fear and desperation lingered in her voice.

"I will see to your mistress," he said, a sense of inevitability settling over him. *At the least, she will not slap me. And if she does, 'twill be naught more than I deserve, involving myself in this black stew.*

Mal took a moment to put on a clean tunic and get out of his chausses; they were dirty and he did not want to be clinking and rattling about in mail in the chapel. And, at the last minute—remembering what Tabatha had said—he procured a skin of watered-down wine and a packet of bread and cheese and tucked them into his belt. Then, with a foreboding he could neither explain nor dismiss, he set about finding the small holy place.

When he reached the chamber—which was out of the way and not easy to locate—he didn't see Judith at first. The space was small and dim, lit only by offering candles on a small altar that was hardly large enough for the paten and chalice. Four benches lined the windowless chamber, and to the side was a crude alcove containing a painting of the Blessed Mother.

There he found Judith, kneeling on the bare floor in front of the shrine, swathed in shadow.

He hadn't seen more than a glimpse of her since dinner the night he returned from the brigand hunt, for he'd made certain not to be in the hall when she might be about. But even now, in the dim light, the sight of her made his heart thump unpleasantly. Warmth, and at the same time, something sharp settled in his belly.

Mal nearly turned to go, silent as he'd come—all at once certain he did not have the strength to become ingrained in whatever this was and yet escape intact. Yet his feet once more refused to listen to logic and he found himself approaching her.

Though he knew how to move silently, he must have made some sound to give himself away, for Judith whirled sharply when he came near. "Tab—" she began, clearly expecting her maid. Her expression when she first turned was furious, then it changed into one of shock. And…guilt? "*Malcolm.*"

He could hardly contain his horror at the sight of her. This was not the Judith he knew. She was…gaunt. Her face was thin and ravaged, her features sharp as blades in the shadows. Dark circles curved beneath eyes that seemed too deeply set to be healthy, and they were laced with weariness. Her lips were pale, her face even more so, and the cut on her cheek was still an ugly red line. He saw that she clutched a string of prayer beads, that her body trembled as she fought to keep herself upright on her knees.

Whatever kept her here, 'twas no mere cowardice.

"I mean, Lord Warwick," she corrected herself quietly. She held herself stiffly. "My pardon."

He moved closer, crouching next to where she knelt. The overwhelming urge to gather her to him—this frail woman who hardly resembled the lady who'd nearly beaten him at chess—had him curling his fingers deeply into his palms. Where was the strong, uncomplaining, vivacious woman he knew?

"What do you here, Judith? What has happened? Do you know the queen has been in search of you?"

She looked at him, her face only inches away. Devastation and pain dulled her eyes. Her lush lips were dry and cracked. She swayed suddenly, and he did what he did not wish to do…but yet desired among all things…and caught her in his arms.

"Judith," he said, ignoring his better judgment and pulling her onto his lap. He eased them both to a seat on the floor. "What is it? You are like to faint."

"Then faint I shall, and mayhap then they will leave me be." Now she huddled against him as if she belonged there, delicate and trembling in his lap. Mal curved his arms around her, his chin brushing the top of her head just before she sagged against his chest. He breathed in the scent of her.

Her fingers were ice-cold and stained. At first he thought the dark spots were blood and he tensed…had she cut herself? Did she meant to slice her wrists open and perish in the chapel? But he rejected that immediately as foolish, and then realized it appeared to be ink stains all over her fingers and wrists.

Malcolm was conscious of how quickly he'd lost his need to be angry with her, but for now, he ignored this realization. There would be time for self-recrimination later.

"They?" he prompted when she stopped speaking. But she remained silent, close against him, still and unmoving but for a hardly discernible trembling. Despite the warm day, she was chilled.

"Come now, Judith. Usually 'tis no hardship to set your tongue to wagging."

This seemed to be the right thing to say, as odd as it was, for she drew in an unsteady breath and spoke in a low, rapid voice. "The queen calls me to her early in the morrow each day. She is a bitter taskmaster, particularly when motivated by righteous fury. I am not permitted to leave her chamber or to eat or rest until I have finished the many, long, tedious tasks she has laid out for me on that day. And when I am dismissed, I return to my own chamber and I find...." Here her breath hitched, and palpable misery flooded from her. "I find my summons to the king awaiting me. I am...with him...." She vibrated in Mal's arms, yet continued on: "...until the early hours of dawn. And so it goes. I do not even know what day it is any longer, or what hour. But at the least," she added dryly and with a spark of the Judith he knew, "Eleanor has not lifted a hand to me again."

Mal could not move. He forced himself to go rigid, to become paralyzed, for if he did not, God knew what he would do. 'Twas a wonder she was not fainted on the floor. Or worse.

"And," Judith said, her voice rough and low, "I am fair certain I carry the king's child." And that was when he felt her release and begin to sob, jolting softly against him. "Now I will never be free of him," she whispered. "*Never.*"

She did not want the king's child, that much was abundantly clear. But was it because she did not want to further anger the vindictive queen, or because she did not, after all, wish to be tied to the king? A royal bastard would ensure Judith of wealth and comfort all the days of her life—mayhap even a permanent place in the royal household. What woman would not want that? She would be a fool not to desire such stability.

She does not look like a woman infatuated with her lover, Lady Maris had said.

Malcolm closed his eyes.

"I brought some food and drink," he said at last, when he could no longer sit with his own thoughts. "Your maid claims you haven't eaten for days."

Judith pulled away, and though he was bereft at losing the scent and feel of her, he helped her sit on the floor, resting her back against the chapel wall. "Or slept," she added.

Or slept.

Mal busied himself by pulling the strings of the wine skin free of his belt. He handed it to her and presented the cheese and bread. "Thank you," she said, taking the offerings gladly. "I will do myself no good if I do not eat."

"'Tis true," he said. Then, after she had eaten some and quenched her thirst—and because he could not help himself—Mal asked, "You do not wish for the king's child?"

Judith's eyes flashed to him and he saw a quickly masked flare of heat and anger. "I do not wish the man to touch me, let alone for his seed to root within my belly. 'T may be treason to say so, but 'tis the truth."

A roaring filled his ears, as it had done when he first learned she was the king's mistress, and his vision clouded red. His hands were tight fists, his muscles so tense they pained him. If the king were present, Mal would gladly commit his own violent treason. 'Twas near impossible for him to get the words out. "*He forced you.*"

Now Judith played with the remainder of the cheese, turning it into crumbles in the lap of her skirt. "I was not willing. He knew I was not willing. But he cared not. Yet he was not…he was not violent. And I was no virgin. But one cannot say nay to one's liege lord and king. The punishment would be far worse than this." She shrugged, looking up at him again. Her pallor had some color now, and in her eyes he could see a spark of life. "I begged the queen to send me away—back to Lilyfare. She would not, for she intends to keep me as her slave until long after Henry is tired of me sucking his cock. Or so she has decreed."

Mal caught his breath at the lewd image and closed his eyes. Rage and arousal battled within him, and he settled on rage. 'Twas safer.

Judith's mouth moved into a flat line and she looked back down at the destroyed cheese. "And if I bear the king's child…." She shook her head. "I would be tied to him—and to her—forever. Hence my fervent prayers." She waved a hand to the room at large, then lifted the wineskin to drink once more.

When she pulled it away, her full lips glistened deliciously and Mal had to avert his gaze. Even unfed and unrested, even wasting away to skin and bones, even painting repulsive mental images of her in her lover's bed, she was a gloriously beautiful woman. His desire for her washed over him, so strong and deep he could scarcely draw in a normal breath. *Dog. You are no better than the king.*

"'Tis a shame you've set your heart on Beatrice of Delbring," she said, those lips curving in a humorless smile. "Else I should throw myself on your mercy and beg you to wed me and take me from here, and then no one would know if I carry the king's babe or nay. I would be quit of him and this court." She dug in the packet and pulled out a corner of the bread. "But, nay. Lady Beatrice's heart is safe. I would not ask that of you—or any man. For the queen's wrath would come upon you…and the king's as well." She bit her lip and stared down at the crumbling bread. "Henry claims he is quite obsessed with me, and that he shall never tire of my company."

Mal was very still for a moment, and then his body rushed alive. Hot and cold and filled with hope, fear…and, God help him, lust.

"What of de Rigonier?" Mal at last found his voice.

Judith looked at him. Her expression had reverted to despair. "I would not ask it of him either. I fear the king and queen would—"

"Nay," Mal said impatiently. "That is not my meaning. What of you and de Rigonier?" She shook her head, clearly at a loss. He tried again. "You were no virgin in Henry's bed…was it de Rigonier?"

Her eyes widened. "Nay, of course not. 'Twas Gregory who took my maidenhead—who had the right to do so, as my betrothed."

Mal's tension eased. "You and de Rigonier are not lovers?"

"Nay." Even in the dim light, the color rising in her cheeks was obvious. "I may now be called whore, but 'tis only that the king has made me thus."

"I will wed you."

She stared at him. "Nay, Ma—*Warwick.* Do not be a fool." Her eyes were wide with consternation and regret. She reached to touch him, her small hand resting on his arm. "'Twas a jest. Only a jest. I would not allow it."

"Allow it? You?" His laugh rang out, echoing eerily in the small, closed room. Yet, desperation surged through him. To be so close to his desire, to have it within his reach…. He would not allow it to be snatched away. "The king himself has granted me leave to wed where I will. You meet all of the requirements, Lady Judith. I will wed you, and take you from here. And none will know that you carry the king's babe. I will raise him as my own. And you know I have no aspirations to the throne, nor to such power as a bastard prince would give."

"Lord Warwick, I cannot…." she began. But she was looking away, down at her fingers twisted and wrapped within her cheese-stained gown. "I could not live, knowing you put yourself at such risk. Nay. We cannot."

He could not see her face. But he didn't care. Reason had deserted him. Reason and prudence. "You said it—'tis the only way you might escape your fate. I will manage it all, Judith. And we will wed."

And even as she hesitated…then nodded, glancing at him briefly then looking away once more, Mal hardly noticed. He was flush, alive, alert, victorious.

And if he was no better than the king, at the least he would be entitled to her in his bed in the eyes of God and the Church.

TEN

I **WILL** wed you.

Even after Malcolm had gone and Judith was alone, she could not erase those words from her mind. They were the answer to a prayer...a solution of which she'd hardly allowed herself to dream. To be Malcolm of Warwick's wife.

And yet she could hardly look at him, for fear he'd see the truth in her eyes. How she'd trapped him. Gently, innocently...but entrapped him nevertheless.

Deceitful woman!

I did not intend to lead him that way. She spoke silently, directing her thoughts to the image above her of the Virgin Mary, who surely thought her an unconscionable wench. And truly, Judith hadn't been thinking clearly when the words poured from her mouth. She hadn't considered what it would mean to him, putting himself at odds with not only the queen but the king as well. Nay, they had been foolish, capricious words, half in jest, half in despair...her thoughtless mouth running off on its own, leaving her brain behind once again.

And Malcolm, being the honorable man he was, would never deny the chance to assist a lady in distress. It was his responsibility. And part of what made him a good man...a man she had come to care for far deeply than she realized until now. For though he had offered her everything she wanted, she knew she must not accept it, knowing what it could do to him.

Thus, guilt and relief warred with fear and delight. She could be Malcolm's *wife*.

Nay, I cannot do this to him. She couldn't drag him into the mire of her life and affix him alongside her, betwixt the warring faction of queen versus king. He was a powerful lord, a wealthy and important baron—but just as easily, the king could find reason to disseisin him from his lands, to seize Warwick and his other estates. Throw Mal into prison....

Nay, I must not do this to him. Her belly, tight and empty for so long, felt heavy with the stones of nausea and guilt.

Judith felt the cold, hard floor beneath her knees once again as she rose upon them. She clutched the prayer beads so tightly they left marks on her skin. And she prayed for a different way, another answer to her petition. *Show me another path.*

Before Mal left the chapel, he warned Judith to say naught to anyone of their plan to wed. Not even to Tabatha. "I must make careful arrangements," he said, his face intent, his mind clearly working. "So as not to bring the king's wrath down on us."

"There is naught you can do," Judith protested. "He will be furious." *I tried again*, she cried silently, arguing with her conscience. *I tried to talk him from it, but he would not listen. Foolish, honorable man.*

Foolish, honorable man with whom she'd fallen in love.

Oh, aye. Alone, naked to herself, brutally honest, she must admit the truth. She'd opened the door and forced him to walk through it not only to free her from the bed of the king, but because she wanted Malcolm for herself.

"I will send to Mal Verne," he told her. "He is your closest relative. Tell me true—will he have any reason to oppose our match?"

"Nay," Judith replied. "Gavin would be pleased to see me wed. He has no claim to Lilyfare or Kentworth, and he has pressed me to find a husband more than once. And he knows you well, of course." She could hardly believe they were having such a conversation.

"And he is close to the king. I have much to do. Stay you here," he said almost absently, pressing a firm hand onto her shoulder to stay her from rising. "I will send Father Anselm. The queen cannot tear you from sanctuary—"

"Eleanor will not stand for it," Judith argued. "She will demand my attendance."

But Mal shook his head firmly. "She will not dare cross Father Anselm. Not now, not with the unrest rising betwixt her and Henry with Canterbury and the Church. The tension grows, and the rift between them is widening. 'Tis too dangerous for them to cross the archbishop—now. And," he added with satisfaction, "the archbishop himself was present and witnessed to my writ, granting me the freedom to wed as I might."

He turned his attention back to Judith. "Do you remain here for this day. You will rest and sleep and eat. I will send Tabatha with a pallet and more food. And you will better be able to face the queen's demands on the morrow. It will take some time for me to arrange things and I do not wish her to be suspicious or otherwise on her guard, for our wedding must happen quickly before they can stop it."

Darkness crossed his face and his jaw shifted. "As for the king…." Malcolm stopped, his lips compressing, his expression turning deathly cold. "I shall do what I can to keep the king distracted. He will not call for you this night."

Judith did not respond. Instead, she swallowed the thick lump in her throat and refused to look at him again. Pray God his plan would work. "Very well, my lord Warwick. I will remain here."

"I will not return," he said, rising slowly to tower over her. "Nor seek you out. There can be no hint of our plan, Judith. But know that I will make the necessary arrangements. If you need to contact me, send quietly from Tabatha to Nevril."

He turned to leave, then paused, the sole of his boot grinding softly on the stone floor. "Malcolm. I am not Warwick to you, my lady. Only Malcolm."

~*~

THE SECOND day after Judith and Malcolm spoke in the chapel, her monthly flux began.

Her first reaction was one of wild relief and delight. Tears of joy sprang to her eyes and she had never been more thankful for the monthly inconvenience. She would not bear the king's child after all! And, thanks to Lady Maris's special tea—which Judith made certain she drank every day—that would likely not change.

But quickly on the heels of this great reversal of bad fortune came a dismaying realization.

There was no longer any need for Malcolm to wed her.

Ah. Thus and so is my prayer answered...yet again.

Now he could be freed of the black muck of her life, and he could go on his way and wed Beatrice of Delbring as he always intended. For it had not escaped Judith's notice that, despite the wealthy beauties at court and the pressure from herself and the queen to consider other than Lady Beatrice, none seemed to have caught Malcolm's eye.

I am not Warwick to you. Only Malcolm.

She shook her head. *Nay. He must be Warwick to me again. And I must send word to him.*

Judith sat down, suddenly cold.

As it happened, she was in her chamber alone in the midday. The queen, miraculously, had not summoned her this morrow because she and her ladies were meeting with a new fabrics master to pore over bolts and bolts of new materials—silks and fine cottons and even something called gossamer—from Antioch, Cairo, and Jerusalem. The news was that *six* wagons had brought the goods into the castle, and that another three more were imminent. Once, Judith would have been in the midst of such excitement—and delighted to be there. But no longer; the queen wanted her nowhere about during such an event.

Thus, she had the perfect opportunity to send a message to Malcolm. And yet she sat on her stool by the fire, staring into the anemic summer flames. Her lungs and chest felt tight and heavy. *I am still trapped. And he will soon belong to Beatrice of Delbring.*

Judith was not certain which of her two fates was worse.

A knock on the door brought her wearily to her feet. The sound heralded only bad news as of late and she dragged herself to answer it. What more could happen?

But to Judith's surprise, Lady Maris stood on the threshold. "May I come in?"

"Of course," Judith replied after a moment of confusion. She stepped away from the door and closed it behind her friend. "I did not know you'd returned."

"Aye. Only just some short while ago." Maris's shrewd green-brown eyes searched her countenance. "What is it? You have been ill. I can see it in your face—you are thin and weary. You are with child, then?" Her voice was grim.

"Nay. Nay, I have just this morn learned I am not with child," Judith confessed.

"But you are unhappy?" Maris's tone was neutral, though her expression didn't quite succeed in matching it.

Judith took a deep breath and then before she could stop them, tears began to flow. All of her weariness, frustration and fear came tumbling out. She told Maris the whole of it—of Eleanor's punishment of her and Judith's servitude thus, the intimate details of Henry's increasing demands, how she was trapped in a never-ending struggle of power between the king and queen…and, finally, of her conversation with Malcolm.

During Judith's speech, Maris helped her to sit on the bed. She settled next to her, holding her friend's hands as she listened. Her face betrayed no expression until Judith finished speaking. Then she blinked and said ruefully, "Less than a se'ennight I was gone and all of this has happened. 'Tis glad I am that this court is not my home."

Judith wiped her eyes and blew her nose, feeling more than a little foolish for her mad torrent of words and tears. "Forgive me, Lady Maris. I had no cause to pile all of my worries on you." She realized with a stab of fear that she'd done what Malcolm warned her not to do—to tell anyone of their impending marriage. Not that it would matter any longer, but she had betrayed his confidence. *Again my foolish tongue!*

"Very well. So we must reassess the situation. First," Maris said, digging in a small pouch hanging from her belt, "I have brought you something to assist with the king. And now that I have learned the whole story, 'twill help you with the queen...at the least for a time. I meant for you to have a rest from the king's attentions, but now that you are bleeding, you can send word to him of that. Surely he will give you a reprieve of some days."

"Aye," Judith said, hoping Maris was correct. As the queen had pointed out, however, there were other ways to pleasure a man aside of copulation. And Henry never seemed to tire of her.

"But this," Maris said, giving her a small vial, "will ensure you have at the least three days of peace. Mayhap longer." Judith took it and looked at the dark brown liquid, then back up as her friend explained, "'Twas my great luck to come upon an herbary during our journey. 'Tis a rare plant, and I paid a grand sum for it—aye, you shall find a way to compensate me betimes, for Dirick bellowed quite loudly when he learned of the cost—but when you drink it with some small bit of water—take care, for 'tis foul-tasting and bitter—you will soon show red patches all over your body. They will itch, but they are harmless and will disappear after some days. But I promise you, the king—and likely the queen—will not wish to be in the presence of aught so ugly and contagious. And I will assure them that 'tis not a deadly disease, but they do not wish to be exposed." Maris's eyes danced and she looked as if she would love such a jest.

Judith took the vial, herself smiling at the thought. "Thank you, my lady. 'Tis very thoughtful of you. I shall use it as needed and I will most definitely repay you."

"Now. To your other, larger issue." Maris clicked her tongue and pulled her knees up to her chest, easing back further onto the bed as her bliaut and kirtle bunched up around her. "Ah," she said with a smile, "'tis long since I've been able to this—for having a babe in the belly made it impossible to even see my feet, much less pull them up like this."

Judith nodded, but her thoughts went immediately from large bellies carrying babes to the niggling knowledge of what she must tell Malcolm.

As if reading her mind, Maris said, "You are considering not telling Warwick."

Though her friend's tone was neutral, Judith flushed. "Nay. Not truly. Though 'tis a fantasy, I confess."

"You could wait to tell him. What harm would there be—another day or two. Mayhap he will make the arrangements and you will be wed...and then your flux will come. And then he will know any babe planted in your belly is his."

Judith felt a sharp stab at the thought of Malcolm planting a child in her belly—a pleasant, yet disappointed thought. "I cannot do that," she said, shaking her head. "He does not deserve to be trapped along with me. 'Twas wrong of me to say such a thing in the first place, to capture him so."

Maris *tsk*ed and sat up. "But it would solve your problem quite handily. And if your flux comes later...well then, you will already be wed. And he will have obtained a beautiful, wealthy wife for his troubles. 'Tis no bad bargain."

"Along with the king's wrath and the queen's spleen," Judith replied. "I could not bear that that burden be thrust on him, Maris. I truly could not."

"I've found," her friend said, "that betimes, the workings of a man's mind is not the same as that of ours. They yearn for violence and bloodshed, for battle and war...and sometimes, their perception of honor is much different than that of ours. Methinks they oft prefer the chance to be honorable in a difficult situation than to have a quiet, simple life. He would do it for you."

"'Tis true," Judith replied. But her mind was made up; speaking with Maris had removed any last bit of doubt. As painful as it would be, as dark as her future might seem, she would release Warwick from their agreement.

_*_

"I DO not know what it is has taken the stick from up his arse," Nevril said to Gambert, "but I am near ready to praise it as a miracle."

They stood in the bailey, just on the other side of the training yard's gate. Both sweating, out of breath, and bare of torso, they'd just cleaned and put their swords away for the day. But they were smiling and in good humor, for their lord had not only *not* cursed them roundly—whilst pointing out each one's failings on the field for all to hear—but neither had been landed on the field with his face plowed into the dirt, thanks to their ill-tempered but skillful master. Which had been happening with great regularity for nearly a se'ennight, and always accompanied by more bellowing and cursing from Lord Malcolm.

Gambert glanced to where his master was speaking to Lord Dirick, who'd returned to Clarendon with his wife only hours ago. "Praise God indeed," the squire said. "Lord Mal is in such fine spirits these last days, I fair expect him to break into song."

They both laughed heartily at the image of the staid, sober Malcolm of Warwick bellowing a bawdy tune in the training yard. Though with his change in mood, 'twas possible even the inconceivable could happen.

"Mayhap I shall find the man a lute," jested Nevril.

Gambert chortled. "Methinks we'll soon be on our way back to Warwick. Another cause for celebration, for I am sore weary of sleeping on a pallet in a hot chamber of farting, snoring men. At the least at Warwick, I have only to share with you and a half dozen others."

"And we have our own pallets," allowed Nevril.

"With the number of missives my lord has been sending as of late—to Mal Verne, Rittenbridge and Salisbury and, most importantly, Delbring—I suspect we shall make a detour there for a wedding. 'Tis apparent he has at last settled on a bride, and soon we shall have a new lady at Warwick. And my lord shall remain in his good humor whence he has a woman in his bed every night."

"Aye," Nevril said, but he sounded much less enthusiastic. He couldn't help but glance at the stable where the irritating Bruin continued to have the temerity to exist.

Tabatha the maid had hardly given Nevril anymore than a nod and a glance since he brought her to Lord Malcolm two days ago—the ungrateful wench. But since he would soon be bound for Warwick, Nevril concluded, 'twas just as well. For some unknown reason—likely stemming from his bad choice of rabbit stew jests and skill with the bow—she continued to show only loathing toward him.

Still…when he left the training yard, Nevril slowed his pace as he passed the stable. It would make for an even finer day if he found reason to pique the hard-hearted maid once more. For when she glowered and her eyes flashed, he found it more entertaining than the thought of Warwick playing the lute.

As luck would have it, this dallying brought his very desire to pass, for as he walked toward the keep, he spied Tabatha walking toward him. In the light, her bright golden hair gleamed as if drawing the sunbeams toward it. To his surprise, when she saw him, instead of changing direction or even turning her face to a glower, she increased her speed…coming straight to him.

"Sir Nevril," she said. "Good morrow."

He blinked. That was nearly the most civil thing she'd ever said to him. "Mistress Tabatha. Are you in search of another critter in need of your tending?"

She looked at him oddly, but replied, "Nay. I have a missive for your master." She handed him a piece of parchment, folded until it fit neatly into the palm of her hand.

"I will see that he receives it. And how fares Sir Rabbit?" Nevril asked, loathe to allow her to be on her way.

"He is freely roaming the meadows again, for all I know," she replied. "I released him back to the wild only four days past, for he was hopping about the chamber." She glanced at the message he held. "Do you know where Lord Malcolm might be? The missive should be delivered at once."

"Walk with me, if you will, so you may see for yourself that I deliver it posthaste," he suggested. "Warwick is at the training yard."

She made a moue of distaste, but nodded. "Very well."

Nevril was so surprised at her easy acquiescence that he nearly didn't know how to respond, but he recovered quickly. "This way."

The walk back to the training yard was much too brief in his estimation, and all the while, Nevril struggled with something on which to converse that had naught to do with rabbit stew…but his mind was curiously blank. Tabatha had nothing to say either except for a mundane comment about the weather.

"Lord Malcolm," Nevril called when he saw his master, still in the yard. He hadn't yet sheathed his sword or donned his *sherte* or tunic, and was still in conversation with Ludingdon. His master turned at the hail and when Nevril held up the parchment, he walked over to meet him at the gate. "'Tis a message for you. Delivered by Mistress Tabatha."

Malcolm nearly snatched it from his hand, then, walking away, unfolded the parchment. He began to read it, then came to a dead stop in the middle of the mucky, empty training yard. He hissed audibly, staring at the paper. He read it again. "*There is no longer a need?*"

For a moment he didn't move. Then all at once, a change came over him—like a fast-moving cloud covering the sun. His expression darkened, his body tightened visibly. His face thunderous, he tucked the missive into the collar of his tunic.

Warwick looked over and saw Nevril standing there. "Why are you there? Where is your sword? Who gave you leave to remove your hauberk? To me! At once! There is much work to be done on your skill with a broad-blade, you lazy dog!"

~*~

"I SPOKE with Judith today," Maris said as her husband came into their chamber shortly before the evening meal.

She rose to put the fed and sleeping Rogan in his crib, feeling the weight of Dirick's interest on her backside as she bent over. Smiling to herself, she took her time arranging the blankets over the chubby babe. It had, after all, been nearly a se'ennight since they'd had a moment of privacy.

When Maris finally turned, she found him sitting on a stool, unwinding his crossgarters. Still watching her. A thick curl of dark hair fell over his forehead and there was a hot gleam in his eyes. She knew what that portended. His boots were in a heap next to the hearth and, *tsk*ing, she picked them up so no one tripped on them and landed in the fire.

"Warwick told me of their intent to wed," Dirick said. "Then moments after he told me of this, he received a message from Lady Judith, telling him there was no longer a reason."

Now she made a sound of satisfaction. "Excellent. I did not think she would do it so quickly, but I hoped in the end she would. I gave her every opportunity to talk herself out of it, and she did not. I am very pleased."

"What have you been plotting?" her husband asked, kicking off his hose and leaving *that* in a pile as well. He was still looking at her with that gleam. "'Tis glad I am to be back to Clarendon, for sleeping on the ground and in a shared men's chamber did not suit me."

"I found Canterbury quite comfortable," Maris told him with a teasing look. "And I don't plot." She snatched up hose and crossgarters as he gave a bark of laughter at her pronouncement. "Mayhap you could find another place to put these in the stead of the floor?"

"Is that not what you have a maid for?"

"Oh, aye. I'd forgotten. I shall call her now, then," Maris said with great innocence as she slipped away from his greedy grasp. "Sally can pick up your clothing, sweep, and tend to the fire." She started toward the door.

Dirick laughed ruefully, knowing he'd been trapped, and moved to block her way. "Oh, no you don't, my love. We have some time before the meal, and I do not wish to be disturbed." He leered at her and began to undo the lacings on her gown. They were already loose because she'd just finished feeding Rogan. "I rather like this style of dress," he said, opening the front of her bliaut. "'Tis ready access."

"As I was saying," Maris continued, giving him a saucy smile as he slid his hands through the widening opening, "I do not plot. I was merely…measuring Judith."

"Measuring?" He hefted her breasts as if doing so to her.

She rolled her eyes at the poor jest. "Judith may have goaded Warwick into offering to wed her, but 'tis clearly because she loves him, not because she wishes to…quit…the king…." Her words trailed off into a sigh as Dirick found her sensitive nipples with his thumbs.

"Indeed." His voice had gone very deep and low. "Warwick was not pleased with the reversal," he said, his mouth moist and hot against her throat. "He was nearly beside himself, though he tried to hide it."

"So he cares for her? That is why he agreed?"

"Oh, aye. Warwick is besotted—and 'tis not for only her lands. He is adept at hiding it, but as a man who is besotted himself…I can see the truth."

"Very good," Maris sighed.

He smiled against her lips. "I know."

She smiled back and arched a little as he shifted to take a nipple into his mouth. "That is not what I meant."

"Is that so?" His words were muffled, but she felt the heat of them against her sensitive skin.

"Oh…aye…." she murmured, choosing the double meaning apurpose. But then she refocused her mind and shifted away a little. "And now how will they finalize this match if she has declined him? We must help them."

"Nay. I do not know why one should meddle in such a thing," Dirick said. He pulled away, his eyes warm but irritated and his mouth full and sensual. "Busy-body."

"But if we did not have the grace of the king—and the meddling of the queen—we would not be here together at this moment," she reminded him. Then bit his shoulder to let him know she was not wholly distracted from the real matter at hand.

He groaned softly, combing his hands up into her heavy hair. "That is not like to happen for them," he said with a half-laugh, half-groan as she reached to cup his stones.

"Aye, 'tis the truth," Maris said, fondling him gently. "And that is why mayhap a bit of *plotting* on their behalf would be a good turn."

"I do not know *why* we are talking about them when there are *other* things at hand." As if to emphasize his words, he gathered up her breasts and gave them a little jiggle. And then he bent to give them all of his attention.

Maris lost her trail of thought for a moment, and the next thing she knew, the bed was behind her and Dirick was hiking up her skirt. She looked up at him and saw the fierce, desirous expression on his face as he slid his hands up along her thighs, easing them open. A pang of lust shot through her, adding to the heat that rolled through her body at his familiar, comforting touch…and that was why.

This. Love.

"We are talking about them…because…." she murmured, helping her husband into position. They both sighed as he fit into place and slid deep. His fingers curved over her hips and pulled her close as she wrapped her legs around his firm arse.

"Who?" he asked. But it was more of a gruff laugh than a real question. Maris couldn't answer, for by now he was moving in that familiar, hot rhythm. She had no thought for anything but pleasure.

~*~

JUDITH WAS indeed offered a reprieve from the king; however, the queen did not do the same. So it was late in the evening when Judith was released from a long day of writing and rewriting and allowed to return to her chamber.

Her fingers were crabbed tightly from the tedious work, and she flexed them open and closed as she walked back through the dim corridors. While she was grateful to at last have a night alone in her own chamber, she couldn't help but feel the strain of knowing there was no longer an avenue of escape from her fate of being trapped between Henry and Eleanor.

She'd sent word to Lord Warwick yesterday, immediately after Maris left the chamber. There had been no response from him. Not that she'd expected one, but mayhap in the deepest part of her soul, she had *hoped* for one. Instead, she could only come to the conclusion that he was relieved to be released from their agreement.

Nevertheless, she had been thinking of other ways to free herself from her predicament. The king had given her jewels and other baubles that were worth a small fortune. Mayhap she could find a way to leave Clarendon and take them with her to Paris. King Louis might allow her to join his court—for there was no love lost betwixt him, his former wife Eleanor, and the man for whom she'd divorced Louis. Of course, if she managed somehow to do that—for a woman traveling alone was a problem in and of itself—she would never see Lilyfare or Kentworth again. She would never be welcomed back in the English court. And—

A large, shadowy figure detached itself from a small alcove as she walked past, and Judith gasped in surprise.

"'Tis I," said a familiar voice immediately.

"Mal—*Warwick*," she managed to say, her heart pounding. "You startled me." Walking through the twisty, dim corridors late in the evening was nearly as dangerous as walking through dark streets or alleys in town.

"'Twas only my intent to speak with you privately and unseen," he said. But he remained in the shadows, his face partly obliterated.

"Very well," she replied. "Now that I have swallowed my heart back to its place, speak."

"Your message—I received it. You claim there is no longer a need for us to…continue on our previous path."

"Aye," she said, her voice low and unsteady. "I am not with child. And I have the means to prevent it for the future."

"And therefore you are pleased and willing to remain the king's concubine and the queen's slave?" His tones were odd; she couldn't read them. Nor his face, for he had not moved into the light.

Judith drew in a deep breath. *Nay, oh nay!* "'Tis not the urgent matter it was when we met three days ago."

"You agreed to wed me. I would hold you to that promise."

She gnawed on her lip as her insides warred with her brain: cautious hope battling guilt and fear. "I tricked you into offering for me," she replied flatly.

"Do you wish to remain the king's concubine?"

"Nay. Of course not!"

"I have already made the arrangements. 'Tis late to change them. I would hold you to your word."

She realized her hand was pressed against the rough stone wall as she peered into the shadows. All she could see was a part of his shoes and hose and the corner of one sleeve. Her heart beat steadily in her chest as she closed her eyes. *God forgive me.* "Aye," she said at last. "I will keep my word."

Though her words were low and sober, inside she danced and leapt. But in the back of her mind, there was still the worry of what her acquiescence might mean for him. And guilt. For if aught happened to Malcolm because of her.... "If you are truly certain you are prepared for the king's wrath," she was compelled to add. "I fear what he and Eleanor will do."

"I am willing."

"Very well," she replied, wishing he would step into the light. Wishing she could see his face, read what was there.

"I will send word to you anon." And then he was gone, swishing into the darkness, down a side hallway and into the shadows.

ELEVEN

THREE DAYS later, Lady Judith of Kentworth developed a horrible rash with red splotches all over her face and arms, and one presumed, elsewhere.

She was sent to her chamber after an examination by the queen's trusted lady and healer Maris of Ludingdon, and there she was confined to be certain she spread no contagion to Eleanor and her baby.

For Judith, this quarantine was both a blessing and a curse. While she had some much-needed privacy and an opportunity to rest, she was also left alone with her thoughts and fears. She heard naught from Malcolm, nor did she know what to expect.

Nor was Judith even able to take the time to visit her raptors, which she had been forced to neglect since she attracted the attention of Henry. Fortunately, she communicated with Tessing through Tabby and knew that Hecate and the others were doing well. The eyases were growing and their baby feathers had fallen away. Soon they would be flying far and wide, and would need to be moved from the hacking house into the main mews.

While in her chamber, Judith had ample opportunity to look down from her arrow-slit window, watching the men training in the yard far below. She was certain she spotted Malcolm more than once—he was nearly always bare of torso and taller than all but Ludingdon—but on this day, well after the midday meal of her third day in confinement, she did not see him. In fact, the yard seemed to have fewer men than in days past though the weather was clear and sunny.

Maris had visited briefly on the morrow of each day, providing her with a salve to keep the splotches from itching. She also insisted Judith bathe daily in a tub with soaking oats and lavender to help keep the rash from irritating her further. By now, the patches were hardly visible and no longer itched, and Judith knew she would have no excuse to hide for much longer.

A knock at the chamber door had her turning eagerly from the window. Maris had already visited several hours before, and Judith expected no one but Tabby. But just as she reached to open the door, she hesitated. It could very well be a page from the queen or the king, come to assess her health.

The knock came again, more loudly and firmly. "Judith!" demanded a masculine voice.

She flung the door open. "Gavin?" she cried, shocked and delighted to see her cousin. She threw herself into his arms, which came around her tightly after an instant of hesitation, for he was not normally a demonstrative person. "What do you here?" she said, pulling away to look up at him.

Without responding, he stepped into the chamber and closed the door behind him. "I've come for your wedding, of course," he said, looking at her closely. "You seem healthy enough, despite the story throughout the keep you've contracted some worrisome disease. Though a little peaked, as Maddie would say. But Ludingdon tells me it was all his wife's doing."

"Madelyne! Is she here too?"

"Nay, she did not come. I traveled too swiftly and she has just delivered herself of a baby only one month past. A girl," he added, with a flash of pride and affection in his eyes. "Rosalind."

"I am happy for you, Gavin," Judith said, squeezing his hands. He'd been so troubled for so long, and the serene, beautiful Madelyne de Belgrume had brought love and light into his life.

"And you, Judith. You are to wed Warwick. Is this what you wish?" Gavin was looking down at her, his expression particularly serious. "If you mean to wed him only to be free of the king, tell me now. I will extricate you from this place if need be, and you will not be required to barter yourself in marriage." His features, always dark and forbidding, were as stern as she'd ever seen them. "Now tell me true—do you wish to wed Warwick or nay?"

"I would wed him, Gavin. Not only to be quit of the court. He is a good man, and kind, and I believe he will make a fine husband. I have long wished to return to Lilyfare and to leave the queen's side, but she would not allow it."

Her cousin relaxed. "'Tis glad I am to hear of it, Judith. I was most pleased when Warwick sent word, requesting my blessing and explaining the circumstances. But I wanted to hear it from you myself."

Malcolm had asked Gavin for his blessing? For some reason, that information made Judith even more content with her decision. "But I fear what Henry and Eleanor will do to him when they learn of this."

Gavin shook his head. "Do you not worry. Warwick has laid his path neatly, and only part of it was sending word to me. And the marriage contract he had prepared is more than fair. Now, if you are willing, we must go at once. We haven't much time."

"Go where?"

He looked at her in surprise, a smile crinkling the corners of his eyes. "Why, to your wedding. Your groom awaits."

‿*‿

JUDITH NEVER imagined her wedding would take place in the tiny, out-of-the- way chapel where she and Malcolm had first agreed to marry.

Nor did she anticipate it being crowded with so many people she could hardly see her groom, who stood at the tray-sized altar.

And she certainly did not intend to be wearing nothing more than a simple gold bliaut covered by her best cloak—the fanciest article of clothing she could grab before Gavin ushered her out of the chamber. And her hair...! She did not want to think on the sight of her hair, for surely she'd mussed the simple braids when she lay down on her bed for a nap after Tabby fixed it up after her bath.

"You look beautiful," her cousin told her when she balked at leaving in her state of attire. "But we cannot wait. We must go now. If there is a delay, Henry may learn of the plan and put a stop to it. Once you are wed, 'tis a different matter—but if he halts it, I fear you will never be free of him."

This was enough of a threat to get Judith out of her chamber in a swirl of cloak—even leaving behind her gold link girdle and emerald earbobs. And when she and Gavin arrived at the chapel, Maris was there at the doorway.

Maris ordered Gavin to step aside. "I'll set her to rights...just one moment," she said. A twitch, a pull and a tug later, she had pinned combs bejeweled with topazes and emeralds into Judith's hair. "There," she said. "Now you look lovely. And your rash is all but gone."

Gavin took Judith's arm and before she knew it, he was leading her down the short, narrow aisle to the altar. She recognized many of the faces who lined the route—Hugh de Rigonier and Castendown, Lord Rittendon, Alynne and Ursula...even Salisbury and Peter of Blois.

Judith nearly gasped aloud when she saw Father Anselm and the Archbishop of Canterbury standing at the small altar. Her eyes widened and she glanced at Gavin, who murmured, "Warwick takes no chance that the wedding will not be recognized."

At that, Judith had the courage to look at Malcolm for the first time. He stood towering over everyone in the chapel, helped by his great height and broad shoulders as well as the small dais. She noted at once that his sable-brown hair had been trimmed and was shorter than she'd ever seen it, just past his chin. It was shiny and combed neatly, and his jaw clean-shaven and smooth.

Unlike Judith, he wore fine clothing: a tunic in the colors of Warwick—gray and blue—with detailed embroidery that must have taken many hours of work. Beneath the tunic was a *sherte* of dark blue, embroidered at the end of the long, tight sleeves in gold, red and white. He wore a heavy, ornate sapphire and emerald brooch at his throat, anchoring a shimmering gray cloak lined with dark red fabric. His boots were well-tooled dark brown leather, more costly than a good mare. On his right hand was a heavy signet ring with a square stone of onyx.

At this imposing sight, Judith swallowed hard—for she'd never seen him dressed befitting his station as a great and wealthy baron. He was both breathtakingly handsome and intimidating all at once. She managed to raise her gaze to his, mortified that she should be presented to her future husband dressed as she was whilst he was garbed in all finery.

But when she met his hazel eyes, she saw only anticipation and blatant approval. Judith held her chin high and when Gavin transferred her hand to Malcolm's, she gave a brief curtsy to her soon-to-be husband, then pressed a kiss to her cousin's cheek.

Malcolm's large hand covered hers easily, his fingers warm and steadying around hers as they turned to face the priest and the archbishop, kneeling on the *prie-dieu* in front of them.

The ceremony was too brief and yet interminable. Judith, who'd attended mass countless times in her life, and nearly as many weddings, struggled between nervousness and pleasure as the clergymen led them through the familiar rites. Throughout, Malcolm's fingers remained curled around hers, offering stability and comfort.

When at last Canterbury released them to the room at large, she and her new husband faced each other. He bent to press a brief, soft kiss to her lips, then turned to present the new Lady of Warwick to their friends and peers.

And then all at once, the chapel went dead silent. Everyone was turning toward the rear.

"What is happening here?" demanded a familiar peremptory voice.

Judith went instantly cold, her insides puddling into fear and her knees weakening as she looked up to see King Henry standing on the chapel's threshold.

"Good evening, your majesty," said Malcolm in a smooth, calm voice. 'Twas Judith's good fortune that he had a strong hold around her waist, else she might have sagged to the floor.

"Your majesty," said Gavin, interrupting when Malcolm might have continued. "You have arrived just in time to congratulate Warwick on his new bride."

Judith swore the chamber held its collective breath as the news sunk in. Even from across the small way, she saw an array of emotions pass over Henry's face: shock, disbelief, fury. She noticed Dirick of Ludingdon and Hugh de Rigonier shifting their position so as to be visible to the king.

"Canterbury?" the king demanded, looking about. "What have you to say?"

"Congratulate Warwick, Henry. He's made a fine choice in wife," said Thomas à Becket—who may or may not have been aware of the undercurrents now seething in the holy place. "I have just finished officiating the ceremony—and now I wish to eat and drink."

"Indeed." The king's voice was frosty and his expression like granite. He looked at Judith, meeting her eyes from the other end of the aisle, and she shivered at the expression therein. She clutched Malcolm's arm more tightly, and he gave her a little squeeze.

"Very well then," said Henry in a falsely jovial voice, "'tis off to the hall we go, for much celebration!"

~*~

HENRY PLANTAGENET, King of England, Duke of Anjou, had never been foiled so neatly and truly as he had been today.

He simmered during the loud, raucous evening meal, wherein he was required to pretend to happily endorse the marriage of the woman with whom he was obsessed to a wealthy baron who had powerful friends. Even dressed as she was—in a simple, loose gown, with her brilliant fire-gold hair in a variety of braids—Judith of Kentworth was magnificent. He could still taste the sweetness of her skin and feel the perfect heft and weight of her breasts. The image of her hair spread over the white coverings of his bed, and her ivory body splayed on dark, sable fur were burned into his mind.

He was not yet finished with her, and though she'd been snatched from beneath his nose by Malcolm of Warwick, Henry was not about to stand down. Nay. He was *King*. It had been more than a se'ennight since he'd had his fill of her, and he would wait no longer. He would not be denied.

And so as the evening progressed and his court drank itself merry and stuffed itself with the extravagant meal he provided, Henry waited. He imbibed little, ate less, and watched. Eleanor, who sat next to him at the high table, coldly ignored him. Yet she was no happier with the events of the day than her husband.

And when Judith of Kentworth—now Lady of Warwick—stood at last to go to her chamber to prepare for her wedding night, Henry noticed. And when he saw that Malcolm of Warwick seemed not to notice or care—for he appeared well into his cups and wholly entertained by Hugh de Rigonier and a raucous game of dice—Henry rose.

The hall had begun to empty out, for it was late. Men-at-arms snored, their heads resting on the tables. Most of the ladies had sought their beds. But the bridegroom seemed in no hurry to do so. Canterbury was gone as well, Henry noted with relief. He and Becket had been close once upon a time, but since being named archbishop, Becket had become holier-than-thou.

Henry left the hall, eluding a trio of pages and one of his men-at-arms who meant to accompany him abovestairs. He was not bound for his own chamber this night.

The corridor that led to Judith's chamber was silent and empty. Henry's heart began to pound and his cock shifted in anticipation as he approached her door. Once inside, he could bolt them in and take his pleasure all the night. Warwick would have no choice but to allow it...and mayhap after this night, he would no longer want the woman.

Aye. That would be it. Henry would give her lands to Warwick and keep her for himself. He smiled, adjusting the weight of his cock inside the vee of his hose, knocked on the door, then shoved it open.

His anticipatory step across the threshold was halted by the sight which greeted him.

A well-lit chamber it was. And crowded. Henry's eyes bounced around like coins in a pouch as he saw Ludingdon, Mal Verne,

Salisbury, Castendown…*Canterbury*. Mayhap a dozen or more men, all of whom he knew, stood in the chamber. He could not speak and all feeling drained from his face and body, surely seeping into the floor.

"Good evening, my lord," said Ludingdon, stepping out from the crowd. His excessive height always annoyed Henry—and even more so in this instance.

"What is this?" the king blustered.

"'Tis obvious why you are here," Ludingdon—one of his most trusted barons, a long-term friend and confidante—replied. His voice was firm, his eyes dark and serious. "And methinks 'tis just as obvious why we have chosen to greet you thus. There is not one of us who wishes to believe our king and liege would help himself to our wives or daughters at his whim. Thus, we are certain the purpose of your visit this night is to extend your felicitations to Lady Judith. And for no other reason…despite any past…arrangement…you may have had. Is that not so, my lord?"

Henry looked around the chamber, meeting the cold, steady eyes of every man there. Every one of them were important, powerful men. Vital to him and to the stability of his kingdom. They swore fealty and brought armies and fought his wars and paid his rents. And in this, he recognized, they were united against him.

If, in this small matter they could unite against him…what more could they do on a grander scale if they were angered and betrayed?

Henry was no fool. He was not the most powerful landowner and ruler in all of Christendom for no reason.

"Indeed," he said then, making a grand gesture that encompassed the chamber. "If the lady is within, I would be delighted to extend my congratulations to her on her new marital status."

With those words, it was as if a signal had been made. The crowd of barons parted, revealing the bed on which Judith sat. She looked at Henry, her expression remote and cool, and bowed her head regally. Just like a queen.

"Thank you, my lord," she told him. "I am honored."

There was a moment then, when Henry nearly allowed his fury and desires to overcome his rational mind, but he quickly subdued it. "Blessings to you and Warwick, and many children to you," he said.

And then, with one last cold scan around the chamber to look at each one of his audacious barons, Henry turned and left the room.

He knew when the battle—and the war—had been lost.

~*~

JUDITH HAD been nervous while awaiting the king's expected arrival, but after her champions quit the chamber, her apprehension grew.

When a firm knock came once more on the door, she felt her belly drop alarmingly. *My wedding night. My husband.*

She moved slowly to the door, opening it with cold fingers, and was relieved to find Maris there. Behind her was Tabby, and behind *her* was a lineup of pages and serfs with a bath.

"Oh, bless you," she told Maris and Tabby. "I have felt so out of sorts, being wed in such a state." She gestured to her garb, still the same simple bliaut she'd donned early this morrow when she expected to remain the whole day in her chamber.

"'Tis a shame you were forced to marry in that gown," Maris told her, wrinkling her nose in tacit agreement that her attire was, indeed, an unfortunate matter. "But there was no help for it. But now we shall prepare you for a beautiful wedding night. Your groom has agreed to give us no more than a half hour, so we must be quick."

Judith was grateful not only for the companionship, but for the flurry of activity. It took her mind off Malcolm's imminent arrival and made her feel less as if she were waiting like a lamb being brought to slaughter.

Maris must have sensed her apprehension, for shortly after she and Tabby helped Judith from the bath, she said to the maid, "Go you now—take your small zoo with you. A wedding bower is no place for a dog and cat, methinks. You may attend your mistress on the morrow. But not too early, mind you."

Tabby nodded and did as she was bid while Maris helped Judith dry. Her hair was washed earlier, so they'd pinned it up for the bath. But now Maris helped her take it down and let it fall freely about her shoulders, over her breasts and to her hips.

When the chamber door closed behind Tabby, Maris offered Judith a small bundle. "Since you did not have a pretty gown for today, I bethought you would like something for this night."

Giving her friend a grateful smile, Judith unwrapped a fine, shimmering swath of blue cloth. She held it up and saw that not only did the light filter through it, but she could see her fingers from the other side. It was very nearly sheer, shot with gold and silver threads fashioned into intricately embroidered flowers. Little more than a loose, flowing tunic that skimmed the floor, the gown's shoulders were gathered together by palm-sized clusters of topazes, garnets and sapphires set in ornate gold.

"Oh! But this is too much," Judith gasped. "Why, it must have cost a fortune! Maris, I cannot accept this!"

But her friend was shaking her head. "Nay, my love. The fabric is my wedding gift to you, but the jeweled brooches are a bride's gift from your husband." Her eyes gleamed with satisfaction. "It shows the extent to which Warwick values you."

Judith felt her cheeks flush hot. "I am not so certain of that," she murmured, suddenly nervous again. But she couldn't take her eyes off the fine, gossamer fabric and the heavy, glittering clasps.

Maris wisely chose to say nothing about her comment. Instead, she unraveled Judith from the drying cloth and helped her into the sleeping gown. "You will entrance him," she told her, surveying the bride critically. "He will be beside himself when he sees you."

"Oh," Judith said, suddenly no longer able to keep quiet. "I am so nervous! Why am I so nervous? I am no shy virgin, that is sure." These last words came out choppy and bitter, and she looked away in shame.

Maris took her hand and squeezed it. "But of course you are nervous. Surely there has never been a bride who is not so on her wedding night. But I tell you true…you are a virgin in the true sense of the word." When Judith would have interrupted, she *tsk*ed and shook her head. "Nay, listen you. 'Tis a whole world different lying with a man whom you love than one you do not."

Judith looked at her with wide eyes. "How…why do you say I love him?"

Her friend rolled her eyes and *tsk*ed again. "'Tis there for anyone to see who might look. And that, dear Judith, is the most wonderful gift of all. Enjoy your husband, for I trow he will do the same with you. If he does not, the man is addled!"

Before Judith could respond, another knock sounded at the door. Firm, spare, and yet demanding.

"He is here. Our half hour has passed." Maris stood and patted Judith's hand. "Have no fear. All will be well." With a swirl of gown and quick, energetic steps, she went to the door and opened it. "Good evening, my lord. And good night."

Suddenly Maris was gone and Judith and Malcolm were alone.

The door closed with a quiet scrape, and the latch clunked into place. Judith's new husband walked into the room, his head nearly brushing the ceiling. The chamber seemed to shrink, becoming very small and warm.

Malcolm turned to look at Judith, who was still sitting on the bed with a lap filled with gossamer blue fabric and fiery-red hair, and he stilled. His gaze, heavy and hot, slid over her slowly, raising little shivers on her skin as if he actually touched her. She saw him draw in a deep breath, then he released it in a long, low exhale.

"Good evening, my lady wife," he said at last, cutting into the silence even Judith wasn't certain how to break. "I trust you fared well during the king's visit?"

"Aye," she replied, unable to take her eyes from his broad shoulders and chiseled lips. "Thank you for…arranging such a warm reception for him."

Malcolm's lips tightened as he unpinned the heavy brooch at his throat and put aside his cloak. "'Twas Ludingdon who insisted on handling the welcome, as I was forbidden by himself and Mal Verne to be present at all. Mayhap you wish to get into bed?" He sat on Judith's stool, his movements stiff and slow, and began to work off his knee-high boots.

"Do you not wish me to assist you?" she asked, already sliding off the bed. Her nightgown slid and shimmered lightly against her bare skin, rippling around her as she made to kneel at his feet. "Gambert isn't here tonight. Of course." She sounded breathy, even to her ears.

"Nay," he said quickly, almost sharply. "I can manage on my own. Are you not…*chilled*…in…that?" His voice was gruff.

"'Tis a summer's night! Of course I am not chilled." She stood in front of him, their faces nearly level, for he was sitting. Suddenly she remembered, and blushed at her lack of manners. "Oh, Malcolm…thank you for the jewels. They are beautiful, and beyond anything I could have imagined. I've never had anything so lovely in my life."

"Nor have I," he murmured, reaching to touch the end of one of her curls where it rested against her arm. Then he withdrew his hand and said, "They are your colors. The blue of your eyes, the gold and fire of your hair. Now, get in bed, Judith." His voice was clipped, and as she turned to obey, he bent to untie his cross-garters.

She slid under the coverings and watched him unwind the garters, then pull off his fine tunic. The *sherte* beneath molded to his muscular shoulders and upper arms, falling flat over his belly— unlike that of the king, whose clothing rounded out a small bit at the stomach. Judith felt her heart begin to pound at the thought of seeing…and touching…her husband's bare torso, which she'd had the opportunity to admire in the training yard. A flush of warmth had her cheeks heating and a little pleasant squiggle in her belly.

Mayhap Maris was right. This would be utterly different than lying with the king. Judith smiled to herself as Malcolm extinguished the candles on the wall, leaving only the small fire as illumination.

He stood at the end of the bed near the window and pulled off his *sherte*, leaving him clad only in hose, now sagging without the cross-garters. As he laid the *sherte* neatly over a trunk, the bit of moonlight able to slide through the narrow window cast a silvery glow over his nude chest and sleek arms. She could see the slabs of muscle, the way they shifted and slid as he walked over to look out the window.

Judith realized her heart was thudding—but rather than apprehension, it was anticipation that caused her mouth to dry and her belly to flutter. And yet, he made no move to come to the bed. He stood, staring out the window, into darkness.

"Malcolm?" she asked after what seemed like a long while. "Do you not come to bed?" Her heart was in her throat. What was wrong? What bridegroom would delay entering the marriage bed?

His shoulders moved; she saw the subtle lift and slight drawing together. "Go to sleep, Judith."

Her heart dropped and she went cold and light-headed with confusion...and fear. Was he regretting their marriage already? Or....

Was it her? Had her *affaire* with the king despoiled her so much that Malcolm was repulsed by the thought of coupling with her? Of taking the king's leavings? They were wed and he'd never even kissed her, she realized with a sudden, nauseating shock. Even today, at the end of their wedding, he'd barely touched her lips with his.

But she'd sworn she'd seen desire in her husband's eyes...even just now, when she stood in front of him. The fire behind had surely outlined her figure beneath the light fabric of her gown. He'd noticed. She'd felt his attention, slow and heavy, as it caressed her. *Surely* he'd noticed, surely that was why his breathing had changed, his voice had tightened. She was no stranger to a man's expressions of lust.

So why?

It was not in Judith's nature to remain quiet, to wonder and worry. She had to know, even if the knowledge was painful. For she surely wouldn't sleep until she did. "You do not mean to consummate our union, then? We are to be wed in name only?"

Once again, she saw him still, his silhouette freezing in the moonlit window. He raised one hand and settled it on the wall next to the opening, leaning even more into the night air. He tipped his face up and she caught her breath at the beauty of his profile, glazed in silver. His torso expanded as he drew in a deep breath.

"I bethought you would wish for…a time of reprieve. I would not follow in the steps of the king and…force you into my bed."

"Force me?" Judith's voice cracked with surprise. "But you are my husband. You have the right—"

"Aye. I have the *right*." His voice was hard, as if he spoke from between an unmoving jaw. "As did the king so believe. But I would not exercise that right merely because I can, Judith. Now, I tell you, woman…go to sleep."

The tension that had flooded her drained away as if a cork had been removed. She was out of the bed in a swirl of hair and gown, moving toward him even before he turned at the sound.

"Judith," he snapped, looking back out the window. "Do not try me. Get back in bed."

Of course she ignored him, continuing to approach until she was close enough that the edge of her night rail brushed his legs. "'Tis true the king forced me to lay with him," she said, resting her hand on his bare arm as she stood just behind him. His bicep was hard with muscle, and warm, and she slid her palm along it in a soft caress. "But you are my husband, and I would welcome you in my bed—right or no right."

He'd stopped breathing and she felt the faintest quiver from beneath his skin. His muscles were taut and still. Encouraged and emboldened, she settled both hands on the tops of his shoulders— higher than her own eyes—and slid her palms along the broad, warm width, then lightly down over his shoulder blades. Tiny little bumps erupted in the wake of her touch, and she felt another deep tremble from inside him.

"If you are willing…."

"Aye," she said, curving her arms around his waist, pressing herself into him from behind. His hard, flat belly leapt and shifted beneath her touch, and she splayed her hands wide over its muscular ridges, tickling the patch of hair that grew there. Her breasts pressed into his back, her cheek rested on his spine, just between the shoulder blades. His heart slammed beneath her ear.

Then Malcolm released a great gust of breath and gently but firmly removed her hands from his waist. With a smooth movement, he drew her around in front of him, and before she could speak or even think, he had her angled up into the edge of the window, eased against the wall, kissing her.

His large hands cupped her chin and curved around her neck as he settled in, covering her mouth with his. He was hot and hard, his lips mobile and tender, easing hers open to kiss her with deep, slick movements. He ate at the corner of her mouth, delved deep with a strong, thrusting tongue, smoothed the pads of his thumbs over her cheeks.

Judith lost sense of time and place, vaguely aware of a cool breeze over her bare shoulder and the harsh stone edge along her back as heat enveloped her, rushing through her like hot liquid. She had her hands up in his silky hair, bracketing his strong neck as she took what he gave her—their mouths sliding and nibbling and molding together. She could hardly find a breath, hardly cared to draw it in as he moved to nuzzle her throat and the side of her neck.

She sagged against the wall, her head lolling to the side as he drew the long, heavy swath of her hair away. A fresh breeze from the window caressed her warm, sensitive skin before he pressed his lips to her again, his mouth hot and sensual, sliding along the length of her neck. Judith was aware of her ragged breathing, of the soft, panting moans she made as she settled her hands on the solid planes of his chest. He was warm and smooth, hair- and scar-roughened, and yet sleek with muscle. Such muscle…so hard and firm and powerful.

Malcolm had settled the side of a hip against her belly, holding her firmly in place as he devoured her mouth, tasted her throat and nuzzled beneath her ears. But now, with a soft, deep groan, he shifted, sliding himself and his hose-covered erection fully against her. Judith shivered, a bolt of desire stabbing her deep in the belly when she felt the hard, immense bulge pressing against her abdomen. She was flushed, damp and hot everywhere, her body awake and alive.

She arched a little, pushing her hips against him, rolling her belly against his erection, shifting so one of his thighs fit between hers. He stilled, his hands tightening over her shoulders, then slid down to cover her breasts, crinkling the gossamer fabric against her hot skin. Her nipples were hard and ready, and he molded the material in a rough, textured caress over them. Then she felt something loosen, a soft, tearing sound…and her night rail slipped away, falling to the floor with the soft clink of metal and gemstone.

Once again Malcolm paused, his hands, rough with calluses and scars, settling on her arms as if to hold her in place. He looked down and dragged in a rough breath as he traced the tip of one nipple with a fingertip. Judith tilted her head and saw the silvery moonlight outlining her high, ivory breasts and the dark valley between them, then filtering onto the darker, hair-dusted skin of his bare torso. She trembled at his light touch, pleasure and anticipation wending its way south.

"Judith," he whispered, his expression intent—almost reverent—as he gathered her naked breasts into two large, dark hands. "I would take you to bed."

"I would go," she said, then arced closer to him as he raked his thumbs gently over her straining nipples, sliding over the very tips of them in tiny, delicate swirls. She shivered, sighed, smiled as pleasure rolled through her, down to the full, swollen place she rode against his thigh. He bent to kiss one of her breasts, his tongue sliding over and around its sensitive, engorged nipple. Hot curls of desire undulated through her, throbbing and pounding and wanting some sort of release.

Then she was airborne, hoisted and gathered up into strong, warm arms. The bed appeared beneath her nearly at once, and she looked up as he stood over her. A dark figure, outlined by the moonlight from behind, shoulders wide and square, hair mussed from her own hands.

Judith realized belatedly that she was completely naked in front of him, and for a moment, modesty and nervousness rushed through her as she lay splayed on the blankets. Malcolm's gaze was riveted on her as he shoved down his hose then eased onto the bed with sharp, impatient movements.

The bed shifted under his weight, tipping Judith into his long, solid body even as he pulled her close. Now she felt the insistent nudge of his cock, hard and warm against her thigh. His hands seemed to be everywhere, his fingers sliding between her legs, parting them gently...then finding her hot, damp center. Judith gasped in surprise at the sensations—bold, sharp, luscious—as he touched her in the intimate place, his fingers slipping and exploring urgently.

She quivered and shook, her eyes closed, her skin slick and hot as her breathing turned to desperate panting. "*Mal*," she whispered once, in a low, desperate sigh. He made some guttural sound of response, then pulled his hand away and shifted into position over her. He settled between her legs, which had fallen open, ready—oh, very ready—for him. His hips were sleek and strong, his thighs like tree trunks...and his erection incredible.

"Oh," she whispered, her eyes closing again as he pressed into her. She arched a little to help, then her eyes flew open wide when he slid all the way home. "*Oh*," she said again...but this time it was more of a moan. A satisfied moan.

Malcolm muttered something she couldn't hear through the roar of lust sweeping her as he moved, thrusting long and deep in an urgent rhythm. Judith was unaware of anything but the sensations building, flowing through her like a fiery liquid...centered at her core and rolling through her limbs.

It was like nothing she'd ever felt before. Nothing like the twinges of pleasure, the little pangs, the quiet insistence. This sensation was deep and lush and intense, and it grew, billowed...hot and liquid and seemed to charge through her body...then shatter.

He gave a sharp groan just as her body exploded. Judith cried out as pleasure and satiation undulated through her, her heart racing, her breath wild, tears trickling from her eyes.

Malcolm arched over her, shuddering his own release, propped on an arm so he wouldn't crush her. She glanced up to see his eyes closed, his face taut with effort, then Judith collapsed into a puddle of skin and bones, still trembling and shaking, hot and breathless... satisfied. *Never*, was her only coherent thought. Never before.

It was as if she'd saved this ecstatic moment forever...as if she'd been waiting for it, teased and titillated, but never seized it, never knew how to grasp it, until now. She lay there for a moment, basking…waiting for her body to come back to itself. Then, as Mal rolled over and off, separating from her, she brushed away the tears with the palms of her hands and lay there, drawing in deep, shuddering breaths.

Never, she thought to herself again. Never before had she been so pleasured and sated. Never had she thought it could be so *good*.

Malcolm was moving—up and off the bed. Judith opened her eyes; but he was merely lifting the coverings to slide inside. Before she could gather up the strength to move, he picked her up and gently deposited her under the blankets.

Then, without another word, he climbed in on his side of the bed.

TWELVE

MALCOLM LAY next to his bride. His body still hummed, his breathing was just slipping back into normal. His muscles trembled and shuddered gently beneath his skin, little twitches of the orgasm continuing to lick through him.

He should have been snoring by now, easing into the paradise of slumber, empty of tension and stress, fulfilled after enjoying his new wife...but nay. Though his body still basked in the afterward, his thoughts were cold and heavy. He'd seen the tears. They poured from her eyes as she lay beneath him, her face contorted, her eyes closed.

Fool. You are no better than Henry to use her so.

He'd come out of his stupor of lust and desire, hardly remembering what had occurred. Had he hurt her? Been too rough? But earlier, Judith had seemed to be enjoying his touch—her head tipped back to give him access to her neck and throat; soft, panting breaths...her fingers, curling into his hair, around his shoulders, his arms...those proud, glorious breasts, bathed in moonlight... tantalizing with their jutting nipples, perfect in weight and shape.

Malcolm remembered all of those things—the sweet taste of her, at last, after a decade of awareness and desire...the softness of skin, the shiver of pleasure, the softness of her curves...the sensual way she'd pressed herself against him at the window.

What had happened? Had he misunderstood, misread her desire? Was she remembering her time with the king and equating the two men? Mal went cold at the thought.

There'd been no mistaking the tears—they were so profuse she'd had to wipe them away. She hadn't looked at Malcolm after. Now she slept, curled up in a ball under the covers where he'd placed her. That river of fire-gold hair was spread out over her pillow and his, all but covering one tempting breast.

She was as ripe and beautiful as he'd always believed. Lush, sleek, sweet. Already Mal felt himself stirring again. He'd had only a sample—a mere taste of his wife.

His *wife*....

He could scarcely believe it. He was wed to Judith of Kentworth. What had been inconceivable only a month ago had come to pass, and he had gained a prize beyond expectation.

But at what price? Mal felt the niggle of guilt he'd tried to subdue for a se'ennight. He'd fairly forced her into wedding him. She tried to renege, tried to break their agreement. An honorable man would have allowed it to happen…mayhap.

She despises the king. And wedding Malcolm was an escape from a dangerous and untenable situation.

Or so he told himself. Judith didn't want to remain the king's concubine or the queen's servant. It would kill her, if one of them didn't do so first.

He proposed the perfect arrangement. She gained freedom, and the ability to return to her beloved Lilyfare, and Malcolm gained… *her*.

He'd very nearly convinced himself of this—that it was the right thing, that it was the only way to protect her. And then Gavin of Mal Verne arrived at Clarendon, coming in response to Malcolm's letter.

"You do not have to wed her," Gavin told Malcolm, his tones serious, his dark gaze probing. "Though I cannot thank you enough for making the offer, and doing what you can to protect her. I did not know…." Gavin was obviously disgusted with the situation—but also with himself, for not taking better care of his cousin's interests.

"No one knew," Mal told him.

"She could have written me," Gavin said, shaking his head. "But now—I can take her from here. I will extricate her from the king. You do not have to wed her to save her, Mal….Unless that is truly your wish."

"I would wed her," Malcolm told him after the slightest hesitation. He did not wish to appear too desperate. "If she will have me."

At that, Gavin smiled with genuine pleasure, sending a bounce of relief through Mal—for if his friend had any doubt of their match, Malcolm would have stepped aside. "Felicitations, then, Warwick," Gavin said, thumping him on the back fiercely. "I wish you the best of luck taming my wild cousin."

With that, Mal's spirits had lifted. He was exuberant as the pieces fell into place and at last, later that very day, Judith became his. Even the king was thwarted after his visit to her chamber this night. Dirick was confident the king was no longer a threat, for the unification of the barons and their challenge had subdued him.

But now…Mal could only wonder. Had Gavin *insisted* she accept him? Had she done so only to escape the king? And to once again see her beloved Lilyfare? Did she already regret not finding another way out of her conundrum?

But you are my husband and I would welcome you in my bed—right or no right.

She'd lured him to her, breaking through his shield of honor, coaxing him to couple with her. But now she wept over it. Had she done so, had she forced herself to accept him only to ensure a consummation of their marriage? So they would be truly wed, and even the king couldn't cleave them apart?

As he lay there—staring at the canopy fixed to the bed posts, feeling the warmth radiating from her, smelling the intoxicating scent of their coupling, still among the sheets—Mal wondered why he even cared what was her intent. She was his wife. Just as it had been with Sarah, Judith's duty was to give him an heir or two and to warm his bed while doing so. She would be chatelaine of their lands if she knew how to manage an estate; if not, he could employ a steward.

But as he'd told Judith when they went hunting, he cared not whether his wife had any other pleasant attributes—if she could converse, or if she were comely or if she had any other skills as Lady Maris did. It was the way of the world, of the matches between ladies and great lords like himself. So if Judith was unhappy with her decision, why should it matter to him?

Because you coerced her. You made it near impossible for her to deny you.

The small gnawing in his chest bothered Mal and he shoved away the taunting voice in his head. Judith had agreed to marry him and now she was his wife. 'Twas done.

He would do his part and take her back to Lilyfare. Beyond that….

Malcolm rubbed a hand roughly over his forehead, then let it rest, covering his eyes. *It matters not why she wed me. She is mine now.*

~*~

THOUGH HIS thoughts were heavy, Malcolm eventually fell asleep. But he didn't sleep long, for it had been four years since he'd had a wife, and even then, he and Sarah rarely shared the same bed. So when he felt the nudge of something against him, he bolted awake with the same intensity he would have done if sleeping on a blanket in the forest.

But this, he realized instantly, was a much more pleasurable situation. For the brush of soft, warm, sweet-smelling skin against him was from his wife. No sooner had this information penetrated his brain than his body responded. Quickly and fully.

And then Mal had no other coherent thought beyond touching, tasting…taking. He moved Judith's hair out of the way and eased himself up behind her, as if he were a large hand cupping her body. Her arse curved into his lap, brushing against his cock, which was already full and throbbing. But he took his time, sliding his hand around to cover her breast, letting his manhood slip along the

warm juncture of her legs. She shifted and shivered, half asleep…
gave a soft sigh…and he felt it when she became fully aware, for she
stiffened against him.

At first he feared she meant to push him away. It was too
dark to see her expression, but Mal wasn't about to be denied. His
wedding night, his wife.…

He kissed her shoulder, slipping his tongue out to slide over the
delicate muscle and tendon there as he nibbled her sweet, salty skin.
She trembled a little, but she didn't move away or resist. His leg slid
between hers from behind as he gently fondled her breast, finding
the nipple there and teasing it into a firm shape. A little quiver
rushing through her gave him the encouragement to slide his hand
down between her parted legs.

When he felt her soft, damp center—wonderfully slick and
hot—when she gave a soft gasp and vibrated softly against him, he
nearly lost control of himself right then and there. The subtle scent
of her musk mixed with his made him feel heady and desperate, and
he would wait no longer. With a swift, sure move, he pulled himself
up and shifted Judith toward him so she was on her back and he
was poised over her. In the dim light, he could see her eyes were
open and her lips were gently parted.

She murmured something; it could have been his name, but it
wasn't a demand or a protest. Nothing to stop him, nothing to keep
himself from easing between her thighs. Nothing to keep him from
sliding into her warm, damp sheath.

His breath left him in a gust, and he began to move. Judith
moaned beneath him, a titillating sound. One that sharpened
his desire. She had her hands on his chest, planted there with her
fingers curling up over his shoulders, holding him in place as he
moved, in and out, faster and faster. In the back of his mind, he
tried to remember to hold back, to keep himself from driving her
into the head of the bed. Judith cried out, her fingers digging into
his upper arms, her hips slamming up to meet his. The very sound
sent him over, into the rocking waves of orgasm. Malcolm thrust
home, straining with effort as he poured every last bit of himself
into her.

My God…. It was half prayer, half curse…and he collapsed next to her, his body wrung out, his mind empty, as if it had been shattered. A warm, rich contentment settled over him like a blanket, and he gathered her in his arms, pulling her against his chest.

And then he stilled, the last bit of contentment sliding away… for he could feel it: her face was wet. With tears.

~*~

WHEN MAL opened his eyes again, it was past dawn. The summer sunlight poured into the chamber, bathing it in a soft, yellow glow.

He realized with surprise that not only had he slept for several hours, but that Judith had slipped from the bed without disturbing him. *One night as a husband again in a warm bed, and already I grow soft and slow.*

Mal pulled himself to a sitting position just in time to see his nude wife rising from a crouch, having slid the chamberpot back into place. She turned in a swirl of hair and bounce of breast. When she saw him awake and watching her, she squeaked in surprise.

"Oh," Judith said, and then her face turned a charming pink. So did the upper part of her torso, over her freckled shoulders and breasts, and he noticed her perky nipples with delight. "Good morrow, my lord husband." Her voice went a little husky on the word 'husband,' and Mal wasn't certain what to make of that.

"Good morrow, Lady Warwick," he managed to reply, realizing with a sudden burst of pride that he was uncommonly pleased to have given her his name. It was, however, nearly a miracle that any words escaped his suddenly dry mouth and tight throat. For what he'd seen of his bride's lovely body in the moonlight was naught compared to a full sunlit view, with her slender, ivory limbs bathed in golden warmth and the blaze of light setting her hair to fire. It was no surprise the king had been obsessed, he thought darkly.

"I expect Tabby is waiting outside the door," she said. "Or nearby." Her words almost ran together, as if she were nervous or unsettled. "Shall I call her in? Would you like a bath or are you in need of…aught? Shall we break our fast?"

"I have a hunger for aught other than bread and cheese," he said, patting the bed next to him. "Climb back here, Judith." Mal was aware that, despite the throbbing of his cock and the hot anticipation thrumming through his body, he had an underlying apprehension…a niggle of concern. Would she agree, or would she make some excuse?

To his relief, Judith smiled bashfully, her cheeks growing pink again, and climbed back onto the bed. That in itself pleased him, and yet was cause for confusion—for she was no shy virgin.

But she was here, and with him, and he easily pushed those concerns away as he reached for her. She came willingly, and even—to his surprise and great delight, as well as near embarrassment—closed her fingers around his great, stiff cock. Her firm touch nearly sent him over the edge before he even began, and it was only with great control that he saved himself from spilling his seed so easily.

"Not so fast," he muttered, sliding a hand between her thighs. She was warm and full and moist, and though it didn't seem possible, he grew harder. Her breasts, dusted with golden and amber freckles, were lovely in full daylight, and he took his time kissing and sucking on pert nipples, teasing them with his tongue until they were tight and sharp. Judith curled her fingers into his hair as if to keep him in position, making delicious little panting moans and shifting her hips as if impatient for him to join with her.

And though he fully intended to give her much more attention, before he knew it she was guiding him between her legs and he was thrusting home. She writhed and moaned beneath him, shifting and shuddering. Just as he groaned out his release, there was an imperious knock on the door.

Praise God, he thought, peeling open his eyes after the passionate storm had waned. Judith was already scrambling away from him, for the peremptory knock had continued.

"It cannot be Tabby," she muttered, reaching for a blanket to wrap about herself. "She wouldn't dare—"

"Open the door in the name of the queen!" demanded a voice from the other side.

Malcolm sprang from the bed at that, the rest of his pleasure whisked away like the blanket Judith had just pulled. "I will answer it," he told her, grabbing a wad of cloth to hold in front of him for basic modesty as he brushed past her to the door. He caught a glimpse of her expression, pinched and pale, and wondered whether it was due to their visitor…or to their morning activities. She'd leapt away and out of bed so quickly he hadn't been able to see whether she'd cried this time or nay.

Ignoring those thoughts for now, he opened the door. "Is there a message from the queen?" he demanded of the page who stood there with one of the queen's men-at-arms. Behind them was the maid Tabatha, who looked terrified. It could have been because of the interruption—for fear she would take the blame—or because of Mal himself: large, naked, and furious.

"Aye. Lady Judith of Kentworth is required to attend her majesty the queen immediately. I shall escort her," said the man. He looked at Mal and an uneasy expression filtered over his face, for Mal took no pains to hide his feelings about his wife being summoned from her marriage bed to attend the woman who'd fairly tortured her.

"I shall escort her," Malcolm told him coolly. "As her majesty surely knows, you have interrupted our wedding night and we have not yet risen nor broken our fast. Pray give my honor and good wishes to the queen and inform her I shall bring my wife to her within the half hour."

"Aye," replied the man-at-arms, his eyes darting from Mal to the chamber behind him, then back again to the livid man in the doorway. "I shall bring the message."

Malcolm would have slammed the door to punctuate his opinion of the man but for Tabatha, who looked as if she would prefer to be cowering in a corner. "*You.* Your lady will be in need of you anon. Go find aught to break our fast, and call for my squire. He must attend me at once."

"Aye, my lord," she whispered, and hurried off.

When Mal closed the door and turned back to the chamber, he found Judith looking at him with wide eyes and raised brows.

"Well, then, my lord," she said, still holding the blanket. Despite her demure position, her words were tart. "If you continue to speak to my maid in that manner, you will frighten her to death—or at the least, cause her to fear being in your presence. And that will make me quite unhappy, for 'tis no easy task to find a competent, trustworthy tiring woman who doesn't faint when encountering her lord."

Mal glowered at her, but gave a brief nod. "Very well." His attention slipped to her long, loose hair, falling nearly to her waist, the curve of her collarbone and the mounds of her breasts, only half-hidden by her wrap. *Mine.* He drew in a deep breath. "You heard the summons?"

"Aye," she replied, her shoulders and arms tensing. "And that you will accompany me. Thank you, my lord."

"Malcolm," he said, his voice tight. "I am Malcolm to you when we are private."

"Very well, Malcolm," she replied, and her mouth seemed to relax, almost smiling.

There was a knock again—this one easier and less demanding. But he went to it, flinging the door open to find Tabatha standing there. She squeaked, but collected herself and gave a brief bow. "I have aught to break your fast," she said as he saw Gambert behind her. "Your squire had already anticipated your needs, and I came upon him on my way to the kitchen," she added, gesturing to the bundle he carried.

"Very good. Gambert, wait in the antechamber whilst my lady is dressed," Mal told him, stepping aside for Tabatha to move past him into the main chamber. He closed the door after her and took the food from Gambert. "Now. Go you and speak to Nevril. Lady Judith and I will be leaving Clarendon as quickly as possible. Have the maid pack what my lady will need immediately, and send for her master-at-arms. Some of you will come with us, and the maid and others will follow with all of her trunks."

The sooner we quit this place, the happier I'll be.

-*-

THE HEAVY double doors to the queen's chamber loomed in front of Judith like a hangman's scaffold. As they approached, the two men-at-arms who guarded the entrance drew them wide.

She drew in a deep breath and willed her palms to stay dry and her knees strong and sturdy. Malcolm's solid presence behind gave her support as she walked over the threshold into Eleanor's chamber.

"Your majesty," Judith said, sweeping into a curtsy. Mal bowed to the queen, but even Judith, who could not see him as he was slightly behind her, could sense the underlying insolence in his gesture.

"My lady queen," he said as he straightened.

"I did not expect to see you, Warwick," said Eleanor. Her voice was frosty, and the chill was echoed in her posture and expression. "I called for Judith to attend me. Not her husband." She fairly spat the last word.

The queen sat on a large chair at one end of the chamber, which, as Judith took a moment to notice, had no other occupants. A wriggle of nervousness clutched her belly as she recalled the last time she'd been called privately to the queen's presence.

"I thought it expedient that I escort her to your chambers. To ensure she didn't lose her way, or be otherwise circumvented." Malcolm's voice was supremely polite and sincere.

"Excellent thinking, Warwick," the queen replied. "And now that you have completed your mission, you may leave us."

"Under the circumstances, my lady, I would prefer to remain present," Malcolm said, shocking Judith so that she hardly contained a gasp at his audacity. He moved to stand very near her, his hand resting possessively on her shoulder.

"You may wait outside," Eleanor said, her voice steely. "What I have to say to your wife is for her ears only. But do not fear. She will be returned to you momentarily, and intact."

Malcolm looked at Judith, and she read question in his eyes. He would stay if she wanted him to, disobeying the queen—and that knowledge made her heart swell large and full inside her. "I would hear what the queen desires to say," she told him. "If you would wait without, I will come to you when we are finished."

"Very well, my lady," he said, bowing first to Judith, and only then to the queen in another show of power. He turned smoothly and strode from the chamber, closing the door behind him.

"If he was not such a close friend of Ludingdon and Mal Verne, I would have him jailed for such insolence," Eleanor said when Judith returned her attention to the queen. "For more than one reason." Her eyes were sharp with banked fury, yet Judith, who knew the queen as well as anyone, saw a deeply buried vulnerability. She felt a pang of guilt, for she knew that, at least in part, she had caused some of that pain.

"What did you wish to say to me, my lady?" she asked, wanting to finish the interview as quickly as possible.

Eleanor's eyes narrowed. At first, she didn't speak, but after a long moment of looking at Judith with that cold gaze, she said, "I see that you've healed from your illness. Just in time to wed."

Judith kept her expression blank as she replied, "Aye, my lady. Nearly all of the marks are gone from my skin."

"How fortuitous." Once again, the queen waited before speaking. Then when she did, her voice was filled with venom. "So you have chosen to marry. To bond yourself to a man. To become his chatelaine, his servant, his property. Do you love him, or is it that you wish merely to be quit of this court? To make an escape?"

Judith swallowed but remained silent. Did the queen truly believe she'd give her more ammunition for her vengeance?

"You will answer me, and truthfully, Judith," commanded the queen.

"He seems a good man. And I have come to miss Lilyfare very much. It has been more than five years since I have seen it."

"Pish. How long do you think it's been since I have been to Aquitaine or Poitiers? The lands will always be there—and you have a good steward. But…you and Warwick. Methinks you have some affection for him. And some day you will regret accepting his offer, selling yourself to him. Mayhap sooner rather than later."

The queen stood and began to pace with short, hard, rapid steps. "If I could have remained unwed, I should have done so. But nay—I was married to a prude of a man, a living saint who sought to impose his own piety on me and all in his court. Then, rather than being abducted and forced to wed a man I could not stomach, I chose my second husband. Now I am tied to him who I once loved and trusted—and who has shown me little regard in the last years. Despite the fact that I brought him wealth and power, and that I bear his children, and help him rule his lands. This will be my last child with him," Eleanor said fiercely, cupping her round belly. "He will not find my bed again. Henry has betrayed me for the last time."

Much of what Eleanor said, Judith knew, was spoken in anger and hurt—for Henry had always treated his queen with respect and listened to her advice and thoughts—at least in relation to his rule. She acted as chancellor for him whenever he was absent. But the king's regard, Judith realized with a sharp pang of guilt, was not extended when it came to affection and love. Mayhap the king appreciated his queen for her lands and her astuteness in managing them as well as his own, but he did not show her his love and respect in the bedchamber.

"Oh, Henry shall see the wrath of a woman. And soon. Does he not know I have his sons close in my heart, and I in theirs? And so 'twill always be. One of them shall be king some day—mayhap sooner than my husband wishes."

Her mind whirling, Judith did her best to follow the queen's tirade. Prince Henry was eleven, and Prince Richard was only nine.... It would be years before either of them could lead a revolt, which seemed to be what she was implying. *Dear God, the queen is speaking to me of* treason!

"You were a friend to me, Judith of Kentworth," Eleanor continued. Her voice had quieted and she had stopped her pacing, but was turned away. "I trusted you, and I wanted only the best for you. What I could not have—freedom. Independence from a man's rule. Why do you think I never allowed you to leave me, or to wed? Because I knew only heartache and pain awaits a wife. I sought to protect you of it, to keep you from such a fate. You could have remained with me for all time, independent and a woman of your own."

"My lady," Judith said, her heart squeezing with guilt. "I am so sorry for the pain I have caused you. I would never have done such a thing had it been in my power to refuse."

The queen made a sound of disdain. She turned, straight and proud, and looked at Judith with eyes that glittered with anger and unshed tears. "I loved Henry once. You may love your husband as well, but know if you do, 'tis naught but a curse. For you will find only pain on that path. Pray to God you ne'er look upon the *last* woman he takes to his bed—for there will be one. The one he would keep forever. The one he would set you aside for if it didn't mean giving up half his lands." Her face appeared brittle, and with a start, Judith realized Eleanor was speaking of *her*.

"Nay, your majesty, I do not believe that," Judith said. Her insides felt as if ice flushed through them. "Not I. He would always return to you."

"So I once believed—anyway, I will not allow it," Eleanor snapped. "He will never touch me again. And know you this, Judith…if you had not been such a friend to me all these years, I would not have been so forgiving of your misdeeds. Now, leave this court with your new husband. And allow me never to set my eyes on you again. And pray that *you* must never look upon the woman your husband loves."

"Aye, my lady," Judith whispered. Her heart pounded and her belly swished unpleasantly. She could hardly swallow. "And God be with you on the rest of this pregnancy."

She turned to go, walking with a straight spine and firm chin to the door. Just as she reached it, the queen spoke once more. Her words were cold and flat.

"If you had come to me at once, Judith, I would have stopped it immediately. Henry would never have touched you again."

‑*‑

THE QUEEN'S words echoed in Judith's mind as she exited the courtroom. *"I would have stopped it immediately."*

Was it true? All at once, she felt chilly and lightheaded. Could the queen have intervened? Could she have saved Judith from the horrors of the last fortnight? *How could I have been so foolish? Of course she would have helped me.* What a fool she'd been!

"Judith."

With a start, she looked up to find Malcolm in front of her, a dark expression on his face. "Is all well?" he asked, taking her arm and casting a quick, dark glance at the hovering guards.

"Let us away from here," she replied from between lips that hardly moved.

Her husband fell into step with her, taming his usually long strides to match hers. As soon as they were out of earshot of the men-at-arms, he demanded, "What did she do?"

Judith looked up at him, a tremor of warmth rushing through her at the knowledge that whatever she now faced, she no longer faced alone. She had a powerful husband to help and support her. "She sent me away. We're to leave as soon as possible, and never to be seen by her again."

An expression of obvious relief crossed his face. "I could not have asked for a better punishment. 'Twas my intent to leave this very day, as soon as I could extricate you from her—whether she allowed it or nay. The sooner we are away from here, the happier I shall be." He glanced down at her, his happiness seeming to falter. "Did she strike you?"

"Nay, she did not."

"Do you...do you not *wish* to leave Clarendon?" His lips flattened unhappily, as if he actually believed she'd *want* to stay.

"Oh, my lord, you know I wish to leave! More than nearly anything I want to see Lilyfare again," Judith told him, forcing her lips into a smile. "Indeed, I am well ready to be quit of this place. But, Mal, she was...she...." Judith stopped there in the corridor and looked up at him, unable to form the words to explain how badly she'd handled the whole mess. She shook her head; she could never explain her confusion. Nor did she wish to speak of Eleanor's dire predictions about love, for that would mean admitting to Malcolm how much she cared for him. "The queen...she was...overset."

"Of course the queen is overset," he said, looking at her as if she'd confessed that the sky was blue. "And 'tis why we must leave anon. Come. We have privacy in the chamber to discuss your conversation. And I have more preparations before we leave."

"Aye, of course. But I do not have a mount," she said, suddenly remembering her other loss. "And I've not packed, and—"

"Your maid is packing for you and I will soon introduce you to a very sweet-tempered but strong and brisk mare by the name of Socha. She is your new horse."

"Oh!" she said with great delight, stopping again in the corridor after only two steps to look up at him. "Thank you, Malcolm."

"She's gray and has a white forelock," he said, almost smiling now. "I hope she will suit you."

"If you have chosen her, I'm certain she will suit me well," Judith told him as they started off once again. "Will we truly leave this day?" Hope colored her voice.

"Aye," he told her as they reached the chamber. "I shall come for you in an hour. Take only what you will need, for we travel with speed. I will not be at ease until we are safely behind the walls of Lilyfare. Your maid and the rest of my men will follow with the remainder of your possessions. I trust you will be comfortable traveling without your maid?" he added, opening the door. "We will likely be on pallets in an abbey or monastery during our journey, or if we are fortunate, one or two nights in a friendly keep."

"Aye," she replied, understanding his meaning. They would have no privacy and little comfort for the journey. But she cared not, for she was going home! "I can easily manage without Tabby for a se'ennight or more. And my men? Do you wish for them to stay or accompany us?" she asked, looking up at him from just inside the chamber. "I will order them accordingly."

Malcolm hesitated. When he spoke, he seemed to choose his words carefully. "We travel lightly and with speed. 'Tis best to have a small but well-armed group for our purposes."

Judith's heavy heart lightened even further. Her husband was allowing her to make her own decisions about her men and give her opinions about their journey. "Of course, my lord. I will leave it to you to determine which of my men should travel with us, and which should come with Tabby and the others. Send Holbert to me and I will give him this direction."

Her husband's expression relaxed. "Very well. I will return in an hour, Judith. Do not delay." His eyes flitted over her, and for a moment, Judith thought he might kiss her…but then he turned abruptly and strode down the hall.

She closed the door behind him and turned to find the chamber in disarray, for Tabatha seemed to have upended every one of her trunks into piles on the bed. It took nearly the full allotted hour for Judith and her maid to determine what should leave immediately and what should come later, during which time Holbert arrived as directed. Judith gave him instruction that he was to obey any orders from her husband on this day, and then further direction about how to help Tessing prepare Hecate and the other raptors for travel.

"As for the the two eyases," she said in hard voice. "I do not believe they will travel well. Make a gift of them to de Rigonier from me." Better that she never again see the birds which would remind her not only of Piall's death, but also her ill-fated relationships with Henry and Eleanor.

"Aye, my lady," Holbert said with a bow, then left.

"Tabatha," Judith added, turning to her maid, "go you to Lady Maris and return this to her. I am no longer in need of it." The pouch she handed her maid still contained a fortnight's supply of the special tea Maris had given her. "And bid my friend farewell, for I do not know whether I will have time to say goodbye before we leave."

After Tabatha had gone, leaving Judith alone, she surveyed her chamber one last time. Though the court had been here at Clarendon for only six months at this time, the contents of her chamber—which followed her from place to place—had made each location seem the same. Now, she would bid farewell not only to this room, but also her nomadic life of following the queen on her many travels.

Alone and unseen, Judith fairly danced about the chamber, whirling from fireplace to window to bed, and back again. She was going *home*. She was *married*. A whole new life was about to begin.

She hugged herself, spinning around like a small wooden top as tears of joy and relief filled her eyes. *I cannot say farewell to this place soon enough.*

When the door opened, she was startled and turned quickly, mortified to be caught in such a ridiculous activity.

Of course it was Malcolm who had to find her thus, and Judith immediately stilled and tried to appear more decorous, surreptitiously wiping at one of the tear streaks on her cheek. But his attention swept over her, and his expression changed from questioning to a dark, irritated one.

"More tears, my lady?" he said enigmatically. "Regardless—your hour is up, my lady," he continued in a flat voice, as if preparing himself for some argument. "We leave now."

"Of course," she said, keeping her voice modulated. He was likely as embarrassed as she at finding his wife dancing and leaping about like a child. After all, had he not mentioned—more than once—of his desire for a meek and mild wife? *Oh dear.* Under the guise of pointing in the general vicinity of her maid's whereabouts, she managed to stifle a giggle by half turning away and covering her mouth. "Tabatha should return in a moment."

"As your maid is not leaving with us, it matters not to me when she returns." He strode into the chamber, once again making it seem smaller and closer. "Where is your baggage? I warn you, it must be small and able to fit on the back of your horse. And if you are not yet ready, we shall leave it all behind."

"'Tis only this packet here," Judith told him mildly. "I am ready to leave."

Malcolm nodded, then swung up the large cloth bundle. "Let us quit this place."

Judith very nearly held her breath during the last few moments of preparation. She had no opportunity to bid her friends or acquaintances farewell, and though it saddened her, she knew she could write to them. But, just as Malcolm seemed to be tense about their departure, so she understood his worries. Until they were out of the walls of Clarendon and well on their way to Lilyfare, she would feel a prickling on the back of her neck as if someone waited to stop them.

But when, only a quarter of an hour after leaving her chamber for the last time, Judith and Malcolm rode beneath the portcullis and onto the road, surrounded by their men, she could nearly believe they were free.

THIRTEEN

MALCOLM WASN'T certain when to expect it, but he knew it would come. And it did, just as twilight fell on the second day of their journey.

He rode next to Judith, who had disdained traveling in an enclosed cart in favor of a saddle on her new mare Socha.

"I've traveled with Eleanor for years. I ride on horseback," she had informed Malcolm pertly, just as they started out from Clarendon.

He had no issue with this decision, for that meant they journeyed faster and more efficiently. At the front of the party were his man Lelan and five other men-at-arms, and at the rear were another four, including the trusty Holbert. These were men Mal had chosen for their intelligence and prowess with a sword, as well as their ability to follow orders. Five were his own, and the others were from Lilyfare—picked with just as much care by Holbert.

They were trotting along in the falling darkness, another hour from the hidden Lock Rose Abbey where they intended to stop for the night. On either side was deep, heavy forest—the perfect place for an ambush. Thankfully, Judith was becoming tired after her first full day of travel, and she had lapsed into a stretch of silence. This allowed Mal to focus on their surroundings while attempting to ignore his other dark, guilt-ridden thoughts.

The only sound was the clip-clop rhythm of hooves along the beaten-dirt road, and in the distance, the hoot of an owl. Though

Malcolm watched, listened and even sniffed the air, 'twas Alpha's ears going sharply forward that called the warning. Then the destrier snorted, and Malcolm needed no other signal to draw his sword.

"To arms!" he cried, just as a group of shadowy figures on horseback emerged from the thick forest in front and behind them. Another cluster of silhouettes dropped from overhanging branches.

All at once, the still night was filled with action and sound: shouts, whinnies, metal clashing and sliding, grunts and groans and one female cry.

One of the silhouettes had landed on the back of Mal's horse, and even as Mal drew his sword to fight off a mounted attacker at the fore, he swung his shield around sharply. It connected with the man behind him, who'd gripped the back of Mal's hauberk as Alpha reared and snorted at the unexpected weight.

With a shout of fury and effort, Mal slashed down with his blade at the man at his front, and slammed his head back into the face of his rear attacker. At the same time, he whirled to look at Judith, who was the single unarmed, unprotected person in the group, even as he slammed his shield into the stunned man behind him. "Ride!" he shouted. "Judith, *ride! Lelan!* To her!"

She was holding onto her reins, bent over Socha's neck and gripping tightly as the mare reared then kicked, sidestepping and rearing again. But the horse was penned in by the wild melee and had nowhere to go. Socha screamed and whinnied in terror, for she was not a warhorse and was unused to such activity. Mal watched in terror as he fought off another attacker, praying Judith would hold her seat and keep from tumbling beneath the group of furious, lethal hooves and that a stray blade wouldn't strike her, even as he fought to get near enough to strike Socha on the flank and set her off.

"The woman! No harm to the woman!" cried a male voice in front of Malcolm. One of the attackers.

"Seize the lady!" cried another.

That was when his worst fears were confirmed, and a red haze settled over Mal's vision. *The king's revenge.* He struck out blindly, his sword slamming broadside against a mailed torso, sending the man flying from his saddle. Rage drove Malcolm—rage and fear—as he fought through the assailants, his mind blank as he focused on the fury.

Though there were nearly two dozen attackers, they were not as well-armed nor as practiced of fighters as the men from Warwick and Lilyfare. Still, it was a well-matched battle.

Malcolm slammed the flat side of his sword against someone's skull, and the man fell away…and suddenly, Judith was there.

"Mal!" she cried, and all at once, she seemed to be scrambling through the air toward him.

He cursed at her disobedience, but snatched her up in mid-launch as she flung herself from Socha's saddle toward Alpha's. Slamming her into position in front of him, he curled his shield arm around her. "Stay down!" he ordered, spinning to greet another flash of sword. It whaled into his shoulder and bicep enough to send a shuddering pain through him. Mal grunted, but he didn't hesitate as he brought his agonized arm up and out with a strong return blow.

The man cried out when the tip of Mal's sword found the unprotected spot beneath his arm. With a sharp jerk, Mal thrust his opponent away and the man tumbled off his horse.

And then, just as quickly as it had begun, all was quiet again except for the whuffling and agitated dance of hooves of their horses, and the gasps of exertion and pain from those men left standing or mounted.

"Judith. Are you hurt?" Mal asked, pulling his shield away from where he'd crushed her between it and his body.

"Nay," she said, her eyes wide and her breathing rapid as she came out of the safe cocoon of arm and metal. "But you—"

"Holbert!" cried Mal, his mind still blank—though blind fury curled at the edges. "Lelan! *À moi*! To me!" He couldn't look at her, couldn't speak to her…not now. Not at this moment.

The men clattered over, and the others surrounded them. "Casualties?" Mal demanded, looking about, counting heads as well as he could in the dim light of dusk. *Damn Henry. By God, he might be my king, but I damn him to the bowels of Hell.*

"No dead of ours," Holbert told him, his face streaked with something dark. Probably blood. He was holding his arm as if in pain. "But some injuries."

"Any of their survivors?"

"Duncan went after one who slipped away," said Lelan, speaking of another man from Warwick.

Mal nodded sharply. "Aye. Good. I want answers and Duncan is one to get them. Though I suspect I already know all I need to know." Judith, still clutched in his arm, tensed and he knew she was about to speak. "Be still, woman," he snapped, tightening his grip enough to squeeze the breath from her. "My lady and I will go on now. The abbey is an hour's ride. Holbert, Ulreth, Robert—you attend to this here. The rest of you, close in tightly. Can everyone ride? I expect no further problems—but I am not such a fool as to be careless."

Malcolm could have put Judith on Socha for the ride to Lock Rose Abbey, but he found he could not release her. Instead, Lelan led Socha behind and Mal pushed Alpha into a steady canter on the road. Aside from increasing their speed, it also made it difficult for Judith to speak.

He didn't want to hear her talk, ask questions, wail about her fears, sob over the terror of the battle. He needed to calm himself, keep his thoughts clear, and praise God that he still held her—this woman who'd turned his mind inside out—in his arms. Living, warm, soft and safe.

This woman who cried after coupling with him. Whom he'd come upon crying *again* in her chamber the morrow after, hiding her face from him as he came upon her in preparation for their departure.

And now she disobeyed him.

Anger over her foolishness teased the edge of his mind, threatening to flood into his thoughts. But he kept it at bay for the whole of the ride to Lock Rose Abbey. They would be safe there for the night, for even if those who'd come after them were still determined to have Judith—

He drew in a deep breath, aware that his knees were shaking and his grip around her was iron-tight. He exhaled, retraced his thoughts. *'Tis done. For now.*

They'd be safe in the abbey, for not only was it well protected, it was well-hidden in the depths of the forest. Few people knew of its existence—and the only reason Malcolm knew of it was because Gavin Mal Verne had told him. It was there that Judith's cousin had come upon Lady Madelyne, who eventually became his wife. She'd been hiding there for a decade, protected and safe until Gavin discovered her identity and brought her to the king.

Indeed, even though he knew 'twas there, Malcolm would have ridden past the stone wall if Gavin had not given him explicit direction. It was well-hidden with ivy and climbing roses, shrouded by thick trees with low-hanging branches. Yet, when he rang the bell and used Mal Verne's name, they were immediately given entrance. The nuns didn't wait to be asked, but instead ushered the injured off to their infirmary and gave direction to the others—where to put the horses, where to get food, where to lay their pallets.

Malcolm was calm and quiet during all of this, giving commands, answering questions lucidly, dismounting and helping Judith down. He even pressed a generous handful of coins into the mother abbess's soft, wrinkled hand when she came to greet him, having learned he was a friend of Gavin and Madelyne.

But he never released Judith's arm, and he kept her close to him as she trotted along, trying to match his long strides. And at last, when all had been attended to and they were walking into the abbey to sup, he hung back then pulled her into a shadowy alcove.

"Malcolm," she began, clutching at the edge of his hauberk. "I—"

"What were you thinking?" he demanded. "What on God's vast green earth *were you thinking?*" His voice shook with fury, and it was all he could do to keep from taking her by her slender shoulders and shaking *her*—trying to knock some sense into her stubborn, red-headed brain.

Judith gaped up at him, her eyes wide. "I do not know—"

"I told you to *ride*," he seethed. "They were after *you*, you bloody fool of a woman! I told you to *ride away!*"

To his surprise, instead of cowering in the face of his anger or even going demurely silent, she wrenched her arm from his grip and poked him in the chest. "Of course they were after me. And they meant to *kill you*. Why do you think I climbed onto your horse?"

"You didn't climb onto my horse," he bellowed. "I dragged you over *because you were about to fall and be trampled.* You *fool!* They meant to take you, Judith—"

"And they meant to *kill you*, Malcolm. Did you not hear them? 'No harm to the lady!' they said. 'Twould be near impossible to kill you and not harm me if I was on your horse next to you, would it not?" she said sharply. "Who is the fool now? They could not take me from your arms, and they dared not slash out at you for fear of striking me!"

Malcolm gaped down at Judith as her words and meaning sunk in. "Do you mean you meant to *protect* me?" he roared. "*You? Protect me?*"

"Hush," she told him, but her voice wasn't quite as strong as before. In fact, she sounded a little nervous. "You'll have the sisters wondering what harm you are inflicting on me."

"Harm? On you? By God, woman, you are fortunate we are in a holy place, or I'd as lief   " He bit off the words, knowing they were a worthless threat, and turned away. His teeth ground audibly, his jaw creaked from the pressure, his eyes felt as if they were going to bug out from the pressure of his fury.

"Malcolm," she said, touching his arm. Though he still wore his cloth hauberk and the mail *sherte* beneath it, he swore he could feel the heat of her touch, filtering even through the protective chain links.

Aye, he thought grimly to himself. *I have no protection from her. She can slip betwixt my links and into my soft spots and I cannot fight her off. I am well and truly slain.*

"We were in battle," he said from between tight jaws, still turned away. "I gave you a command. I expected such an attack, and I'd prepared Lelan to be the one to follow you." He stopped, realizing he'd said too much.

"You'd expected an attack?" Judith repeated. Her fingers grew heavier and tighter around his arm. "As did I."

"You?" Now he turned to look at her.

Judith looked up at him as if he were addled. The light was dim and her lovely features were limned with the mellow golden light from a trio of candles on a sconce above her head, but he could still read her expression. "Of course. But I do not know whether 'twas the king or the queen who ordered it."

Malcolm felt as if his breath had been snatched away. Clearly, she was just as jaded—and realistic—about their liege lord and lady as he was. And clearly, she was not about to succumb to vapors or hysterics because of what happened. Nay. She only cried when he touched her.

He gritted his teeth, shoving away that dark thought. Burying the niggling guilt. "You disobeyed me, Judith. You cannot talk your way out of that."

"'Tis true, but I had my reasons. Which I've already explained to you. The more troubling concern ought to be—I should *think*," she added in that tone which suddenly made him want to tear his hair out, "is whether it will happen again. And who was behind it. And how we may defy such a plot."

"Methinks the king," he replied, then stopped before he said anything further. This was not the sort of conversation he should be having with his wife. With a woman. She needn't worry about such things, nor should *he* voice them....

But he wanted to share this with her, he realized. He needed to talk with her, to listen to her, to understand what was in her mind—and that she might know some of what was in his. *Now* he understood, all at once, the relationship Dirick had with his own wife. It was more than coupling and begetting an heir, and seeing each other in passing.

"And I am nearly as certain 'twas the queen." Judith held up a hand to keep him from speaking, and he was bedamned if he didn't close his mouth. "My lord, please. My reasoning is sound. First, I cannot believe the king would order you, one of his most powerful barons killed—"

"I doubt he meant for me to be killed outright," Mal argued as handily as he would have done with a peer. "Though he surely wouldn't have shed a tear if I had. He is playing David to your Bathsheba."

"But you are no Uriah, sent off to war to die," she told him. "And after the events in my bedchamber on our wedding night, I do not believe Henry would wish the suspicion—and ire—of the barons to fall upon him. You are too well known and admired. I believe 'twas the queen who set those men on us. Do you listen to me, Malcolm," she interrupted when he would have argued. "I have given this much thought. On what road did the ambush lie in wait? On the road to Warwick? Nay, 'twas the way to Lilyfare. Did you not tell me we turned from Warwick early this morrow? And took the direction to Lilyfare? 'Twas the queen who knew how badly I wish to return to my home—not the king. Had he ordered such an attack, would the men not have expected us to go to Warwick? Would they not have laid in wait on that roadway?"

Malcolm had opened his mouth to speak. Now he closed it. "'Tis possible," he mused, thoughtful and pleased by her clear-headed argument in spite of himself. And with her logic came a semblance of relief. 'Twas much more palatable—and would be easier to combat—if it were Eleanor who was behind the ambush rather than his liege lord. They may not ever learn the truth, but at the least Judith's argument was sound.

"I told no one of our travel plans," he said. "Henry would have thought us to go to Warwick. I will send word to Ludingdon and Mal Verne. Mayhap one of them can learn something. And put a word in the ear of the king. For, as you said, he would not wish suspicion to fall upon him—and surely he can rein in his wife. Though, the fact that we were more than a day's journey from Clarendon would help prove the king innocent should anyone look his way."

"Aye. He is blinded by obsession and lust," Judith said, "but even so, I do not believe he would be so rash as to order such an attack."

Mal shook his head. "I cannot agree completely. All know of his hot temper and thoughtless rages."

"And 'twould be more likely that one of his rages was heard and the directive was taken seriously, even if he did not mean for it to happen. But even knowing that, I suspect if some of his men had decided to take matters into their hands, they would have met us on the road to Warwick."

"You may be correct. And I do not think we will ever know for certain," Malcolm said. Now as he looked down at her, he realized his rage had ebbed, his fear had eased…and he was alone in a shadowy corner with the most beautiful woman he'd ever known. And she was his. Still his.

And not only was she beautiful, but she was foolish and brave and spoke her thoughts and had good arguments. And she disobeyed him and thought she could *protect* him…and she wept in his bed.

Had she cried thus after coupling with the king?

"What is it?" Judith said suddenly.

Malcolm blinked, pulling himself back from thoughts and images he did not wish to entertain. "What?"

"Suddenly your face turned dark and angry again," she said. Her slender hand was on his chest, covering the center of his hauberk where he wore the crest of Warwick.

"Aye. I am angry. You disobeyed me—"

"I was not going to ride off and leave you to be slaughtered," she retorted. "And…'tis the truth: I didn't trust anyone else to protect me as you can," she added, causing his anger to wane. She was looking up at him with intense blue eyes, her lush body very close to his all of a sudden.

He drew his ire up around him again. She must understand her error—and, more importantly, he could not give in to the temptation she presented. Not here, in the midst of an abbey. In a public corridor. "In a moment like that, you must listen to me. You know naught about such things as war and battle, and 'tis unseemly for you to even *think* of shielding me!" He was becoming furious once more. "How would that look to my men—and to yours?"

Judith looked up at him, her hand still resting on his chest, her gaze unblinking. Then she looked away, her lips folding in on each other in irritation. "Aye, my lord," she sighed in capitulation. "You speak the truth. I know little of battle, and I should have listened to you in those harrowing moments. I likely endangered you as well as myself."

With that unexpected acquiescence, the last bit of Mal's anger evaporated, leaving him with naught to shield himself from her seductive proximity. "And well you did," he said, reaching to touch one of her loosened braids. "But 'tis done for now." He slid his fingers along its thick length, then over the curve of her collarbone. "We are both safe."

His hands didn't seem to want to stop, for the next thing he knew, both of them had curved around her shoulders. Malcolm drew her close, and to his mild surprise, she came willingly into his arms. His body shot to hopeful attention, heat and desire trammeling through him as he covered her mouth with his, pulling her up against the length of his body. Her lips were sweet and pliable, and he devoured them with a deep, sleek kiss. She made a soft sound, raising her arms to wrap them around his neck, pulling herself up against him. Her breasts lifted and pressed into him, and his hands settled at her hips then slid down over the curve of her arse.

Dimly aware of the soft rattle of mail and its metal barrier between them, Mal shifted, crushing her gently against the wall. His hands were filled with long, heavy hair and lush curves. She tasted like wine and mint, she smelled of moss and lavender, and the heat of her fingers at his neck, sliding beneath the linen of his undertunic, sent little prickles of awareness through him.

He covered her breasts, molding them in his hands and finding taut nipples beneath the fabric of her gown as he tasted her neck, nuzzling and gently eating at the sensitive hollow beneath her ear.

Judith shivered in his arms, and her soft sighs and rough breathing ignited him further. His cock filled his hose, pressing uncomfortably against the mail chausses and he fumbled his hauberk out of the way, then yanked at the chausses opening to free himself. Heavy and hard, his cock slipped free, bumping against the backside of his hauberk.

Before he knew it, he had his hands beneath the hem of Judith's gown, sliding it up along her thighs, his cock pressing against her belly, when he heard footsteps.

"My lord? Lady Judith?"

Christ's nails. Malcolm froze as he recognized Holbert's voice. He shoved her away, dropping the hem of her gown as the hauberk fell over his jutting erection. Judith gaped up at him, her eyes wide, her lips full and glistening as she yanked her cloak back around the front of her as her skirt swirled back into position.

"We are here," Mal called just as Holbert came into view. *With* the mother abbess.

And two other nuns.

Praise God Holbert gave us warning of their approach. Malcolm's face flushed hot and he dared not look at Judith as he shifted to the side and maneuvered a large hand over his waning erection, which still bulged insistently behind the hauberk. *God's stones, what was I thinking?*

"Ah, there you are. We thought you may have gotten lost," said the abbess. "For you were behind us, and then you had disappeared. It can be a bit confusing in this labyrinth of hallways."

She was a kind-faced woman with shrewd eyes, but even she didn't seem to notice the discomfort her appearance caused. Her attention was trained on Judith, who, thankfully, looked no more disheveled than she had upon arrival at the abbey, though was slightly out of breath. "I bethought one of the sisters could draw you a bath, Lady Warwick. And then you may wish to have aught to eat before returning to the women's chamber. We have night prayer in an hour."

"Thank you, mother," replied Judith, also taking care not to look at Mal—who was *absolutely* not looking at Holbert either. "I would greatly appreciate that."

"Come with me, then, child," she said. "Sister Pauletta has a jar of wonderful sea salt scented with rose oil and 'tis a most lovely addition to a bath."

Mal didn't have time to wonder about an abbey where the nuns bathed in rose-scented water, for he was too busy putting himself back to rights. And as Judith went off with the well-meaning sisters, he realized he was going to have a very long, uncomfortable night.

It didn't help that Holbert was doing a very poor job of hiding a smirk.

~*~

TABATHA WOULD have been just as pleased to quit court as her mistress, except for two things.

First, that she must leave behind all hope of capturing the attention of Bruin, the fascinatingly silent second-groom…and second, that she must travel with the irritating Sir Nevril.

Why oh why hadn't Lord Warwick taken his master-at-arms with him and Lady Judith and left Sir Holbert to travel with Tabby and the others? But nay. He'd not only left Sir Nevril of the poor jests and the long scar to ride with Tabby and the rest of the baggage, but he'd put Nevril in charge of the small caravan.

Which meant that not only must Tabatha travel with the man, but she must also abide by his commands. And that, she decided, glowering from her perch in the cart on which she rode, was the very worst part of the situation.

She could see Sir Nevril near the front of their group, jouncing along on horseback. His hair curled in small, tight frizzes, and his mail-covered arms gleamed in the sunlight as he conversed with two of his peers. It occurred to Tabby that she would be seeing more and more of the man now that her lady was wed to his lord, and that did not sit well with her at all.

"He is a beast," she informed the amber-striped kitten—who was hardly a kitten any longer, but more of a young, lanky cat. "If he mentions rabbit stew once more, I shall run him through with his own sword!"

The cat, who was curled up in the lap of Tabby's skirt, purred loudly as she stroked the stripes into a neat pattern. She'd been surprised when Nevril hadn't argued about bringing Topaz—as she'd named the creature because of her stripes. Nor had he suggested she leave Bear behind, even though the poor hound was nearly blind and might not last the journey. In fact, Nevril himself had carefully lifted the graying dog into the cart, making certain he was settled comfortably with a bone on which to gnaw.

But it was the man's comment about having rabbit stew for dinner, cooked over a firepit, that caused Tabby's irritation. "He knows just what will overset me," she said. "And methinks he says it apurpose, just to turn me red!"

And so Tabatha was determined not to allow Nevril to overset her any longer. She would ignore his comments and avoid him as much as possible.

No sooner had she come to this conclusion than the party stopped in the center of the road. She craned her head to see what caused the delay—a broken wheel on one of the carts, an oncoming travel party, or any number of things—but no obvious answer was forthcoming. She could see Nevril dismount and watched as he walked near the edge of the roadway, joined by another man-at-arms. They conferred for a moment, then to her surprise, he glanced back—and looked directly at Tabatha.

When he hailed her, commanding her to come to the front of the group, she frowned mutinously. But climbed out of the cart, nevertheless.

Making her way along the edge of the road, walking in the grass to avoid the heavy-footed, impatient horses, she approached the two men. Both were now crouched, looking at something on the ground, but it wasn't until Tabby was nearly upon them that she realized it was a fox, lame and unmoving on the side of the road.

And she understood at once why Nevril had called for her. She glanced at him in surprise, then back at the rust-colored creature, squatting next to him. The fox panted harshly and his bushy tail twitched like that of an angry cat. She saw right away that his two back legs had angry, bloody wounds on them—as if he'd been caught in a metal trap and somehow escaped.

"Can ye help the beast or should he be put from his misery?" said Nevril. His voice was gruff and he avoided looking at her.

The fox bared his sharp teeth, lunging at her hand as Tabby reached toward his leg, and Nevril moved quickly to block the attack. His mailed glove acted as a shield and restraint, allowing Tabby to examine the wounds.

"I can help him," she said carefully, still stunned that the man had even thought to ask her. "But I must get a cage from my grandfather. I do not believe Master Fox will enjoy the journey in my wagon."

Tessing was riding in a cart with the raptors and their equipment, and Tabby knew she could borrow one of the bird cages to accommodate her new patient.

"We must get on our way," Nevril told her. "I mean to reach Treadwell by sunset. I will fetch a cage and bring the beast to you there, and you can tend to him while we travel."

She looked at him once more, still confused but happy with the arrangement. "Aye. And…now we are stopped, may I go into the woods for a moment? I am in need of water for the poultice, and also…a moment to myself."

He rolled his eyes, but nodded abruptly. "Do not dawdle. And there is a stream yonder."

She grabbed a small wineskin from her cart and trudged into the forest, glad to be moving her legs after a long day of travel so far.

When she came back out of the woods a short time later, she found Nevril waiting for her, just out of sight of where she'd sought privacy. For some reason, she flushed slightly at the realization he'd been waiting and watching for her, and she sailed past him without a word. But when he helped her climb back into the cart, she had no choice but to thank him before he turned to speak with Sir Gilbraith about their route for the rest of the day.

The fox was already in a cage in the cart, waiting for her, and Tabby turned her attention to his care. She was surprised to find that someone had tied a falcon jess around the beasts's snout in a sort of muzzle, then tied it to the cage so she could care for his hind legs without fear of being bitten.

Had Nevril done that? She glanced at him as the cart started off again with a jolt. He was on his mount near the front of the caravan, but stood off to the side as it began to travel past him. When her cart reached him, to her surprise, he urged his mount into position alongside her.

At first, Tabby was able to distract herself by applying the poultice to her patient's wounds. But when she was finished wrapping them up in strips of cloth, she had naught to occupy her mind—and he still rode along next to her.

"Do you mean to remove the muzzle now?" Nevril asked, clearly having been watching her work. "Have a care, for the beast was none too happy when I put it on." Without further explanation, he pulled off his mail glove and handed it to her.

"Thank you," she said, taking it. She'd never worn mail before, of course, and had hardly ever handled it. The last time she'd done so, in fact, was when her father was still alive. It was heavy and cool, and all at once, Tabby was struck with a wave of a memory she'd forgotten until now...actually wearing her father's chain mail *sherte*, storming about their chamber with a wooden sword, pretending to be a knight herself.

She was no more than eight, and the edge of the *sherte* dragged along the stone floor. The sleeves were too long for her, of course, and the weight of the garment was substantial. But she'd managed to tramp about quite a bit before she tripped on the hem and fell. Father had picked her up and bundled her into a hug, mail and all.

"What is it?" Nevril demanded, pulling her from the reverie.

Tabby wiped her eye. "'Tis nothing," she said, turning her attention to the beast in the cage. She slid her hand inside the glove. It was warm from Nevril's hand and so large, it would have slid right off if she hadn't held it in place.

"Do you need help?" he asked.

"Nay," she replied, using the glove to hold the fox's head in place as she untied the muzzle. Despite the ungainly size, it worked quite well and she withdrew her hand with no injury. The poor fox panted and looked around, but now he was bandaged and safe—even though he likely didn't know it.

Tabby handed the glove back to Nevril, hoping that he would ride on back to the head of their train. But he did not.

"He will heal?" the master-at-arms asked after a moment.

"I am sure of it," she replied. "If for no other reason than to make certain you do not wish to turn him into a hand muff."

Nevril chuckled. "I do not think you would allow it, Mistress Tabatha. I believe I have learned my lesson from your sharp tongue."

She smiled. "Well, at the least the old saying is not true: an old dog *can* be taught new tricks."

He glanced at her sharply, then returned his attention to the road ahead. His bearded jaw shifted. "An *old* dog? I am not so very old."

Tabby looked at him in surprise. His tone was odd and mayhap there was a little ruddiness on his cheeks. "But I did not mean you were ancient," she replied. "Only that you are…no young pup." His hair had no gray in it—though it was hard to tell for certain, as it was light in color and tight with curls. But mayhap it was the scar that made him seem old. Or, at the least, older than her.

"I am only one score and a half," he told her, still looking straight ahead.

"Ah," she replied. Then, feeling the need to change the subject—for 'twas clear he had no intention of leaving her to ride along in peace—she said, "Yestereve, when we were stopped for the night, I heard you jesting with Sir Galbraith. About a lute for Lord Warwick? Does my lord play the lute?" Tabatha knew she sounded incredulous—but after all, picturing her lady's new husband crooning a song over a lute was nearly as ludicrous as picturing Queen Eleanor begging forgiveness of Lady Judith.

Now Nevril looked at her once more and she saw a hint of humor in his expression. "Nay, Warwick doesn't play the lute. 'Twas only a jest we had some time ago when he was preparing to wed Lady Beatrice. He was in a fine mood all the time for several days, after having been an angry bear for a fortnight. Gambert and I jested that mayhap he could be playing the lute for us, he was so light of heart."

"Warwick was to wed Lady Beatrice?" Tabatha said in surprise.

"Aye. He was sending messages nearly every day from court—to her father, the Lord of Delbring, Peter of Blois, Salisbury and others. The contract was being negotiated and we were all very happy for that—for 'twas the reason we'd come to court."

"How did he come to wed my lady then?" she asked, a niggle of unease settling in her middle. Did Lady Judith know this?

Nevril shook his head. "I am not very certain what happened, but 'twas after that day—that day when you brought a message for Lord Malcolm. Gambert and I had just made our lute jest, for Lord Mal had been so very light-hearted for nearly a se'ennight. Then I came upon you, and you asked that I deliver the message from Lady Judith." He shrugged. "My lord went in to a black mood after that, and then some days later all at the nonce he was wed to Lady Judith. I knew naught of it until the deed was done—nor did Gambert or Gilbraith or the others." His expression was grim. "I do not know what happened to change it all. Mayhap the woman denied him at the last moment—though I cannot imagine why she should. Warwick would have brought her family much power, and their lands are very close."

"Indeed," Tabatha murmured, gnawing on her lip.

"And Lady Beatrice has visited with her father several times since Lady Sarah died four years past. They were cousins, and she knew Lord Mal quite well. 'Tis a complicated world, the wedding of great lords and gentleladies." He shrugged and looked straight ahead once more. "'Tis glad I am that a simple knight like myself has little to consider when choosing a wife—only her comeliness and personality. And whether she might bear a son or nay."

And to Tabatha's surprise and consternation, he looked purposefully at her—then kicked his horse into a leap, cantering off toward the front of the caravan.

It was only after he'd left that she realized her heart was pounding and her cheeks were *hot*.

‑*‑

"THERE," CRIED Judith, pointing into the distance. "Lilyfare!"

Malcolm drew back on his reins and halted Alpha next to his wife's mount. In the midday sun, the green hills undulated in front of them, brilliant as a swath of emerald fabric. They were dotted with yellow, white, and orange flowers, and on the top of the largest hill—but a much smaller rise than any at Warwick—sat a dark gray enclosure. Jutting up from inside was the keep, a single, crenellated column made of the same iron-colored stone as the wall. Flags of yellow and gray fluttered in the breeze.

"It hasn't changed at all," Judith said, blinking rapidly as she strained to see from her side saddle. "Not from here, anyway," she added, looking at him with glistening blue eyes. She blinked and a tear fell, and she used her palm to wipe it away. But she was smiling and her gaze was filled with open delight. He'd never seen such a beatific expression on her face. "It may have changed within, surely it has some bit—it's been six or seven years—but from here, it looks as it always has done."

Mal's attention was divided between the lush landscape in front of him and the glowing beauty next to him. Judith looked so luminous and carefree. A sense of comfort and completeness settled over him; a settled, swelling feeling of warmth—and not, this time, in the crotch of his hose.

"Shall we ride on? I'm eager to see the rest of this heaven of yours," he said, smiling down at her.

Since they left Lock Rose Abbey, the last four days of travel had been both difficult and surprisingly pleasant for Malcolm. He no longer feared an attack—for now the first one had failed, there was no time nor ability for the queen—or whoever—to arrange for another one. While at the abbey, he'd sent messages to Ludingdon and Mal Verne, as well as Salisbury, about the experience. He outlined his suspicions carefully but in subtle terms—for who knew whose hand the message could fall into—and knew his peers would spread the word through court in their own way. He also trusted Duncan would soon meet up with them, and Mal hoped his man would have information from the runaway attacker, whom he'd attempted to follow.

The difficult part of the journey thus far, however, had been the temptation of her company. Thanks to her years of traveling with the queen, Judith journeyed for long hours and without complaint—all on horseback. And though at the beginning of their journey, Mal was uncertain whether he could stand to listen to her chatter day after day, hour after hour as they rode along, even after nearly a se'ennight he found himself enjoying her company as well as her conversation. She was interesting and intelligent, and he realized he was more than content with her company and her thoughts. Being in her company thus nearly made him forget the fact that he could not bed her. It was nearly as satisfying.

They discussed everything from falconry and fox hunting to horse breeding, the best crops to raise on each estate, whether the women serfs should have access to Judith's private solar for sewing (where the light was the best, but where they also invaded her peace with their constant bickering) and what sorts of punishments or fines should be meted out for a variety of criminal offenses. To his relief, she also lapsed into long stretches of silence, giving his ears and mind a rest and allowing him to contemplate other business he must attend to, now that he was wed again and going home with two new estates to manage. He'd received word of an outbreak of disease among the cattle at Warwick, and he must investigate that as soon as possible.

Judith also sang or hummed to herself on occasion, and quite often, instead of Malcolm, she rode with Lelan, Holbert or any of the other men-at-arms and conversed with them as well. Betimes, she and the others broke out into song as well, and if some of the tunes were bawdy and lewd, she merely sang the louder.

If the days of travel had been easy and entertaining, it was the nights which Malcolm found the most troublesome. For though he spent all the day feasting his eyes and attention on his vivacious wife, he was relegated to the mens' chambers at the abbeys and keeps that gave them respite for the night. The single night spent in her bed had been too fleeting, and memories from their brief interlude at Lock Rose Abbey haunted him.

When he looked back on that moment, however, Malcolm was filled less with desire than with self-loathing and disgust. He'd had his wife pushed up against the wall, ready to use her like a whore, *in the corridor of an abbey.*

Had his mind completely deserted him?

And all the while, even as he tried to push away the self-recrimination, he heard an echo of Judith's own words: *He is blinded by lust and obsession.*

Aye, she'd been speaking of Henry…but, God's truth, those words could just as well have been about Malcolm himself. He was no better than the king, hampered by his own lust and obsession.

Malcolm gritted his teeth. He should have given Judith time to get beyond her *affaire* with the king before crawling into bed with her. Aye, she'd insisted on it, but he realized she was determined to consummate the marriage so it could not be drawn asunder. She was a practical woman.

And she had not denied him, nay. He did not believe she would; for she knew her duty. But Judith's silent tears were a clear indication of her feelings about the activity.

Now, as they cantered across the last hillock to the portcullis of Lilyfare Keep, Mal fought an internal battle with himself. Tonight, he could sleep in a bed and seduce his delicious wife, hoping there would be more than mere acquiescence from her….

Or he could do what he'd planned to do—what he knew in his conscience he *should* do—and leave her at Lilyfare as he traveled on to Warwick. Mayhap putting some space between them would help to ease his own obsession and give her time to come to terms with their arrangement.

Aside from that, he must see Violet. It had been nearly three months since he'd left her. What if she'd forgotten him? A sharp pang stabbed him in the belly. He couldn't bear the thought of returning to find only blank curiosity in her pale blue eyes when she looked on him.

"They are waiting for me!" Judith suddenly cried. She kicked her mare into a full gallop, tearing down the low incline toward the roadway that ribboned through the small town. Her firelight hair shone in the sun, wisps fluttering free and her braids bouncing loosely over her shoulders and down her back.

Villeins and serfs lined the village's main thoroughfare, waving their caps and shawls, and Judith slowed Socha to a trot as she approached. She waved and called to some of the people she knew, blowing kisses to the children and tossing coins from a pouch as she paraded down the street. Further on, flags flew, men-at-arms lined the wall's ramparts and drawbridge, and serfs and other household members filled the small bailey, welcoming home their lady.

Malcolm watched all of this with interest and appreciation. Such a welcome was a clear indication of the satisfaction and ease of the villagers and farmers, who were tied to the land and must accept the rule of their overlord—or lady. Clearly, though she'd been absent for years, Judith was much loved by her people and the estate had been well-managed by her castellan.

"You sent word to them," Judith said, turning Socha to face Mal as he rode up behind her. "I sent word that I'd wed, but you must have written that we'd arrive today. Thank you, my lord."

He shrugged it off. "But of course. I was fair certain you'd wish to sleep in a clean chamber with fresh coverings on your first night home—and to have a feast prepared to celebrate your arrival."

"And my marriage," she said, turning her horse so that they rode abreast. "They must meet their new lord anon."

Her smile was so brilliant, her eyes sparkling so happily, that Malcolm nearly lost his internal battle at that very moment. *Surely I can spare one night here. She* is *my wife.*

Nay. What of Violet? And you must attend to the matters at Warwick. The cattle are dying. And people as well. Violet could be next.

And Judith's smile is not for you... 'tis for Lilyfare.

And so he checked his desires and rode alongside her, determined not to give in to his own obsession. He would ensure Judith was safely home and welcomed, and then take his leave immediately. Mayhap some time apart would allow Judith to accept their marriage and his bed, and there would be no more tears.

Sir Roger of Hyrford, who'd managed the estate for years, met them just inside the bailey. Malcolm observed the man closely—both in the way he greeted Judith as well as himself. The castellan had been wholly in control of the estate during his lady's absence, and as oft as not, a man in such a situation might resent the return of his overlady—particularly if she brought a new husband with her.

However, Malcolm caught nothing in the man's expression or demeanor to indicate anything but pure delight at seeing Lady Judith again. The grizzled Sir Roger was well over two score years of age—mayhap nearer to three—and according to Judith, had been steward for her father for years. In fact, she appeared so fond of her castellan that when he helped her down from Socha, she treated him like a long-lost uncle, throwing herself into his arms.

If Mal was looking for any reason to delay his departure for Warwick, he did not find it in Sir Roger's face—for the older man had happy tears streaming from his eyes as he embraced Judith.

"Ah, how you've grown! In beauty and in stature," he told her, looking down like a proud papa. "Lady Judith, how we've missed your sunny face and happy voice. And now you've returned with a husband too!" Sir Roger, who hadn't knelt to his lady in favor of the more emotional greeting, now turned and made a formal bow to Malcolm. "Lord Warwick, felicitations and greetings. You are well come to Lilyfare, my lord. All in the village and keep are happy to find our lady so well wed."

"Many thanks to you, Sir Roger," Mal replied. "For your gracious welcome to me and upon the return of your lady, as well as your attention to the lands during her absence." He met the castellan's eyes meaningfully, allowing appreciation to show in his expression—as well as taking a good measure of the man—and letting him see that he did so.

"I am eager to swear fealty to you as well, my lord," the man said, meeting Malcolm's eyes fearlessly. "And, in truth, 'twill be a boon to have someone with whom I can discuss several issues that have lately arisen. A new mill, for one, of which we are sad in need."

"Very well," Malcolm replied. "I look forward to receiving your fealty. But not, it appears, on this day. For," he said, glancing at Judith, "I fear I must press on to Warwick at once."

"What say you?" she exclaimed, turning from her conversation with a group of men-at-arms and ladies. "We must leave so soon?"

Mal saw a flash of defiance in her expression as she edged him a few steps away from the others. There was disappointment there as well, and he was unaccountably relieved he wouldn't need to fight that battle with her, at least, today. "Nay, my lady. You shall stay, of course. 'Tis I who must ride on."

Now her expression changed to shock and confusion. "I see," she replied slowly. The few freckles sprinkled over her cheeks stood out sharply. "And I'm to remain here?"

"Aye. Are you not pleased to be home? I did not think you'd wish to leave so soon after arriving," he said. *Ask me to stay.* The thought came from nowhere.

"Aye. I mean, nay. I do not wish to leave. I did not expect… ah, well, very well, my lord. I am certain you must attend to any number of things at Warwick, having been away for several months yourself." She smiled up at him, but it was a smile much less warm and spirited than a moment before.

A small flicker of hope warmed him inside. She did not seem pleased that he was to leave. *Ask me to stay, Judith. Tell me you do not wish me to leave!* But he could not allow her to see the hope in his eyes, and so he glanced over at the cluster of men-at-arms. "I do have some urgent matters to attend at Warwick. But I expect to return well before the snow falls."

"Will you not sup with us?"

His determination wavered, but in the end he knew 'twas best that he not even do that. For the longer he stayed, the more likely he would be never to leave—and being asked to sup was little more than a routine hospitality. "Nay, Judith. I hope to reach Delbring by nightfall, and from there, 'tis only a day and a half ride to Warwick if I travel unencumbered."

"Very well, then. I need not even see to a parcel of food for your journey, since 'twill be so short. God speed to you, Malcolm," she said.

"My thanks, my lady," he replied, unable to read her expression. Her eyes were neither cool nor warm nor distressed. "I shall return before the snowfall. Have a care for yourself."

With that, he turned and called his men—who appeared shocked and disappointed at their short reprieve—to mount.

Moments later, they rode out of Lilyfare.

FOURTEEN

DELBRING. THE moment Judith heard the word pass from Malcolm's lips, her insides turned to ice. He was leaving her at Lilyfare, then riding hellbent for Delbring…where Lady Beatrice lived.

He made no excuses, no explanations. And she was much too proud to ask, afraid to demand—particularly in the hearing or sight of her people.

And so she turned away after a brief wave of farewell, allowing herself to be brought into the great hall—which seemed so small after the ones visited by the royal court over the last years—and to a celebratory feast. If she was sad and confused over the absence of her husband, Judith allowed no one to see. She laughed and jested and ate and drank, and at the end of the meal, she accepted the renewal of Sir Roger's fealty, along with that of each of her men-at-arms.

It wasn't until she was in her own chamber—that which rightly should be occupied by both the lady *and* the lord of Lilyfare—and between the coverings of her own bed that Judith allowed herself to weep. And rage.

Finally, in the dark quiet of the night with the bed curtains drawn tightly against the world, she slept.

The next days at Lilyfare were so filled with activity that Judith hardly had time to stew or worry over her husband's seeming abandonment of her. She was home. She was with her people. She was where she belonged, freed from the confines and dark tendrils of the royal court.

And for that, at the least, she must be grateful to Malcolm.

Late the following day after Judith's arrival in Lilyfare, a lone knight approached the gates. When he announced he was from Warwick, he was immediately brought to Judith, who was in her solar with the seamstresses.

"My lady, 'tis I, Sir Duncan," said the blond man as he bowed.

"Of course. I remember you, Sir Duncan of Merrywerth. You are well come to Lilyfare," Judith told him, submerging the initial spark of hope that he might have come from Malcolm's side with a message for her—for she recognized him as the man who'd pursued one of her would-be abductors. There had not been time for Duncan to find her husband at Warwick and then ride here. Unless he was still at Delbring. Her heart squeezed sharply.

"I understand my lord is not in residence," Duncan said, answering her unspoken question. There was a note of confusion and surprise in his voice, but it was subtle and he kept his expression blank. "I knew he intended to travel to Lilyfare in the stead of Warwick, and I have news for him. Where can I meet up with him?"

"Aye," Judith replied in an easy voice. "He left for Warwick shortly after arriving here—there were some urgent matters he must attend to. But, Sir Duncan, please sit and give me your news. Then I shall feed you and provide you a bunk for the night. And in the morrow, you may leave for Warwick, or we may send a messenger to Lord Malcolm with your information." She spoke sweetly, but made certain there was an underlying thread of command in her voice.

After all, she did not wish for him to leave without learning whatever he had gleaned from his investigation—if anything.

"Thank you, my lady," he said. "But I have very little of import to share."

She smiled, realizing he likely felt as most men did—that women had little interest or need to know unpleasant details. "Very well, then, Sir Duncan. Then it shall take you no great time to tell

me what you've learned. You followed one of our attackers and what
did you discover?"

If the circumstances would have been different, she might have
found his consternation amusing. He was hardly able to control a
grimace of confusion, and she could nearly read his expression as
he struggled with how to obey her implicit command. In the end,
however, honor and respect won out.

"Aye, my lady. I followed him to an inn. I bethought 'twould
be best to listen and see what I could learn, rather than to engage
in battle. I overheard enough conversation betwixt him and some
others to learn that a message had been given out that a particular
lady would be traveling on a certain route. And that if the lady were
to be—er—removed from the presence of her companions, there
was a very powerful person who would be most appreciative. And
pay a large ransom." Duncan glanced at her apologetically, and
Judith gestured for him to continue.

"Was there any indication who this powerful person might be?"
she asked when he hesitated. Her voice was calm, for none of this
was new information to her.

"It was stressed that the lady should not be harmed and that if
she was, there would be no appreciation shown to the ransomers."

"I see. And there was no further information given? How was
the ransom to be paid? How were the abductors to contact this
powerful person?"

Duncan seemed more than mildly surprised at her
interrogation, but he recovered quickly. "Those were the very same
questions I wondered myself, my lady. To take the time to explain
how I learned the answers would be tedious—"

"Aye," she agreed. "So you may simply tell me what you learned,
rather than the method used."

"There was to be a message sent through the inn at Perrymont,
for the name of Thurston." Judith's expression must have betrayed
her, for Duncan ceased speaking. "My lady?"

"You need say no more," she told him. "For to speak anything
further could cause danger to us both. Now, I bid you take your
ease. They will serve you in the hall, and you may ask Gerald for

direction to a chamber for rest and any other need you may have—a bath, a woman, your armor seen to. Thank you, Sir Duncan. You have given me every information I need to know." And though her heart was heavy with the knowledge that it had, indeed, been Eleanor behind the attempted abduction, Judith managed a warm smile for her husband's loyal man.

She knew that Thurston was a mercenary who did particular types of tasks for the queen. Few knew of his existence because of the matter of work he did—carrying out orders and commands that the queen preferred to be done in the dark and private. She doubted even King Henry knew of Thurston's existence, for Eleanor was a very canny woman.

Judith immediately called for one of her men, then for parchment, a pen, and ink. Grateful that Malcolm could read and write himself—for such a skill was oft reserved only for the clerics and monks, and 'twas the rare lord (and even rarer gentlelady) who was schooled in such learnings—she composed a letter to him.

My lord husband, Malcolm de Monde, Lord of Warwick, Baron of Beesley, Baron of Huntesmeade, Lord of Kentworth and Lord of Lilyfare....

I am in receipt of conversation from your man, Duncan of Merrywerth. He shall be traveling to Warwick on the morrow, but I wished to preface his arrival with some information you might find valuable. Thus I am sending this missive ahead of his departure. A particular personage who is well known to both of us, and in fact was the subject of my *position in our recent discussion, has on many occasions been known to travel to a shire by the name of Thurston.*

Here Judith paused, looking down at her neatly inked words. She must take care not to write anything that could put her in danger, nor clearly divulge what she knew so well in the event this message fell into the wrong hands Accusing the queen of such perfidy was not only tantamount to treason, it was simply dangerous.

But even if Mal did not at first understand her reference to Thurston, surely he would quiz Duncan about it and the pieces would become clear to him. Judith returned her attention to the missive, thought for a moment, then added, *I pray this missive finds you well and safely traveled to your destination.*

Then, a flare of irritation spurred her to add, *And that you had an enjoyable visit at Delbring.*

Judith looked at the words, sprinkling sand over the ink to help it dry. After a moment, she tipped the parchment up and the loose sand slid onto the table. She was tempted to add 'Give my regards to Lady Beatrice,' but she did not have the courage to do so.

Instead, Judith dipped her pen in the ink and, in another moment of contrariness, signed the missive: *Your ever-faithful wife.* Then she added the formality: *Judith of Kentworth, Lady of Kentworth, Lady of Lilyfare, Lady of Warwick, at Lilyfare, this date of July 28, 1166.*

She sanded those last words, then once she was certain the ink was dry, Judith closed the message with her wax seal and gave it to the waiting Sir Waldren.

"Deliver you this to Lord Warwick and no other. Travel first to Delbring, where he...where he may still be in residence," she forced herself to add smoothly, "and then look for him at Warwick—or whatever path he may have gone, according to those at Delbring. You may wait for a response, but if none is forthcoming, you will return to me within one day."

At the least, then she would know how long Malcolm remained at Delbring. With Lady Beatrice.

~*~

THERE WAS much to do at Lilyfare since Judith returned. Over the next fortnight, she met with Sir Roger many times, going over the ledgers, reviewing a list of improvements and repairs that must be done, sitting in judgment over issues rising between the villagers, inspecting the household inventories, and taking the maids, seamstresses and cook staff to task. Her years with the queen served her well, for she'd learned much about managing a household—as well as its people—effectively.

After seeing the state of affairs in the kitchen, in fact, Judith was astonished that her welcoming feast had been so extensive and delicious—for the day-to-day activities therein didn't bear out the excellent meal she'd been served. And so she attended to the most pressing problems there, naming a new head cook and rearranging the tasks of the cooking serfs.

She also spent a considerable amount of time examining the mews. Tessing and the falcons should arrive any day, and it had been years since the mews had been used. There were many repairs to be done, and Judith and her mentor had learned much during their exposure to the Far Eastern methods of falconry through the royal court. She wished to prepare the mews for some of these more modern techniques.

'Twas just in time that she had the mews put to rights, for only five days after Sir Duncan's arrival at Lilyfare, the caravan from Clarendon arrived bearing Tessing, Tabatha, and the remainder of Judith's belongings.

Judith managed to hide her loneliness and confusion at first. She showed Tessing the improved mews and directed a delighted Tabby to the small lean-to structure she'd had repaired near the stables for the promised animal infirmary. Then she gave direction for which trunks were to be carried where and unpacked, and made certain all in the party—whether they be from Warwick or Lilyfare—had comfortable places to sleep and sustenance.

But when she and Tabatha were alone in the large bedchamber she should have been sharing with Malcolm, all pretenses were dropped.

"Where is my lord?" Tabby asked nearly as soon as the door was closed behind them.

Judith could hold her emotions back no longer. "He is gone. He has left." She swiped roughly at sudden tears, wondering when in her life she'd ever been so easily set to weeping as she had been in the last months.

"What has happened? Did you quarrel?" Tabby asked even as she began to tidy up the chamber.

"Nay! He hardly darkened the threshold of Lilyfare before he was off…to *Delbring*."

Tabatha started and looked over at her. "What do you say? He has left you to go to Delbring?"

"Nay...at the least—I don't...know. He said he was going to Warwick, but would stop at Delbring for the night. He could not even sleep one night here in Lilyfare, but he had to leave for *Delbring* at the nonce." Now Judith was beginning to rage about the chamber. "And I have heard naught from him, nor from Sir Waldren, whom I sent after with a message."

She paced the chamber, going to the window and peering out over the yellow and white dotted heath, then back again. Why had Sir Waldren not returned with a message from Malcolm? She'd given him strict orders, and it had been enough days for him to have found Mal and returned.

Judith realized Tabatha had gone surprisingly quiet. Most oft, the tiring woman usually had plenty of unsolicited advice or questions, but now she was uncharacteristically silent. "Tabby," she said sharply when she saw the expression on her maid's face. Something lurched in her belly. "What is it? What do you know?"

Tabatha slowly finished folding the bliaut she'd removed from one of the traveling boxes, sliding it into place in the permanent storage trunk in the corner of the chamber. "Ah, my lady...I do not know—"

"What is it?" Judith demanded, her heart seizing. "There is something. Tell me."

"'Tis only that I heard some information from Sir Nevril on our journey. How Lord Warwick was in a fine, light-hearted mood for some time while at Clarendon...and that he was sending many messages to Delbring, negotiating a marriage contract with the lord there. And then all at once, he became angry and bad-tempered again. And on the next, you and he were wed."

Judith's heart dropped to her knees and she suddenly felt ill. *Beatrice of Delbring? That mouse?* The queen's words and Judith's own jests rang in her ears. *Nay.*

But had she not suspected it all along? That Warwick had wed her out of pity and honor, and that 'twas Beatrice of Delbring who held his heart and interest?

She sank onto the bed, crossing her arms about her belly, nauseated and light-headed. She'd believed Warwick held her in such high esteem he took her to Lilyfare before even going to his own home, despite the fact that Judith's estate was a longer journey from Clarendon…but now it made all the sense. For he meant to abandon her there and go to his lady love as soon as he could.

Nay, oh nay.

The words of the queen rose suddenly in her mind, tolling darkly like an insistent bell. *"You may love your husband, but know if you do, 'tis naught but a curse….Pray that* you *must never look upon the woman your husband loves."*

Judith closed her eyes, hardly believing the sharp stabs of pain, the depth of the agony rolling through her body. *How could I have come to care for him so much? So much that he has this power to hurt me so?*

So much that even being at Lilyfare, being home and free of the queen, was no longer enough. She wanted Malcolm. All of him.

‐*‐

YOUR EVER-FAITHFUL wife.

Over the last se'ennight, Malcolm had read those words countless times in the missive Judith had sent. *What did that mean?*

Likely it meant nothing; mere words. A dashed-off formality. But he could not cease from wondering. Worrying. Even hoping… that there was some sort of message therein.

And there was another line in the letter he stumbled over as well. *And that you had an enjoyable visit at Delbring.*

That had set him to scratching his head, seeking to read some other meaning therein. She'd already given him what he needed to know—that Eleanor had been the one behind the foiled abduction. But was there some other message he was missing? Why did she mention Delbring? He could almost hear the odd note in her tone, the discord in this out-of-place sentence.

And this, Mal told himself as he shoved the crinkled parchment into the depths of a trunk, was of such little import that he could hardly fathom giving it his attention. For matters at Warwick were grave enough that he needed spend no time gnawing over a few words from his wife.

Since arriving a fortnight ago, Malcolm had been faced with a myriad of difficult and unsettling decisions. What had seemed at first like a simple ague that took root in a cattle herd, had, by the time Mal arrived, spread from the cows to some of the people of Warwick, making them ill. Three villeins and one maid had already died.

Thus only yesterday had Malcolm made the difficult decision to send Violet to Lilyfare in hopes of keeping her safe from the bad humors.

"Poppy," she'd said, looking up at him with guileless blue eyes. "You not coming wif me?"

His heart creaked as he scooped her up and bounced her energetically in his arms. She giggled and clutched at the top of his head as he said, "Nay, sweetling. But I will come along as soon as I can. Clara will keep good care of you, and you can ride in this nice little bed." He showed her the cart he'd had prepared for her. "You can sleep all of the day or play with your beads. And think of all the sights you will see!"

"I never go away from Warrick," she said. "I like my home."

"I know," he told her, patting down a fly-away blonde curl. "But think of all the sights on your journey. I will come as soon as I can, sweetling. And when I come to Lilyfare, I will introduce you to the great and beautiful lady there. She has hair of fire and is very kind. And she lets a large hawk sit upon her fist, like so." He spoke easily and lightly, but deep inside, Malcolm felt uneasy.

What would loud, brisk Judith think of his daughter—this simple-minded, joyful little girl who would never attain full womanhood and who could never fully grasp the travails of life? Violet was sweet-tempered and kind, and though she would grow physically taller and curvier as young ladies did, she would never have the mental capacity to wed—and she certainly would never go to court. He would never allow it.

Therein lay part of his trepidation of sending her off without him. Mal had spent most of her childhood keeping Violet's existence and simple-mindedness a secret outside of Warwick. The last thing he needed was some greedy, enterprising man to abduct his daughter and wed her in an effort to eventually gain control of Warwick and his other estates. Let alone what would happen to his sweet girl. She was only eight, but girls were betrothed and wed as early as ten or twelve, and he wanted to take no chances that anyone knew of this vulnerability—his *or* hers. And there were those who believed simple people like his daughter were cursed by the Devil, or were some sort of punishment for her parents' actions. They looked in askance at them, and were often dismissive or even cruel.

And as much as he'd come to enjoy Judith's company—her conversations, her opinions, even her jests—he wasn't certain how she would act around a simple child like Violet. His wife was so quick and energetic, impatient and opinionated…would she have the patience and empathy to interact with the girl? 'Twas best for all if he were there to smooth the way, to make certain Judith would not cause Violet to feel overset or frightened.

"There you are, sweetling," he said now, pressing a smacking kiss onto her round cheek before gently tumbling her into the soft pile of bedding in her cart. "You shall have a great adventure, and I want you to pick one flower for me every day. You can show them all to me when I come to get you."

"But what if I forget?" she asked, thrusting out her lower lip.

"Then Clara will help you," he said, glancing for affirmation at the woman who'd been Violet's nurse since she was born.

"Indeed I will, Lady Violet," Clara agreed. "We shall keep them all in a box and you will show them to your Poppy when he comes."

"Now," Mal said, turning away from his daughter to face Clara and Lelan, who was to lead the traveling group. "You must keep Violet out of the sight and notice of Lady Judith until I can arrive. Do you understand? Nevril has come to Lilyfare by now, and he will assist you to find a place where Violet will not be noticed or underfoot. I must be the one to introduce the two of them. Do you understand?"

Though both of them looked at him with trepidation in their eyes, their responses were affirmative. Mal gave them, and the rest of the men-at-arms in the party, a steady, meaningful look. "I say to you—do you not allow them to cross paths, or you will feel the depths of my ire. And though Lady Judith's man Waldren travels with you, do you not allow him to learn of Violet's identity. She is Clara's daughter, sent away to be safe from the plague."

"Aye, my lord," they said—each of them—in succession as he looked at them.

Satisfied that he'd done all he could to protect Violet from any discord, and also from being recognized as his daughter until he could prepare Judith, he returned to the cart to give his child one last smacking kiss and a hug. "Be a good girl. Papa will come soon and I will wish to see all of the flowers you have collected for me."

"Flowers. Aye, Poppy. Clara will help me." She beamed and bounced up in his arms, narrowly missing his chin as he bent to embrace her once more to hide the sudden sting of tears. He blinked rapidly, drawing in her delicate, little girl scent.

"Fare thee well and Godspeed," he said to Lelan when he recovered, setting Violet away. "You shall send word to me every se'enight without fail."

"Aye, my lord. And we shall protect her with our lives," his man replied.

"And more," Malcolm told him frostily. "Godspeed."

He turned and went back into the keep, feeling the same sense of bereftness he'd experienced when leaving Judith behind at Lilyfare. *Pray God my daughter is safe until I can see her again.*

And now that Violet was safe—or would soon be safe—he had other matters to attend to. The ailing cattle, the sickening villagers…and the fact that the Queen of England had attempted to have him killed.

-*-

THE DAYS passed both slowly and quickly at Lilyfare.

Tabatha was delighted her lady had recalled her whimsical promise to allow her a space for her own animal infirmary, and whenever she was not attending Lady Judith, she was at the small structure. The fox had healed and been set free in the meadow, and poor Bear was completely blind so he was corralled in a large area so he did not accidentally get trampled by the horses. Topaz the cat had free reign of the stables, and was just as free with his own gifts of fat mice or squirrels—which Tabby preferred not to receive.

As oft as not, Sir Nevril happened by, usually with a poor jest about rabbit stew (would the man never cease?), but occasionally, he brought something he thought would interest her. Once, a four-leaf clover he informed her was a sign of good luck. Another time, he brought two daisies twined with a dandelion stem. Only two days ago, there was a sparrow with a lame wing, which he carried to her carefully on his large hand.

After she had been at Lilyfare for well over a fortnight, one day Sir Nevril appeared at the doorway of the infirmary. Without even looking over, Tabby knew it was he because of the way his shadow fell, showing the bumps of his curly hair and the breadth of his shoulders…and the way he stood. Casually leaning against the doorway as if waiting for her to notice him.

Quelling the pleasant little flutter in her chest—the one Tabby had begun to notice more oft as of late when he made his appearance—she took her time finishing the project she was doing: sewing a small, warm pocket for a very young rabbit found abandoned inside a small depression in the meadow.

When she looked up and their eyes met, Tabatha felt a quirk of something hot and unfamiliar rush through her. This caused her to speak sharply, "Aye? And what do you there, blocking all of my light, Sir Rabbit Stew?"

Nevril seemed to take this as an invitation and stepped into the small space. He wore no mail today, and so his movements were silent except for the soft grinding of his boot in the dirt. "I bethought you would find this helpful," he said, pulling something out of his tunic.

It gleamed dully in the middling light, but its subtle rattling was familiar to Tabatha. She rose and took the object—a small silvery thing made of chain mail. "What is it?"

He hesitated, then released his breath. "Put it on."

By now she'd unfolded it and saw that it was a mitten, made of mail. Small, much smaller than the one of his she'd borrowed when unmuzzling the fox. Tabby's heart began to beat rapidly as she realized the mitt was just the size of her own hand. "Nevril," she breathed, staring down at it. Then she looked at him in surprise. "I...is this for me?"

He nodded abruptly, but his eyes did not leave her face. "Mayhap you will keep from being bitten when you do your work." He seemed awkward and tense.

Her face had gone hot and her insides shuddered with delight and shock. Not only was this an expensive gift, but it was so... thoughtful. Tabby couldn't remember ever being given something so perfect. She could hardly breathe as she looked down at the mitt, then back up at him. "Nevril...I...thank you." She blinked hard, suddenly filled with some indefinable emotion. "'Tis a most wondrous, wondrous gift." She swallowed and slipped on the mitt.

It fit perfectly, as if someone had formed the mail precisely around her hand whilst she waited. Tabby looked back up at him. "I do not know how to thank you, sir," she whispered. And all at once, her heart was ramrodding in her chest.

"I can think of one way," he said, his voice quiet...yet very loud in the close, dim shelter.

"How?" she asked around the sudden frog filling her throat. The flush of heat grew stronger and her stomach flipped around like a fish out of water.

"Might you...might you answer a question for me?" Nevril replied.

Tabby was aware of a wave of disappointment, but she said, "I would attempt it."

He nodded. "Haps you would tell me, Mistress Tabatha, what 'tis about an armored man that stirs so much loathing in you."

Oh. She snatched in her breath, feeling her eyes go wide. "'Tis...was...my father. He was a knight. A skillful one. He loved to fight, he was always the first to draw his sword or to lead a siege. Every day, it seemed, he looked for a chance to die. My mother hated it. She begged him not to leave, then wept when he did, always certain he would never return. And one day...he didn't." She swallowed, her throat burning. "My mother...she went a little mad. For five years, I cared for her like a child. At last she died, finally at peace. I do not wish to be like my mother," she added fiercely, aware, at the same time, of a strange, ill-fitting chill settling over her. A disappointment, an emptiness. But she grated out the words—words she'd repeated over and over throughout her life. "I will never love a man of war. I cannot."

A long silence stretched, and for a moment, she thought he might leave. His posture stiffened and he was staring at the ground. "'Tis a great shame, then," he said at last. His voice was low and grated like metal over stone. "For this man of war…*loves you*."

His words hung there for a moment, raw and taut. She could think of naught to say, for her insides churned with heat and nausea, mixing and battling. *I cannot.*

"Good day, Mistress Tabatha," he said, turning on the ball of his booted foot. The grinding sound was like a roar in her ears. "I shall not encumber you with my presence ever again."

"Wait," she said, grabbing for his arm. Then she dropped her hand, fearful she'd overstepped. The chain mail mitt slid to the ground in a soft thunk.

"Aye?" he said, and in the low light, she saw a flare of hope in his eyes. She swallowed hard, forcing her heart back down into its proper place.

"Mayhap…mayhap I should thank you in some other way," she said, forcing the words from her suddenly dry throat. "Other than answering a question."

His expression closed off. "Indeed?" He sounded impatient now, irritable; tension emanated from him. The muscles in his jaw were tight.

But before she could think of aught to say, there was a commotion in the bailey. Nevril looked down at her for another instant, then firmly pulled his arm away. "Good day, Mistress Tabatha."

Wait! She cried the word inside, but she could not force her lips to move. And then he was gone, out of the lean-to and into the sunny bailey.

When she would have gone after Nevril—though for what purpose, she was uncertain—she found him greeting new arrivals from Warwick. Though Lord Malcolm was not among them, Tabby noticed a pretty blond child riding in a cart, along with her mother. Nevril greeted them warmly and lapsed into a long, intense conversation with the girl's mother.

Afterward, Tabby watched as he bounced the girl-child from the cart and, settling her atop his shoulders, took her and the mother off into the keep.

~*~

"I HAVE *oft seen this malady of the red-orange spots,"* wrote Maris of Ludingdon. The note was enclosed within a message from her husband, Dirick, to Malcolm. *"It begins with the cattle, on their tongues, as you have noted, and at times is known to spread to men. And though it can be devastating, there is a treatment that will keep it at some bay and decrease the chances of death. You are right to confine those who have it, and to send away those weak and old who have not yet been afflicted."*

Mal read on, appreciating the legibility of Lady Maris's neat script compared to the scrawl of her husband's. Both messages, however, were of equal use to him. Dirick was responding to Mal's message regarding the certainty that Queen Eleanor had attempted to take matters into her own hands regarding his marriage to Judith, and Lady Maris detailed a recipe of bearberry leaves steeped with rosemary as a remedy for the illness at Warwick.

Dirick's words, however, were not as optimistic. *"I will confer with Mal Verne and Salisbury as to the best course to take while ruffling no feathers or turning over no ugly stones. At the least, if there is any news or rumblings, I shall send to you at once. In the mean while, 'tis best to stay close at home."*

Malcolm's mouth flattened grimly at Dirick's last sentence. He was home, aye, but filled with discontent. While at Clarendon, he could only anticipate returning to Warwick, to his home—but now he was here, away from the politics and people, surrounded by his land, attending to his domain…and yet he was discontent.

It was no difficult task for him to realize why. And his foul mood wasn't simply because he'd been sleeping in an empty bed for the two months since his wedding. That could easily be remedied—there were plenty of willing women in the keep or the village who would be happy to see to those base needs. Every man utilized whores when his wife wasn't available—or even, sometimes, if she was.

But Mal found he had no interest in such a simple solution. And that realization alone was enough to make his chest tighten, and his mood more foul. Yet, it wasn't merely the lack of coupling that had him pacing his chamber at night, or feeling unsettled when he sat to meal. He found himself actually missing Judith's company, desiring to confer with her about problems and issues that arose about the estate, and—most telling of all—wondering about her, wishing to hear about her thoughts and experiences during the days.

It was a shocking realization to a man who'd meant to marry only for the purpose of breeding an heir…and yet, he was filled with a sense of inevitability. For ever since the morrow Judith had manipulated him into playing chess, he sensed he'd been fighting a losing battle.

Indeed. He had no armor against her. No protection.

If only she could come to accept him as well.

~*~

TABATHA EASILY healed the wing of the sparrow which Nevril had brought to her; it was a matter of making certain the bird rested while the bent wing vein mended itself. And though, true to his word, he no longer visited her in the animal infirmary, she did make much use of the chain mail mitten and could not help but think of him regularly.

For oftimes when she came to the small lean-to in the mornings after attending to Lady Judith, Tabby would find a basket or cage with an injured animal waiting for her. Or at times, a serf-boy or villager would bring a cat, dog, or even a hen, to her for care.

And though she tensed hopefully every time she heard the rattle of chain mail or the heavy footfall of a man outside of the infirmary, and though she looked for Nevril's curly head in the hall, she never saw him. An ache in her chest that had begun when he walked away continued to swell and grow over the next weeks.

Tabby also noticed that the blond girl who'd arrived from Warwick with her mother often played in the herb garden behind the kitchens. Though she was young, the child, whose name she learned was Violet, reminded Tabatha of an old man named Gentle Ned who used to help her grandfather sew the jesses for Judith's father's hawks. Violet liked to wander among the flowers in the herb garden and orchard, but Tabby noticed the girl only ever picked a single blossom.

"My poppy says I must save them for him," Violet told her one day as she examined a cluster of golden calendula. "One each day."

"And where do you keep all these flowers for your papa? Does your mama help you find a place?" Tabby couldn't help but feel a kinship for the girl, for surely her "poppy" was off fighting some war somewhere.

"My mama is with the angels," Violet told her matter-of-factly, crouching down to get a better look at one of the flowers. She seemed to have honed in on her choice.

"That is not your mama?" Tabby asked, gesturing to the woman named Clara, who was chatting happily with one of the kitchen maids as they shelled peas.

"Nay, my mama is in heaven. That's only Clara," said Violet, who'd transferred her attention to a fuzzy orange and black caterpillar. "Soft!"

"Aye, but do not touch him very hard," Tabby warned as a pudgy little finger came out inquisitively. "Else you might squash him."

"Oh," Violet said, retracting her hand immediately. "But could you not fix him then?"

"I? Oh, I could not do that."

"But Sir Nevril says you can fix any creature," Violet told her, now fixing her guileless blue eyes on her.

A sudden warmth blossomed through Tabby's chest, then waned into emptiness. "Only God can fix any creature. I can merely help them. Sometimes. If they are not too sick."

"My poppy says I had to come from Warwick to stay away from the sick cows," Violet informed her, once again looking at the flowers. "He didn't want me to get their sickness."

"I see," Tabatha replied. But her thoughts were elsewhere, stuck suddenly on the realization that the little girl's papa might be off fighting a war…but it was her mama who'd died and left her alone. Not her papa. "Does your papa miss your mama? Is he sad, now that she is with the angels?"

Violet paused from her examination of the calendula and turned to look at Tabby. "I miss my mama. But I have Clara. And my poppy is not sad except when the cows die."

Tabby drew in a deep breath and might have responded, but a heavy footstep behind her made her turn. She looked up into Nevril's familiar, bearded, scarred face, and all at once a rush of heat and shivers washed over her. Her cheeks went hot and her knees felt weak.

And all at once, she realized what a fool she'd been.

But Nevril wasn't looking at her; his attention was fixed on Violet. "Come now, little one. Do you not be underfoot here. The mistress is working."

"But I must get a flower for Poppy," said Violet, her lower lip coming out mutinously. "He said one every day. And I must find one for him before he comes from Warwick."

"Now, Violet," Nevril began.

"My name is *Lady* Vio—" But her words were cut off as Nevril swooped her up into his arms, then the girl was overcome by a gust of laughter following by shrieking giggles.

Tabby felt a quiver of something in the back of her mind and looked up at Nevril. He seemed unusually tense, even as he bounced the child in his arms. "Clara!" he bellowed, stalking away without a word to Tabby.

Tabatha rose to her feet, watching them…and listening. At the sound of her name, Clara looked over from the earnest conversation with some of her friends. Her eyes widened and she scrambled to her feet, coming toward Nevril and Violet.

When Tabby heard something that sounded like "Lord Malcolm," she frowned. Nevril glanced over his shoulder at her, and both he and Clara had guilty looks on their faces. Then they seemed to be arguing—or at the least discussing something very vehemently.

By now Tabby had approached, and she was close enough to hear, "He will be furious when—" before Nevril stopped himself. He thrust the giggling Violet at a frightened-looking Clara, then turned.

"Mistress Tabatha," he said. "Is aught amiss?"

She looked from him to Violet to Clara and then, that quivering growing stronger in the back of her mind, she said, "Sir Nevril. If you might walk with me a moment?"

He hesitated, causing an icy hand to grip her insides and then squeeze, but then he said reluctantly, "Aye."

Tabby was aware that her palms had gone damp and her mouth dry. What was she to say? How could she tell him…what she wasn't quite certain of?

Nevril walked with such lead feet that she was nearly moved to set him free. But instead she continued until they were in a quiet place in the garden, beneath a shadowy rose arbor.

"I hope the girl didn't bother you," he said stiffly. He stood apart from her, his hands on his hips, looking just over her shoulder. His cheeks were ruddy and his expression emotionless.

"Who is that girl?" Tabatha asked, seizing on the topic at hand. Though it wasn't the reason she wanted to speak with him, it would do to begin, while she worked up her courage. "She is from Warwick. Is she your daughter?"

"Nay!" Nevril replied, startled, his attention coming back to her. "I have never been wed."

Tabby looked at him, and then all at once comprehension dawned. *Lady* Violet. There was only one lady at Warwick, aside from Judith. "She is Lord Malcolm's child, isn't she?"

Nevril's jaw tightened and his lips curled into each other. "Mistress Tabatha, you need have no worry about the girl. She won't bother you again."

Tabby looked at him, and all at once she no longer cared about Violet or Lord Malcolm or even, for that moment, Lady Judith. Her insides were aflutter and her heart pounded roughly. She swallowed hard and stepped closer to him, looking up into his stony face. "What I said, Sir Nevril…about—about never loving a man of war…? Do you recall?"

He blanched, then that harsh expression returned as he made a sound of derision. "Do I *recall?* How could I *forget?*"

She shook her head, drew in a deep breath. This was not what she meant to say, how she meant to go about this. Trying to keep her words steady and strong, she whispered, "I…'tis possible…I might find that my mind has changed."

He stilled, his eyes widening a fraction. "Indeed?" His voice came out in low, rough syllables.

Holding her breath, praying she hadn't waited too long, Tabatha stepped toward him and rested a hand on his chest. She looked up, suddenly lost in his gaze. Then, very slowly, one of his large hands reached out, sliding around to cup the back of her head…and he lowered his face toward hers.

The prickle of his beard and mustache was pleasant and soft, but it was the firm touch of his lips that had Tabby's eyes closing and her heart thudding madly. Warmth exploded inside her, rushing through her limbs as, after a moment, he slid his arms fully around her, pulling her up against him in a long, earnest kiss.

When he lifted his head, looking down at her with searching eyes, he said, "Mayhap your mind has been changed, Mistress Tabatha?"

"I am not certain," she replied breathlessly. "Mayhap I must needs more convincing."

His surprised, delighted laugh was smothered when he gathered her up again for another very long, very thorough kiss.

It was not a long time later when Tabby confessed that her mind had most definitely been changed.

FIFTEEN

IT WAS two months since Judith had been unceremoniously dumped off at Lilyfare.

Several things had come to pass during that time, including the confirmation that she was not carrying the future Lord Warwick. Nor had Judith received any messages from her husband, other than one that had been delivered when Sir Lelan and a group of others had arrived from Warwick, nearly a month ago.

My lady wife, read the message, *from your devoted lord husband, greetings.*

I have received your letter and I beg apology for keeping your messenger longer than intended. If you are reading this, then Sir Waldren has returned, bearing this missive from me, and I trust you will not punish him for his seeming disobedience.

I found it necessary to keep him at Warwick for a fortnight to ensure he did not carry with him the orange-spot illness that has wreaked havoc among my cows, and is now beginning to infect the people here. I did not wish him to carry this plague to Lilyfare and endanger you and others. 'Tis also the reason I cannot, in good conscience, return to Lilyfare at this time. I do not wish to leave whilst my people are ill and dying. I hope and pray this ague does not rise at Lilyfare, and I beg you send word at the nonce if the cattle there take ill with red-orange spots on their muzzles.

I thank you also for the information contained in your previous communication. Though it was appreciated, it was not well-received, as you might expect. I have taken it upon myself to send word to our friends about the situation in the hopes that aught may be rectified by one means or another. Until then, I beg you to remain within Lilyfare and to send word immediately should any visitors arrive, or any summons be sent to you.

I do not know when I shall be able to quit Warwick. As the illness spreads, 'tis less likely that I dare travel. In the mean while, I hope this finds you well. And if there is any change regarding your health, I bid you send me news.

Malcolm de Monde, Lord of Warwick, & etc. 15th of August, 1166. Warwick Keep.

Judith had read the message several times, wondering at the final sentence above the close. *"And if there is any change regarding your health..."* Was he asking if she was with child, or was he referring to the plague-like illness?

She gnawed over that sentence oft during the month since she received the missive. He cared only if she was breeding? If she was not, did that mean he would come to Lilyfare in an effort to get her with child—then leave once more?

A shiver of worry huddled deep in her belly when she realized *he* could contract the frightening illness, and *he* could die. Was that why he stayed away? Because he feared infecting her?

Judith's confused thoughts must have translated to distress or distraction as she swung the lure for Hecate, for the raptor descended unexpectedly, landing on her ungloved hand.

Judith cried out as the bird's sharp talons bit into the top of her hand. She froze as the bird stilled, waiting for the food reward. Despite her pain, Judith flipped the lure enticingly onto the ground, steeling herself as Hecate launched off her hand down to the bit of raw meat. As the raptor took off, her talons dug in a little more with the effort, but then released her mistress's hand.

Blinking back tears of pain, Judith looked down at her fist. Blood trickled from the deepest cut—but she was fortunate, for she'd been footed several times in the past, and Hecate had been gentle with her today.

"'Tis only what I get for being distracted," she said aloud, turning to go back inside the mews for a clean cloth—then stopped abruptly.

A young girl, surely no more than a decade old, stood in a corner of the falcons' flying yard, watching her. She had wispy blond hair and huge blue eyes and the expression on her innocent face was a combination of concern and curiosity.

"Hail there, young mistress," said Judith, looking around for any sign of the girl's friends or family. The child didn't look familiar, but Judith was not acquainted with every child of every serf, villein, or freeperson in Lilyfare after her long absence.

But she thought it strange that the girl was unattended and in an area of the courtyard restricted only to those who cared for the raptors and the horses. While Judith wasn't particularly strict about such things—for she herself had roamed among the mews, meadows, and stables when she was a child, mixing with the children of serf and freemen alike—she did find it odd the girl was alone and unsupervised. It could be dangerous in the stable area.

"Are you the lady with the bird on her hand? My poppy told me about you," said the girl, still watching her with those huge eyes. She had edged out from the corner but still kept a respectable distance. "Why are you bleeding?"

Judith's fist was throbbing with pain, and the blood dripped in large plops onto the ground. "The falcon cut me with her talons," she told the girl. "I must attend to it." She whistled for Hecate, who'd finished her reward, then turned to go into the mews. Inside, she kept cloths and a paste for such situations, for one could not be called an experienced falconer if one's hands had no scars.

"Is it hot?" asked the girl, coming closer.

Judith stopped, holding up her gloved hand for Hecate to light. "Hot? Nay, it stings a bit, but it isn't hot." She gestured with her injured hand, showing the nameless girl where Hecate had gripped her as she went into the mews.

But the girl wasn't looking at her hand. She touched her wispy curls as she stared at Judith. "Your hair. Is it hot as fire? Does it not burn your head? And your pillow, when you sleep?"

"Ah," Judith replied with a little laugh. "Nay, 'tis not hot." She smiled ruefully at the girl. "I must bandage my hand. Will you watch?"

Inside the structure that included the mews as well as a working room, Judith released Hecate into the coop area, then closed the door. When she turned, she saw that the girl had wandered in and was standing near the entrance, watching silently. It was then that Judith realized the girl wore the same expression and had the same wondrous look in her eyes as the man she'd known as Gentle Ned.

"What is your name, young mistress?" she asked, remembering the man from her youth. Gentle Ned had been the son of one of the house servants, and he would sit for hours weaving baskets or repairing fishing nets near the fire. His thick fingers had been nimble and quick while his mind remained simple and childlike all the days of his life.

"I am Lady Violet," said the girl, drawing herself straight with a puffed-up chest.

"Very well then, Violet," Judith replied as she opened the jar with her salve. "I am Lady Judith."

"I am *Lady* Violet," the girl said with a stamp of her foot. "My poppy says I am a lady."

"Indeed," Judith replied, spreading the paste over her wounds. The blood had begun to coagulate and soon would stop, but the salve would help to keep the bad humors for getting in through the open skin. "Very well, then, *Lady* Violet. I shan't forget that," she said gravely, wondering which of her men-at-arms had fathered such a pretty little girl.

"May I touch it?"

Judith looked at her. "What do you wish to touch?"

"Your...." The girl moved her hand over her head, pulling a handful of her own hair.

"My hair?" Judith hesitated, then shrugged. "Very well. Allow me to finish wrapping my hand."

"You have ughies," Violet said, creeping closer with her attention trained on Judith's hand.

"Ughies?"

"Aye." Once again, the girl moved her hand in a gesture in place of words to indicate the talon marks. "My poppy says they are ughies when they bleed."

By now, Judith had more than a mild curiosity about Violet's "poppy," but she was more intent on the matter at hand. "Aye, but this will make it stop bleeding, God willing," she said, finishing with a bandage. "It is not the first time Hecate has expressed her irritation with me."

"Hec-ty?"

"My falcon. Did you not see her?"

"Oh, aye," Violet replied, her eyes wide as she looked toward the mews door. "I should like to pet her and hug her. She is nice."

Judith gave a little chuckle. "I do not think Hecate would appreciate your hugs. Falcons don't much like people, and they certainly don't wish to be hugged. But mayhap some day she will allow you to touch her feathers. If you are very careful and you allow me to help you."

"Oh, aye," said the girl, seeming to have forgotten her desire to touch Judith's hair.

All at once Judith heard a commotion outside and she went to the door of workroom, opening it to see what was happening in the bailey.

"Violet!" called a strident female voice. "Violet! Where are you?"

"Violet!" came another shout—this one from a man. "Where can you be?"

Judith looked at her new friend. "Someone is looking for you. Mayhap your papa and mama?"

Violet, who'd been nibbling on the side of her forefinger, shook her head. "Nay. Mama is in heaven, and my poppy isn't here now." She looked at the door, as if only mildly interested in the fact that her name was being shouted about.

By now, Judith had gone out into the courtyard, gesturing for the girl to follow her. "Here," she called when she saw a frantic-looking woman running down the thoroughfare. "Are you looking for Violet?"

The woman stopped and gaped when she saw Judith standing there with Violet, and all at once the woman was curtsying and bowing. "Oh, my lady, oh, I am so sorry! Oh, my lady, please forgive me…I did not mean…."

"Violet!" called a deep voice, and just then Sir Nevril came barreling around the corner of the nearby stable. Judith was surprised to see Tabatha in his wake, followed by two other men-at-arms.

When they saw her, both Tabatha and Nevril froze, their eyes going from Judith to Violet to the older lady and back again. The other men stumbled to a halt, and everyone seemed to be looking around as if lost.

"What is the meaning of this?" Judith asked sharply. She felt as if she'd walked into the middle of a chamber and everyone had stopped talking at the sight of her—not so very different from the way she'd felt that night at Clarendon when it first became known she was the king's mistress. 'Twas not a pleasant feeling.

"'Tis nothing, my lady," Tabatha said, speaking first after exchanging a glance with Nevril. "Clara was watching little mistress Violet, and she somehow slipped away. I hope she wasn't—uh—bothering you."

"Come now, little poppet," crooned the other woman hopefully—presumably the erstwhile Clara—as she crooked her finger at the girl.

"I am *Lady* Violet," said the urchin, her hands going to her hips. "Lady Violet de Monde!"

Everything stopped at that moment. Judith's breath caught and she looked at the horror-stricken faces around her. Something inside her pitched unpleasantly, and she turned to look at the girl. Bending so they were nearly eye-to-eye, she said, "What is your papa's name, Lady Violet?"

"Lord Malcolm de Monde, Lord of Warwick," pronounced the little girl proudly.

Judith straightened abruptly and looked around at the circle of guilt-ridden faces surrounding her. "I see," was all she said. Her mind was awhirl, her insides a storm. "And how long have you been here at Lilyfare?"

This question was not directed at the girl, but instead at Sir Nevril—who seemed the most likely person to have a truthful answer.

"My lady," Tabatha said, putting out a hand as if to shield Nevril from needing to respond.

But he would have naught of it. He stepped forward, pushing Tabby behind him as he bowed to Judith. He shifted himself protectively in front of Violet, who'd been dragged firmly to Clara's side by the wide-eyed woman. "My lady, please do not take your fury on the girl or her nurse," he said. "'Tis only the fault of me, for I was supposed to be watching her whilst—"

"Silence!" Judith ordered. "I do not wish to hear any explanation or excuses." For the only person on whom she would take her fury would be Lady Violet's "poppy."

Judith looked down at Violet, who did not appear to be cowed by the tension going on around her. "I shall see you on the morrow, Lady Violet. Here. Just after the midday meal. And I shall properly introduce you to Hecate."

With that, she spun about and stalked off.

~*~

"**TELL ME** what you know of Violet," Judith demanded of Tabatha later that evening.

"What do you mean, my lady?" said the maid, industriously shaking one of the bed coverings out the chamber window. Summer was waning and soon the cool days of autumn would fall. She'd replaced the bed curtains with ones of heavier material to keep the cold out, and now fur blankets would cover the mattress.

But Judith would have none of her evasion, and when she did not respond other than slamming down a metal goblet on the table, Tabatha turned slowly. She held the fur blanket in a bundle protectively against her middle as she looked at her mistress. Then, drawing in a deep breath, she exhaled and said, "I do not know much, my lady. Truly. Other than what Nevril has told me."

"And so it is Nevril now—no longer Sir Rabbit Stew?" Judith's tones were sharper than usual. Knowing she was in a bad temper did little to alleviate it, for after meeting Violet, she had spent much of the day stewing about the situation and the mood had settled over her like a heavy cloud.

"Aye," replied Tabby. Her eyes were downcast and her cheeks flushed pink. "He has asked me to wed him…."

"A man of war? A man in chain mail? Surely you set him on the right path and told him nay." Judith heard how brittle her voice was, but at the moment, she simply couldn't care. She was empty, bereft, confused.

"Uhm…." Tabatha was silent for a moment, then she turned. "I agreed. To wed him."

"Indeed. And when were you going to approach me on this subject? Or was this meant to be yet another secret kept from me?"

Tabby shook her head, misery in every element of her posture. "Ah, my lady. 'Twas only just this morrow that he asked me. And then…everything happened. Now he fears you will not allow us to wed, and you will send everyone from Warwick away."

Judith hmphed. The thought had indeed crossed her mind during the fit of rage that caught her up some time ago. But of course that was not practical. Nor was it necessary. Still. Once roused, she had a temper to match her flaming hair, and Nevril was right to be wary of her—at the least until her husband was there to bear the brunt of her fury, hurt and confusion.

Would he never return?

"What do you know of Violet? Why is she here? And why was her presence and identity kept from me?"

The maid snapped the fur covering over the bed and watched it settle into place. "Lord Malcolm sent her here, to be away from Warwick. He commanded that she be kept from your sight and out of your way. I do not know why, my lady," Tabby added quickly as Judith opened her mouth to speak. "I truly do not."

"I do not understand," Judith fumed. "He has never spoken to me of a daughter—or of any child." She recalled asking him, that very first night they'd spoken in the bailey at Clarendon. He'd never answered her.

Then a thought struck her, slightly easing her concern. She looked at Tabatha. "Is Violet his legitimate daughter?" If she had been born out of wedlock, that could explain why Mal hadn't told her, and why he would have little to do with Violet. Many men did little more than acknowledge their natural children.

"Aye, she is the daughter of Lord Malcolm and Lady Sarah. The only child of their issue."

Judith's heart fell. *He never told me of her. Why did he never tell me?*

Was he ashamed of Violet? Of the simple little girl who could never be a great lady? Did he simply mean to ignore her existence because she would never be more than a gentle, childish girl? Though it did not seem like the Malcolm she'd come to know, Judith was well aware of the import men set upon their heirs. Particularly sons.

One thing was certain. She was not about to neglect the girl as much as her father appeared to have done. Whether Mal liked it or not, Violet was a lady of Warwick.

_*_

AT LAST. By God, at last Mal could return to his wife.

The disease that filtered through Warwick had died away, in the end killing fifteen cows and bulls as well as six people, though several more had been infected. But there had been no new instances of the illness for over a se'ennight, and that was enough to give Mal the confidence to leave.

Back to Lilyfare. Back to Judith. Back to Violet. The rhythm of those thoughts, which he'd done his best to bury since arriving at Warwick, settled in his mind as he rode along. He felt a combination of trepidation and anticipation at seeing his wife again. But, by the rood, it had been well over two months since he'd touched her—and as he'd had no word from her otherwise, he must assume she was not with child.

Malcolm could not summon even a bit of disappointment over that conclusion, for that only meant he must try again. And she could not deny him that, tears or no tears.

At the least, that was what he told himself.

Malcolm pressed his party of men-at-arms to travel as quickly as possible. They had more than a day's journey to Delbring, where they could take succor for the night, and then another half day to Lilyfare.

But Mal did not wish to delay even for a night of sleep on a soft pallet at Delbring. They would push on and rest for some short hours beneath the stars, well past Lady Beatrice's estate, which would bring them to Lilyfare before the midday meal on the second day.

Yet the best-laid plans are oft disrupted, as Malcolm well knew, and later on when they were not far from Delbring they spied a fast-riding messenger bearing the standard of that estate.

"Ho there!"

Malcolm's group paused when they were hailed by the Delbring messenger, a man-at-arms who was well-known to them. "Lord Warwick, greetings!" said Sir Gilard.

"Where do you go in such a hurry?" Malcolm asked, even as he eyed the sun's distance from the horizon. Eight hours and he would be at Lilyfare…and in his wife's bed. Just after midnight, but well before dawn.

Once there, he had no intention of leaving the chamber until the noon meal.

"I am come with a message to you, my lord. From Lord Bruse of Delbring."

"Then deliver it, man, for we travel hard and fast," Malcolm told him.

"Lord Bruse sends word of a plague that is spreading through our cattle. One of our villagers has taken ill as well, with the same red-orange spots that afflicted the cows. He is fearful for his wife, daughter, and infant son, and asks for succor for them until the plague has passed."

Peste. Now Mal would be delayed, despite his intention otherwise. "We have just come from Warwick after battling that selfsame illness. I will confer with Lord Bruse, for there is a treatment. Let us to Delbring."

"Aye, my lord. He would speak with you. But Lady Ondine, Lady Beatrice, and the child are some leagues behind me. He has sent them out to be safe from the illness."

"Very well. I shall talk with Lord Bruse, and his family may ride with us. But we are bound for Lilyfare, which is only some hours ride west. I have left Warwick closed, for I do not wish the illness to resurrect there until all have recovered. Mayhap Lord Bruse's family will go with us to Lilyfare, where my wife will offer hospitality."

"Then let us go on," Sir Gilard said, relief clearly on his face.

A short time later, Malcolm was speaking with Bruse, just outside the gates of the bailey at Delbring. Lady Ondine's and Lady Beatrice's traveling party, whom they'd met on the way, waited on the side of the road.

"We had this very plague at Warwick," Mal told him, noting that the older man seemed weary and worried. "Six dead and more than two dozen cattle before I learned of a medicine that will ease the symptoms and save most lives—except those of the very young and weak. 'Tis smart to send your infant son away."

"There is a remedy?" Bruse's eyes lit with hope.

"Aye. I learned of it in a letter from Maris of Ludingdon, who is very skilled in healing. 'Tis bearberry leaves steeped with rosemary. Drink it once the first spot appears. But we will take your wife, daughter and son to Lilyfare to ensure their safety."

Bruse nodded, his face showing relief. "Many thanks, Malcolm. And felicitations on your excellent choice of Judith of Kentworth. I cannot say I am not disappointed Beatrice did not make a match with you, but nor can I fault you for taking a much wealthier bride."

"'Twas due to no short-coming of your daughter," Malcolm assured him quickly.

"Oh, aye, of course," Bruse replied, waving him off. "And I do not believe Beatrice would have been such a good match for you anyway, for she is...ah...quiet. I did not even broach the subject with her, for now that I have an heir in Samuel, 'tis possible she may go to convent, where I believe she would be most happy. You appear weary, Warwick. 'Tis more than a bit exhausting to be newly wed, as I recall." He grinned lecherously, obviously thinking of the recent marriage to his second, much-younger wife, Ondine.

Malcolm felt a pang of frustration and impatience at the reminder. "Aye, but 'tis a wearying of the best kind. Now, as I wish to return to such weary exertion," he said with a hint of ruefulness, "'tis time for me to ride on."

"Very well. Send word once you've reached Lilyfare, and I will advise when all is well here," Bruse said. He went over to bid his wife and son, as well as his daughter, farewell as Mal chafed at yet more delay.

Now he must needs ride slowly because of the ladies, and they would be forced to stop for the night. But, even with that adjustment in his plans, God willing he'd be at Lilyfare by twilight on the morrow. And then he would have all of the night with Judith.

And mayhap part of the next day.

That thought cheered him enough, and as they set out, Mal rode over to greet Ondine, Beatrice, and Samuel—the boy of less than a year old. The fact that Bruse now had a male heir, which would necessitate a smaller dowry for Beatrice, had been only part of the reason Mal had been uncertain about a match with her.

Lord Bruse's family rode in a comfortable, covered cart, which was the cause of the slower pace. But one of the shutters was open, leaving the opportunity for him to trot along next to the ladies and converse.

"Greetings, Lady Ondine and Lady Beatrice," he said. "We shall travel only three more hours and then we will stop for the night. If you wish to ride ahorse for a while, Lady Beatrice or Lady Ondine, I can arrange for it."

"Nay, of course I will stay with Samuel," said Lady Ondine.

"Oh no, my lord," said Lady Beatrice, who, as usual, seemed scarcely able to look at him, let alone speak. "I am content here inside this cart."

"Very well," Mal said. "Is there aught you need?"

"Nay," said Lady Beatrice.

As he looked down at her dark blond head and remembered her docile expression, he was overcome by a sudden, fierce wave of gratitude that she had not become his wife after all. "If you are in need of aught, send word and we will stop."

And with that, he trotted off, intent on hurrying their speed as much as possible.

Despite his attempts, their pace remained excruciatingly slow. If it wasn't Ondine who needed to stop, it was Beatrice. Or the child must be let out of the cart to toddle about, and one must take care that he didn't run beneath the horses or fall into the creek where they drank. The party stopped for the night at a small inn on the roadway a good ten hours from Lilyfare at their rate of travel, and though Mal swore he could see the lights of the village that was his destination, he was forced to make up a pallet on the ground as the inn had only room for the ladies.

He could not sleep that night, and his yearnings to be on the road were so strong that he decided he would ride ahead on the morrow—once they were within several leagues of Lilyfare. He was so intent on this, as he walked through the forest after stretching his legs for the third time in an hour, that he wasn't paying close enough attention.

It was dark and he didn't see the small hole in the ground. He stepped in it, catching his foot at an awkward angle. The next thing he knew, he *flumped* to the ground with a heavy, ignominious thud. He felt a streak of pain along his ankle, and when he furiously pulled himself upright, he found he could not bear weight on that foot.

Letting loose a string of curses that had Rike and Gambert rushing sleepily into the forest after him, Mal hobbled back to the camp, his ankle throbbing with pain. As his squires hovered uselessly, he bound his injured foot up tightly, then lay there on the ground, glowering up at the night sky, livid with himself and whoever had caused him such malfeasance.

As he'd feared, the next morrow his ankle was swollen and so tender to the touch he knew he could not ride ahorse.

When Rike ventured to suggest that Mal could sit in a cart for the remainder of the journey, he exploded.

"*A cart?* I will ride in a bloody cart on the day I am on my deathbed and not before!" he roared, flinging a mug in the general direction of the hapless boy. "Ride into Lilyfare like an ailing invalid? Are you *mad?*"

After that, all of his men avoided him—and his throwing distance—while they packed up and prepared to leave. The ladies came out of the inn and were apprised of the circumstances.

"Lord Malcolm will not travel to Lilyfare with you this morrow," Gambert explained. "But we shall be your escort, and Rike" —who looked miserable, still holding the short straw he'd drawn— "shall remain with my lord until he can travel."

Mal was hardly able to muster a civil farewell to the ladies, but at the least, with their departure, he was offered a chamber in the inn. Rike helped him hobble into the public room where he settled in a chair by the fire, propped up his foot, and commenced with ordering mug after mug of ale.

~*~

JUDITH WAS in the great hall meeting with her steward when the word came. The standard of Warwick had been sighted on the road, and the party would arrive before dusk.

She quelled a rush of excitement, reminding herself that she was still irritated and angry with Malcolm for not telling her of his daughter...but even that small betrayal could not quash her delight at his impending return. Without appearing to do so, she hurriedly finished her business with the steward, then went to her chamber.

Her insides were aflutter and her mind skipped from mental scene to mental scene as she bathed with the help of Tabatha. Of course, she would not rush out to greet Malcolm, skirts flying and hair coming unbound. Nay, that was not meet, and it would not do for him to think her so weak-willed that she had pined for his presence. Even if she had.

But she would have her hair done and don her most beautiful gown, and she would have the most sumptuous meal prepared, and the chamber aired out, and clean bedcoverings put on, and new candles scented with lavender blossoms....

And mayhap she could make him forget about Beatrice of Delbring. The knowledge that he had left her here at Lilyfare to go to Delbring continued to gnaw at her insides, picking away at her as if 'twere a small scab that could not heal. Sir Waldren had assured Judith that Malcolm had not spent more than one night at Delbring. But she could not set the knowledge fully from her mind that he had left her to go to another woman.

Yet she would do her best to do so tonight.

Then, as she arrived in the hall, timing herself to be there just as the traveling party breeched the gate of Lilyfare, Judith heard someone shout: "'Tis Delbring's colors with that of Warwick."

She stiffened, clutching the arm of the chair next to her. Surely she heard wrong. Judith raised her chin, looking about the hall, forcing herself to breathe slowly and steadily even as her insides pitched and churned. Over the mad pounding of her heart, she heard the sounds of arrival outside—the shouts, the calls, the general disruption.

And then the great doors opened and she forced herself to walk toward them, to greet the arrivals, already looking for the head and shoulders of her husband, which would tower above the others.

Instead, she found herself facing two ladies as they were announced, "Lady Ondine of Delbring and her daughter."

Everything else was lost in a roar of sound filling her ears...and then all at once Judith's world narrowed, tunneling into a red-hazed vision of the young woman before her.

Lady Beatrice of Delbring.

-*-

JUDITH DID not know how she managed to negotiate the rest of the evening, but somehow she did. She greeted her guests with all the cordiality of a great, hospitable lady, and when she learned that Malcolm had not even the decency to be present when he introduced his *mistress*, his *love*, into his *wife's home*, she somehow managed to maintain an emotionless expression.

She wasn't certain whether she actually ate any of the feast prepared, but she surely had several goblets of wine, for her head became muzzy and her mouth dry. She must have conversed with Lady Ondine and her daughter Beatrice, but Judith had little memory of the specifics of their conversation.

She did spend time looking at Beatrice, examining every aspect of the woman. She noticed her golden-blond hair, her unexceptional face, her calm, tractable expression, her delicate hands.

It must be love, she remembered thinking to herself. For what else could attract Malcolm to such a quiet, obedient, uninteresting woman?

And with that realization, misery settled over her like a heavy blanket.

It wasn't until she was alone in her chamber—having sent Tabatha off with a sharp command not to bother her until the morrow—that the misery evaporated into rage...then loathing, humiliation, and, finally, anguish.

At last, she fully comprehended Eleanor's unleashed fury... and her warning. *Pray that you must never look upon the woman your husband loves.*

Not only must Judith look upon Beatrice, but she must offer her hospitality in her own home.

So this, then, is my punishment. My penance for the greed of lust, for the disloyalty to my liege lady. For the tricking of a good and honorable man—or one who was once a good and honorable man— into wedding me.

SIXTEEN

MALCOLM FORCED himself up into the saddle less than two days after twisting his ankle. The pain was excruciating, but at the least he could put some weight on it—enough that his still swollen foot would fit in the stirrup and enable him to ride.

Rike could not hide his relief that they were on their way at last—for even Mal privately admitted the two days had been long and filled with his own bad humor, insults and much shouting. And *because* he was on his way at last, Malcolm forgave his new squire the impudence of failing to hide his feelings. And since they were, finally, en route to Lilyfare, he felt magnanimous enough to converse with Rike in a calm, level-headed manner.

For 'twould make the time go faster, and keep his mind off the nagging pain that throbbed and radiated with every one of Alpha's jolting strides. But by God, he would sleep in his own bedchamber with his wife this night if it killed him.

And after riding five of the six hours to Lilyfare, Malcolm was almost certain it would. The agony from his ankle had grown worse, feeding his impatience and frustration—not to mention his fury for being so bloody clumsy and putting himself in such a humiliating situation. He still seethed at the suggestion that he should have considered riding in a cart, but he was even more incensed that he'd stepped in a damned hole to begin with.

The fact that he'd received no word from Judith was only a minor niggling—for what was she to say to his message that he'd be delayed for two or three days? There was naught she could do, and she was likely twittering about with Beatrice and Lady Ondine, gossiping and doing the things women insisted on doing when they were together.

'Twas good, then, that they would get their visiting out of the way, for, ankle or no ankle, Malcolm meant to keep his wife confined and satisfied for at least an entire day. At the very thought of doing so, his blood raced and his body heated, flushing with anticipation and desire. So much so that he not only did not send Rike on ahead to announce his arrival at Lilyfare, but he forced himself to endure the last thirty minutes of the journey at a canter.

By the time he dismounted in the bailey and tossed his reins to the first man-at-arms he saw, Mal could barely walk. His vision was tinted red and filled with flashes of darkness. He snarled out an order not to be disturbed, then gritted his teeth and forced himself to hobble into the great hall, hoping to set eyes on the flame-red hair of his wife.

When he did not see her—although Lady Beatrice and Lady Ondine were sitting in a corner by the fire—Malcolm turned on the nearest serf and demanded to know where Lady Judith was.

"She is in her solar, my lord," said the startled woman.

Of course she was. It was hardly past midday. Still, it was mayhap a bit odd that Judith was not with the ladies from Delbring.

"We are not to be disturbed," Mal commanded—to her and to the chamber at large, catching Nevril's eye as he rushed in to greet his master.

"My lord," Nevril said, nearly sprinting over toward him. "I must tell—"

"*Nay,*" Mal said, grinding his teeth against the white-hot pain and the further delay. "I will speak with you on the morrow. And not before."

Nevril stilled and swallowed, opening his mouth to argue. But he must have seen that Mal was in no mood to be crossed, for he nodded and slunk off.

Malcolm gave his master-at-arms no further thought, for he was already striding painfully toward the stairs that would take him to the second floor. And then he was forced to stop when he realized he didn't know where his lady's solar was, for he'd never even been inside Lilyfare Keep.

A renewed wave of humiliation and frustration washed over him as he turned to another serf, demanding directions.

Thus, by the time he managed to get himself to the second level, Malcolm was very nearly out of his mind with pain, impatience and lust. He forced himself to pause outside the door of the solar, dragging in long, ragged breaths, forcing his mood under control. He was in no fit state to see his wife and he knew it.

For a long moment, Malcolm remained in the corridor. The red haze eased from his vision, the shocking, fiery pain in his ankle ebbed into a mere screaming burn, and he relaxed his jaws, which had been gritted for what seemed like hours. He drew in a deep breath and commanded himself to be easy and patient and take his time. He would even order a bath before going near her. Mayhap he would not even wait for that, and drag her *into* the bath.

Then he flung open the door of the solar. The women— scattered about the chamber sewing and mending—gasped at the sight of him, but his attention went immediately to Judith. She rose from her seat, shocked at his sudden appearance, her face pale, her hair ever-bright, her expression stunned.

Their eyes met across the chamber, and Malcolm felt his heart give a huge thud, then explode into the heat of some deep, consuming emotion. His knees shook. *At last.*

"Leave us," he ordered when all the women in the room gaped at him. "*Go!*"

They scrambled up and off their stools, their embroidery or mending tumbling to the floor amid gasps and stifled shrieks as they fled the room, taking care not to come too near him. Mal fairly slammed the door behind the flock of ninnies, never taking his eyes from Judith.

All thoughts of ordering a bath, of being easy and patient, had evaporated. With three pain-filled strides, he was there, in front of her...and it was only when he looked fully into her eyes that he realized something was very wrong.

"How *dare* you," she hissed. Her face was deadly white, its few freckles standing out like dark stars in a white sky.

Malcolm tried to rope back his shock, but it flared, shifting into impatience. "What ails you? That I dismissed your maids? Do not be a fool, Judith. You would have sent them off any—"

"Nay, you dirt-licking snake," she spat, backing away from him. Her expression had turned cold and her eyes were filled with loathing. "How *dare* you send your mistress to *my home*! Do not touch me!" she cried when he reached for her. "You will not touch me! I will not allow you to lay one finger on me!"

"What? What madness has hold of you?" he roared, suddenly blinded by fury and confusion. She was making no sense, the bitter words tumbling from her tongue like a barrage of poisoned arrows. *What mistress?* But what she said after that was what seized his attention and pride most strongly. "You are my wife, by God, and I will not be denied of you!"

"And all your secrets! And your daughter! How *dare* you! You are not fit to walk upon my land. To come into my chamber!" She shrieked mad, senseless things at him, whirling out of his reach, which was clumsy from his bad ankle. "Or to come near me! Stay away from me!"

He lunged for her again, his injury screaming in pain, and he got hold of her arm, yanking her back toward him so hard she stumbled into his chest. "What are you speaking of?" he demanded, barely keeping a leash on his control. She was his wife. She could not deny him the only thing he wanted from her. Judith's bright hair made her pale face seem even more white. Her lush lips trembled. But her eyes…they were dry and cold and tinged with madness. "Are you ill?" he demanded, trying to pull himself under control. "What mistre—"

"Take your hands off me," she cried over his words, struggling violently to free herself. "You will not touch me! I will not allow it!"

"You will not *allow* it?" Malcolm bellowed, all rationality fleeing. "You are my wife, and you will do your bloody duty to me!"

He pulled her up in front of him, most of his weight on his good foot, his hands gripping her upper arms. In the back of his

mind, he knew he was holding her too tightly, and he forced himself
to loosen his fingers, even as she kicked and jerked about in his grip.
When she slammed a wild foot into his tender, shrieking ankle he
smothered a gasp as his vision went blazing red.

"What is wrong with you?" he snarled, giving her a little shake.
"What has overtaken your mind?"

Apparently realizing she couldn't free herself, Judith calmed
a trifle. Her breathing was out of control, her breasts shuddering
and heaving against him, her hair a wild mess of red-gold curls. She
looked up at him with hatred in her eyes. "Release me," she said in a
low, unsteady voice. "I do not wish you to touch me."

He gave a hard laugh, tinged with his own mad agony. "You
might wish all you want, Judith, but you are my wife and 'tis my
right to touch you. And to have you. You do not say the king nay,
but you say it to me, your rightful husband? How dare *you*."

She recoiled as if slapped, her face going even whiter—though
he'd not thought that possible. And yet, still no tears. He felt her
trembling in his arms, shuddering against him with loathing and
mayhap fear...and yet he still yearned for her. She bewitched him
with her scent, her body, her very nearness, and he was powerless to
resist.

"You are my wife," he hissed. "You cannot deny me, Judith."

He was too rough when he pulled her to him, but he didn't
care. He buried his face in her throat, along the curve of her jaw,
inhaling her scent, tasting her warm, moist skin with demanding
lips. She vibrated against him but made no move, no sound as he
slid his hands to cup her head, shoving his fingers into her thick,
heavy hair, holding her immobile as he covered her lips, tonguing
her mouth open roughly. Drinking, tasting, devouring before he
pulled away to look at her.

Judith's eyes were downcast, and when he eased back, she
turned her face from him. Her lips were slick and full from his
brutal kiss, and she still heaved and trembled against his body. He
could feel the curve of her breasts, the useless dangle of her arms,
the warmth of her thighs burning through hauberk, mail, and hose.

His blood pounded, raging through him, the sensation surpassing even the nonstop agony piercing his ankle.

Grabbing the front of her bliaut, he fisted the material in his hands. With one sharp movement, he could tear it in two, leaving her bare to him. He could fill his eyes and hands, he could take and taste and tease…and slake his lust. Take what was his.

He tightened his hands, the fabric stretching taut between them, her breasts brushing the bottom of his knuckles—and he looked down at her.

"You will not say me nay," he whispered as she turned her gaze toward him.

Cold. It was cold and empty and, yet, lingering beneath those icy blue eyes, was anguish. And aught more he could not recognize.

"Very well, then, my lord. But do not tear my gown."

Something inside him seemed to crack—sharp and deep—and with a low cry, he shoved her from him, spinning away on his bad ankle. The sudden streak of agony nearly brought him to the ground, but with great effort, he kept himself upright as he strode out of the chamber, flinging away a stool in his wake.

Blinded by frustration and confusion, propelled by fury and madness, he trod roughly on his ruined foot, welcoming the acute pain as a relief from this other torture. He stumbled out into the hall, his fingers curled into themselves, his insides hot and aching, his face wet with tears.

He didn't know where he was going, he didn't know what place in this keep might offer him solace and sanctuary, and he staggered along in a red haze until he could no longer bear the pain. His ankle gave way and he tumbled to the ground in front of a small door, wedged open.

Malcolm dragged himself across the threshold and discovered he was in a small, dim chapel. With a hard, ironic laugh, he collapsed in front of the altar.

‿*‿

JUDITH BARELY kept herself from falling when Malcolm shoved her away, and she watched in horror as he spun and limped heavily from the chamber.

She sank to the floor, weak and shaking, covering her mouth with trembling hands. Her lips were full and still throbbed from his kiss, and God help her if she didn't still feel the warmth pulsing through her.

How could it be?

The very sight of Malcolm, suddenly appearing in the doorway, had made her heart lurch and leap with gladness. He'd been so broad and large, so familiar and beloved and powerful…and the look in his eyes. Hot and determined.

But it was only that moment of madness before she remembered all he'd done to her. How he'd betrayed and dishonored her…and that the woman he truly wanted was in the hall below.

Judith would be no woman's substitute. Oh, nay.

Yet, when he pulled her to him, when he kissed her and buried his face in the sensitive curve of her throat, murmuring against her skin, gathering her close as if he meant to devour her, she could hardly keep from sagging in his arms, dragging him to her for her own taste. Tiny licks of arousal battled with her anger and hurt, the heat of desire threatened to overtake her logic and pain. She fought it back, remaining rigid and unfeeling.

Nay, I cannot give in to him. I cannot allow him to take this from me too. For what Malcolm would take from her was much more than any damage Henry had caused.

And now her husband was gone. And she was glad for it. She must be. She must make herself be glad.

For the queen was right. To love a man was naught more than to be cursed.

_~*~_

IF HE could have ridden, Malcolm likely would have left Lilyfare. But his foot had swollen again from the abuse visited upon it, and if he hadn't torn off his boot, he would have had to cut it away. He was going nowhere soon.

As it was, he lay in the middling candlelight of the tiny chapel for some unknown length of time, wracked by agony. He wasn't certain which caused him more pain: his ankle or the ugly, incomprehensible scene with his wife.

Her cries and accusations left a shocked muddle in his hazy mind. His mistress? Beneath her roof? What madness was that? His *daughter*? Well, *that* he understood, but the rest of it…. He shook his head wearily, his anger having ebbed some small bit…until he remembered Judith's loathing and her denial of him. Then white-hot fury incensed him once again, followed by black despair.

Fool. You should have wed Beatrice and been done with it. At the least then you wouldn't have the Queen of England trying to kill you as well.

He leaned back against the wall, tipping his head against the stone, and tried to ignore the incessant pounding of his foot. But that was preferable to thinking on the misery his life had become—and so he meditated upon the constant agony, fairly praying for the pain to increase.

Some hours later—after he had drunk all of the unconsecrated wine he found in the sacristy—he heard the sound of a person passing along the corridor. When he shouted for attendance, a serf poked his head in curiously and Mal demanded his squire and another bottle of wine—not in that order.

This directive brought a cautious Gambert and Rike, and—praise God—more wine. Eventually, the squires helped Mal to his feet and started down the corridor. It was a slow, laborious process, for he was unable to put any weight on his foot and weighed several stone more than either of the young men.

Eventually, they reached the doorway to a room Mal recognized as the master chamber, belonging to the lord and lady of Lilyfare. His rightful place.

"Belowstairs," he snarled. "I would go belowstairs. To the hall."

Gambert and Rike exchanged looks, but neither was mad enough to speak. However, they called for Nevril to assist managing their lord down the narrow stairs. One look at Malcolm and any question the master-at-arms might have died on his lips.

Eventually, Mal was installed in a massive chair in the hall in a corner near one of the large fireplaces. His purple-green-yellow foot, thrice its normal size, was propped on a table in front of him. It was well after the evening meal and the keep was settling for the night, but Gambert brought him a platter of food.

Soon, the hall was empty and quiet, dark of everything but the last embers of his fire.

~*~

JUDITH SLEPT fitfully that night, expecting her husband to storm into the chamber at any moment.

She hadn't dared bolt the door against him, and she warred with herself over wanting him to appear and demand she welcome him back in her bed…or wanting to be left alone to grieve and loathe and rage.

The next morrow, she dragged herself from bed just after dawn, before even Tabatha had risen. When she came down the stairs into the hall, which was just stirring for the day, she saw him and stilled.

From the dim corner where he sat, Malcolm's eyes fastened on her, cold and dark. They glittered, like that of a predator. Judith gave a little shiver and turned away, hastening to the kitchens and far from him, her heart thudding heavily.

What have I done?

She took her time away from the hall, circumventing the area as long as she could. But at last, well into the middle of the morning, Judith had no choice but to return. As she walked through, she saw Lady Beatrice and Lady Ondine sitting with Malcolm in the corner.

Jealousy flared hot inside her and Judith stalked away, head held high, heart pounding furiously. She was just out of sight of the hall when she heard, "Poppy!"

Oh nay.

She spun in time to see Violet charging across the room toward her father. Judith froze and turned, her heart in her throat as she waited to see whether Mal acknowledged his daughter. Her fingers curled into the edge of the stone wall and she tensed, ready to rush over and swoop the naive little girl away from him.

When Violet launched herself into Mal's lap, Judith held her breath. But though a flash of pain crossed his face as the girl jarred his foot, he was smiling as he caught her up in his arms.

Smiling.

Judith exhaled in relief and wonder. Had she ever seen Malcolm smile like that? With such an expression of love and affection on his face? With such eagerness and light?

This was not a man who was ashamed by or neglected his daughter.

So then why...why would he keep her from Judith? Why would he send her secretly to Lilyfare?

She peered around the corner again, watching. Malcolm and Violet were in earnest conversation, him stroking her hair as the little girl jabbed a finger in the direction of his injured foot, then turned to speak to....

Lady Beatrice. Who smiled and nodded and tapped Violet smartly on the nose.

Judith's heart seized, squeezing so tightly she couldn't breathe. Of course. Mal had brought both of his women to Lilyfare...and now they were together. The three of them.

And she...she was merely the wife.

SEVENTEEN

AFTER THREE days in the hall, Mal could stand it no longer. His scalp itched, his clothes were brittle, his foot was nearly back to its normal size, and surely the reason everyone gave him wide berth was because he stank. Even Violet had wrinkled her nose and squirmed away when he tried to gather her onto his lap for a tickle.

But he was not about to bathe in the midst of the great hall, and he surely was not about to allow serf and man-at-arms alike to assume he was unwelcome in his own bedchamber...even though he had never yet set foot over its threshold.

So he waited until the morrow when Judith was off on a hunting trip before he called for assistance to the second floor and ordered a bath.

To his surprise and delight, the serfs brought a massive copper tub—easily large enough for Mal to fit and actually submerge himself with only his shoulders and a bit of knee exposed. He didn't think he'd ever had such luxury, except when once he'd sat in a bubbling hot spring at some Roman ruins. He lost count of the number of buckets of water required to fill the container, closing his eyes as one of the maids scrubbed his head and another shook out a clean tunic and hose, whilst another prepared to shave him. There was even a bundle of rosemary and a cloth of wrapped lemon peels floating in the hot water, offering a fresh, clean scent that mingled with soft soap.

His wife surely knew how to manage a household.

A stab of pain at the thought left Mal breathless, and he closed his eyes. Here he sat, in the chamber that was rightfully his—clean, neat, bright, and sumptuously furnished, smelling of his wife, filled with evidence of her presence everywhere…including a long strand of fiery hair caught on one of the fireplace stones.

Though he'd seen glimpses of her in the hall over the last days, she'd never even approached him. Her railing, shrieking accusations were a blur in his pain-filled, confused mind. *Mistress? Secrets?* Aye, he'd not told her about Violet, but what other madness had settled in her craw? He'd been so enraged and frustrated over her denial of him, so muddled by pain, he'd nearly forgotten about the accusations.

And if anyone suspected aught was amiss between the lord and lady of Lilyfare, no one dared speak of it. But how could they not know? Yet, he was too proud to send for her—for fear she would not come.

He had but two choices: to leave Lilyfare, resigned to their failed match, or to stay and force Judith to accept her role as his wife. At the least until he got an heir or two.

Neither option sat well with him, and he closed his eyes against the sting of angry tears. By now, the maids were done scrubbing and shaving him and more buckets of water had been brought to dump over his head, rinsing away the last bit of dirt. He rose awkwardly to his feet, still unable to put full weight on his ankle, looking about the chamber as they toweled him off.

A chair sat by the fireplace with a small table next to it and a coil of leather that resembled the jesses of a falcon. Thick, woven material covered the floor near the chair and in the corner stood two large trunks. The high, massive bed was piled with furs and pillows, its curtains pulled neatly back.

Nothing had ever looked more inviting and Mal hadn't slept in a bed since leaving Warwick—well over a se'ennight ago. So, while the tub was being emptied by a parade of serfs, the maids helped him pull on his hose and tunic. And then he sent them all away and climbed into *his* bed. He pulled the curtains tightly against the stream of bright sun.

And, surrounded by the scent of his wife, he slept.

-*-

MALCOLM WOKE immediately when the chamber door opened.

"Of all the things—to fall into a bog," Judith was saying as she came in. Her arrival was accompanied by the unmistakable sounds of the metal tub being slid across the stone floor, then the soft rustle of people moving, the sloshing of water.

Mal sat up quietly, his heart pounding, his body alert. He should reveal himself, but…nay. Not now. Not when there were serfs and maids about. He was bedamned if he'd air his dirty laundry for all to see and gossip on.

Now he could smell the stink of algae and mud, he could hear the soft swish of clothing, of trunks opening and closing, the muffle of Judith's voice as she pulled the gown over her head. The bed curtains rippled and twitched from the activity in the chamber and he felt ridiculous, being reduced to hiding in a bed while his wife bathed. And though it would be humiliating to be discovered in such a position, he could not make himself announce his presence.

At last the serfs were gone and only Tabatha remained to serve her mistress. And though he couldn't see what was happening, he could envision it. The soft splash as Judith climbed into the tub, the drips as a washing cloth was brought from the water, the scent of lavender and lily overtaking that of rotting plants and muck. Knowing he was about to fight what was likely the most dangerous battle of his life, Mal closed his eyes, drew in a deep breath, then pulled open the curtains.

Both women whirled, staring at him with shocked eyes. Tabby gasped.

"Dismiss your maid," he said to his wife.

Judith's face, already flushed from the warm water, turned even pinker. Her lush lips were parted and her hair was piled on her head with a few wisps brushing her gold-dusted ivory shoulders. Thank God he could see naught else of her.

He tensed, praying she would not disobey him—for that he could not allow.

"You may go, Tabatha," she said tightly.

The maid's eyes were circles of surprise and confusion, but she said not a word and swiftly left the chamber, closing the door behind her.

Now Mal could return his full attention to Judith, and he did. Silence smothered the room like a heavy tapestry.

"And so you've come to claim your husbandly right," Judith said at last, leveling a stare at him. It was neither friendly nor angry. Merely...accepting.

Hope leaped inside him, then faded. He wanted more than her acceptance. "I needed a bath," he told her. "And I've not slept in a bed for nearly a fortnight."

"Surely your mistress could have provided one for you."

A wave of fury and confusion washed over him. "Mistress?" he snarled in frustration. "What is this madness you cling to? I have not even looked on a *whore* since the day you forced me to play chess."

She gaped at him. Then the shock faded and her expression became pinched. "Your lover then. Mayhap you must worship her from afar because you are not wed. Which would explain the lack of a *bed*," she added sharply. Her face was turned away, but he saw the slender column of her throat convulse as she swallowed.

"I do not know *what* you are speaking of," he said desperately. "My lover? My mistress? Judith, you accuse me of aught I do not understand."

"I am not a fool. I know you wished to wed Beatrice. I know you love her. You could hardly wait to be rid of me, to return to her." Her voice became thready and high. "But *why* did you have to bring her here? Under my roof? Was it not enough that you must pine for *her* whilst wedding me?" Now she looked at him, distraught and devastated, the water sloshing with her vehemence. "I know 'twas wrong of me to open that door, to trick you into offering for me—to use your honor against you—but I tried to release you, Malcolm. I tried and you would not allow it!"

By now he was off the bed, next to the tub, ignoring the streak of pain in his ankle as he crouched next to her. "Beatrice? Of

Delbring? You believe I love Beatrice of Delbring? Is that what this is all about?" he bellowed, half in fury, half in joyful relief.

She merely looked at him and nodded. He was close to her, pressing against the side of the tub, his arms wide, his hands gripping the edge as if to embrace the vessel itself. Water seeped into his tunic and he could see the pulse pounding in her throat and the tempting hint of breasts. His own heart thudded madly.

"You mad, *mad* woman," he whispered, reaching to touch her, curving a dark, scarred hand under her chin. "The only woman I love is you. I cannot even look at a whore because you have so ruined me."

"But...you were negotiating a marriage contract. With Delbring. While we were at Clarendon. Nevril told Tabatha—you were so happy, he said—and then you became angry when you learned you must wed me...." Judith's voice broke. She was looking at him through blue pools of hope, yet her eyes were still laced with suspicion and pain. "And then you left me here to go to Delbring...."

Mal shook his head, his fingers sliding down along her throat and over her delicate collarbone as he tried to understand how she could have come to such wrong conclusions. It took a moment before comprehension dawned. "*Nevril.* That rock-head. He did not know of our plans to wed. But I sent messages, many of them—to Mal Verne, Salisbury, and Peter of Blois and others—and aye, to Delbring. But 'twas only to give off the impression I meant to make a match there. I could not allow the king or queen to get a hint of our plans...and so I allowed some to think that was my intent. And I was happy because a miracle had happened." He brought himself up on his knees, pulling her close. "I had the chance to wed you."

She did not resist when he covered her mouth with his. Her lips were warm and softly parted, and he was gentle, for the fierce desperation he harbored for so long was gone. Judith tasted sweet and lush, and 'twas all he could do to keep from crawling over the edge and into the tub, gathering her damp, sleek body to him.

But she turned away too soon, easing back against the edge of the tub. "But you left me here. Why? And why did you not tell me of Violet? Why would you keep such a secret from me?"

A flicker of shame caught him and it was Mal's turn to shift, shocking his weak ankle as he put space between them. "I had to send her from Warwick, for I wanted her to be safe from the disease there. But I was not…certain how you would accept her."

"But she is your *daughter*."

"And she is not—she will not be…. She will be a child forever, Judith." Mal realized he was holding his breath.

"What have I ever done to make you believe I would be unkind to a child—*any* child?" she whispered.

He shook his head fiercely, shame heating his face. "Naught. I was a fool. I meant only to protect her…for you are so…bright and bold and filled with life. Quick and brisk. And I feared you might not—ah, I was wrong. I misjudged you badly."

"Aye," she said softly. "That you did, Malcolm. But I…I cannot point such a sharp finger, for mayhap I have done the same."

He exhaled and nodded. "Forgive me."

"Aye." She paused, trailing her fingers over the top of the water. "Malcolm…would you help me?"

"Of course. What is it you wish?"

"I wish to climb out of the tub, and I find I need assistance." The flicker of a smile touched her lips and Malcolm felt a rush of heat washing over him.

In one swift, smooth movement, he rose and scooped her up, hardly noticing his protesting ankle. Water sluiced everywhere, and he snatched up a drying cloth in which to wrap her…then looked down into her beautiful, flushed face. His heart pounded and his blood surged.

"I would take you to bed, Judith," he said.

"And I would go," she replied, reaching to touch his face.

He settled her on the bed, whipping away the drying cloth as he came to lie next to her. His fingers trembled a bit as he made a long, light stroke from her shoulder to breast to the curve of her hip, hardly believing that she was his. Then he gathered her close, drawing her up to kiss her with all the tenderness and love he'd stored behind three months of anger and frustration.

She kissed him back, sighing softly into his mouth, teasing him with her tongue. She arched against his damp tunic, which suddenly seemed like more of a barrier than even a mail hauberk. He pulled away to whip it off and froze when he saw the glitter of tears in her eyes. She blinked and one of them tipped free, trailing down into the pillow beneath her.

Malcolm's heart seized and his insides plummeted. *Nay.* By God, surely she would turn him *mad.* "What is it, Judith? Do my kisses remind you of the king? Is that it?"

She frowned, shaking her head, placing a hand on his bare chest. Her touch was welcome, arousing and comforting, but he forced himself to wait for her to speak. "Oh, nay, Mal. There was never any kissing with the king. Ever."

A pulse of disgust surprised him, but he pushed it away. He would not think of his liege now, would not imagine the lecherousness of the man to whom he must be loyal. "Then why the tears, Judith? What makes you so sad and hurt that when I touch you, you must cry?" His voice was edged with frustration and he gritted his teeth.

She dragged herself up on an elbow, wiping away the tears. "Oh," she said, her expression turning from surprise to comprehension and tenderness. She touched his hair, sliding her fingers into it, combing gently along his scalp. "I am not sad or hurt, my love. These are tears of happiness and joy. For I cannot keep from weeping so when I am thus content. And I am content now…or I shall be, methinks, once you have bedded me."

Her smile was a charming combination of shyness and teasing, but Mal hardly noticed through his mingled relief and chagrin. "And that is why you cried on our wedding night? And when we were to leave Clarendon? I bethought you were sad and angry and did not wish—that you wished we had not wed."

"Oh nay, Malcolm. That was not crying. That was *weeping.*"

"There is a difference?" he asked, hardly able to believe he was having such a conversation with his wife when she was sleek and naked, warm and damp from her bath...and ready for him.

"Aye, indeed," she said, sliding her hand down over his chest and ridged abdomen. He was shockingly aware of his skin leaping and trembling beneath her touch, and how his hose jutted out in a most insistent bulge. His breathing became ragged, and he could hardly follow her words. "For when I *cry*, dear husband," she explained with a sassy tilt to her head, "you shall know it. For I am red-eyed and runny-nosed and my face turns pink and I am furious and loud. Very...loud."

Malcolm's breath caught when she curved her fingers around his heavy, thick cock, pulling it gently from its confines. He stilled and nearly lost himself right then.

"And so..." he breathed...and then completely forgot what he was about to say. His mind went utterly blank, aware of naught but the sensation of her hand, sliding tightly, smoothly along his erection and back again. He slammed a hand over hers, halting the movement, and peeled his eyes open. "Nay. You will unman me," he told her.

She grinned, her eyes lighting up into a duo of mischievous, sparkling blue. "Is that a challenge?"

"Nay!" he said, moving swiftly once more, flinging her onto her back. "You are already challenge enough, Judith." He placed a hand over her belly as he knelt in front of her, firmly parting her thighs, lowering his face to taste her in that hot, musky place. "But now, my love, 'tis my intent to make you weep."

EPILOGUE

Four months later.

JUDITH BROKE the seal on Maris's letter and unfurled the parchment eagerly. She always enjoyed hearing from her friend, and hoped Maris would join her at Lilyfare to midwife for the birth of her first child. The babe was not due to come until early summer, but she had already sent word to ask for attendance.

Settled in a large chair by the huge fireplace in the great hall, she settled in to read what she hoped was a gossipy missive, then suddenly found herself skimming quickly through it. "Tabby! Send for Lord Malcolm at once!" she said, rising from the chair. "He is in the training yard."

Her maid, who herself was round with child, bustled from the hall as Judith hurried up to her chamber. She wished to have this conversation with her husband in private.

Moments later, she heard the pounding of footsteps down the hall. Mal burst in, eyes wild, still holding a sword. "What is it?" he demanded. "Are you well? The babe?"

"Oh, aye, all is very well," she told him, holding back a giggle. He looked so very fierce. "So I do not believe you are in need of that...."

He paused and looked from her to the broadsword he held and back again. He frowned. "When you send to me with such urgency, what do you expect me to think?" He shoved the blade into its sheath and unbuckled the weapon from his waist, placing it on a trunk. "Well? You interrupted my training for what purpose?"

"A letter from Maris."

He looked at her sharply. "And….?"

Judith could not hold back a smile. "She is very careful, of course, not to say anything outright—"

"She is coming to midwife for you?" he asked.

Judith rolled her eyes. "I am not even rounding in the belly yet, and you are worried. Aye, she will be here. But that is not what news she sent."

"You might not be rounding in the belly, but I am seeing rounding elsewhere, mistress wife," he said, his eyes settling on her breasts. When she huffed a little, he sighed and said, "Do you mean to tell me or shall I continue to guess?"

She smiled. "'Tis news from court. Eleanor gave birth to a boy, John—"

"Aye, we have already heard that news—"

"Indeed…but not this choice gossip. The queen meant to go into her confinement at Woodstock, but at the last moment traveled on to Beaumont Place. Word is she did not wish to be in the same residence as Mistress Rosamund Clifford."

Mal grumbled impatiently, "Judith, if you do not come to the point very soon, I shall strap on my sword and go back to my men. Even Rike is making progress today, and I—"

"Rosamund Clifford is the king's new leman. Maris claims he is quite besotted with her, and the queen is beyond livid. The gossips say his obsession with Rosamund is beyond anything they have witnessed, and that even Eleanor has naught to say about it. The woman is taking precedence even over his wife."

During her speech, Malcolm's expression eased into one of interest and satisfaction. "And so Lady Maris believes any ill will the queen might still harbor toward you—or me—is now turned upon Mistress Clifford? I do hope the woman does not have a husband," he added ruefully.

"Nay, she does not. And aside from that, Eleanor is leaving for Aquitaine now that she has delivered herself of Prince John. Betwixt the unrest there, the tension between Canterbury and the king, not to mention the fair Rosamund, the queen has other matters on her mind. Both Maris and Dirick believe the viper has been confined to her nest and will not come out for a long while—if ever."

"And so we can draw in a breath of relief ourselves, is that the news?" he said, now eyeing her speculatively. "I cannot imagine a more happy announcement."

"Indeed. I am so relieved…I believe I could be reduced to tears," Judith said, spinning away from him as she tossed a hot, meaningful look over her shoulder.

"Is that so? Well, never shall it be said I cannot bring my wife to weep if I desire it," Mal said, lunging toward her.

She allowed him to catch her this time, fairly climbing into his arms to smack a joyful kiss on his lips. "You are safe, my love. And though I hurt for the queen—for no one should be subject to such pain and disrespect—I cannot be sad that her attention is directed elsewhere. The woman might have all the wealth and power in Christendom, but she is ill-used and—"

"Aye," he said, but his tone was distracted and he already had his hands full of her bountiful breasts. "Now if you will cease speaking about the woman who tried to murder me, I shall see about directing *your* attention elsewhere."

"But what about your training?" she teased. "The men will be waiting your return."

"They can wait. I still have not forgiven Nevril for causing such upheaval with my wife," he said.

And then she could no longer respond, for he covered her lips with his and they collapsed onto the massive, pillow-covered, becurtained bed he now called his own.

˷*˷*˷

˷*˷

A Note from the Author

Although Judith and Malcolm's story is, of course, a work of fiction, there are several elements that are true to the history of King Henry II and his wife Eleanor.

I've always found Eleanor of Aquitaine—wife to two kings and mother to two more—to be a most fascinating historical figure. She is my hero, not only because of her attachment to so many powerful royals, but also because of her own legacy in a world ruled by men. She went on Crusade, leading her own army of women, managed her own vast lands in Aquitaine and Poitiers, bore ten children, and lived to nearly eighty—while acting as Regent for her son, Richard the Lionheart.

It's a well-known fact that her husband Henry had many mistresses over the years, and although they might have begun their relationship as a love match—for they met long before she divorced from Louis, and clearly had an attraction to each other—their marriage obviously ended unhappily. Although the first obvious and lasting rift between them came when Henry fell in love with Rosamund Clifford, who became his final and most long-lasting mistress, it widened over the years after the murder of Thomas Becket, Archbishop of Canterbury.

But the schism between Eleanor and Henry was irreparably cast when she joined with their sons Henry, Richard, and Geoffrey in a rebellion against the king—an event which she foreshadows to Judith in *A Lily on the Heath*. Henry reacted to his wife's perfidy by imprisoning her from 1174 (after the failed rebellion) until his death in 1189, when Richard took the throne.

Also foreshadowed herein is the strain between the Plantagenets and the clergy, which grew uglier during the late 1160s and reached its breaking point after the death of Thomas Becket in 1170. It is well known that the murder of the archbishop occurred because two of Henry's men-at-arms heard him raving about the man, and when he said, "Will no one rid me of this curse?" the knights took his words to heart and assassinated Becket.

Malcolm considers the possibility of such an event when he considers whether the king might have been ranting about Malcolm himself, and thus caused the attack on himself and Judith after they left Clarendon.

Mal and Judith's story ends in late 1167, when Eleanor cloisters herself at Beaumont Place to deliver the future King John (instead of at Woodstock, where her rival was in residence). By this time, Rosamund Clifford has publicly overtaken Henry's affections—and by most accounts, it was a truly loving relationship—and one can assume that any reconciliation between the king and queen was unlikely.

Colleen Gleason, January 2013

Don't miss any new releases!

Sign up for New Book Alerts on Colleen's website
(ColleenGleason.com)
or send an email to alert@colleengleason.com

Colleen Gleason is the international best-selling author of the Gardella Vampire Chronicles, a historical urban fantasy series about a female vampire hunter who lives during the time of Jane Austen. Her first novel, *The Rest Falls Away*, was released to acclaim in 2007.

Since then, she has published more than twenty novels with New American Library, MIRA Books, Chronicle Books, and HarperCollins (writing as Joss Ware). Her books have been translated into more than seven languages and are available worldwide.

Visit her website at ColleenGleason.com or find her on Facebook at Colleen.Gleason.Author

CPSIA information can be obtained at www.ICGtesting.com
Printed in the USA
LVOW11s1724090214

372970LV00005B/870/P

9 781931 419123